Lena Diaz was born in Kentucky and has also lived in California, Louisiana and Florida, where she now resides with her husband and two children. Before becoming a romantic suspense author, she was a computer programmer. A Romance Writers of America Golden Heart® Award finalist, she has also won the prestigious Daphne du Maurier Award for Excellence in Mystery/Suspense. To get the latest news about Lena, please visit her website, lenadiaz.com

Nichole Severn writes explosive romantic suspense with strong heroines, heroes who dare challenge them and a hell of a lot of guns. She resides with her very supportive and patient husband, as well as her demon spawn, in Utah. When she's not writing, she's constantly injuring herself running, rock climbing, practicing yoga and snowboarding. She loves hearing from readers through her website, www.nicholesevern.com, and on Twitter, @nicholesevern

AGENT UNDER SIEGE

LENA DIAZ

THE FUGITIVE

NICHOLE SEVERN

MILLS & BOON

First Published in Great Britain 2020
by Mills & Boon, an imprint of HarperCollins*Publishers*
1 London Bridge Street, London, SE1 9GF

Agent Under Siege © 2020 Lena Diaz
The Fugitive © 2020 Natascha Jaffa

ISBN: 978-0-263-28317-4

0121

MIX
Paper from
responsible sources
FSC™ C007454

This book is produced from independently certified FSC™ paper to ensure responsible forest management.

For more information visit: www.harpercollins.co.uk/green

Printed and bound in Spain
by CPI, Barcelona

AGENT UNDER SIEGE

LENA DIAZ

My prayers and condolences to all who have lost loved ones and friends during the horrendous, unimaginable pandemic that gripped our world in 2020. I hope that this story gives you a few hours of escape and that it puts a smile on your face. God bless.

Chapter One

Long before the shadow fell across the end of the dock and hovered over Bryson Anton's wheelchair, he knew the man was there. Motion sensors and security cameras had made Bryson's watch buzz against his wrist when the man parked his car in the driveway. More messages warned when the man crossed the back patio. And again, when he'd descended the gently sloping lawn that ended at the creek. Bryson didn't care who was now standing behind him, as long as he didn't have to engage in conversation.

"Nice place," the man's voice rang out. "Probably one of the highest views in the Tennessee side of the Smoky Mountains. I'll bet at night you can see nearly every light in downtown Gatlinburg from here."

Bryson sighed but didn't turn around. "My former boss took pity on me after I got myself hurt on the job. He gave me a boatload of money, and I was selfish enough to take it and buy this property. But that doesn't mean he can drop by any time he wants."

"I'm still your boss. I haven't accepted your resignation."

"That's not how it works, Mason. I resigned, whether you accept it or not. I'll never be a Justice Seeker again. I'm not going back to Camelot. You and your knights of the round table are better off without a washed-up former profiler jacking up your investigations."

"Is that why you're sitting out here drinking like a fish, because you think you jacked up everything?"

"Something like that." Bryson grabbed a can of beer from the cooler beside his wheelchair and popped the top. He took a deep long swallow, more to irritate his unwelcome visitor than because he wanted it.

Mason retrieved a beer and eyed the label, then tossed it back unopened. "Fish biting?"

"Do you see a fishing pole around here somewhere?" Bryson emptied his can in the water and dropped it on his lap before wheeling around. "Enjoy the view as long as you want. You paid for it." He rolled his chair up the flagstone walkway toward the house.

"Dalton and Hayley missed you at their wedding last week." Mason fell into step beside him.

"Yeah, well. I didn't have time to learn the latest dance steps." He stopped at the sliding glass doors and tossed the empty beer can in the recycle bin. When he reached for the door handle, Mason leaned past him and held it closed.

Bryson swore. "What do you want from me?"

"I want you to do your job. A new client came to Camelot yesterday. She specifically wants to hire *you*."

He scoffed. "You expect me to believe she asked for a washed-up former FBI agent to screw up her case so someone else will die? If she did, send her on over. I can accomplish that without lifting a finger."

Mason leaned back against the door. "That's a heck of a guilty conscience you're nursing. Or are you just feeling sorry for yourself?" He waved toward the wheelchair. "If you'd actually go to your physical therapy appointments instead of being a no-show half the time, you'd be out of that thing by now. Don't look so surprised. I pay your in-surance premiums. I see what's billed. And there've been a surprising lack of medical invoices lately. You've given up, Bryson. The question is why?"

"Why?" he gritted out. "Let me remind you that when I was the FBI's golden boy, everyone treated my profiles like biblical text. So when I presented them with a profile for the Kentucky Ripper, they focused all their efforts on Avarice Lowe, the suspect at the top of my list. Meanwhile, Leviathan Finney—the real Ripper—was no longer under surveillance. To celebrate, he kidnapped and *gutted* another woman. Because of me, he was able to kill again."

"*Because of you*, the police were able to significantly narrow their list of suspects much faster than they could have otherwise. The choices they made after that weren't your fault. Hell, Bryson. If it wasn't for the work you did, it would have taken far longer to catch the Ripper and put him in prison."

"Tell that to the family of the last woman he killed."

Mason shook his head. "I hear someone anonymously sends money to the last victim's family every month. While I admire the generosity and kindness of the gesture, that person is making payments on a debt he doesn't owe. The only person responsible for that woman's death is the man who killed her—Leviathan Finney."

Bryson fisted his hands on the arms of the wheelchair. "Are we about done here? It's getting late."

"Big plans tonight?"

"I have to wash my hair."

Mason let out a deep sigh. "Just explain one thing, then I'll go. Why now? You left the FBI over three years ago and started working for me as one of the Justice Seekers. Why is the Ripper case bothering you again after all this time?"

Bryson stared at him incredulously. "Bothering me *again*? It never *stopped* bothering me. But I tried to make

something good from the bad, atone for my sins by working investigations for you. And what did I do? I nearly got
Hayley killed, got myself shot and here I sit with shrapnel
they can't dig out of my hip without risking the loss of my
leg. Do I sit here feeling sorry for myself? No. I don't deserve anyone's sympathy, least of all my own. The people
who deserve sympathy are the ones I've hurt, those who
nearly died because of me, and the one who *did*. Accept
my resignation and leave me alone. I'm not going to risk
hurting anyone else. I'm done."

Mason's jaw worked as he stared past him toward the
creek. A full minute passed in silence before he finally
met Bryson's gaze again. "Sounds like you've made up
your mind."

Bryson arched a brow. "Sounds like you're finally listening."

"Oh, I've been listening. I just don't like what I'm hearing." He pulled a thick neon green folder covered with pink
polka dots out from beneath his suit jacket and dropped
it onto Bryson's lap. "Guess you won't be needing this."

He eyed the folder like he'd eye a coiled rattlesnake.
"What is that hideous thing?"

"I was asked to give it to you. It's from the client I told
you about, the one who requested that you work on her
case. She put her pursuit of a master's degree in criminal
justice on hold to perform research on an alleged serial
killer. She believes that you're the only person who can
convince the police that her conclusions are reasonable
and help her catch him. She provided a summary of her
research in that folder."

Bryson snorted and shook his head. "If she's convinced
that a failed criminal profiler is the key to her theory, then
she needs to go back to school. Her deductive reasoning
is skewed."

"Personally, I found her work intriguing, her theories compelling. And I've already got my master's in criminal justice, not to mention a decade of experience as a chief of police and another seven years after that running The Justice Seekers." Mason straightened and tugged his suit jacket into place. "But I can see that I'm not going to change your mind. The funny thing is, I never took you for a quitter. Even after the FBI."

"Yeah, well. I never thought I'd be responsible for another innocent person almost being killed either. Guess we were both wrong."

Mason stared at him a long moment, then looked past him again toward the dock. "That really is a gorgeous view. Let me know when you decide to go fishing. I can bring a pole, throw out a line." He gave him a hard look. "*All* of your brothers and sisters at Camelot would love to toss you a line, including Hayley. You just have to ask." He shoved his hands in his pants pockets and strode away without waiting for a reply.

Bryson dropped his gaze to the ridiculous-looking pink-and-green folder in his lap. He stared at it long after he could no longer hear the sound of Mason's car driving away. Long after the sun began to set and the mosquitos started buzzing around his ears. Long after the twinkling lights of Gatlinburg reflected in the sliding glass door, studding the night sky like glitter on a black velvet canvas.

Then he tossed the folder in the trash.

Chapter Two

Teagan whistled as she stepped out of her car onto the brick-paved driveway. It was as if she was standing on top of the world, with the entire Smoky Mountains range spreading out around her in 360-degree views. There wasn't another house in sight, just the rambling one-story stone-and-brick mansion set so far back from the main road that she hadn't seen it until she'd almost passed it.

She wasn't sure what she'd expected of the home of a former FBI special agent, but it wasn't this. Either the FBI was paying way better than most people realized, or Bryson Anton's post-FBI career paid *extremely* well. He'd spent three years so far with The Justice Seekers, an agency of former law enforcement officers and ex-military whose professed goal was to obtain justice for people who couldn't get it via the traditional route. Having seen their quirky, state-of-the-art headquarters that they'd dubbed Camelot, she figured it was a safe assumption that's where Bryson had made his money.

When she reached the front porch, she was surprised that in addition to the broad front steps there was a ramp concealed behind the landscaping. No rocking chairs dotted the wide expanse. No flowers decorated the empty cedar window boxes, even though it was the middle of spring. If she had to describe the expensive, sprawling home in one word, it would be…*lonely.*

She was about to knock on the frosted glass double door when the left side jerked open. She blinked in slack-jawed admiration at the incredible work of art that greeted her wearing nothing but a frown and a white towel draped around his hips. His dark, shoulder-length hair was damp. Beads of water clung to the hair on his golden, sculpted chest. It almost killed her not to reach out and trace the trail of one very happy bead that ran toward his six-pack abs and disappeared below the top of his towel. On a scale of one to ten, she rated him sexy-as-hell.

"Hi." Of all the compelling, intelligent, well-formulated introductions that her summa cum laude education could have provided her, she came up with that one-word bit of brilliance. She cleared her throat so she could properly introduce herself.

"It's about time you got here," he practically growled. "I've been trying to work the cramps out of my hip all morning. If the muscles aren't loosened up soon, I'll end up in the wheelchair the rest of the day abusing an exquisite bottle of scotch."

Leaning heavily on the cane in his right hand that she only just noticed, he limped across the expensive-looking shiny white floor before stopping beside one of the biggest black leather couches she'd ever seen. Except for the other couch in the room, which was just as big. The two of them formed an L with their backs to the bump-out of windows near the garage.

"Where do you want me?" he asked.

Was that a trick question? On a bed, on the kitchen counter, *anywhere.* Since he appeared to be waiting for an answer to his ridiculous query, she had to rewind the brief conversation in her head and remember what he'd said when he'd opened the door. Her previously absent brain clicked into gear, and she realized he was likely expecting either a massage therapist or a personal trainer. For his left hip, the one he was favoring as he leaned toward the cane on his right side. Apparently he wanted her to tell him where he should sit, or lie down, or whatever was required so that she could work out his muscle cramps.

Her ovaries screamed at her to say yes to anything he wanted. But it wouldn't be ethical to let this go on any longer when it was obviously a case of mistaken identity. All she had to do was tell him who she was and why she was there.

Now if she could just stop drooling long enough to remember her name.

He frowned. "What's wrong?" He glanced down at his towel. "I've got boxers on if you're worried that I'm naked under here."

"Oh, no, trust me. That wouldn't bother me *at all*." Drop the towel. And the boxers. *Please.* She cleared her throat. "What I meant to say is that—"

The doorbell rang, followed by a knock on the glass.

He swore. "Ever since my old boss came by yesterday, you'd think this was a Walmart on Black Friday. This makes the third person to come by in two days."

"Three visitors in two days. A veritable siege."

He gave her an odd look.

She smiled. It was either that or give in to the barbaric urge to grab his towel and toss it away. She curled her fingernails against her palms, trying her best to keep him safe.

His face was a study in pain as he limped to the door. She wondered at the source of that pain. His employer hadn't mentioned anything about an injury. Mason had only stated that Bryson was on temporary leave, but that he'd be more than happy to return to take her case. She had a feeling that Mason might have stretched the truth. A lot.

He opened the door with a bit of wariness this time, keeping his lower half hidden behind it.

Unable to make out what was being said, Teagan imagined it was far more clever than her conversation since they spoke longer than it took to say, "Hi." When he stepped back, a rather impressive woman entered. Bright, attention-getting red hair floated above baby-blue scrubs. She marched across the room with the authority of someone who had a legitimate reason to be there. Teagan was quite certain that the woman's muscular arms would have made a linebacker blush with envy. After snapping a white linen in the air and tucking it around the couch cushions, she ordered Bryson to lose the towel and lie down.

Teagan debated what to do. Should she go or should she stay?

"You." Bryson pointed at her. "Sit over there until I can stand again without wanting to drown myself in a bottle of tequila. Then we'll find out who you are and what you're doing here."

He dropped his towel and lay down on the couch, his left leg facing out toward the room. His thighs were just as muscular and beautiful as the rest of him. *Wowzah.*

The woman that Teagan mentally dubbed "Helga" placed a pad on the floor by the couch and propped her knees on top of it. Strong, man-size hands were stuffed into latex gloves. Then she shoved the side of Bryson's boxers up his leg and proceeded to squeeze and pummel his hip.

Personally, Teagan wouldn't have bothered with the gloves.

She tossed her purse onto the other couch and plopped down to enjoy the show. It was over far too soon. She almost groaned in disappointment when Bryson pushed to his feet, then pronounced his cramps gone and thanked the therapist. A few minutes later, Helga had left and Bryson returned from his bedroom in a pair of jeans and a black T-shirt.

Since the jeans caressed his muscular thighs and tight rear end and the T-shirt did nothing to hide the perfection of his pecs, Teagan decided that she didn't mind that he'd put on some clothes. It was a pleasure seeing the perfect male specimen in varying stages of undress. She just wished she could see him *completely* undressed for a fair comparison.

He limped to her couch, looking just as adorably grumpy as he had when he'd jerked open the front door and complained about her taking so long to get there. Well, complained that *Helga* had taken so long.

"Spill it," he said. "Mason sent you, didn't he?"

"I wouldn't put it that way."

"How would you put it?"

"I'd say that I went to Mr. Ford and asked if I could hire you. He said he was certain that you'd be interested, but that I'd have to ask you personally. He graciously provided your address and here I am. Technically, I sent myself." She remained seated on the ultra-plush couch and offered her hand. "Teagan Ray. Nice to meet you."

He didn't bother with a handshake. "Bryson Anton. I don't work for Mason Ford anymore. Get out of my house."

Chapter Three

"No."

Bryson stared at the defiant young woman sitting cross-legged on his couch. There was nothing about her sensible flat shoes, her conservative navy blue dress pants and short-sleeved white blouse that buttoned all the way to her neck to indicate that she was a radical militant bent on destroying the rest of his miserable morning. Even her black hair, which appeared to be curly based on the little wisps that framed her face, was mostly tamed in a tight braid that hung down the middle of her back. So why wasn't she cowed by his sour disposition and gruff commands? And why was she still sitting on his couch?

"Perhaps you didn't hear me correctly, Ms. Ray."

"Call me Teagan. I'll call you Bryson." She flashed a bright white smile that probably cost her parents a second mortgage.

"Ms. Ray, you may call me Mr. Anton, or the jerk who's throwing you out of his house. Because that's exactly what I'm doing. Tossing you out. I didn't invite you here so—"

"Actually, you did."

"Excuse me?"

She tapped her temple as if that would explain everything. "I have a photographic memory. I basically see words—"

"I know what a photographic memory is," he bit out.

"Excellent. It's good to use terminology we're both familiar with for the absolute best understanding, with no confusion. A common frame of reference will help us communicate better. Don't you think?"

"You lost me at *no confusion*."

She grinned. She seemed to do that a lot. "Let's go back to the part where you invited me here."

"I didn't invite you."

"When Mr. Ford told you about me, you told him, 'You expect me to believe she asked for a washed-up former FBI agent to screw up her case so someone else will die? If she did, send her on over.'" She spread her hands out beside her. "Here I am. Plus you invited me in at the front door. It's kind of like with vampires, once you let them in, that's it. You can't just throw them out."

"Watch me." He tossed his cane on the other couch, then scooped her up in his arms.

Her dark brown eyes got so wide he could see the beautiful little golden flecks around the irises.

He whirled around, then stumbled and had to steady his shin against the coffee table to keep from tipping over.

She boldly looped her tawny-brown arms around his neck and stared up at him with a look of concern. "I'm not sure you should be holding me like this without your cane. I don't want you to hurt yourself. Plus, even as gorgeous—with a capital *G*—as you are, I still think we should get to know each other better before we jump into each other's arms. Don't you?" She fluttered her impossibly long, thick eyelashes.

Actually *fluttered* them.

"Has anyone ever accused you of insanity?" he asked.

"All the time. It's one of my best qualities—the ability

to act crazy while I outmaneuver and outsmart everyone around me."

He scowled down at her.

She tightened her arms around his neck. "I could literally do this all day. We fit together perfectly. My soft curves, your hard muscles. Very comfy."

"Are you flirting with me, Ms. Ray?"

"I believe I am, Mr. Anton."

"Because you're trying to confuse and outmaneuver me so I'll let you stay?"

"Mostly. Is it working?"

"The jury's still out on that. But my hip's starting to hurt like the devil again, so I'm either going to drop you or set you down. I'm leaning toward dropping."

"I prefer setting."

"No sense of adventure." He let her legs slide down until she was standing. Then he gingerly let her go, trying not to move too fast and lose his precarious balance.

She grabbed his cane and handed it to him. "Is this one of those cool FBI things? Like if you twist the head it opens and becomes a rifle? Or maybe the tip has poison in it? You jab the bad guy and he dies a horrible death a few minutes later. Am I right?"

"It's a gun, of course. Poison is so beneath an FBI agent."

Her grin widened. "James Bond has nothing on you guys."

He rolled his eyes. It was all he could manage with the pain slicing through his muscles. When he thought he could shuffle across the room without falling to the floor in an embarrassing heap, he headed toward the kitchen. He eyed her morosely as she used her two perfectly healthy hips to hop onto one of the bar stools at the marble-topped island.

"Don't get too comfortable," he warned. "You haven't achieved victory. Once I liquor up enough to be able to haul you to the front door, I'll be throwing you out as promised."

"I consider myself forewarned." She motioned toward him. "Mind if I ask what's wrong with the leg? I noticed the ramp outside, and a wheelchair in the corner of the family room."

"You can *ask* all you want. And I can choose not to answer." Bypassing the scotch that he preferred for late-night drinking—alone—he grabbed a bottle of tequila along with a shot glass.

She motioned toward the cabinet. "Can you at least pretend that you have some manners and act like a host for a few minutes?"

"Are you even old enough to drink?"

She rolled her eyes. "I'm sure I don't look *that* young."

He sighed and reached for a second glass. After pouring two generous helpings, he set the bottle between them. "Ms. Ray. You seem like an intelligent young woman—"

She grimaced. "You say young as if you think I'm a child. I can't imagine that I'm more than ten, maybe eleven years younger than you."

He arched a brow. "Meaning that while you were in elementary school, I was losing my virginity to the homecoming queen at my high school."

She hesitated with a shot glass halfway to her mouth. "Can't top that. But I did have my first kiss quite early. Third grade. Behind the jungle gym. Ricky Southernton." She tossed her shot back with one gulp.

"On the lips?"

"On the cheek."

"Doesn't count. I was in *second* grade when I kissed Becky Louis. She bit my tongue."

"Maybe you shouldn't have shoved it down her throat."

He reluctantly smiled. "Maybe not." He tossed his own shot back and reveled at the smooth burn as it went down. A few more shots and he might be able to avoid the wheelchair until at least the dinner hour.

"Have you thought about getting prescription painkillers instead of drowning the pain with alcohol?"

He shot her a look that should have frozen her to the bar stool.

She held up her hands in a placating gesture. "Sorry. The filter between my brain and my mouth is defective. I shouldn't have asked."

The completely unrepentant look on her face, in direct opposition to her words, forced a laugh out of him. How long had it been since he'd laughed, or even smiled? He had no idea. But the novelty of both had him starting to relax, if only a little. "I was on pretty strong pain pills in the beginning, but it was like living in a brain-fog all the time. Had to wean myself off them. Drinking works better for me, and it's a heck of a lot more fun." He refilled his glass, then paused in question with the bottle poised over hers.

"Yes, please."

He topped off her shot, then drained his while watching her. If he hadn't been paying close attention, he wouldn't have noticed the tiny, involuntary shudder when she tossed it back.

"That's a waste of some pretty great tequila for someone who doesn't even like it."

She shoved the glass across the island for more. "What makes you think I don't like it?"

He poured more for himself, but not for her. "When you have ten or eleven more years of experience behind you, maybe you'll figure it out. Go home, Teagan. There's nothing for you here. I can't help you."

"You mean you *won't* help me?"

"The intent doesn't matter. The result is the same."

"Then I guess we're back to drinking. Shots with a hot guy before noon. I can think of worse ways to spend my morning." She grabbed the bottle.

He tugged it away from her. "If you're trying to win me over with the hot guy talk, you can stop right now. Like I said, I'm not going to help with your case. And I'm not buying this over-the-top happy, flirty personality you're presenting. Nobody's that cute. You're trying too hard."

"You think I'm cute?" She grinned and fluttered her long lashes again.

"I think you're nervous and overcompensating. It's time to drop the act."

Her smile dimmed and she seemed genuinely confused. "What do you mean?"

He rested his forearms on the island. "Profiler, remember? At least, I used to be one. It took me a few minutes to realize what was happening. Probably because I'm out of practice and I do my best to avoid people these days. But you don't have to keep pretending, trying to be something you're not. Maybe it's the tequila that I drank, maybe it's that I admire your spunk and the effort you've put into this. Whatever it is, you've earned a slight reprieve. I'll listen to your spiel so you can get it out of your system. *Then* I'll throw you out."

She stared at him, wide-eyed, then grabbed his full shot glass and tossed it back before he could stop her.

He silently cursed himself for not being more careful. Given her small stature and the strength of the tequila, her ability to safely drive herself home was now seriously in question.

"Better?" he asked dryly.

"Better. Although I'll admit that scotch I saw in your cabinet is more to my taste."

"Don't even think about it."

She grinned.

"This is where I warn you that I haven't read the information that Mason left me."

"I kind of figured, since the folder I gave him is hanging half-out of your garbage can on your back patio." She motioned toward the glass doors on the far side of the kitchen.

"Observant, I'll give you that. Then again, it's hard to miss a neon green folder with hideous pink polka dots."

"Not a polka-dot fan?"

"Not in the least."

"Pity."

He shifted his weight to help ease the tightness in his hip. "Maybe you can brief me on what's in the folder. Mason mentioned you think you're on the trail of a serial killer."

She nodded and ran her hands up and down her arms, looking slightly less eager now that the discussion was at hand. She reached for the tequila.

He swore and placed the bottle on the counter behind him. "Trust me. You're already going to have a heck of a hangover. No more alcohol. Now, for a common reference, so there's *no confusion*, what name are you dubbing your alleged killer?"

She drew a deep breath, then straightened her shoulders as if she was about to head into battle. "The Kentucky Ripper."

Chapter Four

Bryson froze, then slowly straightened. "That's not funny."

Teagan's eyes widened. "I'm not making a joke. I'm serious. The Ripper is the killer I've been researching."

"At least now I know why you asked Mason for me, specifically. Well, forget it. Rehashing past failures isn't my idea of fun."

She held up her hands. The overhead lights winked off several gold rings. "Just hear me out. I've been researching this for a long time. I'm not here to cast blame. I'm here for your insight. And I'm here to ask a very important question." She squeezed her hands together. "What if the guy they thought was the Ripper is actually a copycat and the real serial killer is still at large?"

He winced, then eyed his empty glass with longing. "If that's true, then I screwed up even worse than I thought."

"Not at all. *You* didn't make the mistakes during the Ripper investigation. The *police* did."

He tore his gaze from the shot glass. "Maybe I drank too much tequila too because that one went right over my head. I'm lost, in spite of our *common frame of reference.*"

"Then I'll be happy to explain. First, profiles are tools, not biblical text."

He stared at her as his own words were thrown back at him. "Did Mason say that to you?"

She frowned. "No. Why?"

He shrugged. "Just wondering. Go on."

She crossed her arms on top of the island. "When your profile indicated that one of the two top suspects was the most likely killer, the police went after him with everything they had. Meanwhile, their other prime suspect was no longer under surveillance. He took advantage of their mistake to abduct and murder a woman. Instead of thinking of your profile as a divining rod, they should have stayed the course, kept their surveillance on both suspects until some evidence tipped the scales." She motioned in the air as if waving away her words. "Regardless, my point is that, based on my research, I think your profile was spot-on. The first guy *was* the real Ripper. The guy they put in prison is a copycat. The police got sidetracked by the last murder and pursued that killer to the exclusion of everyone else. So, while there's plenty of blame to go around for how everything turned out, none of it should have ever blown back on you."

He was going to filet Mason for giving this misguided, albeit beautiful woman his address. Her theories were bogus. Unfortunately, he could tell how vested she was in them and he didn't want to destroy her confidence before her law enforcement career was even off the ground.

Using his nonjudgmental teaching voice, the one he'd adopted while presenting guest lectures at Quantico, he explained, "For that theory to hold water, the first requirement would be that the Ripper is still active. But no other women have been tortured and brutalized per his specific signature since he was put away. Explain how your theory addresses that."

"No other women *that you know of.*"

"Fair enough. That I know of. But if new cases had popped up, I can't imagine the media not making a connection even if the police didn't. The Ripper case was bread and butter to them. It made for great ratings. If something that sensational happened again, they'd be all over it."

"The media in Kentucky, yes, absolutely. Other places, not necessarily. They don't know about the original cases and wouldn't realize there was a serial killer operating in the area."

"Maybe."

"Definitely," she countered.

He admired her confidence, even if she was dead wrong. "Why would the killer change locations?"

"Because he's smart. He knew he'd been given a tremendous opportunity, that a mentally disturbed fall guy had taken credit for his crimes and turned attention away from him. He knew that if he killed again in the same area, the police would know right away that they'd caught a crazy guy bent on enjoying the spotlight and confessing to crimes he didn't do. They'd be back on the trail of the real Ripper, reassemble the task force. But stopping, not killing anymore, isn't an option either. Our psychopath is driven by an urge to kill that he can't control. So in addition to changing locations, he also changes his MO, his modus operandi, the way he kills."

He could see why Mason had found her compelling. She spoke with authority, like someone who'd had real-life experience with this sort of thing rather than just book knowledge. He decided to press her some more, see whether she'd backtrack and second-guess herself, or hold firm and defend her theory. "Don't serial killers always keep the same MO?"

She gave him a wounded look that almost had him feeling guilty. "You're treating me like a student, testing me, aren't you? Pushing to see if I know what I'm talking about."

"Do you? Know what you're talking about?"

Her gaze dropped to the island. "Yes," she whispered. "I do."

Her ragged tone put him on alert, had him studying her body language. The best indicator of honesty and genuine emotion as opposed to lies and bravado was how a person moved, how they spoke, not the words they used. Her body language told him that something else was at play here, something she wasn't yet ready to say out loud, something that had dread curling in his chest. "You were talking about modus operandi."

She cleared her throat. "What I was saying is that serial killers don't always maintain the same MO, their method, *how* they kill. Modus operandi is a conscious choice. They can change it if necessary. Like if a killer starts out tying his victims with shoelaces. If one of them manages to break a shoelace and escapes, the next time he abducts someone he'll use handcuffs. Different MO, same killer."

"That's a good way to explain it," he allowed. "But I'd add that MO is more about what's necessary, or what the killer *feels* is necessary, in order to carry out his crime. Outside of forensics, with no fingerprints or even DNA, what would convince you that some murders were done by the same killer if the MO had changed?" Again, he watched her closely, trying to decipher the subtext, the meaning beneath her words.

"Signature. A serial killer, a true psychopath, is driven to kill. He can change parts of what he does, but the signature is an intrinsic part of his killing ritual. It's the part of his crimes that he *can't* change. Signature is a subconscious action, something he doesn't choose to do or not to do. It's something he's compelled to do." She clasped her hands on top of the island. "Like the Ripper carving an *X* across the abdomen of each of his victims after he abducts them. That's his way of branding them, of letting them know that he…he *owns* them."

She wasn't meeting his gaze anymore. Instead, she slowly traced the veining in the marble top of the island. Her stark words had his throat tightening as he carefully watched her, weighing every move, even the tone of her voice.

"Signature is often a reliable means for linking crimes," she continued. "But the police often confuse MO with signature, or assume something is the signature when it's just another thing the killer does each time, but isn't *compelled* to do. And even though it's been documented many times that serial killers can and sometimes do change their victimology, go outside their comfort zone and choose a victim that doesn't fit with their history, the police automatically think that means it's a different killer. It's not their fault. Most will never come across a serial killer case their entire career. They're not equipped to evaluate the complexities, dive deeper, weigh a killer's thirst to kill versus his desire not to get caught. They don't understand his willingness or ability to adapt."

"You've circled back to the Kentucky Ripper again." He kept his voice gentle, encouraging her to finish what she came here to say, what she so obviously *needed* to say. And all the while he cursed Mason for sending her, for *using* her to get to him. "His original victimology included Caucasian women in their mid-to late thirties, married, with children. They all lived within the same fifty-square-mile geographical region in Eastern Kentucky. None of them worked outside the home."

She nodded. "Yes, but I'm saying he could have changed all of that. He could have moved to another state, gone after someone who was younger, single, without children. Someone who worked outside the home, even if only to take temporary odd jobs to make ends meet. Even if the signature was the same, most people in law enforcement would think it was another copycat, a one-off, since the alleged real guy is in prison. They wouldn't realize what they're dealing with, or even that they have a serial killer operating in their midst."

What he'd started to suspect just moments ago had solidified into a cold hard knot of dread that had him clenching his teeth so hard they ached.

Holding on to the edge of the countertop to maintain his balance, he limped around the island until he was standing beside her. Then, keeping his voice as gentle as possible, he asked, "How old are you? Don't give me a flippant answer either. I'm serious."

His question didn't seem to surprise her. "Just turned twenty-six. My birthday was last month."

Younger than he'd thought. Her guesstimate of their age difference was off by several years. "You're not Caucasian."

Her perfectly shaped brows rose. "Gee, what gave that away?" Her sarcasm did little to hide the underlying pain in her tone.

"Mason didn't mention where you're from. I'm guessing it's not Kentucky."

"Never even been to Kentucky. My home is in northeast Florida, Jacksonville." Her bottom lip trembled.

He tightened his grip on the island. "Single?"

She nodded, her eyes over-bright, as if she was fighting back tears.

"No kids?"

She squeezed her eyes shut, then shook her head. "No kids."

"You take odd jobs to make ends meet while doing your investigation?"

She slowly nodded.

"Show me," he whispered, still praying that he was wrong, but just as certain that he wasn't.

Without hesitation, she gripped the hem of her blouse, then pulled it up to her chin.

Angry puckered welts marred her skin, forming a five-by-five-inch X on her abdomen. His hands shook as he gently pulled her blouse back down. "When?"

"Two years ago." Pain leached from every word. "I was halfway through my master's degree program. But I had to put it on hold until…until I recovered. But after that, I couldn't focus, couldn't even think about going back. The police had no leads, no suspects. They still don't." She shook her head. "That's when I put my education to the test, began my own investigation. That folder I gave you is a year and a half of my life. My conclusion is that the man in prison known as the Kentucky Ripper killed *one* person, even though he claimed responsibility for many more. The real Ripper changed locales and victimology."

She finally looked up, her tortured gaze meeting his. "I believe that I'm a victim from his second spree. There are probably others as well, cases no one has connected, including me. And more women will suffer and die if I don't stop him. I'm also worried that I'm a loose end for him, that he'll come back to finish what he started." Her gaze searched his, as if looking for answers. "Please, Bryson. Help me find him and send him to prison. I don't want to die." The tears she'd been holding back spilled over and streamed down her cheeks.

He swore and lifted her into his arms. Daring his hip to interfere, he cradled her against his chest and strode from the kitchen.

Chapter Five

Teagan rubbed her bleary eyes and rolled her head on the pillow. She was in Bryson Anton's bedroom. In his bed. But he wasn't there, and his side of the bed hadn't been disturbed. She didn't know whether to applaud his old-fashioned gentlemanly conduct or curse him for it. She sighed and threw the covers off her before shuffling to the open bedroom door.

Bryson glanced up from the couch behind the coffee table, a stack of papers in his hand and more spread out across the wooden surface.

She stretched her arms above her head as she padded across the family room in her dress socks. She had no idea where her shoes and purse were. "Not to bruise your ego, but after you took me to bed, I don't remember anything. Maybe we should have a redo so you can refresh my memory."

He gave her the side-eye. "Trust me. If I took you to bed, you'd remember."

She grinned. "I have a feeling you're right."

He rolled his eyes. "You passed out in my arms, and I generously allowed you to use my bedroom to sleep it off. You're a lightweight when it comes to alcohol."

"Won't argue that." She yawned and gestured toward the cup on the table beside him. "I don't suppose that's coffee?"

In reply, he held the cup out to her.

She took a huge gulp before handing it back to him. "I think I'm half in love with you."

"That's the tequila talking. You're still drunk."

"Can't be. Had to have slept it off by now. How long was I out?"

He glanced at his watch. "Seventeen minutes."

"Oh. Then I'm definitely still drunk. More please."

He handed her the mug without looking up.

She shifted around to see what he was doing, then sat beside him, her thigh pressed to his.

"Boundaries, Teagan." He glanced pointedly at their legs, plastered together.

She sighed and moved over, just enough so they weren't touching. "You're either married, have a girlfriend, or we play for the same team, because nothing I'm trying is working."

"Never married. My girlfriend dumped me months ago because hanging with a guy with a limp cramped her style. And, trust me, you and I are definitely not playing for the same team."

"What is it then? I haven't struck out this many times since high school softball."

"Maybe you're not my type."

"Pfft. Have you *seen* me? These legs go all the way up."

He arched a brow. "We need to work on this low self-esteem of yours."

She laughed and shuffled through some of the papers he'd spread out in front of him. When she realized what he was looking at, hope flared in her chest. "You're reading my file?"

He shrugged. "I was bored. I had seventeen minutes to kill."

"Does this mean you're going to help me?"

"My history of helping people isn't exactly stellar. I'm only committing to looking through your research to offer suggestions that you can take or leave. Maybe I can put a different spin on it so you can think in new directions. I wouldn't get excited, if I were you. Like I said, I don't have a great track record. This ruined hip is because I messed up a pit maneuver a rookie could have performed in his sleep. I managed to knock the killer's vehicle into a ditch, but knocked myself silly in the process. Before I could even scramble for my gun, I'd been shot, shoved out the door, and the killer was taking off in my car with a hostage. The only reason the hostage survived is because one of my coworkers was able to rescue her after I nearly got her killed."

"I have a feeling there's way more to it than that." She started to pat his leg, then jerked her hand back at his reproachful look. "Have I mentioned that I'm a touchy-feely sort of person? I'll try to behave." She bit her lip. "You're still going to help me, right?"

He blew out a breath. "I thought you were *acting* earlier, that you were overcompensating."

"Sorry to disappoint. This is the real me."

"I didn't say I was disappointed."

She stared at him, hoping he'd explain *that* comment. But instead, he turned back to the papers in front of him. After a few minutes, she said, "If you change your mind about you and me, and I miss a signal, just let me know, okay?"

He let out a deep sigh and pinned her with an exasperated look. "Teagan?"

"Yes, Bryson?"

"Shut up."

She grinned and scooted back on the couch to sit crosslegged while he reviewed her research. It was taking him far longer than she'd expected. The folder wasn't *that* thick. She'd brought the summary, not the detailed reports. But he kept thumbing through the pages, comparing things, rereading. She was dying to know what he thought. She was also dying for an entirely different reason.

She climbed off the couch. "Where's the nearest toilet in this monstrosity? I'm about to pee my pants." She hopped back and forth from one foot to the other. "Never mind, I'll figure it out." She ran into his master bedroom and chose door number one. "Found it!" she called back, before slamming it closed.

BRYSON STARED AT his bedroom doorway where Teagan the Tornado had just disappeared. He'd expected a different woman when she woke, figuring her earlier actions were a type of bravado, a coping mechanism because of what had happened to her. Then again, she hadn't slept long enough to sober up.

He took his cell phone from one of the piles of paper on the coffee table, idly rubbing his aching hip as he reluctantly pressed a programmed number that he should have deleted months ago. When the line clicked he said, "You're trying to kill me."

"Delightful, isn't she?" Mason chuckled.

"You mean she's always like this? There isn't a cure?"

"I'm not taking her back. If that's what you want, I'm hanging up."

He turned his head, looking through the glass doors at the back of the kitchen. The creek was too low to see from here unless he stood. But the pilings holding the dock in place reached like spindly fingers toward the bright blue sky overhead, a reminder of his last conversation with Mason. Had it been only yesterday?

"Bryson? You still there?"

"I'm here. You mentioned when I was ready, that you'd throw me a line. Looks like I'm going to at least dip my toes in, whether I want to or not."

"She's a hard person to say no to."

"Yes. She is."

"Whatever you need, it's yours. Just name it." Mason's tone was all business now.

"My files, all those boxes I foolishly—and against FBI policy—saved from the Ripper case with the Bureau. I asked you to store them along with other case files you archived for The Justice Seekers. Is it possible to get them sent here, when you have time?"

"You'll have them within the hour."

Teagan appeared in his bedroom doorway, looking slightly green and more than a little woozy as she gripped the doorframe. She really didn't know how to hold her liquor, which for some reason he found adorable. "Thanks, Mason."

"For the files?"

He tightened his hand on the phone. "We'll start with that, for now." He hung up. Then he grabbed his cane and laboriously climbed to his feet.

Teagan trudged toward him and stopped a few feet away, her hand clutching her stomach. Bryson had a feeling he was about to finally meet the real Teagan.

She looked up at him, misery drawing tight lines at the corners of her eyes. "Did I really tell you I had to pee?"

He smiled. Maybe he'd already met the real Teagan after all. "Come on. I'll make you some fresh coffee and my special hangover blaster."

Chapter Six

When Bryson had mentioned a hangover blaster, the name alone should have warned Teagan to just say no. But she had to admit, even sitting on his master bathroom floor with her head hanging over a toilet, that awful concoction had done the trick. Too bad that meant throwing up everything she'd eaten or drank for the past *week*.

She shuddered and sat back. At least she could be grateful that the man was a neat freak. Either that or he hired really great cleaning people. His bathroom floor was spotless. She winced. Or it had been, until she'd come along. With her tummy finally settling, she pushed herself to her feet and then wobbled to the sink.

After rinsing her mouth out with some mouthwash that she'd found in a cabinet and brushing her teeth with her finger and a dab of toothpaste, she felt almost human again. She washed her face, made sure her stubborn hair hadn't escaped its braid, then did a quick refresh of the bathroom. The sound of voices engaged in conversation had her hurrying through the master bedroom and opening the door.

The front double door was wide open. Bryson was in his wheelchair directing a man with a hand truck full of bankers boxes toward a hallway that ran across the back of the house. Careful not to get in the way, she plopped down cross-legged on a leather padded bench just outside the bedroom and waited.

By the time the man was finished and Bryson locked the door behind him, she'd counted over a dozen boxes.

He wheeled his chair up to her. "Feeling better?"

"Much. Although I'm not sure whether the cure is worse than the hangover." She motioned toward his chair. "I see you ran out of tequila and traded in the cane."

"My liver cried uncle for the day."

"If you strip, I'd be happy to play Helga and massage your hip for you." She rubbed her hands together in anticipation.

"Helga?"

"The masseuse from this morning. What I lack in professional training I'd more than make up for with enthusiasm."

He coughed as if to cover a laugh. "Yes, well. I appreciate the offer but another massage isn't going to do the trick at this point. The hip gives out once the muscles get overworked and won't support me anymore."

"Are you doing physical therapy?"

"Let me guess. You can help me with that too?"

"If I'd known I'd meet you one day, I would have changed majors in college so I could say yes."

This time he laughed out loud. "Let me worry about the therapy, or lack thereof." He waved toward the back hallway. "Go on. Ask me about the boxes. I can tell that your curiosity is eating you alive."

She frowned. "Your earlier theory about your girlfriend dumping you because of your limp probably isn't right. I think she left you because you're always profiling people and reading their minds. Okay, yes, the curiosity is driving me batty. What's in the boxes?"

"I don't read minds. Profiling, or more accurately,

Criminal Investigative Analysis, is science, not art. Although some might argue it's both. And the answer to your question is that the boxes contain my research on the Kentucky Ripper. I was fresh out of polka-dot folders."

"All you had to do was ask. I could have let you borrow some of mine." She waved toward the cased opening where he'd directed the man with the hand truck. "Did the FBI send over copies of their research on the case?"

"The FBI doesn't allow former agents access to their case files. Those are copies I made of everything that passed my desk back when I worked on the investigation. Well, more accurately, when I worked on the profile. Technically, I wasn't an investigator. But the case consumed me and left me with more questions than answers, even after the killer was convicted. I religiously copied as much as I could and snuck it home every chance I got. From start to finish, the case took two years. Those copies added up."

She put her hands on her hips. "I knew it. You don't think the right guy was put away or you wouldn't have risked your career taking that stuff home. Admit it. My theory holds water."

"I admit nothing. But I'm willing to take a fresh look, which is why I had this stuff brought out of storage." He motioned toward the doorway at the end of the room. "Come on. Might as well give you a tour of this *monstrosity* and show you where those boxes went."

"That monstrosity comment I made earlier was under duress. I didn't mean it."

"Yes, you did. And I don't take offense. It *is* a rather large house, too big for one person. But it met my requirements when I was house shopping."

"Let me guess. Requirement number one, no carpet, for easier mobility with the cane and wheelchair?"

"Anyone could have guessed that."

"Requirement number two," she said. "It's only one story. You're not ready to tackle stairs just yet."

"Again, too easy. What about the third requirement?"

She shook her head. "Stumped on that one."

"The isolated location so people wouldn't bother me." He arched a brow at her.

She winced. "Ah, well. Two out of three isn't bad. That's sixty-six percent, still a passing grade, in high school at least."

"Somehow I can't imagine you ever being satisfied with anything less than an A. You were valedictorian, weren't you?"

"Takes one to know one?"

He smiled. "Come on. You've already seen the kitchen, family room, and made yourself completely at home in my master bedroom and bathroom." He waved toward two more doors on the far right wall. "Closet and half bath."

"I was so close earlier. Didn't realize there was a half bath over there."

"At least you made it to a bathroom. Can't complain about that." He wheeled his chair toward the back of the room.

She fell in step beside him. "What is this floor made out of? I can't figure it out."

He leaned over the side of the chair as if noticing the floor for the first time. "Beats me. Came with the house. Come on, right turn, obviously, since the hall starts here."

Along the way, he pointed out the various rooms but didn't stop until they reached the far end.

"He motioned toward the door in front of them. This leads—"

"Let me guess. Man cave?"

"Home office."

"Oh. Kind of anticlimactic after walking all this way."

"It wasn't *that* far."

She gave him a droll look. "Says the man who *rolled* all the way here. I've already gotten my ten thousand steps for the day. And that's just since I walked out of your bedroom."

"Do you want to see the coolest part of the house or not?"

"Coolest? Robert Downey Jr. in *Iron Man* cool or Keanu Reeves in *John Wick* kind of cool?"

"More like Bruce Willis in *anything* kind of cool."

She grinned and they fist-bumped. "Then my answer is most definitely yes."

He shoved the door open. Then he moved back and motioned her forward. "After you."

The excitement on his face had her expecting something amazing when she stepped inside the room.

She wasn't disappointed.

Chapter Seven

Bryson rolled into his office behind Teagan and did something he rarely did these days. He simply enjoyed the moment. He didn't worry about his aching hip or rehash the would haves, could haves, should haves of his life. Instead, he basked in the sheer joy on her face as she turned in slow circles, taking it all in.

There was a lot to take in.

The expansive room was a microcosm of the house itself, fully contained with a kitchenette in one corner, a bathroom, a bedroom intended for those all-nighters if he needed a quick nap before heading back into the main room to continue his work.

On the left side was the library. Floor-to-ceiling cherrywood bookshelves were filled with all kinds of law enforcement textbooks on topics like forensics, crime scene analysis, and profiling. Past the library, nearly every inch of wall space was adorned with matching cherrywood cabinets, drawers and open shelving. Storage would never be a problem here. The boxes that Mason had sent over were neatly stacked beside some of those storage cabinets. Something for him to tackle later, after everything was scanned electronically. That was the real beauty of this room—the technology.

A large round stone table in the middle of the room was

control central for the massive daisy-chained monitors that took up most of the opposite wall. From that table, he could bring up reports or photographs or even the internet and display the information on any individual monitor, or slide it across all of them to form one picture. It was a profiler's dream, to be able to have everything at his fingertips at one time so he could make comparisons and see the entire case at a glance.

Too bad he'd never actually used the darn thing on a case.

Teagan had made a full circuit of the room, opening doors and checking behind them, looking into the storage cabinets. But she surprised him by returning to the library, rather than the round table. She traced her hands almost reverently across the books, like a beautiful butterfly, flitting from tome to tome. When she finally turned around, she motioned toward the two leather wing chairs and circular rug that completed the library effect.

"This is amazing. You have books I've only dreamed of reading, rare ones that my college couldn't even get their hands on when I tried borrowing them through our library system. Two of the books have your name on them. I didn't know you'd authored any texts."

"Neither do most people," he said dryly. "My publisher lost a fortune on those."

"Then they don't deserve to be your publisher. They obviously don't know how to market your work or it would have sold a gazillion books."

"Are you one of the six people who bought a copy? Is that how you know they're amazing?"

She rolled her eyes. "I'm sure you're exaggerating."

"Not by much, unfortunately."

"Well, based on your reputation in the field, I'd love to become reader number seven, if you'll let me borrow them."

"You can *have* them. I've got plenty more. What about the rest of the room? You don't seem as impressed as I'd hoped. My ego's a bit deflated. I thought you'd run straight to the table and start salivating."

"I would have, if it wasn't for your library. I'm a book lover, through and through. But the entire room is incredible." She strode to the table and ran her fingers across it. "You must have enjoyed being a Justice Seeker more than you've let on. This is fit for the *knights of the round table*, just like the one that Mason told me that you all have in some super-secret hidden room at The Justice Seekers' home base."

"Almost. It's not quite as large as his since I don't have twelve Seekers, or so-called *knights*, to fill it up. But I admit I enjoyed his flair for the medieval and the fun of the whole Camelot concept, so I stole some of that for myself. I converted an existing study and two bedrooms into this office with the intention of using it to work from home while recuperating from being shot. But the recovery has been slower than I'd expected, and I ended up with way too much time to think about my failures. Resigning seemed like the reasonable thing to do."

"Wait. Are you saying that you've never used this office, or *great hall*, if you call it that like Mason does? Once it was finished, it just sat here unused?"

"I don't call it a great hall. It's got the stone floors, walls and table, but nothing else that resembles a castle like Mason's does. And, yes, you're absolutely right. I can't remember the last time I've traipsed across the house to this room. If it wasn't for the cleaning company that comes in once a week, there'd be cobwebs and dust all over the place."

"Wow. If I'd known that, I'd have snuck in through a back window and claimed squatters' rights long ago. I

could happily live here for weeks and not come up for air."
She lowered herself into one of the cushy leather chairs at
the round table. "Ahhh. World class. You have great taste."
She waved toward the monitors. "Feel free to feed your ego
by giving me a demonstration. How big are those screens
anyway? Six or seven feet tall?"

He rolled one of the other leather chairs out of the way
and positioned his wheelchair beside her. "Each one is
six feet by three feet. I wanted twelve, to keep with the
Camelot theme. But it seemed like overkill and would have
restricted the space too much, so I settled on nine. They
work together as one monitor if I want, or I can load something different on each one. That's the real benefit, being
able to put up information about different crimes on each
screen and compare them. I can use a computer tablet at
the table to select which screen I want and use a light pen
to draw circles around different items or highlight them,
edit them, whatever."

"Definitely cool. Can I drive?" She held out her hand.
"Give me the reins. Let's do this."

Instead of popping up one of the computer tablets from
a hidden compartment in the table, he adjusted his chair
to face her and took her hands in his.

Her eyes widened and a slow grin spread across her
face.

"Don't," he said. "Whatever sexy, funny, or smart-ass
comment you're about to make about me holding your
hands, just wait. I need to have a serious conversation
with you. Can you focus for a few minutes without any
wisecracks?"

A look of wariness crossed her face. "Why do I feel like
I'm about to be sent to the principal's office?"

He sighed and let her go.

"Okay, okay." She grabbed his hands with both of hers. "No jokes, no tangents. I'm listening."

He arched a brow, not sure whether or not to believe her.

"Really," she said. "I can be serious when I need to. Go on. What is it?"

"I just want you to be sure that you know what you're getting into before we go any further. You've been like a whirlwind, blowing into my life. I met you, what, a few hours ago? And somehow you've managed to make me excited about working again. That's why I brought you to this room, to show you the tools we've got at our disposal so we can work together, if that's truly what you want to do."

"Are you kidding? It's all I've wanted since I first came across the Ripper case and saw your contributions to the investigation. I want to work with you to catch the Ripper before—"

"We're not going to work on the Ripper case."

She blinked. "My turn to be confused."

He gently entwined their fingers, trying to convey that he was there for her if she needed his support. "I'm going to hire a temp to scan in and catalog the data in those boxes. That will take several days, maybe even a week. In the meantime, the only case that I've had a chance to scan is yours. While you were recovering from your tequila binge, I used the scanner in my study to process your folder. That's what I want to bring up on these screens. But there's a world of difference between looking at something on an eight-by-ten sheet of paper, and seeing it on a six-foot-tall screen. A lot of this stuff is deeply personal. Are you sure you can handle it?"

"I don't understand your concerns. I put that folder together. I know what's in it. I want you to see it, to review it with me."

"Your descriptions of the most recent attack that you allege was made by the Ripper didn't mention you by name. That's quite telling. And there's far more detail to what happened to you than what you had in that folder. A lot more. We have to review all of the information, not just some of it, if we have a chance at solving this thing."

"Well of course there's more, all the detailed reports that support the summaries I wrote. I didn't bring those with me."

"That's not what I mean. There are other details, things you didn't reference even at a high level in your summaries."

"Like what?"

He squeezed her hands before letting go. Then he pushed down on top of the table in front of him and the section flipped over to reveal a computer tablet. He typed some commands into the control program, then pressed enter. Teagan looked up at the screens. Her eyes widened and she put a hand over her mouth before turning away.

"Where did you get those?" she whispered.

He tapped the tablet and the screens went dark. "I still have a few contacts in law enforcement."

She crossed her arms over her middle. "Well, they shouldn't have shared my hospital photos with you. They're—"

"Too personal? None of my business?"

She flinched and dropped her gaze.

He rolled back from the table. "Come on. It's okay. Forget all this. You're not ready."

"Wait. Just…give me a minute to catch my breath, okay? I can handle it. Really."

"Teagan. There's no reason for you to have to catch your breath, to handle it. You lived through the abduction, the torture, once already. You shouldn't have to do that again, reopen old wounds. Leave the investigation to me. Maybe because I admire your spunk, or maybe just because I'm ready to jump back in the game and didn't realize it until now. Regardless of the reason, I want to do this. But the only way I can is by going through every piece of data surrounding your abduction, everything that happened to you. *Everything*. It's the only way to make sure nothing was missed, that every possible clue has been considered. Meanwhile, you can go back to Florida, get on with your life. When I have something to report, I'll contact you." He wheeled to the door and held it open for her. "Come on. We're done here."

Chapter Eight

When Teagan crossed her arms and gave him a mutinous stare, Bryson sighed and let the office door close. She'd made no move toward the doorway. She wasn't backing down without a fight. But neither was he. "Teagan, we should—"

"You caught me off guard. That's all. I didn't expect to see…those pictures, okay? You should have warned me."

"If I'd warned you, I might not have received an honest reaction. You would have covered up your true emotions, or at least tried, with false bravado. Now I know the truth. This is all still too raw for you to be involved in the investigation. And there's nothing wrong with that. Victims don't typically work on their own cases, for good reason."

"I'm not a victim," she snapped. "I'm a survivor."

"Fair enough. That doesn't change anything that I said."

She waved toward the stacks of boxes. "Why can't we start with these? I already know the man who attacked me is the real Kentucky Ripper, not Leviathan Finney, the guy in prison. There's no reason to review every nitty-gritty detail about what happened to me. We're past that. We know who did it, that first guy you profiled back in Kentucky, the one the police let get away, Avarice Lowe."

"Did you tell the detectives on your case that you believed Lowe was the one who'd abducted you?"

"Yes. I did."

"And? Let me guess. They did a cursory look at him and either couldn't locate him at all or said he had an alibi. And they went no further than that."

"They couldn't find him. But they didn't try very hard."

"Why do you suppose that is?"

She threw her hands in the air. "I don't know. Probably because they're lazy and wanted to work on easier cases."

He wheeled over in front of her. "Can you think of another reason? Come on. Set aside emotion and use that valedictorian mind of yours."

She gave him another mutinous look. "They don't believe Lowe is the Ripper and had no evidence to tie him to my case. But that's because they refused to listen."

"Detectives, good ones at least, follow the evidence. The only reason you feel that the Ripper is the one who abducted you is because the man who hurt you carved that X on your abdomen. Everything else about your case is different, including the fact that you survived."

"Then let's go through your case files and find more similarities. That's why you brought them here."

He shook his head. "I brought them here to review *after* I review your case, and then, only if we decide the two cases are connected, or highly likely connected. What happens if we do it your way, spend all our time on the Ripper case, and discover that you're wrong? We've wasted weeks, or longer by that time going through all of the Ripper's cases. We'd be starting over at ground zero without having made any progress figuring out who attacked you. If you truly want my help in finding out who hurt you, I'm all in. But I have to do it my way. I follow the evidence. And that means, starting at the beginning, with what happened to you."

She stared at the stacks of boxes for a long moment.

When she finally met his gaze, naked pain radiated back at him. "I spent over a year and a half on this to find the man who hurt me. I don't want to start over. I can't."

Disappointment shot through him, but he forced a smile. "Then don't. Keep doing what you're doing. Follow the leads where you believe they'll take you."

"Without you."

He nodded. "Without me."

"Bryson's way or the highway, is that it?"

He hated the hurt in her voice. He especially hated that he was at least partly the cause. But it would be far worse if he gave in, if he went against everything he'd learned as a Justice Seeker in how to run investigations as well as his profiling experience with the FBI. She'd managed to awaken a hunger in him for justice again, a desire to right the wrongs of his past and prove he was better than the mistakes he'd made. Starting out by making another mistake wasn't how he'd atone for his sins.

Steeling himself against the censure and sense of betrayal in her beautiful brown eyes, he responded to her accusation. "Bryson's way was to enjoy his hermit-like existence and never talk to another human being again. I was perfectly happy here all by myself until you showed up. So don't act like I'm suddenly pushing you to do something that I want you to do. You came here for my help. I was willing to help you the only way I know how, by using my training and experience and following the right steps from beginning to end to build a profile. I would have gathered as much evidence along the way as I could. Then, I would have worked with the police to get them moving on it. None of that is sexy or flashy. It's a heck of a lot of work. But that's the way it's done. Period. And you said you can't do that, which means *we're* done. Follow your own path and I'll follow mine. There's a creek full of fish in my backyard. Maybe I'll get a pole and cast a line. There are worse ways to spend my time. Go home. I mean it. I wish you the best, I truly do. But when I come back inside, I want you gone."

He wheeled out of the room and a few minutes later he was on the dock, nursing a can of beer as if the twenty-four hours since Mason's visit had never happened. But as he listened to the creek splashing over the rocks and watched the cars far below that seemed like toys from this distance, he realized that everything had changed. There *was* no going back. Mason had started a quiet rumble inside him. Teagan had built that rumble into an earthquake that had rocked him from his complacency. She'd reminded him of the thrill of the chase, the satisfaction of solving a puzzle, and the reason he'd gone into his line of work to begin with—to help people. But just as he hadn't helped Hayley when he'd gotten shot, he hadn't helped Teagan.

He swore and crumpled the now-empty can in his hand. He'd been far too rough on her. Every word he'd said had been true, his truth at least. But she obviously wasn't ready for that kind of honesty. She wasn't one of his peers, a hardened or jaded agent who he could talk to without guarding his words. She was a victim, a survivor. She deserved nothing but respect and kindness as she struggled to come to terms with what had happened to her. If going after the Ripper was her way of coping, then who was he to stand in her way? He should have encouraged her. Instead, he'd lectured her on the "right" way to conduct an investigation.

The distant sound of her car starting up in his driveway had his shoulders slumping in disappointment. Not with her. With himself. She'd probably head back to her hotel room, or wherever she was staying, and continue her research like a hamster on a wheel never getting where they truly wanted to go. She needed guidance from someone willing to pursue the angle she wanted to pursue, not the angle that Bryson had insisted was the right place to start. So how could he help her?

It all boiled down to contacts.

He'd joked earlier that he still had a *few* contacts in law enforcement. In reality, he had far more than a few. After all, he'd only gone on hiatus as a Justice Seeker six months ago. Before that, with his combined years as a Seeker and an FBI special agent, he'd worked with hundreds, maybe thousands of peers in his field. Many of them had become close friends that he still had to this day. Maybe, just maybe, he could give Teagan what she wanted—someone to talk to who'd worked on the Ripper cases.

He pulled out his cell phone and placed a call to Special Agent Pierce Buchanan. There was the usual small talk, asking about Pierce, his wife, Madison, and their toddler, Nicole. That was followed by some groveling and apologizing for Bryson having refused the couple's many requests to let them visit him after the shooting. But they worked out an agreement. In exchange for Pierce contacting Teagan and offering her an insider's view of the Ripper murders, Bryson would fly to Pierce's home in Savannah for a long weekend later this summer. Bryson wasn't sure if he was the winner or loser in that negotiation. Three of Pierce's four brothers and his father were in law enforcement. They'd likely show up and grill him about every detail of the shooting and its aftermath.

After ending that call, he made one more.

To the airport.

Chapter Nine

Death and its close cousin, extreme violence, had walked this meandering path before. They'd held hands in the dark shadows beneath these towering live oaks. They'd carefully avoided the bulging tree roots that lifted and cracked the concrete, quietly stalking their prey. Here, in the near-darkness where thick branches and leaves blotted out the hot Florida sun overhead, they'd crouched in this ten-foot-wide space lined on both sides by six-foot-tall wooden fences. The fences were supposed to ensure the privacy of the homeowners whose properties backed onto the nature trail in The Woods subdivision while joggers and walkers enjoyed these paths. But two years ago, these same fences had protected and concealed evil.

This was where Teagan Ray had been attacked, brutalized and then abducted.

There were theories that extreme violence, whether or not it ended in death, left an indelible mark on a place. It tainted the soil, the trees, even the air with its negative energy and could be felt for years afterward. Standing here now with a sense of dread and oppressiveness weighing down on him, Bryson was more inclined to believe those theories than to dispel them. Because it wasn't the GPS coordinates that had made him stop when he'd reached this spot. It was an overwhelming feeling of doom.

He shook his head at those thoughts. It was more sci-
entific than that. He'd stopped here because he'd tried to
mentally place himself in the role of a man stalking prey.
This is where he'd have lain in wait for a potential victim. It
was a particularly dark spot, with thick overgrown bushes
providing the perfect cover. And over two years ago, unfortunately, Teagan was the one who'd happened through
here at just the wrong time. And she'd paid for that dearly.

After the initial attack, the belief was that she'd been
drugged. Still able to walk with assistance, but not coher-
ent enough to fight back or even understand what was happening to her, she was led by her abductor to wherever he'd
parked his vehicle. Or, at least, that was the theory. There
weren't any witnesses to fill in those details.

Her first lucid memories, after the attack on the path,
were that she was blindfolded and tied up in the shack
where he'd taken her. Two weeks later, when he'd left on
one of his so-called supply trips that he took every few
days, she'd miraculously escaped. But she'd gotten lost in
the wilds of the Florida backcountry for days. By the time
a hiker had found her, she was dehydrated and sunburned
and half out of her mind. Once she'd recovered enough
in the hospital to explain that she'd escaped a kidnapper,
over two days had passed. The police used scent dogs to
backtrack to the shack where she'd been held. Turns out
she'd been about an hour and a half from her hometown
of Jacksonville, deep in the woods outside of Live Oak,
near the Suwannee River. But the abductor wasn't there,
and he never came back after that.

The owner of the shack was cleared. Not because Teagan couldn't pick him out of a lineup. She couldn't pick
anyone out of a lineup. She'd been drugged, blindfolded,
deprived of water and food. Her abductor had kept the
shack mostly dark, with room-darkening drapes and few

sources of light. He'd told her from the beginning that he planned to kill her. But until then, he was super careful, obviously in case she somehow escaped, which she did.

Because of his extreme care to conceal his identity, she'd told the police she could probably pass him on the street and would never know it. That was likely one of the reasons she had put her education and the rest of her life on hold to try to find the man who'd attacked her. Knowing he was in prison and could never hurt her again would no doubt be the only way she could ever live without the fear of him finding her again, and finishing what he'd started.

Too bad her abductor hadn't been the owner of the shack. That would have made everything neat and tidy and it would all be over by now. But the owner lived in Canada, where he went to work every day and had plenty of people to vouch for that. The shack was where he stayed two or three times a year when he came down to work at clearing the land around it in preparation for building the retirement cabin he dreamed about.

Bryson made some notes on the police report, marking things on the map of the trail that he'd noticed today. Then he tucked the report into his jacket pocket and took one last look around. He intended to walk all of the paths in this community today if his hip could handle it, or use his wheelchair if he had to, which seemed likely by how badly his hip was already throbbing. He wanted to see whether there were other good ambush spots on other trails. If so, then maybe someone with homes backing up on those paths might have spotted a man walking the trails back then, choosing his ultimate hiding place. There could be some witnesses who didn't even realize they'd seen something important.

There were 4.1 miles of nature walks and trails in this community, according to its website. Other statistics that he'd gleaned about The Woods were that it had 811 homes and 18 man-made ponds. It boasted a so-called natural setting, thus the name. From his perspective, that meant there were a heck of a lot of trees and overgrown bushes, providing great hiding places for would-be attackers. But because the community was gated, the residents had been lulled into thinking they were safe.

Maybe that explained why Teagan had thought nothing of walking through this overgrown, dark, far less traveled section of the trails as the sun was going down. Her parents lived just a few streets away, and she'd been home from college on a visit. Having grown up here without any major crime incidents in an upper-middle-class area that was generally considered safe, she had felt there was nothing to worry about. In a perfect world, there shouldn't have been. But unfortunately, there were some very bad people sharing the same air as the rest of them, and Teagan had the misfortune of coming across one. Wrong place, wrong time.

Or did that really explain it? Could the attacker have been after her specifically?

That was one of the questions Bryson needed to answer. The assumption all along in the police reports, and by Teagan and her parents as well, had been that she was a randomly chosen victim. There wasn't any evidence to the contrary. But Bryson wasn't the type to assume anything.

A low growl had him turning around, leaning on his cane with one hand as he flipped back his jacket with the other to grab the pistol holstered on his hip. But he didn't pull his weapon. Instead, he let his jacket fall back into place and rested both of his hands on the cane to steady himself as he glanced from the impressive, still-growling German shepherd to the gorgeous young woman holding its leash.

Teagan.

The accusation that she might have somehow gotten Pierce to tell her where he was and then followed him to Jacksonville died on his lips unspoken. She hadn't expected to see him here. It was evident by her wide eyes and the way her left hand was pressed against her throat.

"What are you doing here?" he demanded. "I thought you'd be in Savannah by now." His accusatory tone did exactly what he'd intended. It gave her something to focus on instead of the fright from seeing a man standing in the shadows where she'd once been attacked.

She dropped her hand and gave the dog a command that had him sitting on his haunches. His tongue lolled out as if he hadn't been poised to rip out Bryson's throat seconds earlier.

"Why would I be in Savannah?" She sounded genuinely confused.

It was his turn to be surprised. "Didn't you get a call? From FBI special agent Pierce Buchanan?"

She shook her head. "No. But I haven't checked my messages since leaving your place yesterday. My phone number listed in the folder I gave you is a landline at my apartment. It's not one that I share with many people. And it's not registered under my name."

The truth sent a wave of anger and sympathy straight through him. "You carry a burner phone, don't you? You're worried that your attacker might trace you."

Her gaze was her answer, darting toward the fences on either side of the path and the thick trees and bushes blocking the view of anyone behind them. He wondered why the homeowners association hadn't voted to clear out these dangerous hiding places, especially after what had happened to Teagan. But mostly, he wondered why she was here.

He took a step forward, hesitating when her dog emitted another threatening growl.

"Zeus, stop." She shook the leash and the dog quieted, but his dark eyes followed Bryson's every move. "Why would an FBI agent be looking for me?" Her eyes widened again. "Have they found something? In Savannah? Oh no. Someone else wasn't attacked, were they?"

Ignoring the new round of growls from her dog, he limped toward her, stopping just out of lunging distance. "No. I'm not aware of any more attacks linked to the man who hurt you. Pierce is a good friend of mine who lives in Savannah. Because of his experience with serial killer cases, he ended up assisting on the task force in Kentucky. We worked the Ripper case together. After you left yesterday—"

"After you threw me out, you mean," she accused. "I thought you Justice Seekers were supposed to be honorable and help people in need."

He smiled, pleased to see a return of the sassy confident woman he'd met in Gatlinburg. "Yes, well. I was on hiatus from the Seekers at the time. So you weren't officially my client. But I did want to help you. So after I threw you out, I called Pierce and asked him to give you an insider's reading of the Ripper cases and to answer any questions that you had."

Her brows crinkled in confusion. "Why would you do that? You told me that looking into the Ripper case was the wrong approach."

He started to move closer, but Zeus stood up, his ears flattening. Shooting her dog to defend himself was the last thing he wanted to do, so he took a step back.

"I'm glad you have Zeus with you, for protection," he told her. "That's smart."

She winced and looked away.

Understanding had him filled with regret. "I wasn't trying to say that you shouldn't have been out here without him that first time." When she didn't answer, he leaned to the side, trying to get her to look at him. "Teagan?"

She sighed and met his gaze. "What?"

"It wasn't your fault." He waved his hands along the path. "None of this is your fault. A woman should be able to dance naked through the streets without worrying about some Neanderthal attacking her. It's *never* the victim's fault. The only person to blame is the monster who hurt you."

A reluctant smile tugged at the corners of her mouth. "You sound like my parents."

Now it was his turn to wince. "Ouch."

She laughed, then winked, looking more like her old self again. "Don't worry. There's exactly zero chance of me confusing Hot Guy with my parents."

"Good to know. I think. Assuming I'm Hot Guy?"

She grinned. "Definitely." Her smile dimmed, and some of her earlier uneasiness had her glancing around again. "I'm staying with my parents for a few days. And like I do every time I see them, I walk this trail. Not because I want to go…where it happened…some survivor's weird hang-up or something. But because it's the same routine I had before the attack. I've walked these trails almost daily since I was a little girl. And I refuse to change that because of…because of what happened. He took so much from me. It might seem silly, but letting him take away my joy of nature and long walks would be letting him win." She patted the dog beside her. "My only concession now is to bring my mom's dog Zeus and Annie along."

The dog seemed to be licking his lips in anticipation of sinking its teeth into his hide—if dogs had lips.

"Wait. Annie? Who's Annie?"

She slid her hand into the pocket of her jeans and pulled out a compact .22-caliber pistol. "Meet Annie."

"Let me guess. After Annie Oakley?"

Her gorgeous smile made another appearance. "Very good, Sherlock. Maybe you should be an FBI agent." She shoved it back into her pocket.

"Been there, done that." He gestured toward her pocket. "Should I ask for your concealed carry permit?"

"That depends. Did you become a police officer since the last time we met?"

"Touché. Don't worry. Your secret's safe with me. I won't call any of my JSO contacts to tell them about Annie."

"Is that how you got past the gates? Someone from the Jacksonville Sherriff's Office told the guard to let you through?"

"Actually, I got in the old-fashioned way."

"The old-fashioned way?"

"Ben Franklin. A bribe."

He'd expected a laugh. Instead, her face turned ashen.

"Teagan? Are you okay?" Risking the wrath of Zeus, he leaned toward her.

Predictably, the dog barked and pulled against the leash trying to reach him.

She frowned and yanked him back. "Zeus, enough. Friend. He's a friend." She motioned toward Bryson. "Hold your hand out for him to sniff, palm down."

"You're kidding, right?"

"No. I'm serious. Let him smell you." She slipped her hand under the back of the dog's collar. "Friend, Zeus. Friend."

Telling himself he was an idiot, he did as she'd asked, holding his hand out.

Zeus snuffled his hand for a good ten seconds, then his

tongue lolled out and he gave it a long sloppy lick before sitting back on his haunches.

Bryson made a face at the saliva on his hand, then looked up in time to see Teagan trying to hide a grin. He narrowed his eyes suspiciously. "You did that on purpose."

"Yeah, well. It's kind of funny, seeing you dressed up in a business suit with dog slobber all over your hand."

After a quick glance at Zeus, who seemed far more interested in a butterfly flitting around a nearby bush now that he'd supposedly accepted Bryson as a nonthreat, he reached out and wiped his hand on Teagan's shirt.

She gasped in dismay at the wet stain on her formerly white blouse. "I can't believe you did that."

"We're even now. Don't go planning your revenge."

"Hmm. We'll see about that." She glanced around again. "You said you bribed the guard at the gate to let you in? You didn't show him some kind of old FBI credentials or anything like that?"

Now he understood why she'd paled earlier. "You're surprised at how easy it was for someone who doesn't live here to get in. Is that it?"

She nodded. "Not that I should be surprised. After all, the police ruled out the suspect as living in the community. They supposedly researched every single resident. We knew he had to have come from outside somehow. I just didn't think it would be that easy to drive on in."

"Yeah, well. It's not like you have to be a former cop to be a security guard. Pretty much anyone can be one. And they aren't paid enough to make them above reproach, some of them anyway. I'm sure most are great people and genuinely try to do a good job."

She snorted. "Now you're pandering, trying to make me feel better. I preferred it when you were being brutally honest."

"Brutal? Ouch again."

"If the truth fits." She shrugged, then winked as if to soften her criticisms.

"This isn't going at all the way I'd planned when I flew down here late last night."

"You thought I was in Georgia. You didn't plan on running into me."

"No. I didn't. But now that I have, I'm wondering why I did. After being so intent on finding information on the Ripper, why would you come back to Jacksonville? Are you taking a break from the investigation? Returning to school to finish your master's?"

She straightened her shoulders. "No break. I'm digging in harder than before. And I'm taking your advice. I'm starting at the beginning. And this—" she waved her hand toward the trees and bushes around them "—is where it all began."

Chapter Ten

The look on Bryson's face had Teagan stiffening. "Why are you so surprised? I went to you for help and advice because I respected your experience and expertise. Did you think I'd completely ignore your suggestions?"

He nodded, surprising her with his honesty. "I assumed anyone stubborn enough to work past my annoyance over the mistaken identity thing and then pretend they liked tequila enough to make themselves sick would be far too one-track minded to give up over a year of research to essentially start over."

"Yeah, well. Maybe you shouldn't judge people so fast when you meet them."

His mouth quirked up in that sexy half-smile that had her practically drooling again just like the first time she'd seen him. Good grief he was dangerous, the kind of danger that had her wishing she'd worn shorts instead of jeans. She was actually sweating now, and it couldn't be more than eighty degrees. A mild spring day around here.

"Looks like my profiling skills are even dustier than I'd realized," he said. "My apologies for making assumptions." He shifted on his feet, and she didn't miss the telltale wince as he rested both hands on the top of his cane.

"Your hip is bothering you."

"Are you playing Watson to my Sherlock now?"

"Oh heck no. I'll never be the sidekick. If anything, I'm Wonder Woman and you're Steve Trevor."

"Doesn't he die in the end?"

"Everyone dies in the end."

His grin faded. "I didn't mean to bring up bad memories again."

She shook her head. "Trust me. You didn't. They're always there, in the back of my mind. That's why I'm doing this investigation. When I escaped that day, I got out of the shack. But I didn't escape him. He's still out there. Until he's put away for good, I'll never be able to move on. Not really."

He sighed heavily. "I was worried that might be a big part of this for you. What happens if you never find him?"

Zeus whined beside her and she realized she was unconsciously tugging his leash, transmitting her agitation to him. She forced her hand to relax and rubbed his head. "That's a problem for future Teagan to worry about. Right now, I'm on the case, determined to do everything I can to bring this guy to justice. The real question is, now that we're both committed to this endeavor, do we work on it together or go our separate ways again?"

He subtly shifted, resting his back against one of the live oaks lining the path. This was the longest that she'd seen him standing without giving in to his wheelchair, and he'd been out here before she'd arrived. He had to be about ready to collapse.

"How about we discuss it over dinner?" he asked.

She blinked. "Dinner? Did I miss a signal somewhere?"

He laughed. "It's just dinner. I'm hungry, and to be honest my hip is going to give out soon if I don't sit. Rather than fall down in an embarrassing heap on the concrete, I'm inclined to head to my car then off somewhere to eat before my next appointment which isn't for—" he glanced at his watch "—another two hours. What do you say? Want me to drive you home so you can put up Zeus and then go eat with me?"

"What appointment?"

"It was too much to hope you'd let that pass." He pushed away from the tree and leaned on the cane. "I'm interviewing the Brodericks tonight, a couple who used to own one of the homes that backs up to this spot on the path. They moved shortly after everything happened, to one of the homes in the back of the subdivision, on Beautyberry Circle. Tomorrow I'm interviewing some other people who live along this path to see if they've remembered anything in the years since your attack. But also to get more of a lay of the land, try to get more of a sense of what your abductor may have been thinking back then."

She stepped toward him, not stopping until she had to crane her head back to look him in the eyes. "Don't tease me, Bryson. You're mentioning these interviews because you're offering to let me participate. Is that right? You wouldn't be cruel enough to bring them up otherwise, would you?"

He smiled sadly and feathered a hand across her cheek. The touch was so unexpected, so soft and gentle that she'd swear her heart skipped a beat. Even more of a surprise, he leaned down and pressed an equally soft kiss against her forehead before straightening. But he didn't drop his hand. Instead, he left it there, cupping her cheek, his thumb gently stroking her skin as if he didn't want to break the connection between them.

"I'm not teasing," he said, his voice a strained whisper. "And I would never deliberately be cruel to you. I shouldn't have been so harsh, so short with you in Gatlinburg. I thought I was being noble, protecting you. But I had no idea that instead of influencing you to go off in an innocuous direction where you'd be safe, you'd come back here to start over on your own. If the man who hurt you is still around here, and he realizes you're back in town trying to find him, then you're putting yourself in danger."

She frowned, ready to argue. "But I can—"

"Let me finish. While I'm not trying to send any signals…" He dropped his hand, his face reddening slightly as if he just realized that he was still touching her. He cleared his throat. "I'll admit that there's something about you, something special, that has me thinking about you far more than I should in ways I really shouldn't be thinking, not when I'm working a case. It's hell on my focus."

She blinked up at him. "You think I'm special?"

His gaze dropped to her lips. "No question." He shuddered as if waging some kind of internal war with himself. Then he moved back a step. "The point I'm trying to make, and not doing very well, is that it would be really hard to work this case with you and to also stay objective the whole time and not get…sidetracked. But it would be even more impossible to work the case alone, knowing you were somewhere out there potentially putting yourself in danger with no one to watch your back. I'd worry about you the whole time and wouldn't get anything done. So, I guess you've won this particular battle. To be crystal clear, no misunderstandings, I'm inviting you to work with me on your case, starting with the homeowner interview this evening. But only if we agree to keep our relationship professional." His gaze dropped to her lips again. "At least until the case is over."

Her stomach jumped at his last statement. She couldn't stop smiling. But not just because she now realized he was as interested in her as she was in him. Far more important was that he was going to help her find and put away the monster who haunted her dreams at night, who cast a pall of fear over her every waking hour no matter how hard she tried to pretend that he didn't. Bryson was the answer to her prayers. And she was going to enjoy every single minute that they were together, because the man was hopelessly fun to tease. Keep their relationship strictly professional? Pfft. Not a chance. But, of course, she wasn't going to admit to that. He'd figure it out eventually and by then he'd be so hooked on her that he'd be helpless to do anything about it.

That was her hope at least.

"I'll be crystal clear in my response." She hooked her right arm around his left one as if to flirt, when really she could tell he was struggling to remain upright and was probably too proud to ask for help. "I would love to work with you, starting with dinner, and then conducting the interview tonight. But first, as you mentioned earlier, we need to drop Zeus off. Like I said, he's my mom's. I just borrow him when I visit."

They started down the path together, him leaning heavily on the cane, her holding on to his left arm to keep him from falling over, and Zeus happily sniffing and following along at the end of his leash.

When they reached his rental car, she was surprised and a little disappointed to see that he'd chosen a luxury BMW sedan. Its dark blue color and the four doors gave it a decidedly mature, boring appearance even though it was definitely a nice car. Bryson Anton was still a young guy, in spite of his teasing her for being several years younger. And he really was hot. He'd look much better sitting in a red, sporty convertible with the top down than a glorified grocery-getter. Or maybe even a jacked-up four-wheel-drive truck with a gun rack in the back, although that seemed a little too country for him. He was refined, but not upper-crust. Definitely the convertible sports-car type.

But after he insisted on holding the door open for her, then slid into the driver's seat, his deep sigh and the look of relief on his face explained why he'd chosen this car. He needed the plush seats and comfort of a vehicle that would smooth out a bumpy road because of his bad hip.

"Have you thought of getting a second opinion on your hip?" she asked. "I mean, there has to be a way to fix it so it doesn't hurt so much all the time."

"I've had second, third and fourth opinions. The bullet is lodged close to my spine and presses on a nerve that makes the hip ache. Surgery isn't an option. I'm told there's a fifty-fifty chance that it will loosen on its own one day and then be removable and I'll be good as new, or it will loosen on its own one day and nick my spinal cord, putting me permanently in a wheelchair."

She pressed a hand to her mouth. "Oh my gosh. I'm so sorry."

He shrugged. "I'm learning to live with it. Partly thanks to you. I admit to wallowing a bit in self-pity before you came along. Now, if the bullet shifts and I can't walk anymore, at least it will happen while I'm trying to do something good rather than sitting around my house all day drinking tequila." He put the car in drive but kept his foot on the brake. "Enough about me. Where to, Ms. Ray?"

"Do a U-turn, Mr. Anton."

With Zeus taking up the tiny space behind the seats and lolling half-across the console that separated them, Bryson followed her directions to her parents' home, at the end of a long pond on Birch Bark Court, and pulled into the driveway. Beautiful mature crape myrtles dotted the sides of the yard, their hot pink flowers waving in the warm spring breezes. And standing out front on the walkway between the garage and entry were both of her parents, currently in the process of planting a batch of white and pink periwinkles in one of the flower beds.

"Give me a minute to get your door," he said as he popped open the driver's door. "Please don't embarrass me by getting out first. My mother would never forgive my poor manners if you do."

She grinned and gave him a thumbs-up. Of course she didn't need him to get her door. But she didn't mind the show of chivalry and old-fashioned manners, especially since he thought that she was special and made it hard for him to focus. She couldn't help chuckling at that declaration as he leaned on his cane, obviously struggling not to limp very much as he rounded the car to her side. Behind him, her dad and mom were staring with unabashed curiosity at the gorgeous white guy who'd brought her home, no doubt wondering what was going on.

After she and Zeus got out and he closed the door behind her, she gathered the dog's leash to keep him from taking off and looped her arm around Bryson's left one again.

He arched a brow in question. "That's probably not a good idea. You might give your parents the wrong impression about our relationship." He kept his voice low even as he nodded in answer to her father's wave.

Instead of letting go, she tightened her hold. "Did I ever mention that my dad has a bad heart?"

His eyes widened as they started up the driveway toward her parents. "I'm sorry. I had no idea."

"Oh, it's under good control. But it would probably make his heart go into palpitations if he realized that I'm investigating the killer again."

He stopped beside her. "They don't know?"

"Nope. And I aim to keep it that way. To protect Daddy." She tugged his arm to get him going again.

"Then what are you going to tell them about why I'm here?" he whispered harshly before passing his cane to his left hand so he could do the expected handshake with her father. Her mother hung a few feet back, glancing curiously between the two of them.

"I'm Nick Ray, Teagan's father. That's her mom, Sylvie."

"Nice to meet you both. I'm—"

"Bryson Anton, from Gatlinburg." Teagan flashed her best smile at her parents before dropping a bombshell. "My boyfriend."

Chapter Eleven

"Your boyfriend?" Bryson hissed almost two hours later as he was finally driving Teagan away from her parents' house. "And after telling that zinger you left me at the mercy of your very curious mom and dad while you disappeared to take a shower. I haven't had to dance that loose with the truth or change the subject so many times to avoid being pushed into a corner in, well, ever."

"But you did it. You managed to get through the inquisition and dinner while spinning the truth like a practiced politician—minus the lies. I especially liked it when my dad asked how long it had been since we'd first met and you said it felt like only yesterday." She flashed her magazine-cover smile at him.

He swore beneath his breath. "Why did you do it, Teagan? Lying by omission, or by not correcting what someone else said, is still a lie. And why trap me there for dinner when we were supposed to be there just long enough to drop off Zeus?"

Her smile faded and she looked out the window as he wove through the maze of streets toward the back of the development where the newer houses were built, where the Brodericks now lived.

They didn't want to be reminded of what had happened any more than Teagan did. It had taken quite a bit of cajoling to get them to agree to talk to him tonight. Thankfully, when he'd stepped outside of the Rays' home to make a call to ask them whether it was okay to bring Teagan, they'd said it was. He didn't want to surprise them by showing up with her. And he hadn't wanted to disappoint her either, since she was so set on going.

"Teagan?" he pressed, when she didn't answer.

She finally sighed and turned in her seat to face him. "I'm not going to apologize for doing it. Because I'd do it again if given the choice. But I do regret that I didn't warn you, and that it was so difficult for you. Honestly, I was selfishly focused on myself. I love my parents and assumed you'd enjoy their company. And my mom is a terrific cook. I hoped you would love her zucchini lasagna as much as I do and have a fun couple of hours before we—" she waved her hand toward the road as he made the last turn "—dove back into...this. I needed that break, that moment with my parents to prepare for the interview."

The sound of dejection in her voice had him feeling like a jerk. He pulled to the curb a few houses short of their destination, but left the air conditioner running to beat back the heat. He didn't know how people lived here in the summer. The humidity in March made it feel like he was stepping into a sauna every time he went outside.

"I liked your parents very much. Or, I would have, if I wasn't working so hard not to tell a bunch of lies that I'd have to apologize for later. And your mom is a fabulous cook. We couldn't have bought something at any restaurant around here and had better. But that's not the point. I'm already getting over my anger. But I deserve the truth. Why tell them I'm your boyfriend when I could have just been a friend or a friend of a friend? Now, when they ask you about me later and you tell them we broke up—or whatever your cover is going to be when I don't come back around—it will be that much harder. And it will probably make me look like a heel, thank you very much."

She clutched her hands together in her lap, and he suddenly felt like the heel he'd just described. After everything she'd been through, and the upcoming interviews about her ordeal, here he was dumping on her. Regardless of the little drama that had just played out, it was nothing compared to what she'd endured.

He placed his hand over the top of hers. She glanced at him in surprise.

"I'm sorry, Teagan. I'm making it out to be far more important than it was. Let's just drop it and—"

She shook her head. "No. I owe you an explanation. And it was far more important than you realize. Yesterday, at your house, you mentioned that your girlfriend left after your injury. Well you're not the only one. Except it was my longtime high school sweetheart. It wasn't official yet, but we'd always assumed we'd get married after we both graduated from college and got our careers going. He couldn't…he couldn't handle knowing what happened to me. Or how messed up I was for so long afterward."

He took her hand in his and entwined their fingers together. "You don't have to do this. It's okay. I understand—"

"No. You don't. Look, I'm over him. Way over him. Anyone who can't stick around through the bad isn't the one you want with you during the good. It was a blessing that I found that out before vowing to spend the rest of my life with him. The breakup was just a few months after the attack. I barely even think about him anymore. But I've never…since then I haven't…well, it's been hard to—"

"You haven't dated since?"

She squeezed her eyes shut, then nodded.

He waited in silence until she looked at him again. He

tugged one hand free and gently smoothed back a recalcitrant curl that had escaped the long braid down her back. "Since someone as gorgeous and bubbly as you could have a date any time she wants, that's obviously a personal decision. But your parents don't understand your choice, do they? They worry about you because you haven't, in their eyes at least, moved on."

She blinked as if in surprise. "How did you figure all that out so fast?"

He glanced down at his shirt and frowned. "Where's my I'm a Profiler badge? I could have sworn I was wearing that today right along with my Eagle Scout badge."

She managed a weak laugh and it warmed him inside to see her smile again. "You, Bryson Anton, were never a Boy Scout."

He pressed his free hand against his chest. "You wound me to think I couldn't be a scout." He winked. "What gave me away?"

She shook her head, her smile more carefree. "You'd have been bored to tears doing all the things they make you do to earn a badge. Instead, you'd rather be out there in the thick of things, getting lost in the woods just to see if you could find your own way out. Or setting a fire to see if you could put it out. Not exactly good scouts material."

"Looks like I'm not the only profiler around here." He squeezed her hand before letting it go. "If using me helps to make your parents worry less about you because they think you have a boyfriend, then I suppose the subterfuge is okay. Just give me some warning before you throw me in a fire next time, okay?"

He barely had time to blink before she was straddling the console, one thigh plastered against him, her generous breasts flattened against his chest. All his logical, well-thought-out arguments about not getting involved with her, especially while working the case, were incinerated the second her lips touched his.

So much for warning him before throwing him into another fire.

His whole body was being scorched from the outside in, her tongue doing amazing things with his, her long nails raising goose bumps of pleasure across the back of his neck. But he wanted more, so much more. He groaned deep in his throat and wrapped his arms around her sensuous body. Then he half turned, pulling her the rest of the way onto his lap. He kissed her the way he'd wanted to since the moment she'd stood in his doorway looking so adorable as she breathed the word "Hi." If the pain from his hip hadn't stopped him that day, he'd probably have done something juvenile, like drool. Instead, he'd focused on the pain to keep from acting like a letch.

Teagan was unlike any woman he'd ever met. He never knew what to expect from her. Half of him was annoyed that he couldn't predict her reactions even with his years of training as a profiler. The other half of him was sliding his hands around to the front of her shorts, grasping her zipper. Realizing what he was about to do, he drew on deep reserves of strength and forced his hands to release her zipper. Instead, he gently grasped her shoulders and eased her back to straddling the console instead of him. His lungs labored in his chest as they blinked at each other from only a foot apart. And he couldn't help but be pleased that she seemed to be struggling for air just as much as him.

"Holy smokes," she whispered, her voice breaking. She cleared her throat, her hands shaking as she reached up to check her hair. "Lennie what's-his-face was junior high compared to you. Heck, elementary school. That was *amazing*. I can't even remember what he looks like anymore. And we were an item for over eight years."

He grinned, his ego ridiculously inflated by her compliment. "Wait. Lennie? Your old boyfriend's name was *Lennie*?"

"No judging. People don't choose their own names." Her tongue flicked out to wet her lips, making him groan. "Kiss me again, Bryson. Before I start remembering what what's-his-face looked like."

He grabbed her upper arms and gently but firmly pushed her back. "Hell, no. We need to talk about this… thing going on between us before it goes any further. Besides, another kiss like that and I won't be able to walk for a week." He grimaced and shifted in his seat. "As it is, I won't be able to walk for a few minutes, at least."

Her gaze flew to his lap and her eyes widened. "Oh, mercy. Lennie *really* had nothing on you."

He laughed and pushed her farther away. "I'm starting to feel sorry for this Lennie guy."

Her lips firmed. "Don't. Trust me. He doesn't deserve your sympathy." She settled back down on her side of the car and drew a ragged breath.

Seeing her mood change so quickly, as if swimming through a layer of dark memories, had an ice water effect on his traitorous body—which was a good thing right now. But it also had him wanting to punch her ex-boyfriend for the hurt he'd obviously caused her.

"I've got a few friends at the Jacksonville Sheriff's Office," he said. "Where's Lennie live? I bet I could rack him up enough speeding tickets so he'd be riding the bus to work for the next six months."

Her mouth quirked in a reluctant smile. "Mercedes-Lennie on the city bus. Now that might be fun to watch."

"Just say the word."

She laughed, then pointed to the digital clock on his

dash. "Didn't you say the interview was supposed to start about now?"

He noted the time and grimaced. "Hopefully a couple of minutes won't make them change their minds. You sure you want to do this? You can drop me off and pick me up when I call."

"I've never wanted something this hard in my life. I've been in limbo for years. If you can help me end that, put this monster in prison once and for all, it will make all the difference. I can handle it. I promise."

He wasn't nearly as optimistic as she seemed to be. But he wasn't going to argue with her. If she wanted to be a part of this, as far as he was concerned, she had every right to be. Because it was her life and all about making her feel safe again.

"It's that gray-blue stucco over there, two houses down. Close enough to walk but with my hip, I'm going to be lazy and drive the last fifty yards." Once they were parked in the driveway, he grabbed his briefcase from the floor-board behind her seat.

Unlike at her parents' home, she didn't wait for him to open the door. He silently cursed his hip for slowing him down. But there was no way he could go even one more step without his cane. He hefted it from the back seat and limped after her, pain his constant companion.

He'd pushed himself harder today than any day since he'd been shot. And it showed. His hip was so stiff and ached so much that he was running more on willpower than physical strength. And after that little stunt that he and Teagan had just pulled in his car, he was practically a cripple. But he'd grit his teeth and keep going, somehow. At least until this interview was over. And the moment he reached his hotel room he was going to collapse on his bed, down some painkillers and not move until morning.

At the door, he rang the doorbell then started when Teagan clutched his right arm.

"Teagan—"

"Don't fuss at me. I'm not flirting, Bryson. Just give me a second."

He noted the stress lines around her eyes, the ashen gray tint to her brown skin. He wanted to take her hand in his, offer his strength. But he didn't have any to spare. If he let go of his cane he was afraid he'd fall down. All those times he'd blown off a rehab appointment were really coming back to bite him.

"It's okay, you've got this." He offered a reassuring smile. "*We've* got this. We're a team, together. I'm here for you, all right? Trust me."

She blew out a shaky breath and nodded just as the door opened.

A woman stood there, looking even more stressed than Teagan, her face so pale it was shockingly white in the dimly lit foyer.

Bryson lamely nodded rather than hold out his right hand since it was currently clutching his cane so he could remain upright. "Mrs. Broderick, it's nice to meet you in person. I'm Bryson Anton. This is Teagan Ray. Is this still a good time to speak with you and your husband about Teagan's abduction two years ago?"

"Of course." Her gaze darted from one to the other, then behind them before she stepped back. "We've been expecting you. Please, come in." Without waiting, she turned and strode through the long, dimly lit foyer away from them.

Bryson hesitated. "It seems as if this impending interview is far more upsetting to Mrs. Broderick than I'd expected. Maybe you should wait in the car."

"No way. I don't want to blow my chance. If I can't handle the emotions of this first interview, you won't let me go to the ones tomorrow. I'll be okay. You'll make sure of it. We're a team. That's what you said. Right?"

He regretted agreeing to take her with him for so many reasons. But they couldn't stand here waiting and make the Brodericks think they'd changed their minds. He motioned for her to step inside. She gave him a tight smile, and they started down the foyer together.

Mr. Broderick's deep voice sounded from the family room that was just visible through the arched opening a few feet away.

Teagan gasped and stopped.

He turned to see what was wrong. Her eyes were opened wide, a hand pressed to her mouth. She looked absolutely terrified.

"Teagan? What's wrong?"

"That v-voice," she croaked, obviously struggling to push any sounds out. "*His* voice."

Bryson swore as understanding dawned. He dropped his cane and clawed for the pistol holstered at his waist as he struggled to turn around without falling. White, hot pain exploded in his head and his hip crumpled beneath him. Teagan's scream was the last thing he heard as everything went dark.

Chapter Twelve

Teagan stood frozen, the horror of what was happening—again—seeping into her bones like leaden concrete, anchoring her in place. Her pulse hammered in her ears, blocking out the sounds around her. It was as if her mind had separated from her body and all of this was happening to someone else.

Bryson. Sweet, wonderful Bryson lay dead at her feet, his dark hair matted with blood. She'd only caught a glimpse of his battered body before jerking her gaze up toward the man who'd hit him, fully expecting the next blow from the baseball bat to land on her. Even so, she couldn't raise her arms to defend herself. She. Couldn't. Move.

Instead of hitting her, he'd taken Bryson's pistol out of his holster, then shoved his hand in her pocket and yanked out her gun too, all before she could even blink. How had he known she had the gun when even she, in her moment of need, had forgotten it?

He'd been just inches from her but after taking the guns, he'd walked away. She watched helplessly, uselessly still as a statue, as the man—oh God, *that voice*—crossed the family room to the woman cowering in the corner. What was her name? Broderick. Mrs. Broderick. A trap. She'd led Bryson and Teagan into a trap. Why? Why would she do that?

The woman's lips moved. She was looking up at the man, hovering over her with the bloody baseball bat in his right hand. She was saying something, pleading? The words were lost in Teagan's fractured mind, unable to penetrate the sound of her own heartbeat rushing in her ears. *Thump. Thump. Thump.* Her heart pounded against her rib cage, white noise that masked everything around her. The tableau played out like a silent movie before her, a nightmare. Because surely none of this was real. It couldn't be.

Not again. Not again. She couldn't survive this again.

The man lifted the bat.

No. Teagan tried to yell, to get her legs to move. She had to help the lady. But her throat was so tight she couldn't make a sound. Her legs were shaking so hard she couldn't take a step.

He brought the bat down in a deadly arc.

Bam! Bam! Bam!

Oh dear God, please, no! The bat. The woman. Bile rose in Teagan's throat. A low-keening moan filled her ears, and the man jerked around to look at her. She realized that she was the one making that awful sound.

The room around her darkened, like a tunnel, narrowing down to one point where all she could see was the man across the room, watching her. Everything centered on what she'd never seen until this very moment. His face. She'd known that voice, the devil's voice. To this day, it haunted her dreams. But that face. How could such evil hide behind such an average, kind-looking face?

There was nothing remarkable about it. He was white, clean-shaven, his light brown hair streaked with blond that had no doubt cost a fortune at some expensive salon. Which meant this man had money, a job, likely a home, a car. A family? He was just like anyone else she'd pass on the street.

Except that he wasn't.

The eyes. The eyes gave him away. They were dark, almost black, completely devoid of warmth. An abyss of emptiness, a deep well of evil with no soul to warm them. They were the eyes of the monster who'd hurt her two years ago. The same monster who'd just brutally killed Mrs. Broderick. And the wonderful man lying at Teagan's feet.

She couldn't look down. Couldn't stomach seeing the damage the bat must have done. She didn't want that image burned into her retinas. Bryson. Smart, gorgeous, sweet Bryson Anton, who wouldn't even be here if it wasn't for her.

Forgive me, Bryson.

Evil stared back at her from twenty feet away. Blood dripped from the bat in his hand. She shuddered as a wave of nausea gripped her.

He smiled, as if pleased at her distress. Then he started toward her, still holding that awful bat. Slowly. Like a lion stalking the weakest member of the herd, separating it out, readying for the kill.

Her mind screamed at her. *Move. Run. Do something.*

But she couldn't. Why not? She'd run before. Two years ago, when her attacker injected drugs to put her to sleep, but missed the vein, she'd taken advantage of his mistake. She'd pretended to be asleep. And then, after hearing the sound of his car driving away, she'd forced one foot in front of the other. She'd gotten away.

There were neighbors close by. Some of them had to be home. Most of them had to be home. The workday was over for the nine-to-fivers. All she had to do was turn around and…no.

She couldn't leave Bryson.

She didn't deserve to survive yet again when he lay at her feet in his own blood. It was her fault. This, then, would be her penance. Face the monster. Pay the price for bringing Bryson here, for destroying a wonderful man.

Shoes echoed against the floor. Hardwood. Like her parents' house. He was coming closer. Relentlessly. Slowly. Savoring her fear.

She whimpered, and hated herself for it. She was about to die. She wanted to face him with dignity in her last moments. But the wounds of the past were too much to overcome. Her body wasn't her own anymore to command. She couldn't stop shaking. Maybe she was already dead.

Evil stopped three feet away.

She forced herself to meet his gaze, to memorize every line, every bump, every angle of his ridiculously ordinary face, refusing to look away as fate raised the bat once more. If she couldn't run, at least she could stand here and pretend courage she didn't possess. There would be no defensive wounds for her. But as she stared at him, a strange sense of déjà vu swept through her. She'd seen him before. Not at the shack. He'd always concealed his identity back then. So she had to have seen him somewhere else. But where? Who was he?

He raised the bat higher, watching her, as if waiting to see what she would do. As she remained motionless, his smile faded. She wasn't giving him the satisfaction of cowering. She was ruining his fun.

Hooray for her. Finally she'd beaten him. If only in a very small way. This time it was her turn to smile.

Hate glittered in his eyes as he slowly lowered the bat. He tossed it onto a nearby chair and reached behind him. Metal glittered in the overhead lights. A gun? No. Silver circles. A short chain connecting them. Handcuffs. He'd bound her last time, tied her with strips of cloth. But never handcuffs. She'd cut through the strips with her teeth after the drug had failed to knock her unconscious. Perhaps he'd changed his routine since then. He'd learned from his mistakes.

He moved with a swiftness that was terrifying. Too late, she tried to twist away. But the sound of one of the cuffs ratcheting onto her left wrist echoed in the foyer. He yanked her wrist down toward the floor. She fell to her knees, sliding in the sticky wet blood. Bryson's blood.

Dear, sweet Bryson. Lying on the floor, his face turned toward her. Eyes closed forever.

His murderer slapped the other handcuff onto Bryson's right wrist and ratcheted it closed, anchoring her to his body. She looked up in question. He'd retrieved the bat, but instead of slamming it down on her, ending this, he turned away. His shoes clomped across the floor as he headed down the hall to the left. Dress pants. He was wearing gray dress pants and a white shirt. A formerly white shirt. Had he just left work? What kind of person did this—entered someone's house and beat them to death after getting off work, like it was a normal part of their day?

A hysterical laugh bubbled up in her throat, but died before reaching her lips. The monster had opened a door and headed inside. A muffled sound echoed from the room. Was someone else there? The sickening unmistakable crunch of wood on bone had her gasping in horror. The other half of the couple who lived here, Mr. Broderick. He must have been in the room, probably tied up. A bribe so that his wife would do what the monster told her to do.

Bile rose again in her throat. She turned away from Bryson's body just in time to empty the contents of her stomach against the foyer wall. She shuddered and wiped her mouth.

"Dear Lord," she prayed, the whisper finally passing through her tight throat. "Please let me die quickly. And don't let me grovel or beg for my life. Give me strength. Please, God. Help me."

Something fluttered against her shoe.

She gasped and whirled around. The fingers of Bryson's right hand moved against her, tapped her toe. She shot him a look of shock, and met his pain-filled startling blue gaze.

"Bryson," she whispered. "You're alive. Oh my God. Bryson." She lifted her shaking right hand to his face and gently cupped it. "I'm so sorry. Please forgive me."

His eyes seemed unfocused. He coughed and blood dribbled out of his mouth to the floor.

"Shhh," she whispered. "Don't try to talk." She jerked her head up, realizing there weren't any sounds in the other room anymore. He'd be coming out soon. Coming for her and Bryson. "Close your eyes," she whispered. "Play dead. He thinks you're dead. Just, no matter what happens to me, just lay there. Don't move. Do you hear me? Play dead. It's your only chance."

His fingers tapped her again and his lips moved.

She glanced down the hall, then leaned down, trying to hear what he was saying.

"Run. Get. Away." His whisper was so low she could barely make it out. "Go."

Tears splashed onto his face and she realized she was crying. "Oh, Bryson. I'm sorry. I thought you were… I thought it was too late. And I couldn't make myself leave you. And now, I can't." She lifted her left hand, showing him the handcuffs that bound them together. "It's okay, though," she whispered, looking down the hall again. What was taking the monster so long? What was he doing in there? "It's okay," she repeated. "There's nothing I can do to save myself. I accept that. But he thinks you're already dead. Lie very still. No matter what. You'll make it. Just play dead."

His lips moved again, his eyes pleading with her to listen. "Cane. Get. Cane."

"You think you can stand?" A rush of hope flooded through her. "Here. I'll help you."

"Cane," his hoarse whisper was louder now. "Get the cane."

She stretched out their linked hands and scrambled over, reaching out her right hand as far as she could. It took some contorting, but she was finally able to grab it. "Got it."

"I'll take that." The monster jerked it out of her hand and backed up several feet. "Getting feisty, Teagan? Planning on trying to beat me over the head with this like I did your friend?" He chuckled and motioned toward Bryson. "Give me his cell phone. And yours. Hurry."

"Mine is in my purse." She motioned toward her purse where it had fallen to the foyer floor earlier.

"Prove it. Turn your shorts pockets inside out."

She did as he asked.

"Now his. Get his cell phone and toss it to me so I can verify that you don't do something stupid, like try to press 911 before you give it to me. If you do that, you're both dead. Understood?"

She drew a ragged breath and nodded, then dug in Bryson's suit jacket pockets until she found his phone. For the briefest second, she hesitated, desperately wanting to press the three precious keys that would call for help. But the monster was watching. And he'd shifted the aim of his gun toward Bryson's head as if in warning. She hurriedly stood as best she could with her arm cuffed to Bryson and tossed him the phone.

After checking the screen, he threw the phone on the couch, then motioned toward Bryson again. "Take that watch thing off his wrist and get rid of it. I don't know what it can do, whether you can make calls with it. I'm not taking chances."

She quickly took it off and tossed it down the foyer.

"Help him up. We'll bring him with us. I need to know how much he knows before I kill him."

She hesitated. "He's already dead. Just uncuff me and I'll go with you."

He made a clucking, disapproving sound with his mouth. "Now, Teagan. Don't lie to me. I doubt I hit him hard enough to kill him. But if you'd rather I take care of things right now, to make it easier for you so you don't have to help him walk, I can get the bat—"

"No!" She shook her head. "Please. Don't. Just…give me the cane. I'll help him. But I need the cane to get him on his feet, to help him walk."

He tossed the cane down beside her. "I'd help but I don't want to get his blood on my nice clean shirt."

She blinked and realized he was wearing a different shirt now, a light blue one tucked into navy blue dress pants. Even his shoes, which had been black earlier had been exchanged for gunmetal gray ones. He must have washed himself off and changed into some of Mr. Broderick's clothes. Right after killing the poor man.

Swallowing hard, she looked down. Bryson's eyes were open again. He was staring at her.

I'm so sorry, she mouthed, regret heavy in her heart that she'd wasted her chance to get help for him. Had she suspected he was still alive, she would have forced herself to turn around, to run to the nearest neighbor and call 911. Instead, she'd been frozen by fear and the belief that he'd been killed. She'd given up. And because of her cowardly actions, now he was still in horrible danger, when she might have been able to save him.

"Get him on his feet. Now. If you take too long, I'll shoot you both and be done with it."

She wanted to demand that he be done with it right now. But that was no longer an option. It wasn't just her life on the line now. She had to be brave, strong, and somehow figure out how to get Bryson out of this mess. She awkwardly straightened his legs, apologizing profusely every time she jostled him because of their hands being handcuffed together.

Finally she got him into a sitting position with his back pressed against the opposite wall of the foyer from where she'd been sick. White lines around his mouth clearly mirrored his pain. His hip had to be excruciating right now, on top of the awful bump on his head. She reached up to test it and he winced, ducking away from her hand.

"You're not bleeding anymore," she whispered. "That's a good sign."

"Hurry up," the monster ordered. "The daughter will be home soon."

Teagan and Bryson exchanged a look of horror. The idea of a daughter coming home to find her parents slaughtered by this man was beyond awful. But still being here when she got home would ensure that she too would be killed. As if coming to the same realization, Bryson began pushing against the wall, struggling to get to his feet.

She faced him, their hands clasped together as she helped him up the rest of the way. As soon as she was sure he wasn't about to fall, she got the cane and put it in his left hand. He normally held it in his right, to compensate for his bad left hip when he raised his right leg. But with his right hand cuffed to hers, that wasn't an option. It would be rough going. She hoped she had the strength to keep him from falling.

"Come on. Out the back." The monster was holding a

gun now. Bryson's gun. He motioned with it and stepped out of reach of the cane or a well-aimed kick, not that they could manage either one shackled together with Bryson hurt.

More from willpower than physical strength, the two of them managed to hobble out the open French door, across the patio, all while being directed by the gunman. He closed the door behind them, probably to throw off anyone trying to find the perpetrator who'd murdered the Brodericks. But where was he going? He stopped at the six-foot-tall wooden privacy fence that encircled the large backyard.

He motioned them forward with the gun. When they stopped a few feet away, he lifted one of the sections of fence back from the post it should have been nailed to. Perhaps this was the way he'd gotten into the Brodericks' home? He'd come from behind them, loosening the section of fence to act much like a gate.

Just the way he'd abducted Teagan years earlier? Until this very moment, she'd never remembered how he'd managed to get her off the path without anyone seeing her. It had always been a confusing image in her mind—a creaking sound that she'd attributed to the breezes in the branches overhead, but that she now realized must have been him opening a pre-loosened section of fence; her turning around just as the bite of a needle plunged into her neck and a hand clamped over her mouth. Darkness descending around the edges of her vision as he'd tossed her over his shoulder. That creaking sound again. He'd closed the fence behind them. That must have been what happened.

"Teagan?" Bryson whispered, between lips white with pain. "We have to move."

The gunman was pointing the pistol at her. He must

have told her to get going and was threatening to shoot her. She squeezed Bryson's hand, then struggled forward with him leaning heavily against her, their cuffed hands clutched tightly together.

The gunman waved them toward the back of the house whose yard they were now in while he secured the section of fence behind them. As they reached the screened-in porch, the cut screen on the door told the story that she had feared. She exchanged a look of misery with Bryson before helping him through the door that the killer had obviously gone through earlier.

But how had he known that she would be at the Brodericks'?

That question was eating at her. And she had no answers. She wanted to ask Bryson, but doubted he could think much beyond the pain that was clearly radiating through his whole body. It was taking everything he had to remain upright, as evidenced by how hard he was leaning on her and how often he stumbled. It didn't help that the house was carpeted. It was much harder for him to keep his balance, and he fell against the wall more than once.

"To the garage, that door over there." The gunman motioned ahead to the right, then ducked through an archway to their left into the kitchen.

"Where are we?" Bryson whispered as they hobbled toward the garage.

"Bentwater Place," she whispered back. "The subdivision directly behind The Woods. The entrance to this subdivision is about a mile, maybe more, from the Hodges Boulevard entrance to The Woods."

He nodded as they reached the door that led from the house into the garage. It was standing wide open, revealing a small package delivery truck inside. Any hope that Teagan had that he hadn't hurt the driver died when she saw the piles of packages taking up most of the space on the other side of the garage. No driver would have willingly allowed someone to dump the contents of his truck. How many people had to be hurt or die because of whatever sick fantasies this guy had?

"Find the button that opens the garage door," Bryson urged. "If someone's outside, we can try to get their attention."

"Do it and I'll shoot both of you," the killer said from behind them.

Teagan stiffened and looked over her shoulder. His dark, empty eyes bored into hers. The maw of the pistol was pointed directly at the back of Bryson's head.

"What do you want us to do now?" She steadied Bryson's shaking body against the garage wall beside the doorway. He was so pale she was afraid he was about to pass out.

"Get in the back of the truck." The sound of sirens filled the air, coming from somewhere behind them. The killer froze, cocking his head to listen. The sirens got louder. There could be no mistake. They were racing toward the Brodericks' house. The daughter must have gotten home and called 911. And the police had to have been close by to be responding this quickly. Any minute now, they'd be standing in the home that was separated from this one by about fifty feet of grass and a privacy fence.

If she screamed, would they hear her?

As if reading the intention in her expression, the killer shoved the gun's muzzle against the back of Bryson's head. "In the truck. Now. If you scream, if you do anything to alert the police, I'll shoot both of you, him first. Then I'll find another family a few houses down to kill and drive away in their car as the police try to figure out where the shots came from. You'll be dead, another family will be dead, but I'll be just fine. Is that what you want? Me to kill your boyfriend and another innocent family, all because you refuse to follow instructions?"

"We're going." She forced the words out between clenched teeth.

Bryson looked like he wanted to argue. But he was in no physical condition to do so. They hobbled to the end of the truck. The gunman twisted the handles and yanked open both of the doors. Just as expected, it was empty. No windows. No pass-through to the cab. Just a metal box, with no way out but the back doors. Which required getting past their armed escort.

It took some grunting and contorting because of how their hands were cuffed together to get both of them into the back. As soon as their feet cleared the doors, one of them slammed shut.

The gunman paused in the opening of the other door. "I'll take that cane for now. Don't want you trying to poke me with it when I open the door again." He yanked the cane away from Bryson and sealed them inside.

Chapter Thirteen

"He didn't blindfold us," Teagan said.

Bryson hated the fear in her tone. He knew exactly what she was afraid of, that because the man who'd abducted them hadn't blindfolded them, it meant he intended to kill them. He wasn't worried about witnesses, or that they could identify him later. But reassuring her right now was beyond Bryson's abilities. He was struggling just to stay conscious. That blow to his head had really done a number on him.

The darkness in the back of the truck was absolute, which was disorienting enough. But his aching hip and throbbing head were each trying to outdo the other in the pain department, which made his efforts to wrangle his scattered thoughts next to impossible.

"Bryson?" She moved her left hand against his right one and interlaced their fingers. "How bad does it hurt? Your head?"

He gently squeezed her fingers. "Don't worry about me. I'm fine."

"Maybe if you said that without pain making your voice so raspy I'd believe you." She clasped her right hand over their joined hands. "I'm so sorry. None of this would have happened if it wasn't for me involving you. I never should have gone to Gatlinburg and interfered with your life. That was beyond selfish. And now, we're both going to die—"

"Hey, hey. Stop that. You didn't do anything wrong. I'm the professional. I should have been on guard against this type of possibility. But what matters right now is that you don't give up. You hear me, Teagan Ray? Don't you dare give up." He waited, but when she didn't respond he said, "If you're nodding or shaking that beautiful head of yours, or making some kind of rude gesture, your effort's wasted. I completely forgot to pack my night-vision goggles this trip."

A brief laugh reassured him like nothing else could have. He needed her present, engaged, not frozen and helpless the way he'd seen her in the foyer after he'd finally managed to swim through the darkness that had threatened to drag him under. He wasn't sure how long he'd lain there after that awful slam of the bat against his head. He hadn't even seen the bat until later, when they were leaving, lying on one of the chairs. It had shocked him that he was still alive with the amount of blood covering the bat.

Then he'd seen Mrs. Broderick.

She'd been curled in a lifeless heap on the other side of the room. He knew then that not all of the blood on the bat was his. The poor woman had been brutally attacked. Even though it didn't feel like it, he was lucky to be alive. For now.

"Aren't you going to say I told you so?" she asked, interrupting his thoughts.

He had to draw several deep breaths to push back the hazy fog that kept trying to drag him into unconsciousness. What had she said? Something about I told you so. "What are you talking about?"

"Avarice Lowe. I'd pegged him all along as the man who'd abducted me. But I was wrong. It's this man. Whoever's driving this stupid truck. The thing is, Lowe never seemed to fit the image of the monster in my head. I know it sounds wonky. But I always thought I'd know my abductor if I ever saw him, by the way he was built, his profile, something. Nothing ever clicked for me when I saw Lowe's pictures. And, to be honest, nothing clicked when I saw this guy today. Not really. I mean, his voice, yes. Definitely. And yet, even though he seems familiar, he doesn't seem…right. It's still not clicking." He could feel her shoulders move against him as she shrugged. "Listen to me. I'm not even making sense."

"Always…trust your instincts." He swallowed hard against the bile rising in his throat. Obviously he had a concussion. All he wanted to do was lie down and sleep. Or throw up. Or both. He cleared his throat and tried again to follow the conversation. "Instincts. They're telling you something. What did you mean when you said he seemed familiar?"

"His face."

"His face?"

"It just seemed…familiar. He's the kind of guy you could pass on the street a bazillion times and you might think, okay, he's kind of good-looking. Clean-cut. But nothing amazing. Just a typical, white-collar kind of man, you know? And yet, I would swear that I've seen him before. Not just once. Several times."

He rubbed his left temple, desperately trying to beat back the throbbing pain and focus on what she was saying. There was something important here, more important than her thinking she'd seen him before. But he couldn't seem to grasp what was bothering him about what she'd just said. Finally he dropped his hand to his side, giving up for now. Whatever was bothering him would come to him, eventually.

"Maybe he lives in The Woods," he offered. "You've passed him on the street, on the sidewalk. Or saw him at that amenity center. Do you ever use the tennis courts, the pool?"

"The pool sometimes. But I haven't in a long time. Not since, well, I never was a fan of a one-piece bathing suit. Too grandma for me. But I don't think wearing a bikini is exactly a good idea now."

He wanted to reassure her, tell her that no one would notice the X that had been cut into her skin. But people could be cruel. Some probably would stare. Others might ask a question, innocently thinking she'd had that X carved there on purpose, like a tattoo. They might wonder at the symbolism and significance, without realizing they were bringing up a horrific memory that she'd rather forget.

He'd just started to doze off again when she asked, "What are we going to do?" Her voice was a low whisper, as if to keep the driver from hearing them. "Please tell me you have a plan."

He didn't have a clue. He tightened his hold on her hand. "We'll figure it out. Together. Two against one. We've got this."

The truck hit a bump in the road, knocking them against each other. He scooted back against the wall, trying to keep from slamming into her. But she had no such compulsion. She moved closer, her body plastered against his side. But unlike earlier, there was nothing suggestive about her actions. He could feel the slight shaking of her shoulders and realized she was silently crying. Carefully, so he wouldn't hit her face, he maneuvered their handcuffed hands so that he could put his arm around her, pulling their linked hands tight against her belly. She cradled her head against his neck.

He tried to pay attention to the changes in road noise,

traffic sounds, the turns the truck made. But everything was so muffled that he had no clue where they might be. Had it been an hour? Two? He had no idea. With his watch gone, and his mind a fog, time as he knew it didn't exist anymore. His every moment was measured by stabs of pain that shot through his body with every beat of his heart. His hip had long ago gone numb. But, if anything, the pain in his head was worse than before. He felt every shift of the truck's wheels on the pavement, every pothole, every slide of gravel.

Wait. Gravel?

"We're slowing down," she whispered.

He nodded, then remembered she couldn't see him. "Yes. We are. And we've turned onto a gravel road. Wherever he's taking us, we're close." He carefully pulled their linked arms over her head so they were side by side again, instead of nestled against each other.

The brakes squealed as the truck lurched to a halt.

Her fingers clenched his. "Now would be a good time to share your plan."

Right. If only he had one. His thoughts were so jumbled. "Stay alert. Be observant. As soon as that door opens, evaluate your options and react. If he's stupid enough to stand in striking distance, we tackle him. But I don't expect he'll do that."

"So we have no plan."

He sighed. "Pretty much. But that doesn't mean there's no hope. All it takes is one mistake on his part, one moment when his guard is down. Then we'll get the upper hand."

"Do you really believe that?"

"I have to. We both have to. I'm not operating on all pistons right now, and my vision was blurry at the Brodericks' house so I'm not expecting much better when he lets us out of here. I need you to fill in the gaps. Pay attention when he opens that door. Get a three-sixty view. We need to know what's around us. Where to run if we get a chance."

"Okay. I'll… I'll do my best."

The driver's door creaked open.

"Come on," he urged. "Let's scoot to the end in case we can surprise him, take him down."

Getting to his knees was beyond his capabilities at the moment. Instead, he had to scoot across the metal floor of the truck. Thankfully, it wasn't that large and they were soon positioned beside each other at the doors.

The sound of shoes crunching on gravel came from outside. He was heading toward the back.

Bryson could feel her shivering against him. He silently cursed the man with all the power right now, the man who'd hurt her more than most people endured in their entire lifetime.

He gritted his teeth and braced himself, hoping she was ready to dive with him to tackle the man. There was no other option since they were still handcuffed together.

The left door flew back. Bryson hadn't planned on near total darkness and hesitated for a moment. But Teagan was already hopping out of the truck. He hurriedly followed and together they rushed forward, hoping to wrap arms around their attacker. They both met empty air and stumbled against each other before falling back against the closed right door. It was the only reason Bryson managed to remain upright.

Laughter sounded off to the left. A powerful flashlight switched on, forcing them to squint and shield their eyes against the brightness.

"Good try." The man chuckled again. "But I assumed you'd pull a stunt like that so I stayed behind the door, out of reach." He lowered the light to point at the ground, directly in front of them. Dirt and gravel mixed with pine needles and other debris. Since the only sounds were insects buzzing close by, it was a safe bet that they were somewhere outside of town, an hour, two, maybe more from Jacksonville if his judgment on how much time had passed was accurate. But he couldn't be sure. Their captor may have driven in circles to disorient them and then drove to some rural part of town. Jacksonville was the largest city in the country by landmass, so they could easily still be in Duval County but nowhere near any homes or businesses.

Teagan's fingers curled around his. Perhaps she was beginning to realize how isolated they were, and wondering the same thing that he was—what happens next?

Without the flashlight in his eyes, he was able to make out more details now. The moon and stars provided enough light to see that they were surrounded by trees and Florida scrub, mostly small thin bushes and sharp palmettos ready to skewer anyone foolish enough to go for a walk in the woods.

The gunman stood about twenty feet away, out of reach, a dark silhouette with his arm extended, pistol gleaming in his grip. "Get moving." He motioned with the flashlight to their right, aiming it at what was apparently their destination, a tiny cabin.

"I need my cane," Bryson called out.

The flashlight swept back toward their captor. He aimed it up toward his own face, a slow smile spreading across his cheeks as he pulled something out of his pocket. "Let me guess. Because you wanted these?" He shook the two tiny keys on the end of a chain, making them click against each other. "Handcuff keys hidden in the cane's handle. I knew you were awfully insistent on wanting that stupid thing. Took me half the trip fiddling with it to figure it out."

He threw the keys into the trees, then leaned down and grabbed the cane, which had been lying at his feet. "Afraid you'll have to do without it. I'm not risking another trick in that thing that I haven't figured out yet." He tossed the cane into the woods behind him. "Now go on." He swept the flashlight in an arc toward the cabin again. "Teagan, stop standing there like a statue and help your boyfriend before he falls down." He chuckled.

Bryson looked at her. She hadn't moved since they'd tried tackling the gunman without success. Her fingers holding his were cold, stiff. Her body shook as she stared wide-eyed at the little house in the clearing. And then it dawned on him why. He'd seen it before, in crime scene photos.

The killer had brought them back in time, two years to be exact. He'd brought them to the infamous shack where he'd once held Teagan captive.

Chapter Fourteen

The world had disappeared for Teagan. Everything had faded away the moment she'd jumped out of the truck and the flashlight revealed what she should have expected, but hadn't allowed herself to believe. He'd taken her back to the dilapidated shack where she'd spent two weeks in a drug-induced stupor, drifting in a haze of pain from the torture that her captor had put her through.

She pressed a hand to her belly, remembering that first night, when he'd slowly carved the X in her flesh. The pain had been excruciating. With her arms and legs tied and him straddling her, there was nothing she could do to escape the slow awful burn of the blade. She'd screamed so loudly that something in her throat burst and she'd almost drowned in her own blood.

After escaping this hellhole, she'd charted a new path for her life. She'd focused her energies on becoming stronger, both physically and mentally. When the police seemed to be getting nowhere with the investigation, she'd taken it over herself, doing everything she could to try to discover the identity of the man who'd reduced her to the broken woman she'd become for those fourteen days. And she'd thought she had. She'd been so sure that Avarice Lowe was the real Ripper, the man who'd branded her like a steer. The fact that no one else believed her didn't dissuade her.

Instead, it made her angry, and even more determined to find someone who'd help her put Lowe away. She'd thought Bryson was that someone, the one person who would read her file and finally tell her that she was right.

But she wasn't right. Bryson was right, had been all along.

It was as if everything she'd done for the past twenty-four months and nineteen days was a sham, a waste, a farce. Here she was again, where it had all started. And she'd managed to condemn Bryson to share this hell with her. This time, both of them would die.

"Sweetheart, look at me," Bryson's whispered words seemed to come to her from the end of a long tunnel. "Come back to me. Don't give up. Don't let him win."

She couldn't see him, couldn't see anyone, or anything. Not the dark shapes of the trees, or the twinkling lights of the stars, or the moon, or even the gravel rocks at her feet. The devil himself, the one who'd brought them here, had faded too. All she saw was the little shack.

Hovel was more accurate.

Four walls covered in weathered gray wood that was splintered and warped. No electricity, which meant no air-conditioning, unless that had been changed. The inside consisted of a small bedroom and bathroom on the back left corner, a tiny main room and a kitchen up front. Although calling the cooking area a kitchen was being generous. It consisted of a handful of homemade-looking cabinets and drawers, a tiny refrigerator like those in hotel rooms and a compact gas stove fed by a propane tank outside. The bathroom, as she remembered it, was so filthy she'd had to close her eyes when he'd shoved her inside and stood guard at the open door, watching. Always watching. Or touching, hurting her in unspeakable ways.

Dear Lord, please, let me die. Strike me with lightning, something, just don't let him...touch me...not again. Please.

"Teagan, look at me. Open your eyes." Bryson's gentle but firm voice cut through her terror, snapped her out of her semi-stupor.

She openly stared up at him. The moon's light wasn't enough to see the blue of his eyes, but she remembered their beautiful color, and the kindness in them. She remembered how ruggedly handsome he was. He was so sweet and smart and...*and he was going to die.*

A low keening moan slipped out between her clenched teeth. Her hands shook as she started to lift them. But her left hand pulled up short because of the cuffs. He bent his arm to allow her more movement, frowning, apparently wondering what she was doing, but helping her. Always helping her. She lifted her arms again and this time she was able to cup his face.

"We have to kill him," she whispered. "Before he makes us go into that horrible shack. He won't shoot me, not right away. That would spoil his fun. We'll refuse to go inside and he'll have to come close. As long as you duck down in front of me, I can shield you—"

"The hell with that." His clipped tone brooked no argument. "I'm not using you as a human shield." He grabbed her left hand and pulled it down with his, their handcuffs rattling against each other. "I don't have a plan yet but putting you in the line of fire isn't at the top of my list. It's not even *on* the list. Forget it."

"Hey, you two. Get moving." *Bam!*

The warning shot kicked up dirt near their feet. Teagan threw herself against Bryson's chest, desperately trying to shield his body with hers.

He swore and shoved her as far from him as the cuffs would allow. His glare told her exactly what he thought of her attempt to protect him. But without her to lean on, he stumbled. She rushed forward and jammed her left shoulder beneath his right, bracing him again. The pained look on his face told her he hated that he needed her help. But he didn't push her away again.

"Next one goes in your head, FBI guy. Or Justice Seeker. Is that what you go by? Seems I heard that somewhere. You need to do what I say, when I say it. Or you can seek your justice six feet under."

Justice Seeker? Bryson probably mentioned that he was a former FBI profiler when he spoke to the Brodericks to lend him credibility so they'd agree to speak to him. But would he say anything about being a Justice Seeker? Not likely. It had taken her months of digging to track Bryson to the Seekers. How did this animal know about them?

"I need my cane." Bryson's voice was hoarse, a testament to the amount of pain he was in after their little dance in the dirt. "I can't walk without it. Unlock these handcuffs and send Teagan to retrieve it for me."

"So she can take off and escape? I don't think so. Good try though. But I'm tired of waiting." He aimed the gun at Bryson's leg.

Teagan rushed in front of him to his left side to better help him, their cuffed hands pulled awkwardly across his waist. He was really struggling, his left leg shaking as if it was about to collapse.

His look of regret confirmed that he realized the same thing. He gave her a curt nod of thanks, then lurched forward.

The thirty or so feet to the shack felt more like a mile trudging through wet cement. But finally they were at the two steps that led up to the tilted, rotting front porch. There was no railing, nothing for Bryson to cling to except her. But they made the climb together, pausing just outside the front door.

Instead of the dry-rotting wood she remembered, this door was shiny and new, its glass front encased in a black wrought-iron frame with a network of vertical bars just like she'd expect to see on a jail cell. And both of the small front windows, to the left and right of the door, were covered in the same black bars. He'd converted the shack into a jail.

There'd be no escape this time.

She pulled the door open and glanced up at Bryson. His eyes were glazing over, unfocused. He tried to say something, but couldn't seem to get the words out.

She practically dragged him inside as he teetered back and forth. Thankfully the couch was right where it had been the last time, four or five feet from the door. If turned sideways, it would probably scrape both walls, if it would even fit.

He fell from her grip onto the cushions, pulling her down with him. She managed to push off the back cushion so she didn't fall on top of him. Instead, she slid to the floor, her left arm raised to not jerk his right arm. Not that he would have felt it. His eyes were already closed. He'd passed out.

The sound of metal grating against metal had her jerking her head around to see what the gunman was doing. To her relief, he hadn't followed them inside. But to her horror, he'd just locked the door. He grinned as he pulled his key out of the round lock that required a key on both sides—not the kind where you could flip it from the inside.

He aimed the flashlight up, casting an eerie, sinister look across his face. "I'll give you two lovebirds some alone time," he teased, adding a wink that had her wanting to throw up again. "Make sure he's ready to answer my questions when I get back. I want to know what the cops know. If he can't talk, he's of no use to me."

She'd wondered why he'd gone to the trouble of taking both her and Bryson instead of killing him at the Brodericks'. Now she knew it was because he wanted to interrogate him.

"Today caught me off guard, I gotta admit," he continued. "I'm not really prepared. Don't have my…supplies handy. But don't you worry. I remember everything you like. I'll make sure I come back with just the right stuff." He leaned closer, pressing his face against the glass. "How's my mark on your belly looking?"

She automatically pressed her hand against her stomach, her entire body shaking as she stared at him. Hot tears coursed down her cheeks in spite of her efforts to hold them back.

His grin widened, his bright white teeth sparkling in the light. "Don't worry. I'll freshen it up a bit, make sure it hasn't…faded, since our last meeting." He chuckled and hopped off the porch, the flashlight's beam bouncing across the gravel as he headed toward the truck.

Chapter Fifteen

Bryson blinked in the near darkness, a fog of confusion roiling through his mind. Where was he? How did he get here? And why was he lying on a couch that, judging by the lumps and musty smell, clearly wasn't his?

He braced his hands on the cushions to push himself up but the tug of a cold chain against his right wrist had him stopping to look down. A small form lay curled up on the floor, her left arm propped against the couch. As his eyes adjusted to the dark and he was able to make out more details, he noticed the gleaming silver circle around both their wrists. They were handcuffed together. Still confused, he leaned down for a better look. Teagan. She was on the floor, without even a pillow for her head.

What was going on?

Her eyes were closed and she was asleep, albeit a fitful one, her elegant brows drawn into a frown. Having never seen her hair anything but perfect, he was surprised to see curls forming a halo around her face, escaping the tight braid that hung down her back. Even worse, there were dark splotches on her blouse. The color was lost to him in the darkness, but there was no mistaking the metallic smell.

Blood.

Memories slammed into him. Awful glimpses of the

reality that had happened, and where those dark splotches had come from. He softly touched one to make sure it wasn't wet, then pulled his hand back in relief. It wasn't her blood. It was his. Thank goodness she hadn't been hurt. But that would change the moment their captor returned.

Careful not to jostle their joined wrists, he managed to push himself to a sitting position so he could take stock of their situation. It didn't look good. The front iron-barred door was closed, no doubt locked, but the glass provided a moonlit view of the gravel road and clearing out front. They were empty, the delivery truck nowhere in sight.

He studied all four walls in the main room as best he could in the limited light. Both of the front windows were covered in bars. He imagined the one other window that he'd seen in police photos, the one in the tiny bedroom down a short hall, was also barred. The adjacent bathroom didn't have a window, unless that had been changed over the past two years.

The place was too small to be called a hunting cabin, which was what the owner had called it in the police reports. Had he been the one to install the bars and new door after what had happened here? Or had he sold the cabin, unknowingly, to the very killer who'd been using it all along as his own? Maybe the original owner was the killer, and the police had mistakenly cleared him.

Those were only some of the questions going through his mind. Along with the one that had been niggling him since the tragedy that had happened at the Brodericks': How had the killer known that Teagan would be there?

"Bryson, are you feeling better?" Her voice sounded groggy.

She was shoving to her knees, already reaching up to check on him. He grabbed her hands in his and kissed them before letting go.

"I hate that I slept at all. But I needed it. I'm thinking more clearly."

"What about the pain? Your head? Your hip? I could massage—"

He stopped her wandering hands and teased. "Boundaries, Teagan."

She smiled, somewhat reluctantly. "I sure never thought our first time sleeping together we'd actually be, well, sleeping."

"Maybe next time it will be different."

Her eyes widened like an owl's in the darkness. "If you really mean that, I'll bust out one of these walls to get us out of here. And I'll hold you to your word."

He laughed, amazed that he *could* in a situation like this. "Now there's the sassy, sexy, smart woman I remember. I think that sleep did both of us some good. But we can't sit around any longer. We have to get out of here before he comes back."

She moved her arm, frowning when the short chain between their wrists stopped her movement. "You had handcuff keys in your cane. Why didn't you tell me?"

"I wasn't even sure they were still there. It was a gag gift from Bishop, one of the Justice Seekers, after the shooting. He gave me a set of handcuffs and put the keys in the head of the cane, teasing that I could use them to keep my girlfriend at my side through my convalescence. That was after the nurses complained about how bad a patient I was in the hospital."

The corners of her mouth turned up in a small smile. "I can imagine that. I've seen how grumpy you are when your hip hurts."

"I never thought about those handcuff keys again until I was lying on the floor in the Brodericks' foyer and realized we were cuffed together. That's the main reason I kept asking for the cane. But he kept us under such close scrutiny that I never got the chance to get them out. You have to twist open the top and tilt the cane up in the air. Not something you can do on the sly. Once he put us in the back of the truck and kept the cane, I figured I'd lost my opportunity so there was no point in bringing it up."

"I don't suppose there was a gun in there too," she said. "I asked you in Gatlinburg if there was a gun hidden inside and you said there was."

"I was joking. Being a jerk, really."

"No. Never a jerk." She squeezed their joined hands.

"We need to get these handcuffs off. It's the only way we'll have a fighting chance if he comes back before we get out of this shack."

"You really think we have a chance?"

Her left hand clutched his right one so hard that his fingers started going numb. She was trying to put on a brave front. But inside, she was obviously terrified.

He leaned down and tilted her chin up, their eyes meeting with understanding, before he pressed a soft kiss against her lips. He'd only meant to distract her for a few seconds, to make sure she knew that he was here for her and would do whatever he could to protect her. But with both their emotions running high, touching her was like putting a match to gasoline.

Suddenly she was straddling him like she'd done in his rental car. And the temperature went up a thousand degrees as they tangled against each other like two horny college kids on spring break. It was only when she moaned into his mouth that he realized he'd slid his hands up her belly and was working on the front clasp of her bra. The logical part of his brain was yelling at him to stop this madness, that they were wasting valuable time. The rest of him, which seemed to be winning, was arguing that maybe this was exactly what he should be doing in case these were his last moments on earth. What better way to go out of this world than making love to the most amazing, interesting, adorably sassy woman he'd ever met?

"The back," she whispered against his mouth. "The clasp is in the back."

What few brain cells he had left registered what she'd said, that to take off her bra he had to slide his hands around to her back. But if that was the case, what was the hard part in the front of her bra he'd just felt?

Underwire.

He broke the kiss and stared down at her. Somewhere along the line, either she or he had discarded her shirt as best they could. It was hanging over his forearm caught in the handcuff chain. And in the dim light filtering in through the windows and front door, two perfect breasts sat in all their glory, exposed, freed from the cups of her bra that was still fastened beneath them. More than almost anything, he wanted to pull each nipple into his mouth, treasure those soft, warm, incredible curves. But, as impossible as it seemed, there was something else he wanted more.

Her underwire.

He slid his hands around her back and fumbled with the clasp. She sighed with pleasure as he pulled her bra off, but her eyes flew open in surprise when he sat back.

He held the bra up, felt where the underwire ended, then tore at the delicate fabric with his teeth.

She stared at him in confusion. "What...what are you doing? If you want to put your mouth on something, trust me, there are better places to put it." She motioned toward her breasts.

He grinned even with the fabric in his mouth. She was definitely the type of woman who knew what she wanted.

If he could go back in time and keep her at his house instead of turning her away, he'd probably still be in bed with her days later.

"Bryson?" She was frowning now, obviously getting annoyed.

He made one last tear and the wire hit his teeth. He sat back, working at it with his fingers now, pulling it out of the fabric.

She gasped in dismay. "That bra cost over a hundred dollars."

He hesitated. "You're kidding. You wear hundred-dollar bras?"

"It's my only hundred-dollar bra. I was saving it for a special occasion." She arched a brow. "Why do you think I took a shower at my parents' house? Who do you think I put that bra on for?" She waved her hand toward her shorts. "I have matching panties too."

Boy oh boy did he want to see those matching panties. But more than that, he wanted her to *live*. He glanced toward the door, and the blessedly empty gravel road out front. "I'll buy you another hundred-dollar bra, a dozen. And matching underwear. But right now, I need this." He finally yanked the wire free and held it up. "Handcuff key."

Her eyes widened in surprise.

"Hold up your wrist. I'll try your side first."

She did as he'd asked, and he ran his fingers along the flat side of the metal circle until he found the little slot for the key, just where the metal was locked into the hole. He slid the end of the underwire inside, then carefully worked it back and forth. The cuff backed out one slot with a loud click, giving her a little more wiggle room.

"It's working!" Her voice was full of awe.

"Long way to go. Give me a minute. I have to be careful or the wire will break." He ratcheted the metal back one slow click at a time.

"I'm guessing our captor took Annie from you at the Brodericks'," he said as he twisted the wire in the cuffs. "Otherwise you'd have shot him full of holes."

"Annie? Oh, my gun?" At his nod, she shook her head. "I don't understand it. I had so many opportunities to get away, to get help. But I just…froze. In that foyer. He took your gun and mine before I even thought about trying to use them. Or run out the front door to a neighbor's. I can't believe I just…stood there."

The handcuff loosened another click. "It's the trauma from before. If he'd been anyone else, I imagine that wouldn't have happened. But your brain shut down the moment you realized who he was. That's not your fault. It's not something you could control."

"Nice of you to say, but I'm not so sure that—"

Click. He pulled the handcuff off her.

She rubbed her wrist and grinned. "I'm free!"

"Not quite. That was step one. Step two is getting out of this shack. Step three is disappearing into the woods long before he gets back." He slipped her end of the handcuffs over his still-cuffed wrist and clicked them loosely into place.

"What are you doing!" she exclaimed. "Why did you do that?"

"To save time. I can do whatever I need to do with both cuffs on the same wrist. I'll worry about getting them off later." He waved toward her shirt, which had fallen to the floor. "I'm having enough trouble focusing with this concussion without your gorgeous breasts distracting me. Mind putting your shirt back on?"

Her smile beamed at him, full wattage. "You think my breasts are gorgeous? What a sweet thing to say." She winked and grabbed her shirt. "Let's get out of here, Bryson. I want you to buy me those matching underwear sets so you can take them right back off again."

He laughed and tried to shove himself to his feet, but his hip gave out and he collapsed against the cushions. His face heated with embarrassment as he cleared his throat. "Looks like I'll need a little help standing. I should be able to walk but getting up off this couch is beyond my current abilities. I always get stiff after lying down for a while."

"I sure hope you do."

He glanced at her in confusion, then realized what she meant when she winked.

He shook his head, grinning. "You've got a one-track mind. Help me up." He held his hand out to stop whatever she was about to say. "Without another sexual innuendo. We're running out of time."

Her smile faded and fear took its place. He regretted being so blunt, but even though her natural tendency to block out her fears and worries by flirting and teasing was adorable in most circumstances, they were a liability in this one. Especially since the blow to his head had him thinking far less clearly than usual.

She helped him up, and thankfully he was able to limp unaided to the door.

"What do we do now?" She settled her shirt into place. "Try to pull out the hinge pins?"

He was already sticking the underwire into the door lock when her innocent question had him glancing up in surprise. The hinges were on the inside. Because doors like these were intended to keep people out, not in.

Their abductor might have finally made a mistake.

Chapter Sixteen

"You, Teagan Ray, are brilliant," Bryson told her. "I'll try the lock first, but I was worried this metal will be too soft for this. The hinge pins will likely be our ticket out of here. But we have to find something to use to pop them out." He motioned toward the stove, which was only about three feet from the door, and beyond that to the handful of cabinets that formed the tiny kitchenette. "Look through this kitchen, in the bedroom, under the couch. We'll need something we can either wedge under the end of the pin to pull it or something to stick in the hinge on the bottom to push it."

"I'm on it."

She moved past him and started slamming open cabinets and drawers. He could follow her progress through the tiny shack by the sound of her cursing and the sounds of her either kicking or hitting walls.

He blocked all that out and focused on trying to pick the lock using the underwire.

After half a dozen attempts, he realized it wasn't going to happen. The metal was just too soft and kept bending. He tossed it aside as she ran to him holding up a long metal rod and a foot-long piece of wood.

"Will this work?" She was breathing heavily from exertion. "I figure you can stick the metal up the bottom of the hinge and use the wood like a hammer to push out the pin."

"Do I even want to know where you got the steel rod? And why it's wet?"

"Probably not."

"Were you in the bathroom?"

"Like I said. You don't want to know."

He grimaced. The rod looked like one of those old-fashioned toilet-tank float rods that controlled how the toilet flushed. As to the wood, it was either a piece of baseboard or a piece of the floor itself. Judging by the dilapidated shape of the building, neither would surprise him.

The steel rod was the perfect size and slid in place beneath the middle hinge pin with ease. Hope flared in his chest as he slammed the wood against it. He slammed it over and over and over, but the pin wasn't moving. He finally stopped and leaned in close, trying to see if there was something keeping it in place. Then he took a closer look at the hinges in the door frame and cursed.

"What is it?" she asked.

"Locking hinge pins."

"Never heard of them. But I don't like how that sounds."

He tossed the wood and rod on the floor and wiped his hands on his dress pants. "I thought our captor made a mistake with the hinges on the inside. But he didn't. There's an extra screw that prevents the pin from being backed out. We'd need an Allen wrench and a screwdriver to get it out. No homemade tools are going to back out that screw. It's drilled into the wrought-iron frame."

Her shoulders slumped. "That's why he didn't try to drug us, or tie us up. He knew there was no way to escape."

"Don't give up on me now. I haven't thrown in the towel just yet."

She nodded. But he could tell she was rapidly losing hope.

"Talk to me," he said. "Tell me how you escaped the last time while I see what else is in here."

"There's nothing. Just the couch and a few aluminum pots and pans. The utensils in the drawer are plastic or rubber. There's nothing we could use to stab or hit him."

"He's got a gun. Nothing much trumps that. We need to get out before he returns. We have to think outside the box." He limped past the front door and the stove, then yanked open one of the cabinet drawers in the kitchenette. "Tell me about the shack, and how you got out."

"It's basically the same. Well, the bars are new. And the iron front door. There isn't a back door. He tied me up when he left, with cloth. He didn't use handcuffs. Mostly he used drugs to keep me docile. He'd knock me out for hours, and I wouldn't wake up until he was back. I was in detox for weeks after I got away."

He pulled the hardware, tested the corners of the drawer boxes. "Go on. What else."

She sighed heavily. "I was blindfolded whenever it was light outside. And he wore a hooded mask most of the time. That always gave me hope, thinking he'd eventually let me go because he was keeping his identity secret. But I don't know that he ever would have. He was just extra cautious, in case something happened and I got away. He's not worried about us identifying him. He's going to kill us."

He'd just started into the bathroom but turned around when she said that. "Not if I kill him first. Do *not* give up on me."

Her eyes widened, but he didn't stand around talking. The sense of time passing was making him feel edgy and nervous. He couldn't imagine that whatever their captor was doing would keep him gone much longer.

The bathroom was a total bust. It was pitch dark, for one thing, but tiny without even a cabinet under the sink to hide anything. No bleach or cleaners that he could toss in the gunman's face. He didn't know how Teagan had managed to think about the toilet rod or even how she'd gotten it out of the back of the tank in the darkness. He had to give her a lot of credit for ingenuity.

The bedroom was much the same as the rest. Bars on the lone small window. An empty closet. No bed, just a mattress lying on the floor. It looked new, thankfully. Not the one that had been here two years ago.

He paused in the tiny hallway outside the bedroom. As run-down as the place was, maybe they could push through a wall like Teagan had teased about earlier. He doubted it, but he sent her off to look for weaknesses in the walls while he returned to the kitchen corner of the main room. With her distracted, he leaned down to study the two-burner gas stove.

It had caught his attention earlier as he'd considered what he could do given the lit pilot light and the fact that the gas line ran through the wall to a propane tank on the outside. Filling the cabin with gas and causing an explosion would likely burn the dry-rotted cabin like kindling. And the fire could be seen for miles around. It would get first responders out here for sure. But being blown apart in the explosion or burning alive were both wholly unappealing.

"What are you looking at?" she asked.

"Nothing helpful. I'm going to check the bedroom again. Did you find any weaknesses in the walls?"

She followed him as he limped into the bedroom.

"No. But I'm no expert at building construction. And it's still so dark in here that I might have missed something. Unless you want more baseboards."

He straightened from his study of the wood beneath the window where he'd been hoping moisture might have rotted out the frame. "Baseboards. That's what you handed me to use as a hammer. Where did you find it?"

She pointed toward the closet. "In there. The board was broken already so I was able to kick out that piece I gave you." She rubbed her hands up and down her arms. "He'll be back soon, won't he?"

The wobble in her voice had him longing to hold her, to try to comfort her. Instead, he dropped to his knees to study the baseboards, grimacing at the jolt of pain that sizzled through his hip.

"You didn't finish telling me how you got away." He felt along the bottom of the closet as she talked behind him, telling him how her captor had missed the vein the last time when he'd tried to drug her.

"He was going on one of his supply trips," she said. "The injection made me groggy but didn't knock me out like usual. I pretended to be unconscious. After he left I shoved the blindfold up and used my teeth to loosen my bindings and got myself untied. The old front door was mostly rotten so I kicked it until it split away from the frame. Then I took off. Nothing amazing. I just ran until I couldn't. Then I walked. Then I crawled. A hiker found me several days later. Not that any of that matters. Our situation is different. We're good and stuck here."

He tugged on the board he'd been testing, pulling as hard as he could. It broke in half with a loud crack.

She jumped beside him. "What was that?"

He glanced over his shoulder. "The walls might be solid. But the floor isn't. Those baseboards came out easily for you because the whole floor in this section has been eaten up with termites." He waved toward a foot-long, four-inch-wide hole he'd made in the floor. "That's dirt down there. The crawl space under the cabin. This is how we're going to get out."

She was shaking her head before he finished. "No, Bryson. That's not the sound I heard. There was something else, out front."

He lurched to his feet, then limped as fast as he could into the main room. She ran after him and they both stumbled to a halt when they saw the headlights bouncing crazily across the trees. A vehicle was coming up the gravel road toward the shack.

They were out of time.

Chapter Seventeen

Teagan watched the lights bouncing across the trees. The road faced those trees but ran perpendicular to the front of the shack. They wouldn't be able to see the truck until it made the last turn and pulled up. But there was no reason for anyone else to come down this road. The killer was back. And when he came inside and saw they were out of their handcuffs, he'd cuff them again. Then he'd make a circuit of the shack and find the small hole that Bryson had started. He'd decide Bryson was too big a liability to keep around. He'd kill him for sure.

And then he'd come for her.

"Kill me, Bryson." She grabbed his arm. "Please. I can't do this again. Choke me. Hit me over the head. Something. It will be a mercy killing. Please."

He shook her hand off his arm. "This isn't over. You hear me? Don't you dare give up." He pointed to the couch. "We have to block the door. As small as this room is, we should be able to jam one end against the wall and the other against the door. He won't be able to get inside."

She looked from the lights outside to the couch and back again. "We'd just be delaying the inevitable. What's the point? I have a better idea. I'll make him so angry he has to shoot me. Then at least I won't have to bear his touch again."

He yanked her around to face him as the sound of gravel crunching beneath tires echoed outside. "All we have to do is break three or four more boards in that closet and we're out of here. But we have to buy some time. Help me get this couch into place." He grabbed her arm and tugged her away from the door as the headlights turned toward the shack.

"Grab that other end," he yelled. "We'll have to slide it past the hallway to turn it. Hurry."

She ran to the other end and together they slid the couch across the floor.

"It's clear," he said. "Now, turn it, turn it. This end toward the door."

They slid the couch sideways, one end facing the door, the other the hallway.

"He's here! He's here," she yelled. The truck had parked in front of the cabin.

"Slide it back. We have to wedge it between the wall and the door. Hurry!"

She pushed her end but couldn't get it against the wall. "It's too long. It won't fit. He'll be able to push the door and the couch will slide down the hall."

The engine cut off outside. A loud creak sounded. The truck door opening?

She started to shake. "Oh, God. He's here."

Bryson leaped over the back of the couch, stumbling and nearly falling before catching himself. Then he limped to her end. He bent down and somehow lifted the couch in spite of his bad hip, his face turning red as he shoved the couch up in the air. Then he dropped it against the wall just past the hallway opening. It fell down, but stuck with another foot to go. She didn't see how it would hold. When the killer pushed the door, if he pushed hard enough, the couch would slide up the wall and he'd still be able to get inside.

Bryson must have thought the same thing because he climbed onto the end of the couch that was against the wall and hopped up and down, one-legged, favoring his hip. He jumped again, and again. The couch springs squeaked in protest. Then it dropped down into place, wedged tight.

Keys rattled outside. "Hey, what are you doing in there?"

Bryson grabbed her arm and tugged her toward the hallway. "Go, go, go."

"Open the door!" The gunman pounded against it, his voice thick with rage.

Once they were inside the bedroom, Bryson released her and limped into the closet. Jamming his bad hip against the wall to keep his balance, he slammed his right heel down on the boards beside the hole, over and over. Wood crunched beneath his boot, dropping below. But the hole wasn't large enough for them to get through. Not even close.

Bam! Bam! Bam!

Teagan jerked around as bullets burst through the wall from the front of the shack and plowed through the opposite wall, throwing splinters up in front of her face.

"Down, get down!" Bryson tackled her to the mattress on the floor behind her.

More shots exploded through the wall, right where she'd been standing. She buried her head against his neck as he covered her with his body.

The front door rattled, followed by furious cursing and shouting. Then, nothing. Silence fell over the shack like a heavy blanket, except for the sound of their breathing and the blood rushing in her ears.

"What's he doing now," she whispered. "Where is he?"

He lifted off her and held a finger against his lips, telling her to be quiet.

She nodded to let him know she understood.

A thump sounded outside. Bryson grabbed her, stumbling and limping as he pulled her into the corner away from the window. Moments later, a flashlight shone through the glass. They both scrunched up against the wall, watching the light as it moved around the room. Then it stopped, shining directly on the hole in the closet floor. The light flicked off.

"Oh, no," she whispered.

He swore softly. Then he pressed his fingers to his lips again, and edged to the window to peer out.

A thump sounded from somewhere beneath them.

She covered her mouth to keep from screaming.

He grabbed her, pushing her in front of him toward the door, motioning for her to be as quiet as possible. He was obviously struggling to keep up, his unbalanced gait evidence of just how badly his hip must be hurting. But they made it to the hall, then hurried into the main room.

He limped to the door and tugged the handle. It moved just enough to prove it wasn't locked. But there was no way to open it with the couch against it. He motioned for her to put her hand on the knob, then bent down next to her ear. "When I lift the couch, run like hell. Get out of here. Run to the woods and don't stop for anything."

"What about you? You can't run."

"Don't worry about me."

"Bryson, I can't leave you—"

The sound of wood splintering in the other room was followed by a guttural yell. "You're dead, you hear me? I'm going to kill both of you!"

Shots rang out. Glass shattered. He must have shot out the window.

"He'll be through that floor soon. I need you to run. I need to know you're safe. Then I'll run a different way and hide. Our best chance is to split up. Promise me you'll run and won't look back. Promise!"

More wood splintered in the other room.

"Promise me." He lightly shook her.

"Okay, okay. Promise."

Bracing his left side against the door, he grabbed the bottom of the couch and pulled and tugged, wrestling to get it to move after being wedged in so tight.

A shot rang out.

She ducked, then looked at Bryson, who'd frozen in place. "Are you okay?"

His mouth tight, he nodded. "Get ready. Remember what I said. Run as fast as you can. Don't stop for anything."

She nodded and tightened her hand on the doorknob.

He heaved again. The couch finally jerked free and seemed to practically fly upward and over on its side, out of the way. As soon as it cleared the door, she tugged it open and ran. She ran as if the hounds of hell were on her heels, because that's exactly what it felt like. She didn't stop until she reached the far end of the clearing. Even though she'd promised not to stop, she did. She had to make sure he was okay. Ducking behind a pine tree, she peered around it at the shack. The front door was hanging open and the headlights didn't reveal anyone inside. He'd made it. He'd gotten out.

She turned and ran.

As soon as Teagan took off running, Bryson dropped to his knees, grimacing as he scooted himself back against the wall, tucked between the door and the stove. He hadn't lied to her, not at first anyway. He'd thought he could run, or at least limp really fast. With a head start, he would have had a chance. But then things had changed. He slid his hand inside his suit jacket. It came away sticky and wet. That last bullet had hit its mark. He wiped the blood on his pant leg and closed his eyes.

Another shout of rage sounded from the bedroom. The man sure had an anger problem. Bryson wondered what he did for a living, because it would be really hard to hide that type of a temper in a nine-to-five office job. Something or someone would be bound to set him off. Whatever he did, it would be a solo kind of job. He'd have the freedom to set his own hours so he wouldn't be missed for weeks at a time when he was on a sociopathic spree. He'd have made an interesting profile.

A series of loud thumps and cursing echoed from the back room. The gunman was finally breaking through the floor.

Bryson coughed and blood sprayed out of his mouth. Not a good sign. Darkness was closing in on the edges of his vision again. He shook his head to stay awake. He still had one more thing that he had to do. Step one had been to get out of the handcuffs. Step two was to get Teagan out of the shack to safety. Step three was still to come. He had to ensure that first responders came out here to help her so she wouldn't die in those woods. And at this point, there was only one way he knew to do that.

He slid his hand behind the stove beside him, then yanked hard on the gas line. Like most things in this shack, it was old and brittle and much easier to pull loose than he'd expected. Finally something was going his way.

"I'm coming for you now!" the killer yelled from the other room. Shoes stomped on the hardwood floor and a hulking dark shape appeared in the hallway. Dawn was finally breaking on the little glade in the woods. And the first rays of sunlight shone through the door, glinting on the pistol in the other man's hand.

He narrowed his eyes at Bryson, his face red with anger and exertion. He looked left and right, not that he needed to in such a small space. One glance could clearly show that they were alone.

"Where is she?" He lifted his gun, aiming it at Bryson. "Tell me right now or I'll shoot."

Bryson smiled and held up the gas line, which was hissing and spewing out foul-smelling propane. "She's gone. Go ahead and shoot me. The flare from the muzzle will take us both out. And Teagan will never have to be afraid of you ever again, you scum-sucking, piece of human excrement. You're not even fit to lick the bottom of her shoes, pervert."

The other man's gun started shaking. His face was so bright red it looked like he would have a stroke at any moment.

As gas continued to fill the room, Bryson piled on more insults, trying to prod the killer's temper so he'd shoot. He wanted him to shoot. Because Teagan would be safe. She could finally live the life she deserved, without fear. And the explosion would bring the help she'd need to make it back to civilization.

"You stupid cop."

"Is that the worst you can think to say? Really?" Bryson clucked his tongue. "You're dumber than I gave you credit."

He roared with rage, then strode across the room toward Bryson and shoved the gun against his temple. But when he glanced at the gas line, he swore. He tossed a few more curses Bryson's way, then yanked open the door and headed outside.

Bryson swore a few choice curses himself. He hadn't defeated the devil after all. But he'd get the help Teagan needed. Of that he was sure. As soon as the gunman was far enough from the cabin to feel safe, he'd shoot that propane tank. He was too mad not to. The explosion would be spectacular. Half the firefighters and cops in the county would be here in minutes.

"Bryson, what are you doing?"

His eyes flew open. Teagan was running toward him from the hallway. "What the hell? The place is full of gas and he's going to—"

"Shoot the propane tank, I'm guessing? Was that your stupid plan?" She put her hands beneath his shoulders and hauled upward. "Help me. Hurry."

He swore a blue streak and drew on reserves of strength he never knew he had to push to his feet.

"Go, go, go," she yelled, repeating his earlier words to her.

They hobbled into the bedroom and she hopped down into the hole. He winced as he tried to lower himself, then gave up and went headfirst. She was reaching back to help him, but he shoved her toward the patch of sunlight just a few feet away. She hurried forward and he half-scrambled, half-crawled after her.

Out front, the truck engine started up. Tires crunched and the engine roared as he drove away from the cabin.

They cleared the structure, him leaning heavily on her once again as they stumbled toward the tree line. Just past the first stand of trees, palmettos viciously scraped their flesh.

"Down," he yelled. "Over here!" He yanked her behind a fallen tree log and rolled on top of her.

A shot sounded. The shack exploded, turning the clearing into a fiery inferno.

Chapter Eighteen

Teagan restlessly paced the hospital conference room. From the exasperated looks on the faces of most of the men sitting at the table, she knew they were getting tired of her jumping out of her chair. But she was too nervous, too freaking scared about what was going on with Bryson that she couldn't sit still for more than a few minutes.

"Ms. Ray," one of the Jacksonville Sheriff's Office detectives called out to her.

Which one was he? Burns, Rodriquez, Bunting? The names of the other two sitting at the long table had been forgotten right after they'd introduced themselves. How many detectives did it take to question one lone abduction victim? How many did it take to change a stupid light bulb?

"Ms. Ray," he called out again.

Burns. That was his name.

He motioned toward the other side of the table. "Will you please sit and answer some more questions?"

Five against one. JSO on one side, her on the other. Not that they were enemies, exactly. But their lack of interest, or ability, to solve her abduction and torture two years ago didn't make her much of a fan now. The only reason she was talking to them was because Bryson was in surgery after being life-flighted from Live Oak to the trauma unit at UF Health Shands Hospital here in Jacksonville.

It had nearly killed her watching the helicopter disappear in the sky with him on board. And she'd hated being stuck with a Florida Highway Patrolman as her assigned bodyguard, wasting time making her get checked out at a local Live Oak emergency room. When the doctors there confirmed what she'd said all along—that she was fine—the patrolman had finally taken off down Interstate 10 to drive her to Jacksonville. They'd arrived two hours ago, and she still didn't have an update on Bryson's condition other than that he was in surgery.

"Ms. Ray—"

"Tell you what, Detective Burns." She flattened her palms against the table but didn't sit. "How about you get me a real update this time on Mr. Anton's condition. Something more detailed than a simple acknowledgment that he's still in surgery, and then, maybe I'll answer more of your endless questions."

He sighed heavily, then left the room, presumably to get the information that she'd requested.

Another detective motioned toward her seat. "There are three murders attributable to your abductor—Mr. and Mrs. Broderick and the driver of the delivery truck that he hijacked. We need to catch this guy before he hurts someone else."

"Don't you think I know that?" She shook her head at his seeming callousness. Her heart ached over the senseless, brutal murders her kidnapper had carried out while trying to get to her. She wanted him caught just as badly as anyone else, probably more so. Because even though she wasn't the one who'd hurt those people, she'd always wonder whether she could have done something differently to prevent their deaths.

"Ms. Ray," he began again. "I know this is nerve-racking, especially when you're worried about your fiancé. But we really need your help."

A twinge of guilt shot through her over the fiancé lie. But she'd wanted to make sure that the hospital would share information with her on Bryson's condition. Not that it had served her well so far. She'd been stuck in this room, answering dozens, maybe hundreds of questions during this inquisition. There just wasn't anything else she could tell them. Maybe if they'd actually work on the investigation, using the information that she'd already given them, they'd figure out the killer's identity and arrest him.

She plopped down in her chair. "I honestly don't know what else you think I can tell you. We've been over the timeline again and again. I told you the guy looked familiar but I couldn't figure out why, still can't. I sat with your sketch artist and you've got his likeness now. Why don't you put an APB out based on that and try to find the guy?"

"They don't use the term APB anymore, Ms. Ray," a familiar voice spoke from the doorway. "It's called a BOLO—be on the lookout."

Relief had her slumping in her chair at the sight of Bryson's boss from The Justice Seekers, Mason Ford. "Mr. Ford, thank you so much for coming."

He stepped inside the room. "I'm just glad that I was already in the state working a case when you called."

"Who the heck are you?" one of the detectives demanded. Rodriquez, she believed.

"A friend of the family. If you don't mind, I need to speak to Ms. Ray." He opened the door wider when they didn't move. "Privately."

The detectives shot sour looks at both of them but finally got up. As they headed out the door, Rodriquez turned back to Teagan and slid a business card across the table. "When you're ready to cooperate, give me a call. We need to jump on this case fast. Please don't take too long." With that he headed out the door.

She threw her hands in the air. "When I'm ready to co-operate? I've done nothing but cooperate. They keep asking me the same questions over and over."

Ford shut the door behind him and gave her an apologetic look. "And I'm about to ask you to repeat everything you just told them. Sorry about that. But you did call. I'm here, and the full force of my company is at yours and Bryson's disposal. I'm pulling everyone off noncritical cases effective immediately. We'll do everything we can to catch this guy."

Some of the tension that had taken hold of her for the past twenty-four hours began to melt away at his words. "Thank you, Mr. Ford. I can't tell you how good it is to hear someone say that. Those detectives treated me as if I was a suspect, the jerks."

His mouth tilted up in what she assumed passed for a smile for him. Back at The Justice Seekers headquarters he'd never cracked even a shadow of a smile. But he'd been nothing but courteous and had jumped at the chance to help once she'd called him on the way from Live Oak to Jacksonville to tell him that Bryson was hurt.

He set a leather portfolio on the table and sat across from her. "First, please call me Mason. After all, you being Bryson's fiancée makes you family, more or less."

She felt her cheeks heat. "I'm sure you realize we aren't really engaged. I made that up so the hospital would share updates about his condition. Not that they've bothered."

"Since you only met a few days ago, I kind of figured that was a ruse. The offer to call me Mason still stands."

"A few days ago? It feels like I've known him forever."

"Not surprising, given the trauma and emotional turmoil you've weathered together. As to those detectives being jerks, I'm sorry it feels that way. They're under a lot of pressure to solve this thing and probably don't even realize how they come across. Not that it excuses poor manners. As for Bryson's condition, I can update you on that."

She straightened in her chair. "The hospital gave you information?"

"Let's just say that I got the information from the hospital and leave it at that. Sometimes the end justifies the means. Don't you think?"

She grinned. "I like how you work, Mason. Please tell me how he's doing. Is he…is he going to—"

"He's going to be fine."

She dropped her face in her hands, unexpected tears flowing down her cheeks.

He waited silently until she regained control of her emotions. A few minutes later, she drew a ragged breath and sat back. "That's very good to hear. Thank you."

"Of course. He's actually in recovery now and should be awake soon." He placed his cell phone on the table. "The second he's lucid, that's going to vibrate. I'll take you right to him."

"Thank you," she whispered, fighting to hold back more tears.

"The bullet nicked his spleen but no other organs," he continued. "It went through and through. He lost a lot of blood. That on top of the concussion pretty much shut him down. That's why he was unconscious after the blast. Luckily you were both behind a log when the tank exploded, which shielded you from the shock wave. Otherwise, your insides would have liquefied."

She winced.

He smiled apologetically. "Sorry. That was graphic. Bottom line, he's going to be okay, eventually. He was lucky. You both were. If the explosion and resulting fire hadn't alerted authorities so that help arrived quickly, he'd have bled out."

She wrapped her arms around her waist. "Once again, he saved me, in spite of how badly he was hurt. He saved both of us. He's an incredible man."

"Yes. Yes, he is. And I want to do everything I can to protect both of you. We need to catch this guy and get enough evidence to ensure he'll either be executed or locked up so he can't hurt anyone else ever again. I know you're weary of answering questions. But I'm coming in late on this. So I'd very much appreciate it if you'd start from the top, right after you left my office in Gatlinburg." He pulled a computer tablet from his portfolio and set it on top of the table. Then he took out a small electronic device and set it a foot away from her. "To save time briefing my team, and to make sure I don't miss anything, I'm going to record this as well as take notes. If you're okay with it?"

"Absolutely." Covering the same ground yet again didn't bother her since it was Mason who was asking the questions. She believed that he'd actually do something with the information. None of the detectives she'd spoken to earlier had inspired that kind of confidence. "Did the police give you a copy of the likeness their sketch artist came up with?"

"Not yet." He picked up his phone. His fingers practically flew across the screen as he typed out a text. He waited a few seconds, then the phone buzzed. He checked the screen, then set it down. "My team will have the sketch within minutes." He poised his hands over the virtual keyboard on the tablet. "You were going to tell me the timeline. Don't leave anything out."

Half an hour later, a knock sounded on the door. Mason was out of his chair, gun in hand but hidden behind him before the door opened.

The detective who'd gone for a status update stood in the opening, a look of surprise on his face when he saw Mason. He took a quick glance into the room. "Where is everyone?"

"Not here. What can I do for you?"

"I, ah, wanted to let Ms. Ray know that Mr. Anton is out of surgery."

"Thank you." Mason closed the door before the detective could say anything else. He holstered his gun, then sat down. "You were saying?"

She clenched her hands together beneath the table. "You drew your gun. You think he'll show up here? At the hospital?"

"It's possible. Don't worry. I had a guard stationed outside the surgery room. He'll stay with Bryson in recovery as well."

She blinked. "How do the police feel about that?"

"I'm always as accommodating as possible with law enforcement. But I'm not about to leave the security of an injured member of my team to their care. The hospital administrator was more than okay with it after I offered a substantial donation in Bryson's name." He winked. "Now, if you don't mind. Please continue."

"Yes, of course. I, um, I guess I was up to the point of where I ran like a coward for the trees."

"No. I think you were telling me that you did exactly what Bryson asked you to do, so you wouldn't put him in more danger by making him worry about having to protect you rather than make his own escape. But I'm puzzled. If you ran into the woods at the front of the clearing, how did you end up behind the shack when it exploded?"

Her face heated. "I didn't exactly follow Bryson's instructions. I know he wanted me to keep going, to run as far away as I could. But I hadn't seen him leave the shack, and I was worried that he might have been pretending to feel better than he did, just to get me out of danger. All throughout our ordeal, he kept telling me to have faith, that it was two against one, that we could beat the bad guy together. And there I was running away. I just couldn't do it."

He crossed his arms on top of the table. "So what did you do?"

She wrapped her arms around her middle, remembering. "I circled through the woods to the back of the shack."

"Where was the gunman?"

"I wasn't sure. The truck was still parked out front. I didn't see him anywhere."

He stared at her, waiting.

"I got down on my belly and tried to see beneath the shack, through the crawl space. When I didn't see anyone moving around under there, I was terrified that the gunman was inside with Bryson. So I ran to the shack and crawled up into the closet through the hole in the floor."

He still didn't say anything. But his eyes widened slightly.

"I heard the gunman shouting in the other room. And I smelled gas. It was filling up the cabin. A moment later, the front door creaked. I peeked around the corner and saw the gunman running for his truck." She swallowed hard. "And Bryson, he was just sitting there, his back to the wall, holding the gas line in his hand."

She swiped at the tears in her eyes. "For a split second, I thought he was dead. But then I saw his chest rise and realized he was still alive. I yelled at him to get out. We dropped through the hole in the closet floor and made it to the woods just before the explosion." She wiped her tears again. "Like you said earlier, if it wasn't for Bryson getting both of us behind that log when he did, we'd both be dead. He deserves a medal of honor. Not a bullet in the back."

He cleared his throat. "That's quite a story. I gather you sat with him until help arrived?"

"Of course. I know CPR. But that's about the limits of my nursing abilities. He was breathing, and his heart was beating. But he wouldn't open his eyes. I didn't know what to do. All I could think of was to apply pressure to the wounds, even though they didn't seem to be bleeding all that much. I had no idea he was bleeding internally."

She squeezed her eyes shut for a moment and let out a shuddering breath. "Thank goodness the fire department and police arrived so quickly. I heard the sirens and ran to the clearing. They were amazing, ran with me around back, no questions asked. They immediately started an IV and got him on a gurney. I think they flew him out in a helicopter within a couple of minutes. They saved his life."

He slowly shook his head. "No, Ms. Ray. I think that distinction belongs to you. If you hadn't been stubborn enough and brave enough to go back into that shack to check on him, he'd be dead right now." His voice sounded oddly hoarse, and he cleared his throat before continuing. "Thank you. On behalf of all the Justice Seekers, thank you for saving our dear friend and coworker."

She was about to argue that he wouldn't have even been in danger in the first place if it wasn't for her, but his phone vibrated against the table.

He picked it up, then stood.

She shoved out of her chair. "Bryson's awake?"

He shook his head. "Not yet. But I'll go check on him right now. Meanwhile, you have visitors."

"Visitors?" She frowned. "The police are back?"

He hesitated at the door. "When you called me to help Bryson, I took the liberty of calling someone to help you. But I asked them to give me time to interview you first. They've been very accommodating. But they're out in the hall now, demanding to see you." He smiled his first real smile. "You're an incredibly brave and smart young woman. Thank you again for everything you did." Without waiting for her reply, he left the room.

A moment later, two people rounded the corner and paused in the doorway.

She let out a shriek and ran around the table, tears flowing again.

Her mother and father gathered her to them in a bone-crushing hug.

Chapter Nineteen

Teagan sighed deeply and shifted positions in the plastic chair a few feet from Bryson's hospital bed as he slept the morning away. Three days. It had been three days since she'd cried all over him in the recovery room after he woke up from surgery, only to have him gruffly tell her that he needed his sleep. Since then, he'd hardly spoken a word to her. He was acting just like the surly bear she'd encountered the first time they'd met. But they'd moved beyond that. Far beyond it. So why was he acting like they were strangers and he was the grouchy hermit again?

She'd asked him that very thing.

His answers were many. He had a headache. He was feeling fuzzy from the concussion. The pain from his surgery had him feeling bad and he just needed to sleep. All of that was probably true. But he was a strong man, and had overcome far worse to save both their lives. And he'd been at his kindest in the past when he was in tremendous pain, because he'd risen above it to save them. So none of his actions now made sense.

Thankfully, his boss—Mason Ford—didn't seem worried about Bryson's less than friendly attitude that seemed to extend to anyone unfortunate enough to be in his vicinity. He simply ignored Bryson's gruff responses and went about his business. And he kept Teagan up to date on everything going on with the investigation.

Which, unfortunately, wasn't much.

Even with half the Justice Seekers working the case here in Jacksonville, none of them seemed to be making any more headway than JSO. No one had discovered the identity yet of the man who'd abducted them and killed three innocent people. But Mason assured her they were doing everything they could and weren't giving up. And he did something else—he gave her a company credit card to use for all of her and Bryson's needs. He told her the card had no limit and to use it for anything at all, no questions asked.

He'd also ordered Bryson to let her make all the arrangements to get him set up at a local hotel after being discharged so he could get strong enough for the trip back to Gatlinburg. Teagan decided that she liked Mason Ford very much, especially since he made no secret that he was rooting for her to win this little cold war between her and Bryson.

She crossed her arms and waited another half hour before the doctor's morning rounds finally brought him to Bryson's room to perform a final evaluation before giving him discharge papers. Miraculously, he woke up just as the doctor stepped into the room. Teagan snorted and looked out the window, pretending indifference, when she was fuming inside.

The hurt had long ago faded. Or, at least, it was buried down deep. No more crying in front of him. She had her pride after all. And no crying on her mama's shoulder either, given that her mother now thought—along with the hospital staff—that she and Bryson were engaged. That was going to be a huge disappointment for her parents once he went back to Gatlinburg and she told them the "engagement" was off. They'd half fallen in love with him when he'd had dinner at their home. They fell the rest of the way after hearing everything he'd done to protect their only child.

But they wouldn't be the only ones nursing a broken heart.

She kept her face averted, pretending interest in something out the window while she wiped the wetness from her eyes. How could she still have all these inconvenient feelings for a man who didn't return them? She took a few deep breaths and reached down for her anger again, wrapping it around her other emotions like a shield, to keep her safe.

"All in all, you're an incredibly lucky man," the doctor said behind her as he apparently finished his exam. "Any one of your injuries—the blow to the head, the gunshot, the half-dozen pieces of wood that the explosion drove into your back—could have killed you. You might not feel lucky right now, but once the pain fades and you're back on your feet, I think you'll begin to realize just how fortunate you are. Someone was looking out for you."

She turned around, but steadfastly looked at the floor while he thanked the doctor and discussed the discharge instructions. Her anger had evaporated beneath the shock of what she'd just heard. She hadn't known about the wood driven into his back. On top of everything else that he'd endured, he'd basically been stabbed, *six times*, as the remnants of the shack rained down on them. But not one of those pieces of lethally sharp wood had hit her—because he'd protected her. Again. She had no right to be angry with him. And he had every right to be angry with her. He'd be sitting on his dock enjoying a cold beer right now, listening to the rippling water of the stream behind his house if it wasn't for her. Healthy, content, his only worry the ache in his hip when the tequila and scotch weren't enough to dull the pain.

What a selfish immature idiot she'd been, thinking only of herself.

The squeak of metal had her glancing up to see him struggling to lower the railing. The doctor must have left while she was consumed with her own thoughts.

She rushed over to him. "Here, let me." She gently pushed his hands away and lowered the railing. "Just, please, don't try to get out of bed on your own. I know you don't want my help, so I'll get the nurse to help you get dressed."

"Teagan, I—"

"It's okay. I understand. I'll have the car brought up and will meet you and the nurse out front."

He frowned. "What do you think you understand?"

Without answering, she hurried from the room.

BRYSON EASED BACK against the pillows that Teagan had just stuffed behind him so he could sit up in the hotel bed. "Thank you." He motioned toward the impressive fifteen-hundred-square-feet, two-bedroom suite that she'd reserved for them at the Omni hotel. The accommodations were luxurious, but more important, it was close enough to the hospital that he hadn't had to endure the agony of a long car ride. And since she'd insisted on him taking more pain pills after reaching the hotel, he was feeling pretty good right now. Physically at least. "Thank you for everything, Teagan."

She seemed surprised by his words, acknowledging them with a quick nod. Then she turned to finish putting away his clothes that she'd had brought from the other hotel he'd originally been staying in, closer to The Woods subdivision. Her surprise that he'd actually thank her had him feeling like even more of a jerk than he had since the moment he'd woken up in the recovery room.

All the memories of what had happened had slammed into him, stealing his breath. He'd made so many mistakes that could have cost her life. The very first one was in agreeing to take her with him to that ill-fated interview at the Brodericks'. Everything had gone downhill from there.

The worst part was knowing what had driven him to include her, to give in to her request even though he was the one experienced in law enforcement and knew better, knew the dangers. What had driven him was pure selfishness, his ridiculous fixation on her and desire, no—*need*—to be around her as much as possible. His obsession had clouded his reason. And just as soon as he was able to manage on his own, he'd set her free, break this tenuous bond that had developed between them. He'd ensure that none of his bad decisions could ever risk her life again. Obviously he hadn't learned the lessons of his past—from his sloppy handling of the Kentucky Ripper case to his failure to save Hayley from the person who'd ended up shooting him in the hip all those months ago. He had no business thinking he could really protect Teagan.

She was much better off without him.

Finally she stopped running around the suite putting things away, and stood by his bed. "I guess it's good that you already had a wheelchair and had it at your other hotel," she said. "Saved me from having to rent one while you're here. Goodness knows you'll need it for a while until you're back on your feet." She motioned beside the bed where she'd stored it within easy reach. "There's a cane too, for when you're feeling good enough to try to walk. It's nothing fancy. I got it at the hospital gift shop. Your other one, unfortunately, is locked up in evidence. It practically took an act of Congress just to get my purse released after the police took it from the Brodericks' home. They wouldn't even discuss the cane, for some reason. Anyway, in case you've forgotten your discharge instructions, they're in writing in the top drawer of your bedside table. But part of it is that the doctor wants you to try to stand and take at least a few steps several times a day. If you're in bed the whole time you could get blood clots and—"

"Teagan."

"Do you need something? A glass of water? Soda? There's a bar over there but you really shouldn't have any alcohol with the pain meds you're—"

"No. Thank you. I don't need anything. I—"

"Okay, then. I'm going to explore my room, catch up on some sleep. I haven't slept well at the hospital and—"

"Teagan."

"—if you need something, just text me on your phone. I left it on the nightstand. The police have both our phones in evidence so that's a new one. I had Mason program your team's numbers in there, so that should help. My new number's in there too, obviously, so you can text me. I'll check on you in a couple of hours."

"I need to talk to you."

"No, right now you need to sleep. We both do."

"Wait, please. Just give me a minute to—"

She hurried into the other bedroom, shutting the door hard behind her. But she hadn't turned fast enough to hide the tears in her eyes.

He swore and punched a fist into the mattress beside him.

Chapter Twenty

After spending five grueling days and nights in a tension-filled hotel suite with Bryson, Teagan was more than ready to see the last of the place, no matter how amazingly luxurious it was. She could have had a home health-care nurse take care of him while he recuperated. But since part of the reason that Mason had suggested they stay there together was to ensure that both of them were out of sight in case the killer came looking for them, it just made sense for her to take care of him herself.

But it hadn't been easy.

They'd hardly said two words to each other after their arrival. And since it wasn't looking promising that the killer would be found any time soon, it was time for both of them to try to get on with their lives. Well, as much as possible anyway. The police would have someone watching her parents' home while she was here, not that anyone expected the killer to be brazen enough to try to hurt her again. He was long gone, on the run.

Now, as the rented limo pulled up at her parents' home to drop her off so Bryson could fly in Mason's private jet back to Gatlinburg, she was so antsy to get away from him that she was pulling open the door before the driver had even come to a complete stop on the street out front.

"Wait," Bryson called out. "Let me walk you to the door."

"I've got it. No need." She grabbed her one piece of luggage from the seat beside her and hopped out, not even giving the driver a chance to open the door. "Take care, Bryson."

She heard him swearing as she slammed the door shut. Tears were already running down her cheeks by the time she sprinted across the front lawn and threw open the front door. "Mom, Dad, I'm home. Don't get up," she yelled, hurrying toward her old bedroom on the right side of the house. "I'll put away my stuff and freshen up. Talk to you in a few."

"Teagan? Are you okay?" her mom called out from the kitchen where insanely amazing smells were coming from. She must be cooking dinner.

"I'm great. Need to use the restroom, that's all," she lied, hurrying to toss her bag on the bedroom floor then running into the bathroom before her mother could stop her.

She shut the door, then turned around and slid to the floor, finally letting the tears fall that had threatened all morning. She hated crying, especially since she'd probably cried more lately than most people cried an entire lifetime. But it seemed to be the only outlet for her tumultuous emotions. Admitting to her mom that she was more upset over the way the relationship between her and Bryson had ended than the fact that a killer was still out there wasn't something she was keen about. Especially since the so-called relationship had never really begun in the first place. It wasn't real, none of this. It couldn't be. They hadn't even dated. So how could she possibly be in love with him? It wasn't love. It was lust, and shared trauma. In a few weeks, or months, this ache deep in her soul would be gone and she'd forget all about Bryson Anton.

Now if only she could convince her heart of that brazen lie, she'd be just fine.

After crying for a ridiculously long time, she actually felt better. She blew out a shuddering breath, then climbed to her feet. The mirror above the sink was not her friend. Her eyes were puffy and red. Her hair was escaping her customary braid. And her makeup was a disaster.

Thankfully, her mom and dad wouldn't care about her makeup. But they would care if they realized she'd been sitting in here crying for the past ten minutes. She grabbed a washcloth from the cabinet under the sink and washed her face, scrubbing off all of the makeup she'd painstakingly applied in the hotel bathroom. Not that Bryson had noticed. Her throat tightened. *Good grief. Stop it, Teagan. He's not worth it.* She lifted her gaze to the mirror and shook her head. Maybe if she kept lying to herself, she'd eventually believe the lies.

Straightening her shoulders, she drew a bracing breath and headed off to find her parents. Her mom smiled at her from the archway into the kitchen.

"Teagan, baby. Finally you're home." Her mom tossed a dishcloth onto the countertop and wrapped her arms around her.

"It's so good to be here. I missed you and Daddy so much." After a good long hug, she let her mom go and glanced around the kitchen. "It smells amazing in here. Did you cook all my favorites?" She crossed to the stove and bent down to smell the tantalizing aroma rising from the huge pot. "Jambalaya. You're the best, Mom."

"There's apple pie baking in the oven. It'll be ready by the time we finish supper."

She turned around to hug her mom again, then froze. Bryson was leaning against the wall beside the table at the other end of the kitchen, looking like a model out of a magazine in his charcoal gray tailored suit.

He straightened away from the wall and smiled. "Hello, Teagan."

"What…what are you doing here?" she demanded. "You're supposed to be on your way to the airport."

"I wanted to pay my respects to your parents and they invited me to dinner. You don't mind, do you?"

"Well, of course I mind." She put her hands on her hips. "You need to leave."

"Teagan Ray," her mother chided her. "That's not how we treat our guests, especially your fiancé."

"He's not—"

"Teagan!" Her father had just stepped inside from the backyard, holding a pitcher of sun tea that her mom must have had steeping on the porch table. Behind him, Zeus lay on the grass, sunning himself. Her father's mouth widened in a broad smile. "Your mom said you were finally home. Come over here and give dear old dad a hug." He nodded at Bryson, apparently unsurprised to see him, and set the jug on the table.

She reluctantly stepped into his embrace, glaring at Bryson over her father's shoulder. This farce had to end now. No way was she going to sit through dinner pretending everything was okay. When he let her go, she moved back beside her mother.

"Mom, Dad, there's something I need to tell you."

"You can relax," Bryson said. "I already told them."

Her jaw dropped open. "You told them?" She glanced from her mom to her dad. "Neither of you look furious with me. What exactly did he tell you?"

Her mom pressed a kiss against her cheek. "The truth. That you were never engaged, that you weren't even boyfriend and girlfriend. He explained how you told the hospital you were his fiancée so you could be in on his care plan, which I think is really sweet. I was just teasing you a minute ago about being engaged. I shouldn't have done that."

She blinked at her mom, then shot Bryson a confused look. "What did he tell you about why I said that he was my boyfriend?"

"*He* is standing right here and can speak for himself," Bryson teased, sounding lighthearted, which had her even more confused after everything that had happened. "I explained that you didn't want them to worry about you because of the bad breakup with your ex. You wanted to protect them, to keep them from thinking you hadn't moved on in your life."

"You said that?" she whispered, her throat tight.

"It's the truth, isn't it?"

She slowly nodded. "I still don't understand why you're here. You should be on the plane."

He stepped toward her, his limp barely noticeable. Then, to her complete and utter shock, he took both her hands in his.

"I couldn't leave with things the way they are between us," he said. "I need to explain why I've been a complete and utter jerk since waking up in recovery."

Her chin wobbled, and to her horror she realized she still had tears left to shed. She furiously blinked them back and glanced at her parents, who were both avidly watching without making any pretense at not trying to listen. She leaned forward, lowering her voice, even though she was certain they could still hear. "You don't owe me any explanations."

"Yes. I do. We can talk now, in front of your parents. Or somewhere private. But I'm not leaving until I apologize and give you an honest explanation."

"Why are you being so nice all of a sudden?" She leaned

in so close she was almost touching him and whispered, "You don't owe me anything, Bryson."

He slowly shook his head. "I owe you my life."

"Damn it," she muttered, stepping back. "You're making me cry again."

"Teagan—" her mother began.

"I know, I know. Language. Sorry, Mom." She wondered if her mother would still treat her like a kid when she hit thirty. She swiped at her wet eyes. "We'll talk in the backyard, Bryson. Then you can go."

"After dinner," her mother said. "Whatever you two have to say can be settled later. Now go wash up. Henry, show Bryson to the other bathroom so he can wash up too."

Teagan's face heated with embarrassment at being ordered around in front of Bryson. But since he was currently following her father to the master suite to the second bathroom, at least she wasn't the only one being bossed around like a child.

"You can thank me later," her mother whispered. "Now go fix your face before that handsome man comes back."

She gasped in dismay, remembering that she'd washed off her makeup, and ran for the bathroom.

"You DIDN'T NEED to put on any makeup, you know," Bryson said after dinner as they both rested their arms on the top of the picket fence and stared out over the backyard pond.

Her face heated yet again. "I'm amazed you even noticed."

He sighed heavily. "I owe you a tremendous apology. I've been an absolute beast since waking up after the explosion."

She hesitated, his words surprising her. "I didn't think of it that way, that when you woke up in recovery it was your first time being awake since the explosion. You must have been really confused. In your place, I think I would have been terrified. Not knowing what had happened."

He turned to face her, his left hand braced on top of the fence. "I was beyond terrified, about you."

"About me? But… I was right there in the recovery room. You saw that I was okay."

"By the grace of God, yes. Teagan, what were you thinking coming back inside that shack? Just a few seconds earlier and that madman would have still been there to kill you or take you with him. A few seconds later and you'd have been killed in the explosion. You shouldn't have risked your life like that, especially after promising me you'd run as fast as you could and wouldn't stop."

"Sort of like you promised me that you'd run out of the shack too? If you'd told me you'd been shot, I would have helped you instead of running off and leaving you. If you'd been killed, how do you think that would have made me feel? How could I live with that kind of guilt on my conscience? If you think I'm the kind of woman who thinks it's romantic for a guy to die for her, then you don't know me at all. I don't want you to die for me. I want you to live."

His jaw tightened, and he turned to face the pond again.

She did the same, counting silently until she could speak again without her voice shaking. "So that's it then?" she finally said. "You've been mad at me ever since then because I couldn't bear for you to die if there was anything I could do to prevent it? Is this your apology? Because as apologies go, it totally sucks."

He suddenly turned and grasped her forearms, pulling her close. "Don't you get it, Teagan? When you walked in my door in Gatlinburg, you changed everything for me, everything. You made me care when I didn't want to. You made me want…you. And instead of shutting myself away to protect someone else from being hurt by another one of my lousy decisions, I decided to give it another try. I thought maybe, just maybe, I could help you and not be a bringer of doom. But look at how that worked out? I'm a jinx. Bad luck. Whatever you want to call it. If it hadn't been for me, you wouldn't have been at the Brodericks'."

She shook her head. "What you're saying doesn't even make sense. Mason told me what happened with Hayley, when you were shot in the hip. You were the only person for miles around who saw her with the kidnapper. You rammed her truck with your car to try to save her, and paid for it by getting shot." He started to interrupt, but she pushed his hands away to stop him. "The only one who thinks you were a failure in that incident is you. From what Mason said, the delay you caused before the abductor took off with Hayley again was enough of a delay to save her life. It gave other Seekers the time they needed to catch up to them. She's alive because of you. Period."

His jaw tightened. "Are you done yet?"

"No. I'm not. I won't bother getting into the details about the Ripper case. I already told you my own investigation proved to me that you were the only one who had that right. And, hey, look at me, I was the one who was dead wrong on who abducted me. It certainly wasn't Lowe. But as far as me going with you to interview the Brodericks, give me a break. You know me well enough by now to realize that if you hadn't agreed to work with me after running into Zeus and me on that path, I would have continued my investigation on my own. So what do you think would have happened when I took the steps you did, set up an interview with the Brodericks, and others. Eventually I'd have stumbled onto the killer, like you and I both did. But I'd have done it alone. How do you think that would have turned out? Without you to save me, I'd have never figured out how to get out of handcuffs, or thought to make a hole in the floor to escape the shack. Without you, I'd be dead right now. Don't you see that?"

His gaze searched hers. "After everything that's happened, how can you have such faith in me?"

"You've never let me down, not once. Why wouldn't I believe in you?"

He lifted her hands and gently pressed a kiss on the back of each of them. "I've been angry at myself, angry at you, because I care so much about you. I don't want anything bad to happen to you."

She tugged her hands free and cupped his cheeks. "Then maybe instead of pushing me away, you should be pulling me close. Because there's no one I'd ever trust more than you to keep me safe."

He groaned before taking her in his arms and kissing her. The kiss was so sweet, so tender, that she was crying when it was over.

He frowned and gently wiped away her tears. "I'm sorry, sweetheart. What is it? What did I do?"

She laughed through her tears. "You did everything exactly right. These are happy tears, for once."

He pulled her against his chest. "I don't know that I deserve your trust. Or that I deserve you at all. But you make me want to." He pressed a kiss against the top of her head.

She reveled in the feel of him in her arms, finally. The sweetness of his hug, and the kiss they'd just shared, melted away the hurt of the past week. Finally, she was exactly where she wanted to be. And it felt far better than she'd ever imagined it would.

"I'm so glad I took Zeus for a walk that day," she said. "And that you were with me when the killer found me. You're an amazing man."

He grew still, then gently pushed her back. "That's it. The missing puzzle piece. The path where you were abducted the first time, and where we met while you were walking Zeus. That has to be it."

She stared up at him in confusion. "What are you talking about?"

He pulled out his cell phone. "It's always bothered me that the killer knew you'd be at the Brodericks'. And that he had enough lead time to have carjacked the delivery guy and hidden the truck in that garage. He also had time to loosen a section of fence, all in anticipation of us coming over. Who knew you'd be with me that night?"

She shook her head. "No one. No one but you and me. I didn't even tell my parents where we were going."

"Exactly. You and I didn't talk to anyone about our plans. And there's no reason to assume the Brodericks would have told anyone either, or that they'd just happen to mention it when the killer was nearby."

"Okay, then the killer would have had to hear you and me discussing it. Is that what you're saying?"

"Bingo." He pressed a speed-dial number on his phone. "Mason, yeah, it's Bryson at my new number. Listen, are any of the Seekers in The Woods subdivision right now, maybe interviewing witnesses?" He shook his head for her benefit. "Okay, right. That's fine. I can—" He listened for a few moments, nodding. "JSO. Of course. I forgot they were conducting extra patrols out here. I'll call them now. I'll catch you up later. It's just a hunch."

"Bryson, what's going on?"

"Just a minute, sweetheart. One more call." He pressed another speed-dial number. "Detective Burns? Bryson Anton. Yes. I have a favor to ask." He idly turned away, slowly walking down the length of the fence as he explained whatever hunch he had to the detective.

She leaned against a post, smiling as she noted how well he was walking, without using his cane. His limp was barely noticeable. The last several days of rest had done wonders. And thankfully his surgery had been laparoscopic, making the recovery much easier. Still, he hadn't had a miracle cure. If he pushed too hard he'd end up having to use the new cane she'd gotten him to replace the old one. Or, worse, end up in his wheelchair for the rest of the day. What he really needed was to go home, to get on that flight to Gatlinburg, and give his body more time to fully recover.

As he turned back toward her, still talking on the phone, she wondered what was going to happen next. Not with the case. She was content to let others handle it at this point. What she wanted to know was what would happen with them. After all, he'd kissed her, in full view of her parents who were no doubt watching them through the back sliding glass doors this very minute. And he'd called her sweetheart. Twice in as many minutes. That had to mean something serious, didn't it?

He stopped a few yards away and leaned against the fence looking out at the water, phone still to his ear. But he wasn't talking. He seemed to be waiting for something. He suddenly straightened and looked at her, a slow smile spreading across his face. He said something else to the detective, then shoved his phone in his pocket and closed the distance between them.

"What is it?" she asked. "Did they…did they catch him?"

"Not yet. But we've got a great lead. I asked JSO to look for some kind of camera tucked up in the trees that overlook the path, at the spot where we were that day I met you with Zeus."

"And where I was abducted."

"Yes. It dawned on me that the only reasonable way the killer could have known about you going to the Brodericks' was if he heard us talking about it. And the only place we spoke about it was—"

"On the path."

"Exactly. The camera was about twenty feet up in an oak tree, tucked into a juncture with two other branches, with a fake bird's nest concealing all but a small hole for the lens. And it has audio capabilities as well as visual. He was watching and listening. There may be other cameras along the path too. Now that JSO knows what to look for, they'll be able to find them, if they exist. More importantly, they'll be able to get an expert on this, figure out the camera's range and triangulate the area where someone would have to be in order to receive the transmission."

"Wouldn't he have to be close by?"

"Probably. Which means it's likely he lives or works in this subdivision, and I'm guessing he did two years ago, as well. I doubt he targeted you specifically, not the first time. You just happened along the trail and met whatever criteria he has for his preferred victims."

She pressed a hand to her throat. "I'm still stuck on the first part, about him living or working here. JSO cleared everyone back then, everyone in the whole development."

He cocked his head. "They didn't clear everyone in the one next door."

She gasped. "Bentwater Place. The house where he took us and put us in the truck. He might live there?"

He shrugged. "JSO's looking into it. I would have thought if he did, they'd have figured that out already as part of the Broderick murder investigation. But it's possible he lives in one of the homes next door and would have known the house was empty the night we were doing the interview. Then again, he may live here in your subdivision and the police cleared someone they shouldn't have when your case was being actively looked into. Like you,

I'm a bit skeptical since they missed that camera and it's remained there all this time. But from what the officer said who found it, he never would have seen it if I hadn't specifically told him to look for one."

"Wait. Are you saying it's been there for *years*? Not that it was put there recently?"

He clasped her hands in his. "Based on the condition of the outside casing, it was probably there back when you were abducted. My guess is when the police didn't find it, the killer didn't risk going back to get it. And when months passed without it being discovered, he kept it active and checked in on the video every now and then."

"Which is how he knew I was here in Jacksonville, and where we were going that night."

He squeezed her hands. "I believe so, yes."

She stared up at him. "I was bound and determined to walk that path all week for my planned visit with my parents. I naively assumed I'd be okay with Zeus and my gun. But the way I froze back at the shack, and at the Brodericks' house, we both know I wouldn't have drawn my gun in time to protect myself. And knowing what I do now, I don't think Zeus could have stopped him either. Thank God you were there that day."

He leaned down and pressed a quick kiss against her lips. "That camera will hopefully lead them to the killer. And the BOLO they have with the police artist's sketch will ensure he doesn't get very far. But I'm not taking any chances. Pack a bag, Teagan. You're going with me to Tennessee."

Chapter Twenty-One

If any other man had *informed* Teagan that she was going to do something, or go somewhere, without asking her, she'd have ripped right into him. But this was Bryson. She knew his authoritarian dictate wasn't his typical way of operating, that he wanted to keep her safe, which was incredibly sweet. Besides, flying on a private jet to his home for who knew how many days or weeks of seclusion with him wasn't exactly a hardship. Especially since they'd worked through the tensions and self-recriminations of this past week. She was looking forward to this time alone with him.

But as she watched him snoozing in the limo seat across from her on the last leg of the trip to his house, she couldn't help feeling a twinge of disappointment. Between the toll that his injuries had taken on him and the effects of the pain pills and antibiotics, he'd slept most of the way here. He needed the rest to get better. But she was so hungry for time with him, quality time. She wanted that *get to know you* phase of the relationship that they'd skipped during their life and death struggles. She was greedy to learn the little things.

Like his favorite color.

His favorite food.

Was he partial to country music as so many people around here were?

Would it shock him to know that she hated country music but loved classical?

Since he hadn't mentioned his family before, and none of them had called or visited him in the hospital, was that because he didn't have any family? Or was he just trying to keep them from worrying? Did his boss know that he wouldn't have wanted them told about what had happened?

She couldn't help feeling jealous if he had siblings. She'd always wanted brothers and sisters. Well, mostly sisters. Brothers could be so mean, at least from what her dad said about her uncles. But growing up an only child, she'd always longed for more. She wanted a house full of her own children one day. Did he want children too? Would he love and cherish them and protect them from a world that could be hateful and mean when people didn't fit into those neat little racial categories?

"Want to talk about it?"

She met his questioning gaze. "You're awake."

"I am."

"How's your pain level? Need some pills?"

"I need to know what's bothering you." He grimaced as he straightened in his seat, but shook his head when she reached for the bottle of pills in her purse. "Don't. A little twinge here and there is better than sleeping my life away. Those things knock me out." He glanced out the window. "Almost home. But we still have time for you to tell me what has you frowning as if you want to kill someone. Hopefully it's not me," he teased.

When she didn't answer, his smile faded. "Seriously. What's wrong?"

"Nothing. Random thoughts. Silly things."

"You can be outrageous and deliciously sassy. But

you're never silly. What are these random thoughts? If you have questions about the investigation—"

"What's your favorite color?" she blurted out, even though it was the least important question rolling around in her mind right now.

"Ah. Now I understand the frown. You're contemplating some of life's most vexing problems."

"How do you feel about interracial marriages, and children?"

His eyes widened. "Well, Okay. That was unexpected. The answer is gray, by the way."

"Gray?"

"My favorite color."

"Gray can't be your favorite color. Gray isn't a color. It's a...shade."

He shrugged, unconcerned with her assessment. "As to interracial marriages and children, I'm against children getting married regardless of their race."

She stared at him deadpan. "When did you develop a sense of humor?"

"Apparently never. You're not laughing."

She looked out the window. "How much farther to your home?"

In answer, he tapped on the glass partition. It lowered and the driver met his gaze in the rearview mirror. "Yes, Mr. Anton?"

"Take the long way to my house."

"But, sir. We're already—"

"Up and down the mountain, then. We have a few things to settle before we arrive."

"Of course sir. Just let me know when you're ready to get there."

The glass went back up, sealing them in privacy again. He moved from his seat to settle beside her, then took her right hand in his left. "I'm assuming this is a hypothetical question. Or is there something else you want to add, so that it's more specific?"

Her face grew warm. "Forget I asked. It was a ridiculous question and completely inappropriate."

"It's a serious question, a deep question, and it deserves a serious, respectful and honest answer. As to being inappropriate, I can't imagine how it could be, unless maybe it's not hypothetical after all and you're talking about you and me—and you're worried about how I would take it?"

It didn't seem possible for her face to get hotter, but it did. "Like I said, forget I asked. It was inappropriate, because it assumes all kinds of things, like that whatever this is between us could ever grow into something to where the answer to that question would matter."

"You're talking marriage, between you and me."

She crossed her arms. "You don't have to sound so stunned. It's a logical progression in relationships. Not that I'm saying we're in a relationship, exactly, or that it would become a logical step for us. I mean, if we ever even, you know, dated. Which we haven't, really—"

He covered her mouth with his and gave her a slow, lazy and incredibly thorough kiss. When he pulled back, all she could do was sigh, and melt against the buttery leather seats.

"Wow," she finally managed to say. "If I could bottle you up and sell you, I'd make a fortune."

He laughed, then grew serious. "I'm not going to pretend that I can see into the future and tell where you and I might end up. We've had a rocky couple of weeks, and that's the biggest understatement ever. But I can say with absolute certainty that we are definitely in a relationship."

She swallowed, and managed a shaky smile. "Good to know."

"As to your other questions, the first one is easy. In case you haven't figured it out, I think you're one of the smartest, funniest and hottest women I've ever met."

She blinked up at him. "You think I'm hot?"

"Oh. Yeah. And that's not *in spite* of your brown skin or any other feature that makes you different from me. It's *because* of those features, because of all the things that make you uniquely you. You're an amazing, sexy, wonderful woman, Teagan Ray. Whoever you end up marrying, if you decide to marry, that man would be incredibly lucky and should feel honored that you chose him. And if he doesn't feel that way, then he doesn't deserve you."

She settled against him, resting her head in the crook of his shoulder as he put his arm around her. "You're an amazing man, Bryson Anton."

"You're not so bad yourself. And, Teagan?"

"Yes, Bryson?"

He kissed her neck just below her ear, making her shiver. "I couldn't begin to understand the ugliness the world may have shown you, the prejudice you've likely faced in your life, or the fears you live with every day about things I would never encounter, simply because we were born looking different from each other. But I can tell you this. Hypothetically, if you and I, for example, were to marry and were fortunate enough to have children, I would do everything in my power to protect them in every way. Above all, I would love them, and make sure they knew they were loved, always, unconditionally. And that I've got their backs, no matter what." He kissed the top of her head. "Does that answer all your questions?"

She shook her head. "Not even close. I have dozens more."

"Dozens?"

"Scores, actually."

He laughed. "Then I guess we'll be riding around this mountain for a good long time." He settled back more comfortably, pulling her with him. "Go ahead. Ask your questions. But be prepared. I might have a few of my own."

Chapter Twenty-Two

Teagan had learned so much about Bryson during that conversation in the limo two days ago. It had been fun learning about his family, his rather *large* family of three younger brothers and two older sisters who were both married and had six kids between them.

His family was spread out across the country from coast to coast. While his parents split their time between Canada and traveling all over the US, fully enjoying their retirement, they popped in throughout the year to visit their children and grandchildren.

Bryson had explained that after seeing how difficult it was for his family when he'd been shot during his last Justice Keepers assignment, he'd made Mason promise not to tell them if he got hurt again. That was why they hadn't been at the hospital. While she couldn't fathom not keeping her family informed about something like that, she respected his decision.

But in spite of the many new details that she'd learned about him, she realized she'd already known everything that really mattered. He was smart, loyal, considerate, and a million other wonderful things rolled up in an incredibly mouthwatering package that she wanted to devour.

Except that she couldn't. Not yet.

It was torture not being able to move their relationship

forward the way she wanted to. But he couldn't stand the way the pain pills made it hard to focus and concentrate on the investigation, so he'd all but stopped taking them. And that meant he was hobbling around on an aching hip again in the mornings, stuck using the wheelchair most afternoons. Her heart ached for him as she watched him limping across the family room right now with the aid of his cane, smiling at her and pretending he wasn't in pain. But the small white lines around his mouth weren't something he could hide.

"Ready?" He paused by the front door where she'd been waiting for him.

"Ready." She took his cane so he could grab his suit jacket from the hall tree and shrug into it.

She picked up her purse and let him open the door. It seemed to matter to him to open doors for her, so she'd stopped trying to run ahead or open them herself. As they crossed the front porch, she asked, "You really think a brainstorming session with the Justice Seekers is going to crack the case open?"

"We have to try something new to shake things loose. Plus Bishop texted me that he's back from interviewing Leviathan Finney and wants to talk about what he found. He'll meet us at Camelot."

"First of all, I forget, who's Bishop? Second, he interviewed the Kentucky Ripper in prison?"

He stopped on the walkway at the end of the porch. "Gage Bishop. He's one of the Justice Seekers, the first one Mason hired when he created the company. Everything I know about him would fill about a third of a sheet of paper. He keeps to himself, doesn't socialize with the others outside of work. Mason's the only one who knows whatever traumatic event ended his law enforcement career before he started over as a Justice Seeker."

He limped down the path again, toward the driveway.

"I'm confused. Traumatic event? I thought you didn't know anything about him."

He stopped again, leaning heavily on his cane. "I assumed if Mason was impressed enough to give you carte blanche with a company credit card after I was discharged from the hospital that he would have confided in you. I thought you knew."

"Knew what? I'm lost."

"The Justice Seekers. The whole reason the company was formed was to give a second chance to people who'd had their law enforcement careers destroyed through no fault of their own. It's a second chance for all of us."

"I had no idea. But I guess it makes sense. You felt you'd failed as a special agent—"

"I did."

"No. You didn't. But I understand now why you became a Justice Seeker. After you quit the FBI, you felt you had something to prove. And Mason gave you that chance."

"Not that I've done much with that second chance. He probably regrets hiring me."

They'd started down the path again, but she moved in front of him, blocking his way. "Don't you dare talk like that. I'd have been killed half a dozen times by now if it wasn't for you. I'm not going to listen to any more self-recriminations. You're an amazing guy with fantastic instincts. It's time you gave yourself some credit."

His jaw tightened, telling her he didn't agree. But to his credit, he didn't argue.

She stepped aside and followed him toward the driveway where she'd backed his metallic-blue Ford pickup out of the garage in preparation for the drive into town. It was decked out, with all the options. It wasn't the red convertible she'd pictured him driving. But Hot Guy in a pickup revved her engines even more than she'd thought possible.

A luxury car, like the rental he'd had in Jacksonville, would have been much easier on his hip. But the car that he'd owned, a classic older car he'd planned on restoring, had been totaled that day he'd been shot trying to save Hayley from a kidnapper. So it was either take his truck or hire another rental. She wished he'd opt for the rental because she knew it would be easier for him to climb in and out, and the bumps in the road wouldn't hurt so much in a car. But she also knew he was a proud man and didn't want to look weak in front of the team. To him, renting a car to drive when he had a perfectly good truck in his garage would be a neon sign that he wasn't okay.

At least he was letting her drive. That was the one concession he'd made. She was pretty sure he was relieved when she'd asked, even though he pretended to debate her question. Her insistence that she loved trucks and wanted to drive this one, which was certainly true, wasn't completely accurate since her main reason to drive was to help him save face. It was obviously much more comfortable to be a passenger than to pump his foot on the pedals.

Twenty minutes later they were at The Justice Seekers' headquarters, an enormous two-story modern-day castle that fully lived up to its nickname of Camelot. Even though she'd been here once before when she'd met with Mason Ford about hiring Bryson, she was still in awe. Especially when Bryson took her into a secret passage to a room few clients ever got to see, a truly medieval looking meeting room with an enormous round table in the middle. It had been dubbed the Great Hall. It was a much bigger version of Bryson's so-called office at his house. And judging by the enormous monitors forming a semicircle a short distance from the table, this Great Hall had all the technological gadgets that Bryson's did, maybe more.

"Welcome to Camelot," he whispered in her ear as they stood off to one side, just past the secret passage they'd walked through. "What do you think of Mason's pride and joy?"

"Stunning. A bit overwhelming, really. But supercool." She waved toward the round table, where three other people were seated. "Are those Justice Seekers?" At his nod, she said, "I thought they were in Jacksonville."

"Five of them are. The rest were working cases here and couldn't leave right away. There's one more Seeker we're waiting on before we start. When fully staffed, there are twelve of us, plus Mason, our fearless leader."

"Fully staffed?"

"One of our Seekers was killed last year. Mason's just now looking for a replacement. But let's not dwell on that. Like I said, there are basically twelve of us, plus the boss."

"The knights of the round table. And King Arthur?"

He smiled. "Yes. But if you call Mason King Arthur he'll never forgive you. That's the one part of his little game he hasn't adopted. He thinks it's pretentious." He motioned toward the right side of the table where a man just as broad-shouldered and tall as Bryson was pulling up a chair. "That's Bishop over there. When we sit down, you'll see that everyone has an assigned seat with their name and their moniker engraved on the stone table in front of them."

"Moniker? Like, what, Hot Guy?"

He laughed. "Don't say that too loudly or I'll never hear the end of it. The monikers are based on their former occupations. Bishop is The Bodyguard."

"I thought you didn't know what he did before he became a Justice Seeker?"

"We know he protected people, but we don't know who he worked for. A good guess is one of the alphabet agencies—FBI, CIA, NCIS. But only Mason knows for sure. That extremely extroverted lady on the left who's waving at you is The Cop, Brielle Walker. She used to be a Gatlinburg police officer."

She smiled and returned Brielle's wave. "And the guy beside her?"

"Han Li, The Special Agent."

"You both have the same moniker? Special Agent?"

"No. He was a special agent with Homeland Security. And he started here first, so he got to choose The Special Agent for his title."

"Then what are you?"

His mouth tightened. "The Profiler. Not my choosing. Mason stuck me with that title."

She splayed her fingers against his chest. "You're an amazing profiler, Bryson. If I have to tell you that a hundred times until you believe it, I will."

He arched a brow. "A hundred times, huh? That implies you're planning on sticking around for a while."

"If you want me to stay, I'm sure I'd enjoy you trying to convince me." She gave him an outrageous wink.

He was about to say something but the door to the hidden passageway opened and another man, wearing a Stetson, stepped into the room. Bryson's grin faded and his answering nod in response to the other man's friendly "hello" was decidedly cool.

"Who's that?" she kept her voice low.

"The Cowboy, Dalton Lynch."

"Why don't you like him?"

He gave her a surprised look. "What makes you think I don't like him?"

"Oh, I don't know. Maybe because it felt like a polar

vortex descended on the room when you barely returned his greeting."

His jaw tightened. "I have no problem with Dalton. But I don't go out of my way to inflict my presence on him. His wife is Hayley, the woman who almost died because of me."

She blinked in surprise. At the table, Dalton's expression as he eyed Bryson seemed to be more of regret, maybe even frustration. But there was absolutely no animosity or reproach. When he caught her looking at him, he nodded, then turned toward the others.

"Bryson, I don't think he blames you for what happened to his wife any more than you should blame yourself."

He put his hand on her back. "You're sweet to worry about me. But the only thing that matters right now is figuring out the identity of the man who almost killed you. And putting him away for a very long time. Come on, they're waiting."

He introduced her to the others. Then they all got really serious, really fast. She sat in the chair beside him, in the seat for Zack Foster, The Tracker. He'd whispered that Zack was the one who'd died, which had her feeling like an interloper. But he insisted no one minded her sitting there and it seemed to be true. They were all very respectful and nice to her.

Each of them had a computer tablet in front of them, and what they brought up was displayed on one of the huge screens at the front of the room so they could see everything at the same time. As efficiency went, it was amazing. They shared reports, pictures, investigative notes, all at the touch of a button or the swipe of a finger across their tablets that were each-hardwired into the computer for security.

She was a bit overwhelmed hearing what they'd been

doing. Every one of them was working her case now. It was humbling that they were all so vested in helping her. But then again, they were doing it for Bryson too. He was their brother-in-arms. The man they were after had almost killed him. And it was obvious that none of them were going to let a stone go unturned in their quest to bring the killer to justice and avenge their friend and fellow Seeker.

The hours ticked by, with short breaks here and there so everyone could use the restroom or make phone calls.

Lunch was brought in by some efficient person who suddenly appeared from the secret passageway and quietly set the food and drinks down on a table against one wall, then quietly disappeared.

They seemed to have exhausted just about every lead and angle possible by midafternoon. But there was one person who hadn't presented his findings yet—Bishop. The others sat back and the room went quiet as his notes from the prison interview with Finney, the Kentucky Ripper, filled the screen.

[faded text from previous page visible through paper]

Chapter Twenty-Three

"A few days ago," Bishop began, "Bryson requested that I look into Leviathan Finney in relation to this case. The reason is obvious. Ms. Ray was abducted two years ago by a man who carved an X on her stomach, just like the Kentucky Ripper did to his victims. But since that same man abducted her again, and Finney is in prison for the Ripper's crimes, the question is whether Finney is the real Ripper or a copycat. The reason that matters is that if he's a copycat, then it's possible that the man who abducted her is the Ripper. Knowing that provides a lot more data to use to find this man. But we don't want to send ourselves, or the police, down the wrong investigative path. So it was important to figure out whether we could rule in her abductor as the Ripper, or rule him out."

He typed a few buttons on his tablet, then a table of dates, names and comments appeared on the screen.

"Those are the Ripper's victims," Teagan said.

"They are," Bishop agreed. "Along with the dates of their abductions and murders. I created this table to keep track of what Finney was supposedly doing at the time of each abduction or murder. It's his alibi list, basically. Or it was supposed to be. When I checked through court transcripts, the alibi information was rather thin. His lawyer didn't present much of a defense. Regardless, I dug as deep as I could in the time that I had. And then I went to the psychiatric hospital where Finney was being held before being deemed fit enough to be placed in the general prison population. I spoke to his doctors and was able to convince them to share information to help with my victim/alibi matrix."

Teagan blinked and shot Bryson a look, but he didn't seem fazed by Bishop's last statement. As far as she knew, doctors, especially a psychiatrist, would never disclose that kind of information about a living patient without a warrant. She wondered what Bishop had done to "convince" them to talk.

"After that," Bishop continued, "I spoke to Finney, for hours." He highlighted a handful of rows in the table on the screen. "After piecing together witness statements from the investigations, court transcripts, what his doctor said, and then interviewing people to corroborate what Finney told me, these four rows are the only ones where I couldn't positively alibi him out. But even these I'm fifty-fifty on." He sat back and glanced around the table, apparently finished speaking.

Teagan looked at the others. Brielle was furiously typing on her laptop. Han was swiping through screen after screen on his, as if searching for something. And the guy in the Stetson, Dalton, had jumped up from the table and was standing off in a corner on, of all things, a wall phone. She hadn't seen one of those in years.

At her questioning look, Bryson asked, "The phone? Most of Camelot is a giant Faraday cage."

"Fair a what?"

"Faraday. Electronic signals can't get in or out. We have to use dedicated landlines. It's for security. Even the computer tablets are hard-wired through the table to the main computer."

She thought that seemed like total overkill, but didn't really care at the moment. What mattered was that she was completely lost. "Why does everyone else seem to understand whatever Bishop just said about Finney? I'm confused."

Bishop remained silent, apparently content to let someone else explain.

Bryson took her hand in his. "To sum it up, he was able to prove, maybe not court of law proof, but proof to us, that Finney couldn't have killed most of the victims that he's accused of killing. He had solid alibis that either weren't presented at trial or weren't known at trial. There are only a few that Bishop couldn't speak to. Which goes to say that you were right all along. Leviathan Finney very likely isn't the Ripper. But he's not a copycat either. He was set up. Framed."

"By the police?"

"Doubtful. Most likely the real killer, to take the heat off."

"An innocent man is in prison. That sucks."

"We'll contact one of the Innocence Project groups to look into his case."

"Already did," Bishop chimed in.

"Great," she said. "I guess. But what does all this mean as far as finding the guy who abducted us? Are you saying he's the real Ripper?"

"It's a definite possibility, highly likely actually. The police never linked your case with the others in spite of the signature X because the Ripper was already in prison. But now that we know the Ripper was never caught, all of the murders attributed to him have to be reexamined in relation to your abduction. This is a huge break. There's an FBI field office in Jacksonville. Once our team brings them up to speed on this development, they'll be back in the game, looking into your case and reopening the Ripper investigation. Obviously there are formalities, like convincing JSO to call them in to help. But Mason will get that done. Just a matter of time. The number of people working this case is about to quadruple, easily. With some of the brightest law enforcement minds around. They'll catch this guy in no time."

Dalton returned to his seat. The others turned their attention toward Bryson.

"What about you?" Dalton asked. "Any theories about who this guy might be?"

"A few," Bryson said. "It's been bothering me that he was able to abduct Teagan two years ago without anyone seeing him. She was apparently drugged. She thinks she remembers him injecting her right after he accosted her on the path. After that, her memory is blank until she woke up at the shack. But that path through her neighborhood is well-traveled. And the entrance to the path on both ends is in even busier sections of the neighborhood. It seems far-fetched that he could have led or carried a drugged woman from the path without anyone seeing her. Which is why I called Mason early this morning and asked him to have our Seekers in Jacksonville re-interview everyone who lives close to that part of the trail and ask very specific questions."

"Like what?" Dalton asked.

"Like whether he could have loosened a section of fence like he did behind the Brodericks' house and taken her through the opening to someone's backyard. From there, if he did the same trick he pulled with us, he could have gone through someone's home while they weren't home and into their garage where he had a car waiting. Then, all he had to do was drive out of the subdivision. There's a guard shack at each of the two entrances. But the cameras only record people coming in, not going out. If he came in via the subdivision behind The Woods, like he did recently, he wouldn't be on any of the guard gate's cameras."

Teagan raised her hand.

Bryson smiled. "You don't have to ask permission to speak."

She felt her face heat and lowered her hand. "You said earlier that you thought he might live in one of the houses in Bentwater Place, near the one we went through to that delivery truck. Did anything ever come of that?"

"The police ruled that out. He definitely isn't one of the homeowners on that street or the neighboring streets. But one of those homes was vacant because it's for sale. He could have seen that for sale sign and broke in to conduct quick surveillance on the house next door. Once he was sure the owners weren't home, he used that house as part of his plan to abduct you."

Dalton tapped on the table as if in deep thought. "How close is that path to the Bentwater subdivision?"

Bryson looked at Teagan in question. "What do you think? Half a mile? The Woods is huge. That path is in the center of the subdivision."

She nodded. "Maybe even a mile, or more really if you consider all the twists and turns you'd have to take because of all the streets in between."

"He didn't walk from Bentwater to the path," Bryson concluded. "It's too far. There would have been multiple reports in the interviews that the police conducted after your abduction, reports of different people seeing a man walking toward that trail. There weren't any reports. None."

"Then how did he get in?" she asked.

He sat back, considering the question. "Getting back to basics, we have two choices. He walked or drove. Since no mysterious strangers were seen on the cameras at the guard shack, driving is out. But since he wasn't seen walking through the subdivision by anyone interviewed after your abduction, walking is out too. Which leads to one conclusion. The time frame that the police covered when canvassing the neighborhood was inadequate."

A few chairs over from him, Dalton nodded. "That's the only explanation. He was already in place. He went into the subdivision before the time range that the police checked." He turned toward the former police officer. "Brielle, I think you had that report on the video from the guard shack. How far back did they check?"

She was already typing. Then she punched a button and a report popped up on one of the big screens. "One week. Our killer had to be in place prior to that." She turned her focus on Teagan. "I haven't been in that development. But from what I've read, there aren't any actual woods where someone could hide out that long and not be found, are there?"

Teagan shook her head. "No. I mean, there are plenty of areas with lots of trees and bushes. But it's all personal property, or it backs up behind a strip mall on one side. The community areas are too heavily traveled, like those walking paths, to allow someone to camp out and not be seen."

"I agree," Bryson said. "And it goes back to the sheer volume of witnesses in that area. Even if he camped out, someone would have seen him at some point and reported it. Nothing like that happened. Which means he was in one of the houses. We already know he's not one of the owners, based on the extensive reports the police did on every homeowner. If he was visiting someone who lives there, again, they would have mentioned it to the police. That leaves one last possibility. He was using someone's house when they were out of town. We need a list of everyone who was out of town over a week before the attack."

"On it." Brielle started typing on her computer again. "I've got all of those types of records already from our earlier canvassing but didn't put it together the way you just did. I just need to cross-reference a couple of spread-sheets and I'll have it."

A few minutes later, the dejection on her face told the story even before she spoke. "Sorry, guys and gals. As impossible as it seems in a place with that many houses, no one was on vacation in that time span. At least, no one who didn't have a house sitter or friend at their place while they were gone."

Bryson sat forward in his chair. "Then the house was empty. Whoever owned it didn't live there anymore. How many homes were vacant, either for rent or for sale during that time frame?"

The tension was palpable in the room as they waited for Brielle once again.

She popped up the latest search results. "Three. All for sale, all vacant."

"Bentwater Place, the house that was empty and for sale that the police thought our killer might have used as his home base with the Broderick murders," Bryson said. "Does anyone have any additional information on that house?"

"Like what?" Dalton asked.

"The realty company. Better yet, the Realtor who listed it."

Dalton smiled. "Of course. On it."

"I'm on it too, for the ones in The Woods," Brielle said.

A few moments later, Dalton sat back. "Pine Acres Realty."

"Dang, I almost beat you," Brielle said. "I'm calling it a tie. Two of mine are with Happy Meadows Properties." She rolled her eyes at the name. "My last one, which happens to back up directly onto the path where Ms. Ray was attacked, is Pine Acres Realty."

Teagan blinked in shock. "He's a Realtor?"

"It appears likely," Bryson said. "And he probably works for Pine Acres Realty. We need pictures."

Bishop, who'd been quietly working on his own computer all along, punched a button. The screens filled with pictures of the smiling men and women who worked for that realty company.

Bryson arched a brow. "Thanks, Bishop."

Bishop nodded.

"Bottom row." Teagan's voice was hoarse. "If the screen wasn't so huge, I wouldn't have even noticed. And now I know why no one in the neighborhood recognized the police sketch."

"Why?" Dalton asked.

Bryson reached for Teagan's hand beneath the table and she gratefully clung to it. "Because he looks completely different in that picture. Hair color, hair style, glasses. There's only one thing that's the same."

"What's that?" Dalton pressed.

"His eyes." Teagan's hand tightened on Bryson's. "Pure evil, dead inside. That's him. It's definitely him. I've probably seen him on real estate flyers in the neighborhood. But I never connected the dots. His name?" She paused to draw a choppy breath. "I need to hear his name."

"Chris Larsen," Brielle announced.

She shook her head. "So average. So…normal."

Brielle started typing again. "I'll get this information to Mason and the team in Jacksonville right away."

"I'll give him a call," Dalton added. "I'll answer any questions he has about our thought processes and how we arrived at this conclusion." He smiled. "How *Bryson* arrived at it. Good job, Profiler. And it's good to have you back."

Bryson seemed surprised by Dalton's statement, but he nodded his thanks. "Call me with Mason's update on the hunt for this guy?"

"You don't want to hang around? If our team's in on the takedown we might get a live feed."

"I would, but my hip's aching something awful." He pushed to his feet, leaning heavily on his cane, and motioned to Teagan. "I know you'd rather hang around, but I don't think I can drive right now. Do you mind?"

She was struggling to maintain her composure with all of this information crashing down on her. And here he was, pretending that he was the one who needed to leave. She gratefully went along with his ruse. "I can get the updates later. I don't mind."

Once they were in his truck, the stress and worry that had been eating at her seemed to magically fade away. He had that effect on her, made her feel safe, more in control. "I know your hip really does hurt. But I also know you'd never admit that in front of your team. You did that for me, because you saw how I was struggling to hold it together. Thank you."

"It was nothing. But you're welcome anyway. How are you holding up? I can drive if I have to."

"I know, but I'm fine. It was all so…intense back there, finding out who he was, and realizing he's just a person. You know? Not some mythical monster impossible to stop. Hearing he's a Realtor kind of takes the drama down a notch. Makes it somehow bearable, especially knowing it's only a matter of time now before this is over."

When they pulled into the driveway, his phone buzzed in his pocket. She parked while he spoke to Dalton. When she got out, he frowned, obviously wishing she'd wait so he could open her door. He'd just put his phone in his suit jacket pocket and grabbed his cane when she opened his door and offered her hand.

"There's no one here but us, Bry. You can suck up your pride for a minute and let me help you. It *is* okay for a woman to help a man sometimes, you know."

He avoided her hand and hopped out on his own.

She rolled her eyes and moved to his side. "What did Dalton have to say? Is JSO cooperating? Did they put out a new BOLO on the killer now that we know his identity?"

He smiled and unlocked the front door. As he pushed it open for her he said, "Yes, JSO is *cooperating*, although I'm sure they think it's the other way around. A new BOLO was put out, but they already contacted the realty company to see if they had a lead on his whereabouts. That's why Dalton called, to give us an update about the realty company." He shut and locked the door, before giving her his full attention.

"They got him, Teagan. He's on his way downtown right now in the back of a squad car. It's over."

She burst into tears.

BRYSON TOSSED HIS cane to the floor and lifted Teagan in his arms. He couldn't make it very far, but he managed to stumble to the couch without dropping her. He settled back with his precious burden and held her while she cried out the hurt and the fear and the anxiety she'd been suffering for years.

It was a long time later before he settled Sleeping Beauty in his master bedroom that he'd given up while she was here. She'd readily invited him to stay with her in his bed that first night. But he knew the dangers. It didn't matter how his head hurt, or the wounds on his back, or his hip, or where the bullet went through him, or, good grief, how sore his belly still was from the surgery. He was a mess, physically. But if he got horizontal next to her none of it would matter. There'd be no stopping either of them from taking full advantage of that situation. And then he'd probably end up in the hospital again. But oh how he wished it could be different.

He quietly shut the door. But he didn't head to the guest room where he was staying. He had another destination tonight. And this one was too far for him to make using his cane. He'd used up the last of his stamina carrying Teagan. It was time to admit defeat, for now, and get the wheelchair.

A few minutes later he reached his office. As he opened files on the computer and began moving bits of information onto the various screens, he reflected on what Dalton had said at Camelot. He'd referred to his old moniker, Profiler. That one word, spoken by a fellow Seeker, had started an avalanche of thoughts in his mind.

Even though he'd been trying to work this case as best he could with a lingering concussion and his other injuries, he hadn't tried to approach it as a profiler. He was too used to scorning his previous profession, thinking of his failures instead of focusing on his successes. But he didn't think of it the same way anymore. Teagan had done that for him, made him start to accept that maybe he wasn't the big failure he once thought himself to be. And Dalton, of course, welcoming him back. That had been a surprise. If Dalton didn't blame him for Hayley's near miss, maybe he needed to rethink that whole episode.

But mostly it was Teagan's faith in him that was giving him a new perspective. Like that maybe he should trust himself, listen to the warning bells going off in his head. They were telling him that something wasn't right.

They'd caught the man who'd abducted Teagan. They'd caught the man who'd killed the Brodericks. So why did he feel like there was something left unfinished? The niggling feeling wouldn't leave him alone. So he was going back to the beginning as he'd once told Teagan to do. He was reexamining everything. And once he did that, he'd do what he hadn't done in years, and had never thought he'd do again.

He was going to build a profile.

Chapter Twenty-Four

Teagan finished brushing her teeth just as the morning sun began to peek through the windows. After giving her braid one last adjustment, she left the master bedroom to find Bryson. Much to her frustration, even though he'd ensconced her in the master suite since she'd come here, he was sleeping in a guest room. She understood it was because sleeping together was too tempting. Neither of them would want to *sleep.* Which would just set his recovery back. But she was getting so frustrated wanting him to get better, and just plain *wanting* him.

Everything about him appealed to her. And the more she got to know him, the worse her obsession became. Whether he was in butt-hugging jeans and a T-shirt or one of those sexy tailored suits that showed off his broad shoulders, she wanted to peel off his clothes and explore *every inch*. As if his sexy exterior wasn't enough of a turn on, Hot Guy was also intelligent, with a kind soul and the heart of a steadfast, loyal, intensely protective warrior. It was becoming nearly impossible not to weep with longing and desire every time he entered a room.

She could definitely fall in love with him. She was more than halfway there already. But she had no clue whether he felt the same. Oh, he liked her, a lot. And he wanted her. There was no denying the hungry look in his eyes that he tried so hard to hide. Clearly he suffered from the same affliction that she did. If they ever *really* got together, they'd probably spontaneously combust. But did he care about her? *Really* care, as in I could love you forever kind of care? She just didn't know.

Shaking her head at her fruitless thoughts, she headed to his room just down the hall. He wasn't there. The bed didn't even look as if it had been slept in. Growing concerned, she checked the main rooms in this part of the house. She even looked out the back door at the dock, where he could be found most evenings. But he wasn't there. She was just passing the little alcove to the left of the TV when she realized it was empty. Each night he stored his wheelchair there and used the cane the next day until the pain forced him to use the chair once again. But the wheelchair wasn't there. Why? Had he suffered a setback to his recovery?

Increasingly anxious, she headed down the back hall and looked in every door that she passed until she reached the end, his office. Light shining under the door had her letting out a relieved breath. He must have come here last night for some reason, then ended up sleeping in the attached bedroom rather than head all the way to the front of the house.

She knocked on the door. No answer. She knocked again. When he still didn't answer, her overactive imagination conjured up all kinds of awful scenarios, like him lying on the floor in a pool of blood, his wounds ripped open. Just the thought of him in pain, needing her, had her opening the door.

He wasn't on the floor dying.

And he wasn't sleeping in the guest room.

He was in his wheelchair at the round table, oblivious to her entry as he spoke to someone on his cell phone. All nine of the giant monitors were filled with documents. But that wasn't what had her gasping in surprise.

It was the pictures.

He glanced over his shoulder, then punched a button on the control panel, clearing the screens. "Mason, I'll call you back in a few minutes. Send me that list of dates as soon as you have it, all right? Yeah, thanks. Bye." He set the phone on the table. "Sorry. I didn't realize you were there or I wouldn't have had those pictures up."

She fought against the nausea the graphic, violent images had awakened in her as she joined him at the table. So many women. So much…carnage.

"I heard you talking to Mason. Does he have you working on a new case already and you stayed up all night studying crime scene photos?"

He hesitated, clearly uncomfortable with her questions. "I'm not working a new case, not exactly. I'm…reexamining an old one."

"Why would you do that?"

Again, he paused.

She glanced at the blank screens, her mind's eye trying to reconstruct what she'd seen seconds earlier. But she'd been too broadsided by the unexpected tableau to recall many details, even with her photographic memory. "How old is this case you're looking into?"

He looked at his wrist as if to check the time. But he hadn't replaced the fancy computer watch yet that Larsen had taken from him. "Is it morning already? I can whip us up something to eat." He backed his chair away from the table. "How about omelets? I can't remember the last time I—"

She leaned past him and punched the same key that he had earlier. The pictures popped back onto the screens.

He swore and cleared them again, but not before she saw a bloody X carved on one of the women's bellies.

"The Kentucky Ripper," she accused. "You're looking at the Kentucky Ripper cases. Why? The FBI is covering that angle. You said so at Camelot yesterday. And don't try to change the subject by acting like you suddenly love to cook. We both know better. You forget we played twenty questions times ten in the limo on the way home from the airport. I know a lot of things about you now that I didn't before. Like that you hate to cook. So spill. Why have you been here all night looking at murders that happened years ago instead of celebrating that the man who tried to kill both of us is sitting in a Jacksonville jail cell?"

He sighed heavily. "I didn't want to wait for a report from the FBI. I needed some answers now, to quiet some doubts I had, and make sure we'd covered every angle."

"What doubts? What angles?"

"Little details that don't add up. With Finney possibly innocent, the FBI is focusing on Larsen as the real Ripper. And it makes sense, given the signature and other details about the crime scenes, plus things we're starting to learn about Larsen."

She pulled out the chair beside him and sat down. "If it all makes sense, then what's bothering you?"

He hesitated.

"I'm not dropping this. You might as well tell me now or we'll be here all day," she warned.

He grimaced. "All right. What's bothering me is the puzzle pieces that don't fit. It's like with the original Ripper investigation. There are things that never matched Finney. But there was enough so-called evidence that some other evidence was basically ignored. And once he was in prison, the murders stopped. Everyone was content to let it drop, to ignore the inconsistencies."

"Not you," she reminded him. "You kept looking at the case long after it was over. You stored all those copies of the case files. That's what you were going through just now, isn't it? I'm guessing that means you hired that temp you talked about when I first arrived, to key everything into the system."

"I had Brielle work with someone while I was in the hospital," he admitted. "I'd always wanted everything digitized to make examination of the evidence easier. With you having been abducted again, I wanted to have the previous case information handy when I got a chance to review it. The obvious conclusion at the time was that Larsen was likely the Ripper, even before Bishop spoke to Finney. I expected when I eventually got home and went through this stuff, that conclusion would be cemented in my mind."

"But it wasn't."

"No. Far from it."

She shivered and rubbed her hands up and down her arms. "The man who attacked me, who attacked us, is behind bars. It shouldn't matter whether he's the Ripper or not. So why do you look so serious? And why am I starting to feel concerned?"

He took her hands in his. "Whatever I've found, or think I've found, there's no reason for you to worry. You're safe here, with me. There are four fellow Seekers twenty minutes away if we need them, which we don't. And I've got a pistol in the nightstand in my bedroom."

"Then why have you been up all night looking at the case file?"

A flicker of unease crossed his face before his expression cleared. "I like being thorough. And, as I said, I don't like puzzle pieces that don't fit."

"Show me those pieces."

"Teagan—"

"We're in this together. And we'll still be in this together when Larsen is brought to trial and we're both called to testify. Don't shut me out now. Show me."

His reluctance was obvious, but he wheeled back in front of the computer tablet. "I can clear the pictures. There's no reason for you to look at those. I was using them to double-check details in reports." His fingers flew across the keyboard as he closed files and moved things around on the tablet in front of him without sharing them to the big screens. Then he punched one of the keys, and the various Ripper case files appeared on the large monitors. True to his word, there weren't any pictures.

He continued to move things around, mostly closing out various documents until he was left with only one screen of data. It was essentially a huge list with different headings with bullets of information beneath each one.

She read some of the headings out loud. "Race, sex, age, marital status, victimology, criminal psychopathy, location, signature…" She shot him a look of surprise. "A profile. You're working up a profile."

"More or less. I compiled the information from the Ripper murders along with what we know about Larsen's recent crimes." He scrolled to one of the sections labeled *Organized vs. Disorganized.* "I'm sure you remember a lot of this from your criminal justice classes. An organized killer is one who plans his crime ahead of time, brings his weapons with him. The disorganized killer grabs a knife out of a victim's kitchen drawer to stab her. He's more spontaneous, less controlled and tends to make a lot of mistakes. A disorganized killer is generally easier to find than the organized one because of those mistakes. Which one would you say Larsen is?"

"Easy. Organized. He planned everything down to the last detail, from the camera hidden in the tree over the path where I went walking to the section of fence he loosened behind the Brodericks' home. He had to have spent months getting that shack set up as his own personal prison, installing the bars on the windows and doors."

"You get an A plus. He's definitely an organized killer, which gives us insight into his mind and how he thinks. Mason confirmed that Larsen purchased that shack over a year ago. I don't know whether he planned to go after you again, or someone else. But he was definitely preparing it well ahead of time for another victim. Knowing he was an organized killer helps predict other things, like that he probably had a steady job."

"He worked for a realty company," she said. "Not exactly nine to five, but he would have had some kind of schedule, checked in now and then, attended meetings." She crossed her arms, remembering what she'd researched on the Kentucky Ripper's crimes. "But that doesn't fit what I know about the Ripper."

"Maybe. Maybe not." He punched a few buttons and a list of names and dates appeared on the screen to the left of the main one they'd been looking at. "You should recognize those."

"The ripper's victims. Six of them."

"What do they have in common?"

"Other than the obvious? The carved X's in their bellies, the fact that they were abducted for days or weeks before being killed? That all of them were stabbed, including the ones you haven't listed. Some were shot too."

"Other than all of that. What type of killer was responsible for the kinds of crime scenes we found in those examples?"

She thought about it, then shrugged. "You're going to say whoever killed them was organized. I remember those crime scenes were pristine. Very little forensic evidence was found. No weapons were left behind. I could go on, but I can't argue that point. Those particular crime scenes were indicative of an organized perpetrator. But there were eight more killings. And those were the opposite of organized. They were…sloppy."

"Yes. They were." He displayed another list of names on the monitor to the right of the main one, the eight victims she'd just mentioned. "All of these were similar because they seemed to be the work of a disorganized killer."

"Right," she agreed. "Given the mix of organized and disorganized crime scenes, the conclusion goes more to a mental disease, like Finney suffered from. He was, is, bipolar. The theory was that he killed some in his manic state—the disorganized killings—and some in his depressive state—the organized ones."

"It's a popular theory, one the police bought into back then." He motioned toward the first list. "Consider these victims again. Although they were brutally killed, the number of stab wounds is low. Only three for the first victim, six on another, and something in between for the rest." He waved toward the second list. "These, however, had anywhere from twelve to thirty-one stab wounds in addition to being beaten in two of the cases. One victim even suffered cigarette burns all over her back."

"I remember." That sick feeling was roiling in her stomach again.

"It's called overkill," he said. "The killer inflicted far more wounds than necessary to kill his victims. Normally, that might suggest that he knew them, had personal feelings of hate toward them. But it can happen with a disorganized killer as well, with or without a mental defect. He kills in the heat of the moment, because of some imagined slight or explosive anger over something seemingly inconsequential to you or me but that is blown all out of proportion in his mind."

Again, he motioned toward the screen on the list, the names of the six victims that he'd grouped together. "Here's another take on these. In each of these cases, there's evidence that the killer spent a lot of time in the victim's home during the stalking phase while the victim wasn't there. What does that indicate?"

"I'm not sure. Maybe I need a refresher course on my college classes."

He smiled. "I'm sure it will all come back to you when you go back to finish your master's degree. Familiarity is the missing link here. We spend time somewhere when we feel comfortable there, because the location isn't foreign or unknown to us."

She stared at him a long moment. "I'm trying to follow, but all that tells me is that the Ripper likely lived in Kentucky, close to the crime scenes. That was part of the original geographical profiling. That's why Finney was such a good fit."

"And Lowe. Don't forget him, the second potential Ripper on the original suspect list. He was from Kentucky too, born and raised in the same general area as Finney."

"Okay. Yes, I remember that. It's part of the reason that I thought Lowe might have been the one who abducted me."

He swiveled his wheelchair to face her. "Think about the other things we know about those crime scenes. In the first list of victims, the bodies were left where they'd be easily found, potentially indicating the killer had some religious background, that he wanted them to get a Christian burial, or whatever religion he followed."

"The bodies weren't hidden in the rest of the killings either. They're the same."

"I'm going to disagree on that," he said. "In the overkill

list, the victims were, well, slaughtered for lack of a better description. Discarded. There was no caring emotion behind that action. The bodies were easily found only because the killer couldn't be bothered to try to hide them. Not so with the organized killer list. Those bodies were treated, after death anyway, with a modicum of respect. Left clothed or covered, lying down, almost as if they were sleeping as opposed to being tossed out like garbage. It's subtle, but it's a difference. If you look at every kind of comparison that can be made, those two lists of victims each present evidence of a very different kind of killer. In fact, it's my opinion that it proves there wasn't one Kentucky Ripper. There were two."

She sucked in a breath. But it really shouldn't have been a surprise after everything he'd just shown her. She glanced from list to list, read the headings on the middle screen, the bullets beneath them. "But, if you're right, then your original profile was wrong."

He surprised her by smiling. "Don't look so worried. You're not dashing my newly found confidence. There's more to the original profile than appeared in any police reports."

"Okay. Now you've lost me."

He shifted in his chair, a quickly hidden grimace telling her how much his night of research had cost him physically. His hip was aching. He needed a hot soak in a tub and a long nap. But she didn't want to embarrass him by pointing out the obvious, so she remained silent.

"When I profiled the murders allegedly attributed to the Kentucky Ripper," he continued, "I presented the police with *two* profiles. Two different killers. When Finney was arrested, it was the profile I gave them that most closely matched his characteristics that they used. The other profile I gave them was ignored. That's why you never saw it in any of the official case files that you researched."

"I still have to wrap my head around this. You've turned the investigation I did upside down."

"No. I haven't. I've proved that your original conclusions were right all along."

She threw her hands up in the air. "Now I'm beyond lost."

"Sorry. I'm not explaining this very well. To try to put it succinctly, if I look at Larsen and everything we now know about him, including that he used to live in Kentucky, he fits that first list of victims to a T."

"Larsen is the Ripper."

He sat forward in his chair. "He's one of them. That's where your research comes into play. Everything about that second victim list—if we consider that Bishop is right and Finney was a mentally ill fall guy who didn't kill anyone—that second list fits the man you believed all along was the Kentucky Ripper."

She pressed a hand to her throat. "Avarice Lowe."

He nodded. "All I'm waiting on for confirmation is a list of dates and alibis for Larsen. Mason's working on that to see if Larsen was on vacation or sick or whatever on the dates when the first set of victims was abducted. I've already cross-referenced everything I had on Lowe."

She glanced up at the dates he'd mentioned, the ones beside the disorganized list. They all had check marks beside them. "Lowe doesn't have alibis for the second set?"

"No. He doesn't."

She sat back. "Two Kentucky Rippers, and a third guy in prison who had nothing to do with the murders."

"It's worse than that," he told her. "There's one more puzzle piece that you haven't seen." He typed on his computer tablet again.

"What could be worse than two killers?" she asked.

He hesitated with his finger poised over one of the function keys. "How about this?"

A picture displayed on the screen. She stared at it a moment, trying to figure out what was supposed to be significant about what she was seeing. There was a small crowd of people standing behind yellow crime scene tape. Behind them were homes and police cars parked up and down the street.

"One of the Ripper's crime scenes? A crowd shot?"

"That's exactly what it is. Standard operating procedure in a case like this. The police photographer hides out of sight and takes pictures of any people watching the activity, just in case the killer ends up being in the crowd."

"Because killers often come back to the scene of the crime," she said. "They get a thrill from watching the police."

"Now observe the cropped, close-up version I made of that same picture." He pressed another key and the screen changed. "What's worse than two different killers?"

She gasped in shock. "A tag team of killers, partnering together." She stared at the close up of Avarice Lowe and Chris Larsen standing in the crowd, side by side, watching with riveted interest as the police worked one of the Kentucky Ripper crime scenes.

"Congratulations, Teagan."

She tore her gaze from the screen. "For what?"

"You were right all along. Lowe was the Kentucky Ripper. But so was Larsen. None of us saw that coming."

"You did," she said. "You created two profiles."

"Yes, well. My mistake was in not following through and pursuing both after the police went after Finney. I assumed I'd messed up. Instead, I should have pushed for more investigating. Maybe then, Finney wouldn't be in prison. Lowe would be in prison, along with Larsen. And then you'd have never been hurt. I'm so sorry." His jaw tightened.

She shook her head. "No. Don't you dare go there. What happened to me was not your fault. It was Larsen's."

He swallowed. "Thank you for that. But it gets even worse. I'm not sure it's just Larsen's fault. It may be Lowe's too. Remember that you said, even after knowing Larsen had abducted you, that he didn't seem like the right man, that he didn't fit your memories except for his voice?"

It took a moment for his words to sink in. When they did, she pressed a shaking hand to her throat. "Oh my God. You think that I was abducted by…both of them?"

He gave her a short, clipped nod. "I don't have any real proof. Just theories. But I think we should tell the police and the FBI to consider that they may have been a tag team on some of the same crimes, including what was done to you." He took her hand in his again. "I'm sorry. I probably shouldn't have even told you that."

"No, no. I don't want any secrets between us. I want to be included in everything." She forced a smile. "Honestly, it's not as huge of a shock as you'd expect. I was wrestling with my own doubts because some things didn't seem to fit with Larsen. Now, well, it kind of all makes sense." She squeezed his hand. "I assume you already told Mason about this?"

He kissed the back of her hand before letting go. "I was discussing it with him when you walked in. He's corroborating some data, but as soon as he saw that picture of Lowe and Larsen together, he was convinced. He's pulling the Seekers onto this right now."

"I guess everything's in good hands, then."

"The best."

She pushed to her feet, still feeling a bit nauseated and

shaky after the latest revelations. "I need to push all of this ugliness out of my head for now. I'm going to go call my mom and let her know I'm still alive. She's gotten a bit paranoid after this last…episode. She made me promise to call her every day, but I fell asleep last night and never did. I'm surprised she's not already blowing up my phone this morning." Her face heated. "Sorry about falling asleep with you as my pillow. But thanks for putting me to bed. Next time maybe you can join me." She gave him an outrageous wink, desperately trying to lighten the mood.

He gently cupped her face and pressed a soft kiss against her lips. "One day, very soon, sweet Teagan. I'll do more than just join you in that big bed."

She sighed with longing, already feeling better. He always made her feel better, even in her darkest moments.

He put his phone in his pocket before turning off the equipment. Backing away from the table, he said, "Hop on. I'll give you a ride." He arched his brows in a suggestive manner.

She laughed and eased herself onto his lap so she wouldn't jar his incisions. When they reached the family room, she carefully got up. "I'll call Mom from the bedroom."

"And I'll make breakfast. Toast or an omelet? Those are the only two breakfast meals in my culinary arsenal."

"Omelet. Always."

"Good choice. My toast always comes out burned. Meat lover, veggie lover, or deluxe?" He wheeled toward the kitchen.

"Deluxe. With sour cream on top, if you have it."

"You got it," he called back.

She smiled and went into the bedroom. But after three tries on her cell phone without the call going through, she gave up and headed to the kitchen.

He'd left his wheelchair sitting by the island and was leaning on his cane as he pulled ingredients for the omelets out of the refrigerator. He glanced up in surprise when she started helping him. "That was a quick call."

"It wouldn't go through. I think there must be a problem with the cell tower or something."

He frowned as he set a carton of eggs on the counter. "Is your battery low?"

"No. But there weren't any bars. No connection. I tried three times. All I got was static."

"Static?"

She nodded.

He pulled out his phone and checked the screen. Then he punched a button and held it to his ear. He swore and tossed his phone on top of the island. "Run back to the office and lock yourself inside." He hobbled to his wheelchair and plopped down.

"Why? What's going on?"

He wheeled around the island. "Someone's jamming the cell signal. And there's only one person I can think of who would have a reason to do that."

The blood rushed from her face, leaving her cold and shaking as she hurried after him into the family room. "Avarice Lowe. You think he's on his way here?"

"No." He glanced up at her as he wheeled past the L formed by the two couches. "I think he's *already* here. Probably lurking outside, gathering his courage." He glanced at his wrist and swore. "I should have replaced my computer-watch the moment I got back. It would have warned me if someone was on the property. Go to the office, Teagan. Hurry. There aren't any windows in there. Lock the main door, then lock the doors that lead into the bathroom and bedroom. Wedge a chair beneath the door to the hallway. *Go.*"

Ignoring his dictate, she ran after him into the master bedroom. "I'm not leaving you. Come with me."

He wheeled to the nightstand. "I've got this. I'll take care of Lowe. But I have to know you're safe, out of harm's way. Go on."

He yanked open the top drawer.

"Okay, okay." She headed toward the door. "But I wish you'd let me help you instead of—"

He was suddenly beside her in his wheelchair, shoving her back into the room. She stumbled but caught herself in time to see him shut the door and lock it. His face was drawn and pale as he met her questioning gaze. "My pistol's not in the nightstand. *He's inside the house.*"

Chapter Twenty-Five

He's inside the house.

Those horrifying words ran through Teagan's mind over and over as she watched Bryson leaning against the master bathroom counter after ditching the wheelchair because it was in his way. He was using duct tape to secure the thick towels that he'd wrapped around her arms. She didn't ask why. She knew why. The disorganized killer, the one who'd murdered eight of the Kentucky Ripper's victims, was quite the fan of knives. Bryson was using the towels to protect her in case Lowe got past him and came after her next. As to why he had duct tape in his bathroom, that was a discussion for another day. *If they lived another day.*

The psychopath in the main room had already tried to get into the bedroom once. He'd scraped knives underneath the closed door, swiping at Bryson's feet. Then Lowe had used his body like a battering ram, screaming obscenities as he tried to crash through the door. It was only because Bryson had used his own strength against the door that Lowe had given up. But not for long. He was still out there. Planning his next assault. Even now she could hear his shoes thumping and squeaking across the floor as he paced back and forth mumbling incoherent words to himself.

Dear God. Please help us.

Bryson tossed the roll of duct tape onto the counter and reached under the sink. "This is a last resort." He handed her an aerosol can of deodorant. "I don't want you near enough to him to use this. God willing, when you climb out the bedroom window, he'll be so busy with me that he won't get a chance to go after you."

She sucked in a breath, fear for both of them making her flush hot and cold.

"But if he gets past me," he continued, "and he catches up to you, spray his eyes. He won't expect that. It will hurt like hell and he'll be temporarily blinded. Run past him and go for the truck." He dug the keys out of his pocket and shoved them into her jeans pocket. "Drive down the mountain like a bat out of hell. Don't stop. Go straight to the police station. You hear me? Do not stop at some neighbor's house or a little country store. If he ends up following you, he could go after you again. Go straight to the police. It's almost a straight shot once you reach the bottom of the mountain. You remember the directions I told you?"

He lightly shook her when she didn't answer.

"I do. I remember," she said. "But none of this makes sense. Why don't you put towels on your arms too? And climb out the window with me?"

He gave her an exasperated look. "I was up all night. My hip never had a chance to recuperate. I'm not running anywhere. And the towels would make it too hard for me to maneuver in a fight. This is the way it has to be. He's already cracked the doorjamb. The next time he tries to get through the door, he'll be inside the bedroom. While I keep him occupied, you're going to climb out that window and run for the truck."

"I don't want to run away like a coward and leave you. Don't ask me to do that again."

He grabbed a small pair of scissors from one of the

drawers and set them on top of the counter. Next he grabbed a folded sheet from beneath the cabinet and tucked it under his arm. "You have to leave me. It's the only way."

She frantically shook her head and set the can back on the counter. "No. It's not. Two against one, remember? You and me against the world. He can't kill both of us. If we attack him together, we'll defeat him."

"No, Teagan. You heard his roar of rage earlier. You saw the knives he was shoving under the door. Probably the only reason he didn't shoot his way through is that he doesn't want to end his fun that quickly. He's a cutter. He wants to enjoy himself first. But if he sees you running for the truck through the front windows, he'll use the gun. You can't outrun a bullet. I have to distract him, try to get the gun to give you a chance."

He shoved the can in her hand, grabbed the pair of scissors and pulled her out of the bathroom.

A shoe squeaked against the polished floor outside the bedroom door.

Bryson scowled and dropped the folded sheet on top of the bed. He limped to the window and quietly eased it up. Rather than risk the noise of loosening the screen's frame and dropping it outside, he used the scissors to cut an opening. He motioned for her to stand in front of the window.

"The truck will detect the key fob in your pocket," he whispered. "All you have to do is press the button under the door handle and it will open. The engine's a push-button start. You remember, right? You've got this." He framed her face with his hands. "All you have to do is run, sweetheart. Everything's going to be okay."

Tears spilled down her cheeks as she looked into his beautiful blue eyes. "Bryson, I—"

Another squeak sounded outside the room. Lowe was getting restless, working up his courage for another assault.

Then there was another sound, something scraping across the floor. Something heavy. What was that?

Bryson pressed a quick, hard kiss against her lips. "You can do this," he whispered next to her ear. "Don't let me down."

Her pulse was rushing in her ears so loudly that she almost couldn't hear him. She grasped the windowsill. It was awkward with the ridiculous towels wrapped around her arms. But she managed.

Grabbing the sheet off the bed, he shook it out, quickly rolling and twisting it, holding it in both hands like a length of rope. It shook her to her core when she realized what he was doing: planning to use the sheet to defend himself against the knives. Her heart slammed in her chest so hard she marveled that it didn't crack one of her ribs.

She hated this, hated the thought of abandoning him. And yet, if she stayed, she'd be a distraction that could get him killed. All she could do now was follow his instructions and pray he was able to defeat Lowe.

With a concussion.

A bum hip.

Stitches both inside him and outside. Bruises all over.

With nothing but a sheet to defend himself against a madman with butcher knives and a pistol likely in his pocket.

This was insane.

A thump sounded against the door.

Get ready, he mouthed.

She clutched the stupid can of deodorant and prayed that a better plan would come to her than leaving him here to his likely death. But what could she do? How could she help?

Something heavy crashed against the door. The already cracked frame exploded in a hail of wooden shards as a side table from the family room flew through the ruined opening. Bryson ducked, then lunged forward, arms outstretched with the sheet between them as he grappled with Lowe. Both men moved backward into the family room, a flurry of flashing knives and billowing cloth as Bryson ducked and weaved and wielded his sheet in an effort to avoid being diced into pieces.

"Now, Teagan," he yelled, furiously fighting Lowe's flailing arms. "Go!"

She let out a sob and jumped.

WITH TEAGAN SAFELY AWAY, Bryson focused his undivided attention on the psychopath trying to hack him to death with a knife in each hand. Bryson wrenched his left arm up, using the sheet to deflect yet another blow. This time he twisted the sheet, then wrenched it back. The butcher knife in Lowe's right hand flew across the family room, skittering onto the floor with a metallic twang.

Lowe dropped to the floor. Without his weight as a counterbalance, Bryson's hip gave out. He crashed down on top of Lowe. A sickening scrape sounded and white-hot pain lanced through his side. Lowe's mouth curved in a delighted smile as he grabbed the knife now embedded beneath Bryson's ribs and yanked it out.

Bryson gasped, fighting for air now as he twisted and rolled with Lowe, desperately trying to gain control of the knife. He grabbed Lowe's wrist, muscles burning and shaking as he slowly won the tug of war, turning the man's hand. Bryson swiped the blade across the man's neck. A thin red line immediately formed. But it was only superficial. Lowe didn't even blink. He kept straining against Bryson, trying to turn the knife the other way. Muscles bunched and cramped as Bryson fought back.

The floor turned slippery with sweat and blood. They

rolled like two alligators in a death roll, each struggling to get the upper hand. Lowe was strong, and big, but he still wouldn't have been that difficult for a man Bryson's size to defeat. Except that Bryson had begun this match in a much-weakened state. And Lowe's knife had done considerable damage. His lifeblood was seeping from his side. A cold numbness spread across his middle, making him shiver. If he didn't end this, soon, it would be lights out. For him.

He threw everything he had left into fighting back. But his muscles ached. Weakness crept relentlessly through his body. It was a struggle just to hold up his arms.

Lowe gave one of his guttural yells, this one of satisfaction and triumph. He was winning. It was almost over. And he knew it.

Taking advantage of Lowe's distraction, Bryson managed to twist and jerk the man's knife hand again. This time he sliced deep into Lowe's biceps on his right arm. But before Bryson could follow up with a killing blow, Lowe twisted and rolled on top of him. Bryson couldn't get traction on the slippery floor. Blood saturated the knife handle. Bryson lost his grip. Lowe plunged the knife deep into Bryson's side again, and twisted.

Bryson arched off the floor, an inferno of lava-like pain scorching him from the inside out. He dropped back down, gasping, struggling to catch his breath. The rest of his strength seemed to drain away, leaving him limp, muscles twitching in agony as he squinted and blinked, trying to focus.

Lowe was a dark blur, climbing to his feet, staggering and clutching himself as he lumbered out of Bryson's sight-line. He rolled his head to the side, trying to follow the other man's progress. Cold. He was so cold. His teeth chattered as he frantically pushed against the floor, like a fiddler crab, trying to slide away. But all he could manage was a few inches.

His nemesis stopped by one of the couches and leaned down. When he turned around, Bryson blinked, trying to see what was in the man's hand. A gun. Probably Bryson's own pistol.

He held it up, no doubt gloating with triumph. Bryson could no longer see well enough to make out the man's expression. Maybe that was a blessing.

"Chris said you'd put up a good fight and you did." He spoke for the first time since their fight had begun, his words choppy as he too struggled to catch his breath. "I was his one call from jail. Imagine that. He called me instead of a lawyer." He shook his head. "What a gift. And I'm here paying him back. This is for what you did to Chris." He held his gun arm out toward Bryson. "After you're dead, I'll enjoy that girlfriend of yours. I'll gut her like a fish."

Bryson swore and tried to push himself up. But it was as if his body was glued to the floor.

The sound of a roaring engine had both of them jerking their heads toward the front windows. Bryson's pickup crashed through the house, tossing one of the couches across the room like kindling, and slamming into Lowe so hard he flew across the room.

Someone hopped out, but all he saw was a blur.

"Bryson! Bryson, I'm coming. Hold on."

Teagan.

She crawled over the destruction she'd wrought on his house. He wanted to yell at her for risking her life yet again for him. But he was so glad to see her, alive, and safe, because she'd killed Lowe. He didn't yell. He was too proud of his little warrior to risk hurting the tender feelings that she tried to hide with her sassy quips. He despised himself that it took dying for him to realize just what she meant to him.

And that he loved her.

Her shoes squeaked and slid across the wet floor as she scrambled toward him. He tried to tell her that he loved her, that he was proud of her. But he wasn't sure if the words came out or not. He was so tired. And cold. At least the awful pain had faded. He barely felt anything anymore. He closed his eyes, at peace, knowing that she was safe. That she would be okay.

TEAGAN GRABBED THE discarded gun she'd spotted on the floor next to a smashed piece of electronics that she could only guess was whatever Lowe had used to jam the cell signals. But Lowe was no longer a threat. He was lying in a lifeless heap about ten feet away.

After a treacherous slippery slide across the blood-streaked floor, she dropped to her knees beside Bryson, gun still clutched in her left hand as she knelt over him. "Can you hear me? Speak to me," she ordered through a cascade of tears.

He blinked, then slowly opened his eyes. "Teagan?" Her name was slurred. He seemed confused as he struggled to focus on her face.

"I'm here, baby. I'm here." She set the pistol down and leaned over him, pressing her hands against the floor on each side of him to keep her balance. Something bumped against her arm. She pulled back in horror to see the handle of a knife sticking out from his left side, embedded all the way to the hilt. Blood pooled beneath him, forming macabre rivulets across the formerly polished white floor. "Oh, no. Oh, no, no, no."

"You…okay?" he whispered, his lips an odd, bluish tinge. "Where's… Lowe? The…gun?"

She motioned toward the body on the other side of the room as she tore at the duct tape holding the towels around her left arm. "I hit the piece of scum with your truck. I drove it right up the front steps. Your gun's right here." She patted the floor beside him. "Don't worry. He can't hurt you again."

He blinked. "Truck?" He rolled his head to the side, obviously trying to make sense of what she was saying.

She finally freed the towel and leaned across him, pressing it around the wound while trying to not move the knife and make it worse.

"Down!" he rasped.

She automatically ducked as the sound of a guttural yell sounded off to the side. Bryson swept the pistol up and fired over and over and over. Then his hand dropped to his side and the pistol skittered across the floor. It was as if he'd gathered all the strength he had left to protect her, once again, and was completely spent.

She looked over her shoulder. Lowe was impossibly close to them, just a few feet away. She'd thought she'd killed him. She must have only knocked him out. Or he'd pretended to be unconscious. Neither of which mattered now. Bryson's aim had been true. He'd shot him in the head.

A sob escaped her. "I can't believe it. After seeing him through the window, holding that pistol, I drove through a wall to save you. But once again, you saved me." She turned back toward him, smiling through her tears.

His eyes were closed.

His jaw was slack.

"Bryson?" She frantically bent over him. "Open your eyes. Bryson?"

"Move. Get out of the way."

She whirled around, shocked to see Gage Bishop kneeling beside her. Behind him, Brielle, Dalton and Han had just stepped in through the ruined wall and were sweeping their pistols back and forth, looking for threats.

"Move." Bishop none too gently shoved her out of the way. He pressed his fingers against the side of Bryson's neck.

"Come on." Brielle was beside her now. "Let's give him room. The police and an ambulance are on their way. Mason told us he'd tried to call Bryson back and couldn't get through. He called us, then 911."

Teagan pressed her fist to her mouth to keep from screaming.

Bishop was performing CPR.

Chapter Twenty-Six

Three months later

Long before the shadow fell across the end of the dock and hovered over Bryson Anton's wheelchair, he knew someone was there. Motion sensors and security cameras had made Bryson's new watch buzz against his wrist when they parked their car in the driveway. More messages warned when they crossed the back patio. And again, when they'd descended the gently sloping lawn that ended at the creek. But he didn't turn around.

Not yet.

"It's been nearly three months since you sent me away yet again, Bryson. One minute I'm at the hospital, thanking God that Bishop was able to keep you alive long enough to even get you there. Then I'm on my knees thanking God that you survived yet another arduous surgery. Only to visit you in recovery to discover you're acting like a grizzly bear, just like last time, proving you're the worst patient ever in the history of the universe. And then, when you're finally in your hospital room and we're alone, I'm ready to pour my heart out to you, and what do you do? You tell me to get out! You order me back to Jacksonville to work on my master's degree. What the heck, Bryson?"

"The summer semester was about to start. I didn't want you to have to wait until fall to start back again."

She said several unsavory things. "No phone calls from you. When I tried calling, you didn't answer. I don't even count the pathetic, generic texts you occasionally sent me. Then I find out that you've been talking to my dad every few days, asking how I was doing. If you were worried, all you had to do was talk to *me*, Bryson. Not my family."

"I was busy."

"Really? What's her name?"

He turned the wheelchair around to face her. She was wearing hunter-green shorts and a lime-green tank top in deference to the warm weather. As always, her rich brown skin was flawless, her full high breasts a reminder of the incredible body beneath those clothes. But his favorite part of her was that gorgeous bright mind of hers. And her beautiful, sassy mouth. He never knew what outrageous thing she was going to say next.

"Helga," he said.

She frowned. "Excuse me?"

"You asked me her name. Her name is Helga. Or, well, I actually don't even know her real name. But that's what you called her when she was here that first day you showed up on my doorstep."

She put her hands on her hips. "Does this mean that you've been doing the rehab the doctor ordered?"

"It does. I have."

She crossed her arms, looking only slightly less aggravated than before. "Well, that's good. But I still don't see why you couldn't text me a real hello, with feeling, every once in a while. Or actually speak to me on the phone. What makes you think you could just text me last night to come back and everything would be fine?"

He smiled. "You're here aren't you?"

She narrowed her eyes, then whirled around.

He caught her arm just before she could get out of reach and yanked her backward.

She let out a little squeak and landed right where he wanted her. In his lap.

"Let me go, Bryson. I'm not kidding."

He gently turned her face so she'd meet his gaze. "Is that really want you want, Teag? You want me to let you go?" The flash of unshed tears in her eyes surprised him. "Sweetheart?"

"You already have. You wouldn't let me stay to help with your recovery. You sent me back home like some child—"

"While I could never mistake you for a child, not even close—" he gently stroked her arm, unable to resist touching her "—there's definitely an age difference between us. Something to think about. You're young, still working on officially starting your career, although I heard the FBI is interested in grooming you as a future candidate."

She smiled. Not full wattage, but enough for him to know that he was right, that the FBI opportunity was important to her.

"There might be a nibble there," she admitted. "They were impressed with the detailed investigation I conducted, and that I was right about Avarice Lowe being a serial killer. Apparently my notes on him have helped them narrow down facts that blow apart his alibis for some of the killings. He may not be around for a trial. But at least some of his victims' families will have true closure now."

He pressed a kiss against her cheek and settled her more comfortably against him. The fact that she didn't resist being snuggled close was encouraging. "You have the most beautiful mind I've ever had the pleasure of knowing. It's about time the rest of the world figured that out."

She gave him the side-eye before looking away. "I'd say thank you, but it sounds like you're building another excuse to justify why you wanted me to leave you."

"Not leave me. Go back to school. Huge difference."

She shrugged.

"Teag, you're young, energetic, just starting out in life. I'm more toward the middle of mine."

She snorted.

"Okay, maybe not quite the middle just yet. Hopefully."

"Is this going somewhere?"

He motioned toward the wheelchair. "I wouldn't want you to ever regret spending time with a cripple when you could be out with guys your own age doing whatever you want."

She rolled her eyes with a dramatic toss of her head. "I think you're confusing me with the self-centered stuck-up jerk who used to be your girlfriend. I'm a little more creative than her. I can figure out lots of fun things to do with you even if you can't twirl me around a dance floor."

"Does that mean you could be happy if I never walked again?"

Her mouth fell open and she cupped his face in her hands, all signs of teasing and anger gone as she stared into his eyes. "Oh, Bry. Is that what the doctor said? Are you…are you paralyzed?"

He gently pulled her hands down and kissed them before letting go. "No. I'm not paralyzed. I've been very lucky, actually, after being shot twice in my life. Then stabbed. Twice. I just wanted to make sure that if something like that did happen, maybe down the road—considering how dangerous my career can be—that you'd still be okay sticking around."

Her brows arched in confusion. "Love isn't based on how mobile you are or what you can do for someone else.

Love is when your happiness revolves around the other person's happiness. Once again, I think you're confusing me with the ex who shall not be named."

He grinned.

She frowned.

"Did you just say that you loved me, Teagan? In that unique sassy way of yours?"

She crossed her arms. "That depends."

"On?"

"On why you're asking me these stupid questions and why you texted me last night that you had first class tickets waiting for me so I could fly up here today. Thanks for the first class, by the way. That was cool."

"You're welcome. Thanks for coming."

She twisted her mouth as if trying to figure something out. "You're acting awfully strange. And my infinite patience is wearing thin. Out with it. What exactly do you want? Are you asking me to be your girlfriend and you're worried I'll dump you because of the chair?"

"Will you?"

"Be your girlfriend? Are you asking me to be your girlfriend?"

"No."

"We're done here. Have a nice life, Bryson." She hopped off his lap and started up the dock.

"I'm not asking you to be my girlfriend," he called after her.

She raised her hand in the air and made a rude gesture without looking back.

He grinned. "I'm asking you to be my fiancée. For real this time."

She stopped so fast that she wobbled and almost fell into the water. Once she regained her balance, she slowly turned around. "What…what did you just say?"

He leaned down and flipped the top back on the cooler beside his chair. Then he pulled out a red velvet box and held it up in front of him. "I love you Teagan Eleanor Ray."

She gasped in outrage. "Did my mother tell you my middle name? I hate it. It makes me sound like an eighty-year-old."

"Well, maybe that will help with the age gap between us." He winked.

She marched back to him and stopped a few feet from his chair, eyeing the velvet box in his hands. "Be honest, Bryson. Exactly how much older than me are you?"

"Old enough to teach you a few things that I know you'll really, really enjoy. And young enough to demonstrate them with an expertise that will make your toes curl."

Her gaze flew to his. She swallowed, then cleared her throat. "Toes curl?"

He nodded.

"All of them?" she squeaked.

"Oh yeah."

She fanned herself, then wiped her hands on her shorts. "Um. Wasn't there a question you asked me, a moment ago, when my back was turned?"

He nodded again.

She put her hands on her hips. "Don't you think you should ask again? Face-to-face?"

"No."

Her eyes widened. She started to turn away.

He stood.

She froze and stared in wonder as he dropped down on one knee on the dock.

"I think I should ask it down here, do this the right way, on bended knee." He opened the box and tilted it so the ring would catch the light.

She pressed a hand to her throat. "You stood on your own. No cane. And you're on one knee. I don't understand."

"By the grace of God, when Lowe stabbed me, it knocked the bullet loose instead of into my spine. The doctors were able to extract it. And I've been doing everything the therapists ordered me to do. I'm not pain-free yet. But there's a good chance I will be. Eventually."

Her expression turned sad. "Are you in pain right now, Bryson?"

He shook his head. "No. And it's not because of tequila."

"Scotch?"

"Pain pills. Like I said, I'm following doctor's orders this time. No self-medicating with alcohol. No more skipping rehab appointments. And even though I hate how the pills make me feel, I wanted to be able to do this without grimacing. So I'm all doped up and feeling good. Now, about that question I asked—"

"The ring is beautiful," she breathed, stepping closer and eyeing the box again. "But not half as beautiful as you, you frustrating, stubborn man."

He smiled as he pulled the ring out of its bed of velvet. "I wanted something special, something as unique as you."

She moved even closer, then pressed her hand against her chest. "Opals. And diamonds. And rubies. I love opals and rubies. How did you know?"

"All those calls to your mom and dad weren't for nothing."

"Sneaky."

"Necessary. I wanted to surprise you. You just confirmed that you love opals and rubies. Diamonds too I hope?"

She rolled her eyes. "Everyone loves diamonds. Or they

should. I couldn't ask for anything more beautiful. Thank you." She held out her left hand.

He poised the ring in front of her finger. But before sliding it on, he looked up, meeting her gaze. "It's selfish of me to even ask you to marry me, because I think you could do a lot better. But I can't imagine my life without you in it. I love you, Teagan Ray. I think I loved you the moment you knocked on my door and the only word you could get out was hi." He grinned. "Will you do me the honor of being my wife? Will you marry me?"

"Are you kidding? Put the ring on already."

He laughed and slid the ring onto her finger. Then he stood.

Tears glittered in her eyes as she put her hands on his shoulders. "I can't believe you're standing here like this. I'm so happy for you."

"No happier than me, that you said yes. I wasn't sure how this was going to go."

"That makes two of us. I had no idea why you wanted to see me. I believe you owe me a kiss, future husband." She lifted her lips toward his and waited for him to bend down.

"Hold that thought. I have something else for you." He turned back to the cooler and reached inside.

She groaned. "You're killing me, Bryson. I don't want anything else but you."

"Oh, I don't know. I'm pretty sure you want this. And I did make a promise after all." He handed her a pink bag with little pink ribbons tied all over it, and the name of a very exclusive store on the outside of the bag.

Her eyes widened. "You didn't."

"I did."

She opened the bag and peeked inside, then squealed with delight as she shoved her hand in and pulled out an aqua-colored lace bra and panty set. "They're gorgeous, perfect. And they're my size. Oh my gosh, please don't tell me you asked my mother my sizes." She gasped. "Or my dad!"

"Give me more credit than that. I asked your mother for your best friend's name. Then I asked your best friend."

She laughed with obvious relief and sorted through the contents. "Twelve. You bought me a dozen bras and matching panties. Bryson! This cost a fortune!"

"I can afford it. I'd pay ten times that to see your eyes light up and your glowing smile."

The tears that had been threatening spilled over and down her cheeks. "I'm so happy."

"Because we're going to get married?"

She shook her head. "Because you promised that when you replaced my hundred-dollar bra that you'd buy me more, and then you'd take them off me."

He threw his head back and laughed harder than he had in ages.

"Hurry, Bryson. I'm not waiting one more minute for you to keep your promise. I'll strip right here on your back lawn if I have to."

Still laughing, he scooped her up in his arms and ran with her to the house. But before going inside, he let her legs slide down him as he'd done so long ago. And this time, he did what he'd wanted to do since the first time he'd seen her. He kissed her. Really kissed her. Kissed her with all his pent-up emotions, love and longing and lust all rolled into one. And when he was done, he pulled back to soak in the haze of passion in her eyes and the love reflected back in them.

His hands were shaking as he cupped her face. "I don't know what I did to make you love me. But I'll thank God every night for the rest of my life that you showed up on my doorstep. You're a treasure, Teagan. A gift to my battered soul. I love you so much."

She shifted the bag of lingerie to her left hand and grabbed his right in hers. "I love you too, Bryson Anton. But you have one more promise to keep. You have to make my toes curl."

"Challenge accepted." He scooped her up in his arms and kissed her again as he strode through the house.

Her toes were curling before they even reached the bedroom.

* * * * *

THE FUGITIVE

NICHOLE SEVERN

This one goes to Becca Syme and her book
Dear Writer, You Need to Quit for convincing me
to quit everything that wouldn't help finish this
damn book.

Chapter One

Raleigh Wilde.

Hell, it'd been a while since deputy United States marshal Beckett Foster had set sights on her, and every cell in his body responded in awareness. Four months, one week and four days, to be exact. Those soul-searching light green eyes, her soft brown hair and sharp cheekbones. But all that beauty didn't take away from the sawed-off shotgun currently pointed at his chest. His hand hovered just above his firearm as the Mothers Come First foundation's former chief financial officer—now fugitive—widened her stance.

"Don't you know breaking into someone's home is illegal, *Marshal*?" That voice. A man could get lost in a voice like that. Sweet and rough all in the same package. Raleigh smoothed her fingers over the gun in her hand. It hadn't taken her but a few seconds after she'd come through the door to realize he'd been waiting for her at the other end of the wide room.

It hadn't taken him but a couple of hours to figure out where she'd been hiding for the past four months once her file crossed his desk. What she didn't know was how long he'd been waiting, and that he'd already relieved that gun of its rounds, as well as any other weapons he'd found during his search of her aunt's cabin.

"Come on now. You and I both know you haven't forgotten my name that easily." He studied her from head to toe, memorizing the fit of her oversize plaid flannel shirt, the slight loss of color in her face and the dark circles under her eyes. Yeah, living on the run did that to a person. Beckett unbuttoned his holster. He wouldn't pull. Of all the criminals the United States Marshals Service had assigned him to recover over the years, she was the only one he'd hesitated chasing down. Then again, if he hadn't accepted the assignment, another marshal would have. And there was no way Beckett would let anyone else bring her in.

Beckett ran his free hand along the exposed brick of the fireplace. "Gotta be honest, didn't think you'd ever come back here. Lot of memories tied up in this place."

"What do you want, Beckett?" The creases around her eyes deepened as she shifted her weight between both feet. She crouched slightly, searching through the single window facing East Lake, then refocused on him.

Looking for a way out? Or to see if he'd come with backup? Dried grass, changing leaves, mountains and an empty dock were all that were out there. The cabin she'd been raised in as a kid sat on the west side of the lake, away from tourists, away from the main road. Even if he gave her a head start, she wouldn't get far. There was nowhere for her to run. Not from him.

"You know that, too." He took a single step forward, the aged wood floor protesting under his weight as he closed in on her. "You skipped out on your trial, and I'm here to bring you in."

"What was I supposed to do?" Countering his approach, she moved backward toward the front door she'd dead-bolted right after coming inside but kept the gun aimed at him. Her boot hit the go bag she stored on the kitchen counter beside the door. "I didn't steal that money. Someone at the charity did and faked the evidence so I'd take the fall."

"That's the best you got? A frame job?" Fifty and a half million dollars. Gone. The only one with continuous access to the funds stood right in front of him. Not to mention the brand-new offshore bank account, the thousands of wire transfers to that account in increments small enough they wouldn't register for the feds, and Raleigh's signatures on every single one of them. "You had a choice, Raleigh. You just chose wrong."

"Beckett…" She slowed her escape. Her fingers flitted over the gun as her expression softened. "You know me. You know I didn't do this. Find Calvin Dailey, the foundation's CEO. I told him everything when I discovered the funds were being sent offshore. I've been trying to contact him for weeks. He must've gone into hiding when the news about my arrest hit the media, but he can clear my name."

"I'm afraid Calvin Dailey can't help you right now. Seems your boss left his house without about a half a gallon of his own blood. Local police haven't found the body yet, but I don't think that's a coincidence, considering you just revealed he's the only other person you told about the missing money." He locked his jaw against the fire burning through his veins, the easygoing marshal gone. Beckett lowered his hand from above his holster and took another step. "You think you know a person. Then one day you wake up and see them on the morning news getting arrested for embezzlement."

"Calvin's...dead?" Shock dropped her bottom lip. Real dangerous. Either Raleigh Wilde was one hell of an actress, or she honestly hadn't known her former colleague had most likely been murdered. Shock bled to resolution and wiped the confusion from her gaze. She secured the butt of the rifle against her shoulder. Just as he'd taught her. "I didn't kill him, and I didn't embezzle that money. I'm not going to prison. I can't. Not now."

There was the woman he'd let into his life, the one with vengeance in her eyes and her middle fingers raised high. The one who'd stood up to the mugger who'd tried stealing her purse on a Portland street until it'd gotten to the point Beckett had to intervene before she punctured one of the bastard's lungs with her high heel. The one who'd thanked him for his help by intertwining her fingers with his and showing him what real desire looked like. He'd never forget that woman. Too bad she'd never existed in the first place. Instead, he'd gotten involved with a criminal, but she wasn't going to manipulate him again. "That's up to the judge, sweetheart."

"Don't call me that." The words left her mouth between gritted teeth. "You lost the right to call me 'sweetheart' when you disappeared after my arrest."

"And here I was thinking you're the one who broke us up." He pulled a set of cuffs from the back of his holster, shards of reflected sunlight bouncing across her face. "I'm bringing you in."

"I'll give you one chance to walk away, Beckett." She racked the shotgun, her expression softening slightly.

"Please. For both our sakes, don't make me pull this trigger. Turn around and pretend you never found me. It's better for everyone if I stay lost."

"You're going to shoot me now, is that it?" It was possible. Honestly, how well did he really know her? They'd been together six months before she'd gotten arrested. Sure, she'd let her past slip out every once in a while, but, it turned out, nearly everything he'd known about her had been a lie. The deeper he'd dug into her life, the more he'd realized how stupid he'd been to trust her. People didn't change. Once a criminal, always a criminal.

"I'll do whatever it takes to survive." The shadows across her throat shifted as she licked her lips and swallowed. "This isn't just about me anymore."

Beckett stuck his hand in his jeans pocket and pulled out the rounds he'd taken from the gun. Pinching one between his thumb and index finger, he held it up for her to see. "How are you going to shoot me if the gun is empty, Raleigh?"

She faltered, her green gaze lowering to the weapon.

Beckett dropped the cuffs and the rounds and lunged. Ripping the rifle from her grip with one hand, he unholstered his own weapon and aimed with the other. In less than two breaths, he had his fugitive. The shotgun hit the floor, jarring her instantly. Nice to see there were still some things that could get through that carefully monitored exterior. "Now I can guarantee you this gun is loaded." He motioned her to the left with the barrel of his service weapon. "Cuffs. Now."

"You're making a mistake. If Calvin was killed as you said, whoever stole that money is cleaning up loose ends. He's the only one I told about the missing money. Who do you think they'll come after next?" Raleigh crouched, picked up the handcuffs and secured one over her wrist. The cords between her shoulders and neck flexed tight as she moved. She straightened, facing him, her light vanilla scent making its way deep into his lungs. "You take me in, you'll only make it easier for his killer to find me."

He ensured the cuffs were tight enough she couldn't squirm loose, his fingers brushing the inside of her wrist. An electric jolt shot up his arm in response. Hell. He'd forgotten what it was like to touch her, how his body had always craved hers. His heart threatened to beat out of his chest, his lungs pressurizing with the air stuck in his throat. Six months. That'd been all the time he'd needed to fall for her, she'd been that addictive. He'd run to help when some purse snatcher had tried to take off with her bag, but, in reality, she'd been the one to save him that day. She'd changed…everything, given him hope he didn't have to spend the rest of his life alone. Until he'd learned who she really was. Learned it'd all been one long con.

The cuffs ratcheted into place, the clicks loud in his ears as he secured her hands in front, and reality bled into focus. Justice. Integrity. Service. He'd sworn to uphold the law when he'd become a marshal, and the woman in front of him wouldn't change that. No matter how strong her gravitational pull. Or how clever her lies. "No, Raleigh. The mistake was trusting you from the beginning."

"I'm not going back." She stared out the window over his shoulder, almost lost, green eyes ethereal. Seconds ticked by. Then, in an instant, her gaze snapped back to his, and his instincts screamed in warning. Raleigh wrenched away from him, then kicked him square in the gut. "Not until I clear my name."

His head hit the old wood mantel above the fireplace—hard—and he went down. The cabin blurred in his vision as he struggled to his feet; the only illumination came from a beam of sunlight through the now open front door. It was enough to give him direction. The go bag from the kitchen counter was gone. He pressed his free hand to the back of his head, then glanced at his fingers. Blood. Pain spread fast through his skull. Damn, that woman had powerful legs. Beckett charged out the door, gun up, finger on the trigger. He blinked against the brightness glinting off the lake and shook his head to clear the soft ringing in his ears. "Raleigh!"

Movement registered along the lake's shore about fifty feet to his left. Cuffed, she sprinted toward a thick line of trees behind the cabin, all that soft brown hair trailing behind her.

Beckett pumped his legs hard. The sun had already started hugging the mountains. If she evaded him long enough, there was a chance she'd disappear forever. That wasn't an option. Raleigh vanished into the tree line ahead of him. Loose rocks and fallen branches threatened to trip him up, but he only pushed himself harder.

His heart thundered behind his ears as shadows enveloped the small dirt trail ahead. Too many damn places for an ambush. He slowed, sweat beading in his hairline, and forced the adrenaline pumping through his veins to cool. His training kicked in, instincts on high alert. Raleigh might be a criminal, but she wasn't a trained law-enforcement officer. Any family she'd ever had had turned their backs on her a long time ago, and her friends had been advised to keep their distance by counsel. She couldn't hide from him. At least, not for long.

The sound of a broken twig snapping in two twisted him to the right. He took aim as branches of a fir tree swayed with the fresh breeze. Tension tightened every muscle down his spine. Three seconds. Four. A shadow slipped into his peripheral vision off to the left, and he spun, too late.

Thick dried bark scraped across the exposed skin of his arm a split second before he ducked out of the way of the massive branch she'd swung at him. He lunged as she widened her stance for another round, hiking her over his shoulder in a fireman's hold. A sharp jab of her knee knocked the air from his lungs. A growl rumbled through his chest as they hit the forest floor. He pinned her beneath him, all that lean muscle and soft skin. "You're making this harder on yourself."

Raleigh hooked her foot under his shin and shoved, trying to roll him onto his back. Wouldn't work. Struggling for purchase, she bucked her hips up to dislodge his advantage. Fire ignited the subtle hints of gold around the edges of her eyes.

He secured her wrists between his hands and pulled her to her feet. "You're under arrest."

HEARTS WERE WILD CREATURES. Traitorous, deceitful creatures who didn't know the difference between the US marshal who intended on bringing her in and the man she'd envisioned spending the rest of her life with up until a few months ago.

Raleigh Wilde focused on where her boots landed along the trail and not on the fact she'd actually been happy to see him. Those coastal-blue eyes, his thick dark hair she used to tangle her fingers through or his beard that would tickle her throat when he kissed her. Not to mention every ridge and valley of muscle she'd memorized from the first day they'd met all those years ago.

It'd been four months since the last time they'd stood face-to-face, and this was how it was going to end? Beckett would bring her into the Marshals' district office, turn her over to the FBI, and whoever'd framed her for taking that donation money would enjoy their freedom while she served time for a crime she didn't commit. Because, of all the things she hadn't been able to depend on in this world, Beckett and his unbreakable sense of duty was something she could count on.

She sucked in a lungful of clean Oregon air. Dried needles crunched beneath her feet, red, orange and yellow foliage clinging to the thick line of trees around her aunt's small property. It'd been a long time since she'd had the guts to come back out here. Not since her brother's death. Pressing her cuffed wrists against her lower abdomen, she shook her head. She should've known Beckett Foster would be assigned her case. He was the one who knew her best, after all. The only one she'd trusted with pieces of herself. He'd known she'd come here. But she wasn't a criminal. No matter what he believed about her or what the evidence said. She hadn't stolen a dime from the foundation she and Calvin had built together, and she'd prove it. She'd clear her name and get her life back. She slid the edge of her thumb over the growing baby bump she kept hidden. Get her future back. "I never meant for you to get involved in any of this."

"Don't talk to me like we're friends." His heavy steps echoed loud behind her. The sun had gone down behind the mountains, making the dangerous tone in his voice that much more terrifying. The slide of steel against her spine kept her moving. Twenty feet, maybe less, until they left the safety of the trees. "My head is still bleeding."

She was out of time. She couldn't go to prison. She could run again, but he was so much stronger than she was, faster, bigger. Raleigh slowed. His dark, rich scent still lodged in her lungs. Outdoors and man. She hadn't realized how much she'd missed that comforting smell until just now. She dug her nails into her palms against the truth. She hadn't realized how much she'd missed him. They were nearing the edge of the tree line. He'd parked his truck straight ahead. The second he put her in that vehicle, it was over. She had to tell him the truth. She had to make him believe her. "Beckett, there's something I have to tell—"

A gunshot exploded from the trailhead, echoing off the mountains at their back.

Fire burned along the edge of her neck as strong hands ripped her off the trail and into the trees. In the span of a single breath, Beckett shoved them behind a large fir. Protecting her? Raleigh clamped a hand over the wound as he drew his weapon.

Beckett released the magazine from the gun, checked it, then slammed it back into place. Just as he'd taught her when he'd insisted she needed to learn how to handle a weapon. He spun, facing her. Rough calluses tugged at her skin as he forced her hand out of the way and studied her wound. "How bad is it?"

Her heart jerked behind her rib cage as his fingers brushed against the oversensitized skin of her throat. That almost sounded like concern in his voice. But she knew better. He'd protect her because she was a fugitive whose file had come across his desk. He'd get her back into federal custody, even if he had to shoot his way out of here to do it. She was a job. Nothing more. Anything they had together had been destroyed the moment he'd turned his back on her after her arrest. Bright blue eyes locked on her, and her blood heated in an instant. She hissed as the salt in his skin aggravated the bullet's burn on her neck and pulled back. "It's a graze. I'm fine."

"Good." Beckett turned his back to her, all that concern that'd warmed her from the inside turning to ice. "Then you know the drill. Stay behind me, and don't even think about running again."

"Exactly where am I supposed to go?" she asked.

A short burst of laughter shook his shoulders. "Didn't stop you from trying a few minutes ago."

Another bullet ripped through the tree at her right, and she flinched away as fear took control. Her fingers tightened in his shirt, the cuffs cutting into the soft tissue of her inner wrists. They had to get out of here. Raleigh patted him on the shoulder. "Where are your handcuff keys?"

"US Marshals Service! Put your weapon down, get

on your knees and put your hands behind your head!"
Beckett pulled the trigger. Once. Twice. The shadow
disappeared from the edge of the trees, but Raleigh
wasn't naive enough to believe the shooter had suddenly
grown a conscience and backed down. Calvin's disappearance couldn't be coincidence, and neither was the
fact someone had come for her minutes after Beckett
showed up. He'd been followed. And he'd led a killer
straight to her. "The cuffs stay on. You're not getting
away from me again."

She focused on the slight bulge beneath his lower
pant leg. Screw the cuffs. She wasn't going to die out
here. She had too much to lose. Hiking up Beckett's pant
leg, she unholstered the small revolver he kept strapped
to his ankle and fired three shots toward the shooter.

Beckett twisted around. "What the hell are you doing?"

"Giving us a fighting chance." She left the cover of
trees along the trail, positioning herself as a smaller target, and backed farther into the woods. They'd have to
find another way out. Whoever'd shot at them had them
pinned down, and they knew it. If Beckett wanted to
get her into federal custody, he'd have to do things her
way. "I know these woods better than anyone. If you
want to get out of here alive, you'll do exactly as I say.
Unless your oversize ego won't let me save your life."

He stepped out from behind the massive fir he'd
shoved her behind when the bullets had started flying,
gun raised at the entrance to the trail. "I don't trust
criminals."

Air lodged in her lungs. Was that what this was all
about? Why he hadn't come to see her in county lockup.
Why he hadn't returned her dozens of calls once she'd
been arrested. She'd taken a risk revealing the pieces of

her past she'd shared with him, her need to have some-one to rely on when so many others—family, friends—had up and disappeared from her life. She'd trusted him, believed the promise he'd made to stick by her side, no matter what happened. But, in the end, he'd been ex-actly like the rest of them. Unreliable. Self-righteous.

Her heart thundered in her chest as she studied his broad shoulders. She didn't have to see those light eyes to sense the disgust surging through him, and her stom-ach twisted with nausea. He'd spent over a decade chas-ing fugitives for the Marshals Service, experiencing firsthand how evil people could be. She sucked in a shaky breath. Was that how he saw her now? As one of the bad guys?

Four more rounds exploded through the trees and hurled her back into the moment. Raleigh returned fire until the gun clicked empty. She tossed his backup weapon. Wouldn't do them a damn bit of good in these woods. She'd stashed go bags all over this mountain-side, including the one she'd hidden a few yards away. Except there was no extra ammunition for Beckett's revolver. She drowned the hurt that'd been bottling in-side for the hundredth time and pulled him deeper off the trail. "I don't think you have a choice."

Needles and leaves scratched at her skin as they ran into the trees. Another gunshot rang loud in her ears but arced wide. The sun had set behind the mountain. There was no way their attacker could spot them now, but hiking through the woods in the middle of the night brought on its own set of problems. She had to get to the first supply bag she'd buried before the shooter caught up with them.

No pressure.

Beckett's strong grip wrapped around her arm and pulled her into his chest. She planted the sides of her hands above his heart for balance, and heat surged into her neck and face at the contact. Hard muscle shifted beneath her fingers, his breath light on her skin, and suddenly the weeks—months—since she'd last touched him disappeared. "You're not going anywhere."

"I'm sorry—I thought we were concerned about the gunman shooting at us." Only the outline of his shadow and the feel of his heartbeat beneath her palm registered in the darkness. Too close. Too real. Too painful. The small life growing inside her fluttered, and it took every ounce of strength she had not to smooth her palm over her stomach in assurance. Raleigh pressed away and wrenched out of his grip. "We need to keep moving."

A small click preceded the beam of a flashlight from behind, but she kept pushing one foot in front of the other. He'd come prepared with a flashlight. Always the Boy Scout. "Whatever you're planning, it won't work."

She slowed, the weight of his attention, even in the dark, a physical pressure along her spine. Insects quieted, a light breeze rustling the dead foliage at her feet. Temperatures had already started to drop, but the emotional pain she'd ignored earlier bubbled to the surface. "All I'm planning to do, Beckett, is survive." She faced him, raising her hands against the brightness of the flashlight. "Because in case you've forgotten, the only person I told about the missing donation funds is presumably dead, and someone just tried to shoot us."

"I'm supposed to believe those two situations are linked? Hell, for all I know, that could've been an accomplice getting even when you took off with the money." He lowered the flashlight to his side, his weapon still unholstered. Would he shoot her? After everything they'd been through, had her arrest really brought her so low in his eyes? "You're one of the most intelligent women I've come across, Raleigh. You could've set up this entire charade to insert yourself back in my life, planning to get a US marshal on your side of things, but it won't work. You and I are done. Pretending you're in danger isn't going to change that."

Guess that answered her question. He'd made up his mind about their future the moment Portland Police Bureau had put the cuffs on her, and there was nothing she could do to change it. Fine. Raleigh swallowed the rejection charging up her throat and leveled her chin with the ground. He wanted the truth? She'd give him more truth than he could handle. "I'm pregnant, Beckett. With your baby."

"What?" The flashlight beam shook in his hand, his voice barely audible over the breeze sweeping through the woods.

"You can accuse me of whatever you want. Embezzlement, orchestrating Calvin's death, planning some elaborate scenario in which I play the damsel in distress to get your protection. I don't care." Lie. What they'd had… It wasn't supposed to be like this. Raleigh rolled her shoulders back, then closed in on him, the fury tearing through her uncontrollable. "The only thing that matters to me is clearing my name so I can give this baby the life they deserve."

He didn't answer. Didn't even move.

She turned her back on him, forcing herself deeper into the forest. "And I'm not going to let you stop me."

Chapter Two

Impossible. It was another manipulation, a poison meant to get into his head and force him to reconsider his assignment. He'd learned fairly young to spot a con a mile off, thanks to his father. Raleigh's attempt to get him to sympathize wouldn't play out like she wanted. They'd been intimate, sure, but they'd been careful—each and every time. "I think you'll say just about anything to keep from paying for what you've done, to not answer for how many people you hurt."

Her retreat slowed up ahead, until she stopped cold. She lowered the back of her head onto her shoulders. Almost in defeat, but Beckett knew better. He knew her, and there wasn't a single bone in this woman's all-too-familiar body that would accept failure. She'd helped build an entire foundation from the ground up dedicated to lowering pregnancy mortality rates throughout the world. She was driven, ambitious and had her eyes on only one goal the entire time they'd been together: to succeed.

She faced him, that mesmerizing gaze meeting his in the dim beam from his flashlight, and right then, he could only kick himself for underestimating her in the first place. He should've known better than to fall for the victim play all those months ago, but if there was one thing he hated more than the criminals who thought they were above the law, it was finding out about the people they hurt along the way. He wouldn't let her or any one of them get away with breaking the law. No matter how much the hollowness in his chest wanted her claims to be true, wanted what they'd had to be true, she wasn't who he'd believed. Raleigh took a step toward him, then another.

He'd cuffed her wrists in front of her, but that didn't detract from the gut-wrenching sway of her hips as she closed the distance between them. Mere inches separated them when she stopped, every cell in his body in tune to her slightest movement, the smallest change in her expression. Just as he'd always been. "Left back pocket."

"Your confession in there? Because that's the only thing I'm interested in." Annoyance deepened the distinct lines between her brows, and he couldn't help but revel in the fact he'd managed to break through that curated exterior.

"Yeah. I carry it around in case you were the one assigned to arrest me and drag me back to the feds." The cuffs rattled as Raleigh rubbed her thumb beneath the metal. Crystallized puffs of air formed in front of that perfect mouth of hers as the temperature dropped, but he wouldn't feel the least bit sorry she hadn't thought to grab a coat when she'd tried to outrun him. She stepped into him. "You want to know what I think?"

Four months should've been enough to shut down the automatic spike in his blood pressure when she got this close, and that reaction left him more unbalanced than he wanted to admit. "Not really."

"I think you're so set on making me the enemy, Beckett, you've blinded yourself to anything that might prove I'm innocent." She maneuvered her wrists to one side and dug deep into the back left pocket of her jeans. Her flannel shirt contoured to the shape of her body in the dim light, and for a second, he could've sworn there was a slight curve around the front of her hips that hadn't been there before. She pulled a piece of folded paper free, setting it against his chest with both hands before shoving away from him. "Is that the kind of marshal you really want to be?"

The accusation hit exactly where she'd intended and threatened to knock him back on his heels. He slid his hand over the thin, glossy paper as she turned away from him and hiked back up the small rise. Deviating course to a large tree off to the right, she collapsed to her knees and used both hands to start digging at the base, but Beckett couldn't move. Couldn't think.

After everything she'd done, she had the guts to question his integrity? He'd spent the past decade chasing down the worst this country had to offer, fugitives exactly like her, in an effort to prove the tree he'd fallen from hadn't corrupted his core. Suspects lied to him on a daily basis, ran to keep him from uncovering their secrets and played mind games any chance they got to convince him he had the wrong guy. He wasn't blind. He saw them for exactly what they were, and no amount of manipulation from Raleigh or anyone else would change his outlook as long as he wore this badge. One way or another, he was bringing her in to answer for her crimes. Just as Beckett's father would answer for his when he caught up with him.

Gravity seemed to increase its effect on his shoulders as he unfolded the black-and-white photo. Air stuck halfway up his throat. He studied the gray blurred shape against the dark background under the flashlight beam, could almost count the individual fingers on one hand of the fetus lying horizontally across the sonogram. No. This wasn't... Couldn't be.

His heart beat hard at the base of his throat as she sauntered back toward him. A dark backpack hung from her grip in his peripheral vision, but he couldn't take his attention off the delicate paper photo in his hand. Raleigh's name, the date and time were stamped in the upper right-hand corner, below that the name of the OB-GYN practice that'd provided the ultrasound. Twenty weeks, a little over five months. She might not have known she was pregnant when she'd been arrested, but now the truth was clearer than ever. Along with the arrow pointing directly at three small white lines between the baby's legs. His gut jerked. "You're having a girl."

"*We're* having a girl." She slid dirt-stained fingers over his wrist.

Heat exploded through him at the contact. His fingers ached to crumple the sonogram in his hand, but he forced himself to breathe evenly, to think this through. She was pregnant, with his child, but that didn't mean a damn in the eyes of the law. His stomach soured. Now they were tied together for life. He held up the sonogram between his index and middle fingers. "What exactly was the plan here? Show me this and I'd suddenly want to use my Marshal status to prove you're not the one who took that money? You keep this on you in case I was the one assigned to your recovery?"

"I don't… What do you mean?" Shock smoothed her expression, her mouth parting. Hell, she was good. Perfect at playing any role she needed to get under his skin. Those compelling green eyes narrowed on him, and somehow a shiver settled under his skin as though she'd physically touched him. Raleigh snatched the sonogram from him, the pack she carried in her other hand dragging her cuffed wrists in front of her. The tendons between her neck and shoulders flexed as she stepped away. "You think me getting pregnant was planned? That I had an ulterior motive to keep you in my life in case I was charged with fraud and embezzlement?"

"It's amazing how far criminals will go out of their way to prove they're innocent," he said.

The sun had already gone down. Cold worked under his clothing, his fingers aching against the metal of his flashlight. They'd have to camp here tonight. No point in getting themselves lost in the middle of the woods when the shooter was still out there. "We'll rest here tonight. Give me your hands."

"I'm not a criminal." Her tone almost sounded as though she'd convinced herself as she offered her wrists.

Instant sensation of familiarity arched through him. Leading her to the nearest tree small enough to get her arms wrapped around, Beckett unpocketed the handcuff key and released one of the cuffs, then wound her arms around the tree. The cuff clicked back into place. "Tell that to your aunt, Raleigh."

Her hold on that legendary control slipped. Her eyes

widened, her sharp inhalation cutting through the silence around them.

"You didn't think I'd find out about that, did you? I have to admit, it took me calling in a lot of favors to have those records unsealed, but in the end—" he turned to collect the pack she'd dug out of the ground, then faced her "—I know exactly who you are, Raleigh Wilde. You're a killer, a thief, and there's nothing you can do or say to convince me you're not exactly like the rest of the fugitives I'm assigned to hunt. Guilty."

"Then I guess there's nothing left for us to talk about, is there?" she asked.

How he'd been so blinded during the time they'd been together he had to attribute to the fact she'd done everything she could to hide her past from him. And she'd done a damn fine job. She'd fooled him and everyone else around her. He should've known the whirlwind romance he'd instantly been sucked into had only been the first step of her plan. Now she'd ensured he wouldn't be able to walk away after turning her over to the feds. Not with her pregnant with his baby.

Unzipping her pack, he emptied its contents onto the ground and riffled through them. A change of clothes, a tarp, flashlight with additional batteries, matches, packages of food and a couple of water bottles. Enough to last them a day, maybe a day and a half if they rationed their supplies. And a Glock 22, most likely from the collection of weapons he'd found in her aunt's cabin. He released the magazine and pocketed it, clearing the chamber before wedging it between his jeans and lower back.

"What's your plan, Marshal?" Shifting, she tried

to put space between her and the tree bark grating against her oversize shirt. In vain. He wasn't giving her a chance to run this time. His head still hurt from the last time she'd caught him by surprise. "Hide out here until the gunman who tried to kill us loses interest, then just walk me through the Marshals' office front doors?"

"If that gets your file off my desk and you serve your time." Beckett collected a few dead twigs and dry grass from another grouping of trees, arranged a circle of rocks around a small cone shape he'd made with the kindling, then used one of the matches from her pack to light the fire. Snow hadn't started falling this late in the year yet, but there was a frosty bite in the air Beckett couldn't chase from his veins. Whether it came from the dropping temperatures or from the woman currently handcuffed to the tree a few feet away, he had no idea. Didn't want to know. "Win-win."

"If you take me back, I'll spend at least the next five years in prison for something I didn't do." Her voice shook. "Is that what you want for your daughter? Our daughter?"

Beckett raised his gaze to hers over the fire he'd lit between them, then stood. No. It wasn't. There were plenty of kids who turned out just fine after learning the people who were supposed to care about them were monsters, but he hadn't been one of them. He'd spent his entire life trying to make up for what his father had done, and there was no way in hell he'd put any kid of his through that same pain. Rounding the perimeter of rocks he'd used to create a barrier around the campfire, he checked the cuffs at her wrists. The sonogram was still clutched in her fist, and his gut clenched. "All right, Raleigh. You say you're innocent? I'll give you one chance to prove it before I drag you back to the feds." He leveled his voice to convince himself he didn't feel anything for her or their situation, anything at all. "But if you're lying to me, I'll make sure you never see that baby again."

RAIN PATTERED LIGHTLY on her shoulder, cut through her hair straight to her scalp. A tremor rocked through her, then another. The fire held on, warming her boots and toes, but even with the exhaustion pulling at her muscles, Raleigh couldn't sleep. Beckett had given his word he'd let her prove she hadn't stolen the funds from Mothers Come First—her foundation—but he'd made promises before.

And broken every single one.

She'd watched countless mothers across the globe receive the help they needed and deserved because of the foundation. Prenatal care, postpartum services, sex education, ambulance services to rural areas. The work she'd dedicated her entire adult life to achieving made a difference. It'd saved lives. If there'd been an organization like hers when she and her brother had been born, maybe their mother would've survived the blood clot that'd killed her two days after childbirth. Maybe their lives would've turned out differently. Maybe her brother would still be alive.

Who would want to destroy that by stealing millions of dollars in donations? Who would try to have her killed to keep her from uncovering the truth? And how could Beckett think she'd had anything to do with it?

Raleigh shifted against the tree he'd cuffed her to, rubbing at the rawness between the metal and skin. She'd gotten into the habit of sliding her hands over her growing belly when she needed assurance, but with the cuffs, she was resigned to studying the man who'd put them on in the first place. The man who saw her as nothing more than a fugitive.

Beckett hadn't changed much over the past few months. Thick dark beard around his jaw, matching hair she'd run her fingers through a hundred times. Rain contoured thick cords of muscle along his chest and thighs as his clothing suctioned to his body, and an answering heat to all his contained power ignited deep inside. The lines around the blue eyes she hadn't been able to get out of her head had gotten deeper. There was a hardness in his expression that hadn't been there before, but under all the bitterness and the invisible wall he'd built between them, he was still the same man who'd come to her aid in the middle of that Portland street less than a year ago. Still committed, defensive and cautious as ever.

"Stop staring at me." That all-too-familiar voice warmed areas where dropping temperatures left her defenseless, and her throat dried. Which didn't make sense. He'd hurt her, more than anyone had before, but her heart hadn't gotten the damn idea. She'd trusted him to keep his word, to always be there when she needed him. Then he'd disappeared the moment news of her arrest went public. Beckett Foster didn't deserve anything from her, and she sure as hell wasn't going to give him the satisfaction of coming quietly.

Keeping the brim of his hat low over his eyes, he

shifted against the tree where he'd taken up guard duty, the butt of his weapon visible from here. He intertwined his fingers below his sternum and crossed his boots at the ankles, perfectly at ease out here in the wild. "If you're waiting for me to fall asleep so you can make another run for it, don't bother."

"You're a light sleeper. I remember." He'd taken the supplies from the pack she'd buried in case she'd needed a quick escape and stripped down her weapon. While she had more packs buried out here, he held on to her only weapon. But she wasn't going anywhere. For now. The last of the fire smoked out as the storm thundered overhead. Her clothes had soaked through in a matter of minutes. A shiver chased down her spine, the major muscles in her legs tightening against the cold. They couldn't go back to the cabin. Not with a gunman hunting them through these woods, but there was a chance she'd freeze to death out here before Beckett could turn her over to the feds.

Pressure built behind her breastbone, and she raised her gaze to meet his. Instant awareness charged every nerve she owned, as though she'd laid eyes on him for the first time. His lips parted on a strong exhalation as he sat up and reached for the tarp beside him. In a matter of erratic heartbeats, he stood over her. Water clung to the sharp angles of his face as he arranged the edges of the tarp overhead so she was protected from the downpour. "You should've brought a coat. Won't do either of us any good if you drop into hypothermia."

"I was more concerned about outrunning you than fashion at the time." She licked the water from her mouth, and his gaze homed in on the action, sending a rush of lightness straight through her. The lack of rain sliding down her scalp and into her collar was already helping her warm up, but her hands still shook. The cuffs rattled around the tree, her jaw aching against the chattering of her teeth. She couldn't feel her fingers, and her toes had started going numb without the warmth of the fire.

He maneuvered under the tarp, taking the handcuff keys from his back pocket in the same move. Strong fingers slid around her arm as Beckett twisted the key and pried the cuffs from around her wrists.

She pulled both hands in to her chest. Red-and-pink scratches puckered down the length of the thin skin of her forearms from the tree bark, but while the physical pain hurt, the bruising in her heart ached more. Crossing her arms over her midsection, she leaned into the tops of her thighs. "Thanks."

"It's one thing not to trust you—it's another to watch you freeze to death on my watch." He sat beside her, muscled arms brushing against her side.

Right. Because this was just another fugitive-recovery assignment for him. When—if—they were able to prove she'd been framed for taking all that money, he still had to bring her in for skipping out on her trial. Best-case scenario, the truth would come out, the charges would be dropped and they'd each move on with their lives. That was the job, and the knot in her stomach constricted as loss tore through her.

The neutrality smoothing his expression didn't show any evidence of the thoughts running through his head. He'd cut her off from the man she'd known, cut her out of his life faster than most people took to rip off a Band-

Aid, and there wasn't a single moment out here on the run when she'd forgotten that choice. She'd known the risk of letting someone close again, known the people she'd cared for the most would have the power to cause the most damage, but she'd been willing to take that risk. For him. Raleigh hugged her knees, the waistband of her jeans fitting tighter than a few weeks ago. Only now she wasn't the only one who'd end up paying the price. "Beckett, I know this situation isn't ideal—"

"Let's get one thing straight. I'm giving you one chance to prove your innocence solely because you claim that baby you've got in there is mine. Anything else is off the table, understand?" He dug his heels into the mud, rain echoing off the tarp overhead, and she bit back the apology at the tip of her tongue. He kept his gaze ahead, on some distant point instead of her, and she nodded. She understood. He was doing this for their unborn child, not her, and if he could have it his way, he would've chosen someone—anyone—else to take on that calling. "You're the CFO of the foundation. There can't be that many people aside from you with access to the donations account. If you're not the one who embezzled it, as you say, then tell me who else could get their hands on that money without raising any red flags."

Raleigh forced herself to take a deep breath as the sickening twist in her stomach intensified. She'd helped found Mothers Come First, had vetted nearly every employee herself. Even after all these months, it was still hard to imagine any of them had stolen from the charity, but she'd mapped out her own suspect list soon after escaping federal custody. "The foundation employs thirteen accountants in Finance and Fund Services. There's Calvin Dailey, the CEO, but…" Bile worked up her throat. But according to Beckett, her founding partner had been killed in his own home. She felt light-headed as reality hit. Calvin would've been the only one who could've cleared her name. She cleared her throat, focusing her attention on the scratches carved into her forearms from the tree bark. Her shirt should've been enough to protect her from the bark while she'd been cuffed, but it'd ridden up when she'd tried picking the lock. At the time, the pain had been worth it. Now, not so much. "Then we have two fund services accountants who oversee the daily donations coming in and the money going out. Plus, my assistant, Emily."

"Then we'll start there." His gaze dipped to her arms, the weight of those hypnotic blue eyes hiking her heart rate into overdrive. Before she had a chance to take her next breath, he reached for her. Rough calluses caught against her skin as he unfolded her arms away from her midsection and smoothed his thumb across the small, angry lacerations. "We're going to have to clean those before they get infected."

"I'm fine." She tugged at her wrist as the hollowness in her chest flared, but he only tightened his hold on her. Blood rushed to the oversensitized skin along her arms.

"I'm not going to risk you getting sick on my watch." Keeping her arm in his grip, he dug into her go bag with his free hand and pulled the small first-aid kit from the depths. In seconds, the antiseptic burn spread across her skin as Beckett brushed the alcohol pad down along the tendons of her forearms and left a relieving coolness in its wake. Dirt lined the edges of his fingernails, that signature scent of wood and earth filling her senses, and a glimpse of the man she'd fallen for all those months ago surfaced. The one who'd put himself at risk to fight off a mugger on her behalf, however unnecessary it'd been at the time. Who'd ensured she'd gotten home safely and bandaged the wound in her palm when she'd cut her hand on the sidewalk after the attack. Her nerve endings buzzed with familiarity as Beckett moved on to the next arm and cleaned the rest of the scratches. "There. Less likely you'll die of infection before your next court date."

The physical pain along her forearms ebbed as he secured gauze and tape over the wounds, but there was an invisible sting in her chest. She'd been fine on her own, taken care of herself for as long as she remembered. Losing her mother right after childbirth, never knowing her father. Then having her brother taken from her right in front of her eyes when she'd been fifteen. Losing Beckett had just been another in the long line of people she couldn't count on sticking around. She'd never known how strong she was until being strong was the only choice she'd had, but right now, a nervous tremor shook through her. "Thank you."

"Get some sleep." His voice deepened as though he'd been affected by his action as much as she had, and that, combined with his proximity, hooked into her senses. "Your one chance to prove your innocence starts at dawn."

Chapter Three

He could still feel her, feel the softness of her skin against the calluses on his fingers. What the hell had he been thinking, playing nurse like that? As far as he was concerned, Raleigh Wilde was exactly what the prosecuting attorney believed, the very thing he'd battled to stop his entire career. A fugitive. Here he was, cleaning her wounds like what she'd done didn't matter.

Her head rested against his arm, the slow rise and fall of her chest telling him she'd finally fallen asleep, but he couldn't move. He could hardly breathe, and he definitely couldn't think. Long, damp hair plastered to the angles of her familiar jawline, and his fingers tingled to sweep it back behind her ear. Rain lightened against the tarp above them. That, along with their combined body heat, had chased back the numbness in his fingers and toes, but it'd take a lot more than her word to break through the caution he'd relied on to keep himself alive. Beckett curled his hands into fists. One minute, she'd been everything to him, and in cuffs the next.

Now a shooter had tried to kill her, one he highly doubted she'd hired herself. Hell, he could admit it'd been one of his weakest moments considering the idea, because despite the proof stacked against her, Raleigh had gotten one thing right. He hadn't been willing to see evidence she might be innocent. Not after she'd run from him.

The past rushed to meet the present, and Beckett squeezed his eyes shut. His mother's scream echoed in his head. Over and over. There'd been a gun, blood. Fear. He hadn't been able to stop any of it. His father had stolen millions of dollars from hardworking Americans, and one of those Americans had broken into their family home to make him pay. Only the gunman hadn't found his father that night. The bastard had taken off a few months before. No warning. No note. Just up and left Beckett and his mother to fend for themselves on the ranch passed down from his maternal grandparents. Instead of finding revenge, with a single pull of a trigger, the man who'd lost everything to Hank Foster had taken away the only parent Beckett had left when he'd been sixteen. It'd all been his father's fault.

"Hey." That sweet voice, the one that'd haunted him the last four months, broke through his defenses as her hand slid across his chest. Stinging heat exploded through his system as his heart rate tried to keep up with his shallow breathing. Raleigh rubbed soothing circles over the left side of his chest, her voice soft as reality bled into focus. "Are you okay?"

Red and oranges crept across the sky and damp earth of the clearing they'd camped in for the night. Damn it, he must've fallen asleep. Beckett scrubbed his face and beard with one hand, his defenses growing stronger second by slow, agonizing second. "I'm fine."

"You still have nightmares." Not a question, but he

couldn't help but tense all the same. There'd been times when he'd woken in a cold sweat from the memories of that night, but having her pressed against him, her rubbing his back in soothing circles the same way she was doing now, had made the transition back to sleep easier. He'd spent years training to become a lawman, ready to balance out the hurt and pain Hank Foster had caused by bringing criminals like his father to justice, but in those moments with her, Beckett had felt safe. Supported. Something he hadn't felt in a long time.

"It's nothing." He brushed her hand from his chest and shoved to his feet. He ripped the tarp out of his way. The smell of cleansing rain, earth and wet wood penetrated his senses, but none of it was strong enough to dislodge her vanilla scent from his lungs. Beckett forced himself to clear his head, to focus. She had a federal warrant out for her arrest and a gunman on her trail. They'd wasted enough time. Because the sooner he proved Raleigh was exactly what he thought her to be, the sooner he could move on with his life—for good. "We need to keep moving."

"You've been having them for years, and that's all you say when I ask. That it's nothing." She got to her feet, those all-too-familiar green eyes searching his expression, but she wouldn't get anything. Not from him. Had they stayed together, there might've been a point where he'd trusted her with the truth, but that day was long past. She'd made sure of that. "I was there, Beckett. In the middle of the night, when you were screaming and shaking. I was the one who helped you get back to sleep, who reminded you that you were safe."

This conversation wasn't happening. "I never asked you to do that."

"You didn't have to," she said. "That's what couples are supposed to do—"

"You're not my therapist, and we're not a couple." He closed the short space between them, internal fire neutralizing the low temperatures. The closer he inched, the more her personal gravitational pull on him intensified, to the point he knew if he wasn't careful, he might never back off. "You can cut the manipulative interest in my mental health. I'm here for one thing—to give that baby of yours a fighting chance." He pointed to her stomach. "If that means proving you're guilty, so be it. At least she'll grow up not knowing what kind of monster her mother really is."

"*Our* baby." Her gaze held his as she smoothed her hands over where her baby belly had started to appear. Raleigh stepped into him, pulling back her shoulders as though she were preparing for war. Hell, in a way, loving her had been war. They'd both brought out a competitiveness in each other and dedicated themselves to their work over their relationship. They might've been living together, but Raleigh had been dedicated to the foundation at the time, and he'd been on the road most days chasing bad guys. When it'd ended, neither of them had recognized the other anymore. It'd just taken seeing her arrest on the news that he'd realized how lonely they'd truly been together. How desperate for contact she'd made him. "You keep saying my baby, but she's ours, Beckett, and it took two of us to make her. That means you have as much responsibility here to protect her as I do, and that's what I'm trying to do. Protect her. With or without your help."

He froze, narrowing his gaze on her. "What's that supposed to mean?"

"I could've run, Beckett. Even with the cuffs on. I've got bags buried all over these woods that would get me out of Oregon." Her voice faltered. "You were asleep, and it would've been easy to run, but I didn't."

"Why not?" Criminals like her—like his father—did anything to keep from answering for what they'd done. Wasn't that why she'd escaped federal custody in the first place? Why he hadn't heard from Hank Foster in over twenty years? Hell, he didn't even know if the old man was still alive. Didn't care. Raleigh was right. She could've run, but here she stood, going toe-to-toe with the man tasked to bring her in. "You had the chance. Why didn't you take it?"

Raleigh swept her tongue across her bottom lip as the last few drops of rain fell from her chin. "I don't want my daughter growing up without her parents. I don't want her to have the same kind of life I did. I didn't want her not knowing the people who are supposed to love her more than anything in this world or being passed around by anyone willing to take her on the off chance they might get a paycheck for their trouble. Do you have any idea what that's like, Beckett? To feel unwanted like that, to feel so worthless not even your own family wants to take you in?"

He'd known about her parents. Her mother had died a few days after giving birth to Raleigh and her twin brother, and no one in the state of Oregon seemed to know who had donated his fatherly genes to their creation. Their birth certificates had been left blank at the hospital, but Beckett hadn't known about the rest. The apparent hurt deepening the color of her eyes, so contrary to the fiery woman who'd pointed that shotgun at his chest back in her aunt's cabin, ripped at the edges of the hole she'd left behind in her wake. "Raleigh, I…"

He'd wanted her. More than anything—or anyone— else he could remember since he'd lost his mother. Hadn't she realized that? How desperate he'd been to keep her for himself? Constantly checking in with her while he'd been on the road, celebrating one-month, three-month and then six-month anniversaries. He'd been a regular romantic, and the drafted letter of resignation he'd stashed in his inner coat pocket revealed exactly how far he'd committed to go down with the ship. Just for a chance of hanging on to her a bit longer.

Beckett took a step back, his heel sinking in the mud, but no amount of distance from her could hide the truth. For as much as he'd blamed her for what'd happened between them, he'd never told her how much she'd meant to him, how afraid he'd been of losing her.

He'd lost everyone he'd cared about and been left to fend for himself from the time he'd been sixteen. He'd worked the ranch as best he could on his own for two years, graduated high school at the top of his class and started taking criminal justice courses before applying to the Marshals Service. No one had helped or been there for him after the shooting. Until Raleigh. She'd blazed into his life and set up residence beneath his skin. She'd shouldered the responsibility to take care of him when the nightmares came for him and never demanded answers. She'd been fearless, driven and everything he'd needed to leave the past behind. She'd been a constant he was willing to defend, and while she'd ripped his heart practically out of his chest when she'd been arrested, the tiny life they'd created together deserved what he'd lost, what they'd both lost: a family.

"I'm innocent, Beckett," she said. "But all I need from you is to believe me."

Believe her. As if that would change anything.

"You've made your point. Neither of us wants this baby born behind bars." Damn it. He was about to do something stupid. Beckett scrubbed one hand down his face as his entire career flashed before his eyes. Guess that was to be expected when the life you'd built died right in front of you, but sometimes you had to take the law into your own hands. Only problem was, he'd gotten a good look at the prosecution's case. The state had done a hell of a job showing no one else at the foundation could've taken that money. All they needed to close this investigation was the woman they'd pressed charges against on the other side of the courtroom. Whatever evidence Raleigh believed was out there that would prove her innocence had been buried deep enough the FBI hadn't gotten their hands on it. That was what they had to find. Fast. The US Marshals' office—more specifically, his chief deputy, Remington "Remi" Barton—wouldn't sign off on investigating a case he wasn't assigned, especially at the insistence of a suspect. Which meant he and Raleigh had two days, maybe less, before his team caught up. He wrapped one hand around her bandaged arm and removed the cuffs from her wrists with the other. "I'm going to regret this."

THE EVIDENCE BROUGHT up against her was irrefutable.

Forged transfer documents, offshore accounts with her name listed as the owner, dates that coincided with her travel plans to meet with other nonprofit organizations across the country. It all pointed to her. Whoever had embezzled all that money knew exactly how to make the foundation—make her—hurt. This had been her life's work, the reason she'd put herself through business school and dedicated herself to changing the course of mortality rates for mothers across the globe. Only now it was all at risk. Everything she'd worked for would be destroyed if they couldn't clear her name, leaving nothing but death and loss in its wake if the foundation went under.

"Just a bit farther." Beckett took position up ahead, leading them west through the trees. "You got any more of your go bags around here? We're running low on water."

"No. I buried most of them north of the cabin. That was the route I was going to take if the Marshals ever caught up with me." She framed her near-invisible baby bump with her hands as they trudged through mud, fallen leaves and the occasional patch of twigs. It was silly. The baby wasn't any bigger than an artichoke right then, but Raleigh found comfort every time her palms pressed against the slightly hardened surface of her stomach. Her boots suctioned at the damper places in the ground, increasing the wear on her muscles when exhaustion had already stripped too much of her energy. Sweat built in her hairline with each step despite the fresh rush of cold in the air. Oregon had always been home, but out here in the middle of nowhere, with no cell coverage, board meetings or the incessant drone of the city, she'd found an invigorating peace she hadn't felt anywhere else. Well, almost anywhere else.

She lifted her attention from where she'd place her next step to the man who'd bandaged her wounds in the middle of a rainstorm while swearing he'd put her behind bars if she so much as thought about running again.

She'd almost forgotten the feel of his gaze on her, the raw intensity with which he handled himself. Then he'd touched her. One touch from him had ignited a sweeping heat deep inside her body she'd been craving since she'd been arrested. He'd cleaned the scratches on her arms with a care and gentleness nobody else had done for her. No matter what happened between them after the investigation was over, she wouldn't forget that. He'd always been cautious, defensive, suspicious even, but not with her. All that power, as though he intended to set anyone and anything on fire if it got in the way of justice, built under his cool exterior until it became too much to handle, but he never let it touch her. That was what made him a US marshal. Not the lifetime worth of education and training he'd gone through but the commitment to do the job in the first place, a deep-seated root of dedication he'd accrued long before he'd swept into her life.

"I need to take a break," she said.

Beckett settled those brilliant blue eyes on her, and her nerves hiked into awareness. The past twelve hours had shown her exactly how much had changed since she saw two blue lines on that drugstore pregnancy test, as well as the five that followed, and he slowed his pace. "We've got to keep moving."

"No, I get it. We're vulnerable out here in the open. There's just one problem with that." She bent at the knees and nearly doubled over as fiery bile worked up her throat. Forcing herself to take deep breaths, she closed her eyes as the leaves under her boots started to sway. And not from the wind. "I have to eat every couple of hours, or your daughter takes it out on me."

"Damn it." Calluses caught on the fabric of her shirt as he coursed one palm over her spine, and in an instant, the nausea's controlling grip eased. "I don't know how all this…you being pregnant works yet. I think we have some granola left. Let me find it."

"If it makes you feel any better, neither do I. This is all new for me, too. Every day is a new surprise." Raleigh reached for the boulder a few feet away and slid down onto it. The coolness bleeding through her jeans helped chase back the knot in her stomach, but it didn't compare to the savagery Beckett used emptying their pack in order to find her something to eat. In less than thirty seconds, he straightened, the thick muscles in his thighs flexing. She took the water and granola bar he offered, careful not to let her fingers come into contact with his as another wave of heat exploded through her insides. He'd made it perfectly clear things had ended between them when he'd refused to return her dozens of calls and messages after the arrest. She wasn't supposed to be noticing the way his veins fought to escape the skin along the backs of his hands as he pinched the top of his hat between his fingers and swept his hair back away from his face. Or was this sudden rush of awareness due to the pregnancy hormones? Didn't matter. Beckett Foster had made his choice, and it hadn't been her.

"Thanks." Draining the bottle, she tore into the granola, speaking around the food in her mouth. "You should drink up, too. It might be the middle of fall, but you're still sweating."

Dehydration would slow them down faster than her swollen, achy body would, but she wasn't about to admit that out loud. Definitely not to him.

"That was the last of it." He stared out into the trees, never making eye contact with her. Replacing his hat on his head, he shouldered their pack, as though the fact he'd given up the last of his water—their water—for her in a moment of exhausted weakness wasn't a big deal. "Unless we come across another of your buried packs, that's all we have until we reach the ranch."

"You didn't have to do that." She chewed the last of the granola bar, the oats and Craisins sticking along her throat. She wiped her mouth with the back of her hand and pushed upright. There were only a handful of properties out here on the other side of East Lake, most of which were owned by horse trainers or wheat farmers. Someone had already gotten to her cofounder, and a gunman had tried to kill her and Beckett less than twelve hours ago. They couldn't involve anyone else. Not without putting innocent lives in danger. "What ranch?"

"USMS manages half a dozen seized properties up and down these parts. The one we're closest to was seized from a drug dealer after we connected him to one of the southern cartels for pushing their product into Eugene." He waved his finger to the right. Beckett slowed his escape along the trail, his jacket shifting over powerful shoulders. Unpocketing his phone, he shook his head. "Don't expect anything fancy. We'll be lucky if there's still running water, but we'll at least have a roof over our heads and be in cell range so I can make contact with the rest of my team."

His team? Raleigh spread one hand under her abdominals as a shiver chased down her spine. She forced one foot in front of the other, fighting to keep up with his long strides, but the fear of going back...of being found before they had a chance to clear her name...tunneled deep. She stopped in her tracks. The confidence that'd waned since she'd realized she'd put him on the wrong end of her shotgun charged forward. She'd been living off the grid for months, and she hadn't made any mistakes. Not on her end. There was only one way that gunman would've been able to find her, and it wasn't a coincidence he'd shown up minutes after Beckett had located her. "You can't do that. You can't involve the Marshals' office."

An inner earthquake shook through her as he narrowed that steely gaze on her. He slowly turned to face her, and suddenly he seemed so much...bigger than he had when he'd offered her the last of his water. Suspicious. "I'm a United States marshal, and you're a fugitive. If my boss finds out I'm interfering with this case, I'll be charged with aiding and abetting a known criminal, and your baby won't just lose one parent. She'll lose us both. Is that what you want?"

"It was you," she said.

"What are you talking about?" Confusion cleared

some of the tension from his expression, but he was still too close.

"I've been out here for four months. I've been off the grid, running my own investigation into who could've stolen that money while making sure none of what I uncovered connected back to me." She fought the urge to increase the space between them as a hint of rain and pine from his clothing filled her lungs. "Whoever shot at us… They shouldn't have been able to find me, Beckett."

"Then maybe you're not as good as you think you are." He swept his coat to either side of his hips, hands leveraged against the lean muscle she'd memorized under those clothes. "Maybe you made a mistake. Your name is on that sonogram you showed me. There's a chance someone in the doctor's office recognized your photo from the most wanted list and called it in."

It was a possibility, but the chances were slim. She'd been careful, met with the doctor after hours for a hefty price, altered her appearance for the nurses. Because it wasn't just her life at stake anymore. She had a daughter to think about now, and she would do whatever it took to make sure she got out of this unharmed. Raleigh raised her gaze to his, the knot in her stomach tight. "Or maybe someone knew about our past connection. Maybe whoever stole that money used you to make sure I'd never walk out of these woods alive."

Chapter Four

"Let me get this straight." The muscles down his spine seized up. He rolled his lips between his teeth and bit down, the rustic tang of blood sliding across his tongue. Spreading his hands palms-down in front of him, he studied her for a sign—anything—that could give him an idea of where the hell she was going with this. "Instead of considering you might've made a mistake and given up your location on your own, which, I'll add, wasn't too hard to predict, you're saying I'm responsible for what went down at your aunt's cabin."

"It's not hard to believe whoever framed me knew about our relationship and used that to their advantage, knew you'd follow those unwavering Boy Scout morals of yours to bring me in." She slid her hand along her lower abdominals, a nervous habit he bet she'd picked up somewhere between finding out she was pregnant and today. "I'd say whoever we're dealing with doesn't just know me. They've done their homework on you, too. They could've easily followed you with the intention of taking us both out to keep me from getting to the truth. They might even have a connection in the

Marshals Service and made sure you were assigned my recovery."

The hairs on the back of his neck stood on end, but Beckett kept his expression smooth as her words registered. Finnick Reed, Jonah Watson and his chief deputy, Remi Barton. They'd all put their lives on the line for him on the job, just as he'd done for them over the past decade they'd been assigned to work together in the Oregon district office. Their team had apprehended a record number of fugitives, dismantled criminal enterprises and aided in more statewide manhunts than any other office on the West Coast. The four of them made up the backbone of the federal government, and he trusted every single one of them with his life. But the fact a shooter had tried to kill him and Raleigh less than fifteen minutes after Beckett had found her grated on his instincts. Damn it. He couldn't discount her theory. Hell, it was the only thing they had to go on right now, and that meant leaving his team out of the investigation. For now. "You obviously have someone in mind. Someone from your list of suspects at the foundation."

She nodded, stringy, damp hair skimming the bullet graze at the side of her neck, and it felt as though blood had pooled in his legs, cementing him in place. Another inch to the left and that bullet would've killed her. He would've lost her, lost their baby. This far out, with the closest hospital more than thirty miles away, he wouldn't have been able to save either of them, and his chest tightened at the imagery. "My assistant, Emily Cline. She's worked for me since the beginning and had access to the donations anytime I had to travel. She would've had the perfect opportunity to transfer those funds when I was guaranteed to be out of the office."

"I remember her from the background checks the feds ran. I assume she arranged all your travel, kept your schedule, had your bank account and Social Security numbers to arrange hotels and car rentals?" A cold bite of wind ripped through the trees, but it was the weary hint of exhaustion playing out across Raleigh's features that held his attention. It took everything inside him to keep himself from chasing back the dark circles under her eyes with the pad of his thumb.

She cast her attention to the gravel under her boots. "Out of all of the suspects I've compiled, Emily is the only one who had the means and opportunity to move that money, aside from Calvin, but I can't see the connection between her and the US Marshals Service. Maybe there isn't one. I don't know."

He hadn't gotten a good enough look at the shooter to rule Emily Cline out as a suspect, but having a name was a start. Looked like their only leads were an assistant who possibly knew too much and a missing CEO, but Beckett couldn't dig any deeper than that without alerting his team to what he and Raleigh were doing out here.

"You obviously trusted her," he said. "Did she give you any reason to think she might be in debt or in trouble? Taking care of a sick relative, or does she have access to a gun?"

"No. Nothing like that. We were…friends." Her voice softened, tugging at some invisible string Beckett had used to sew up the gaping holes she'd left behind when she'd been arrested, but that was as far as he'd let it go. This effect she still had on him, this gravitational pull, was nothing more than his body adjusting to being around her again. Temporary. That was it. As soon as they cleared her name of the embezzlement charges, they could each go their separate ways and work out a custody-and-visitation agreement along the way for their daughter. If they couldn't… Hell, he'd have to cross that bridge when he got to it. Raleigh tucked her hands in her front pockets. "At least, I thought we were friends. Guess it goes to show how little we actually know the people around us, or how blind we can make ourselves when we don't want to see the truth."

Was that supposed to be an underhanded accusation directed at him? Because she was right. They might've been sleeping together for six months, but they'd each kept the darkest part of themselves from the other. They didn't know each other at all. A bird called off to their right, then silence. Warning prickled a trail across his shoulders. He automatically drew her in to his side with one hand as he scanned the trees around them. He couldn't take the risk of another ambush from the shooter. Not with their daughter the perfect target. "Come on. We've been out in the open for too long."

She didn't respond, a first for her, as he led her along the unofficial path carving through the trees. The pines thinned after another twenty minutes of them walking in silence beside each other, giving way to one of the most exquisite sights Oregon had to offer. Jagged obsidian lava rock spread out along each side of the path they'd been following toward the smooth incline of Newberry volcano. Dark clouds cast shadows over the second lake in the area on the other side of the inactive caldera. From this vantage point, he calculated they'd walked approximately four miles around the southern end of East Lake and were nearing the Big Obsidian Flow Trailhead. Miles of green pines smothered the valley floor below, and a lightness he hadn't felt in a long time spread through him.

"My brother and I used to hike out here every weekend when we got the chance. Just the two of us." A wistful smile transformed her features, and for a split second, his heart jerked in his chest at the sight. Her shoulders rose and fell with her heavy breathing, that warm gaze taking it all in. "We'd pack a lunch, bring our swimsuits and make sure the rangers weren't around when we climbed the volcano. I forgot how beautiful this place can be."

"You haven't been back out here?" He wasn't sure why he'd asked, or why he cared much about the answer. The lines between them had been drawn, but every second she'd been near, he could feel that old part of himself—the part that wanted to believe her—rise to the surface.

"Not since he died. I thought about it. I wanted to see if it'd changed any, but…it's not the same without him." Smoothing her hands over her shirt, she shook her head, long tendrils of her hair sticking to the fabric. Raleigh turned toward him, resurrecting the atmospheric hint of rain and her vanilla scent in one move. "Earlier, you said you unsealed my juvenile records, but did you read them?"

"I read enough of the police report to know what happened that day. I was able to piece together the rest." In reality, there hadn't been a whole lot to read. He'd had to track down the autopsy report himself. "Your aunt had taken custody of you both at the insistence of your and your brother's social worker because you kept getting passed from home to home. Reports said you had trouble adjusting. You instigated a handful of fights and were caught stealing from one of your foster parents. Am I right so far?"

The muscles along the column of her throat worked to swallow. "Keep going."

"You, your brother and your aunt were down at the shoreline of the lake. Police found a couple easy chairs, a picnic and an umbrella. The scene looked like it was supposed to be a fun day, but there was a fight. Something your aunt did made you snap." He set his hands on his hips, the bottom of the pack she'd dug up brushing against the space between his index finger and thumb. "You caved her skull in with a rock you found in the water."

She flinched, obviously not ready to hear just how much he'd uncovered about her past, but she couldn't hide from it anymore. Couldn't hide the truth from him. She'd kept her secrets to herself when they'd been together, but Beckett knew her better than anyone else in her life, was the only one who knew exactly what she was capable of. Innocent people didn't run, didn't go into hiding. They didn't hurt the people who cared about them. Directing her attention back out across the valley as the wind rustled in the trees on either side of them, she ran one hand through her hair. "That's all the files say? The police report, the court documents?"

"It's enough, isn't it?" he asked. "Proves you have a history of violence and theft, which, I might add, is what you're up against now, and that you're willing to do whatever it takes to get what you want, even when it hurts the people who care about you."

"You're right. My brother and I were eating lunch together like we always did on the weekends. I wasn't feeling too good that day. I think I was coming down with the flu or something, so he said we should set up down on the beach instead of taking our normal hike, and I agreed. I didn't care where we went. I just wanted to spend time with him. For as long as I remember, we were all we had. Then…" She blinked against the sunlight reflecting off the water of Paulina Lake about a mile northeast of their location. "Then my aunt came charging down to the lake, accusing my brother of getting into her gun safe. I'd never seen her so angry before, and no matter what I said, she didn't believe me."

"Because it was you." Memory of the cabin, of the open armored safe tucked into the room off the main living space, flashed across his mind. Dread curled in his gut. Hell. "You were the one who'd gotten into the safe, weren't you?"

"I'd learned to break into it a few weeks before by listening for the click of the combination cams, and I was so damn proud of myself, I wanted to see if I could do it again." She stared out over the expanse of trees and water. "My brother was everything to me, the only person I'd always been able to count on growing up in all those homes, the only one I had left, and suddenly she was choking the life right out of him in front of my eyes." Nodding, she rolled her lips between her teeth and bit down, as though to keep herself under control, but he could see the pain in her eyes, the crack of emotions bleeding through her expression. Raleigh wiped at her face with one hand. "I tried to pull her off, but she hit me in the face, and I fell back into the water. I wasn't strong enough to pry her loose, so I grabbed a rock I'd landed on, and I swung it as hard as I could." Green eyes focused on him. "But it was too late. She'd already killed him."

He cleared his throat, completely void of a response other than an apology for what she'd been through at such a young age. Guess they both had that in common. Her losing her brother, him losing his mom.

"All those accusations you have of me starting fights and stealing? I was making sure my brother and I stayed together every time we got transferred to a new home. We only had each other, but none of it mattered in the end. I lost him anyway, and now I have no one." Loose gravel slipped down the rocky incline as she stepped into him. "Everything I've done hasn't been to hurt the people I care about, Beckett. It's been to protect them, and I'd do it all over again."

He stared after her as she made her way down the steep hill dropping them onto the main trail carved through the trees, his voice low. "You had me."

THE HUMIDITY OF another imminent downpour stuck to the exposed skin under her collar as they followed the Big Obsidian Flow Trailhead around the southern end of Paulina Lake. This time of year didn't bring a lot of tourists to the area, and she'd never been more grateful for that than now. The idea of pasting another smile on her face, of pretending everything was okay, even for a stranger, intensified the headache at the base of her skull. Sweat built along her hairline and slid down her spine, but she only pushed herself harder.

Those records had been sealed. She'd moved on with the intention of never letting those two adrenaline-charged minutes of her life define her. She'd given everything she'd had left after the incident with her aunt from that time forward to save lives. Not take them, but now Beckett knew the truth. The one person she'd tried to shield from her past knew she was everything he'd accused her of being: a killer. The fist around her heart squeezed tighter. There was nothing she could say, nothing she could do, to redeem herself in his eyes.

"We're here." His words punctured through the sweaty haze that'd taken over for the past hour, and Raleigh pulled up short too fast. Her boots slid along a loose patch of gravel on the incline leading down into a valley nestled between the mountains, and she fell back, arms thrown out for balance. Strong hands caught her under her rib cage. "I've got you."

A warmth that hadn't been there before blossomed inside as she tried to get her bearings. "Thanks."

Setting her upright, Beckett let his hand linger at her waist as she pressed into his chest for balance. Her heart thumped wildly at the base of her throat as his gaze journeyed a trail down along her neck. His outdoors scent dived deep into her lungs, making her lips tingle to close that short distance between them. She could still remember what he tasted like, how safe she'd felt in his arms.

Thunder clapped overhead. A drizzle of rain pelted her face from above, bringing her back into reality. He'd cleaned and bandaged the small scrapes along her forearms from the tree bark and given her the last of their water when she'd gotten light-headed, but none of that healed the invisible wound left behind by his indifference. He was here to bring her back into federal custody, and he'd offered to help because she happened to be carrying his child. Nothing more. Any promises that fell from that mouth, so close to hers, didn't mean anything. She couldn't let them mean anything.

Distancing herself from his comforting weight pressed against her, Raleigh surveyed the seemingly abandoned property fenced out at least a quarter mile back. Two large pines towered over the bright red farmhouse trimmed in white. A few other structures, smaller than the main house, interrupted the smooth expanse of green grass across the flat land. There was a detached garage; maybe even a second, although smaller, house; a large barn and a chicken coop. She followed the outline of white vinyl fencing that disappeared into the tree line off to the right. No visible vehicles. No animals. Nothing within a few miles. She was used to isolation, good at keeping to herself, but if the shooter who'd followed Beckett really did have some kind of connection inside the Marshals Service, there was a chance that isolation could be used against them. "You're sure this place can't be traced back to you?"

"I was one of the marshals who seized the property from the previous owner. That's how I know about this place, but USMS owns the deed. Unless whoever tried to kill us can get into one of the most secure federal databases in the country, there's no way they'd know this place exists." He adjusted his hat, then headed down the smooth slope leading to the main house, lean muscle flexing along the length of his hamstrings. "We'll be safe here while we come up with a plan to get to your assistant. It won't be easy. The FBI will be watching her, waiting to see if you make contact."

She followed close on his heels, hyperaware of every move he made, every scan of the property, every change in his expression. Beckett Foster had one of the highest recovery-and-protection rates his branch of law enforcement had ever seen. If there was a threat, he'd be the first to see it coming. She had to believe that. Had to believe that even though her past had wedged this distance between them, he'd do whatever it took to protect their daughter.

The ground leveled out under her as they approached the farmhouse's front door, and her fingers automatically curled into her palms. Exposed wood pillars added to the country feel lining the wood wraparound porch, large windows peering out over the rest of the property. Glancing in, she searched the first level of the two-story structure but couldn't see anything more than a few pieces of furniture, crisply painted white walls and the floor-to-ceiling windows at the back of the home. No movement inside. Nothing to suggest he was walking her into a federal ambush made up of marshals and FBI agents, but she wouldn't discount the possibility.

Beckett keyed in a code on the electronic keypad where a dead bolt usually fit, and the sound of a lock disengaging reached her ears. He swung the door inward, motioning her inside past him and the raw wood door at his back. The weight of his attention pressurized the air in her lungs as she stepped over the threshold. "You can get settled in the larger of the two bedrooms on the main floor while I check the perimeter. Shouldn't take more than a few minutes."

"Okay." She nodded, not knowing what else to say as she took in the large expanse of the main living space. Dark wood flooring stretched the length of the house all the way back to the windows she'd spotted before, with bright white couches and a modern wood-and-metal coffee table set between them. Blue chairs caught her eye from the dining room table beside two more support columns welcoming guests into the modern kitchen. Hard to believe a drug smuggler had run his business for the cartel through a home this beautiful. It looked too…welcoming. Homey.

Beckett closed the door behind him, leaving her alone for the first time since he'd broken into her aunt's cabin, and an instant hollowness fisted in her gut. Which didn't make any sense. He'd ripped through her life as quickly as a hurricane, leaving her decimated, ruined and empty. The pain—the longing—she'd felt after he'd walked away shouldn't have dug its claws in this deep. She was supposed to be an ocean, able to survive anything, supposed to withstand the strength of the storm, but then she'd heard him yelling in his sleep. And everything inside her had broken. The walls she'd built, the anger she'd held on to… They'd evaporated as fast as clouds shifted in the sky. In that moment, with her hand over his heart soothing small circles into his chest, the past had sped up to meet the present.

Raleigh folded her arms across her midsection.

Modern black-and-white tile adorned the fireplace off to her left. Her fingers and toes tingled with the need for warmth, but that was nothing compared to the heat still burning through her from when Beckett had placed his hands on her hips after she'd slipped. It was one thing to ask for his help, but to hole up under the same roof again while a shooter hunted them down trailed goose bumps across her chest. She trod deeper into the house, passing the kitchen and a small home office until she came to the first bedroom in the long stretch of hallway. She ached at the sight of the bed, but she couldn't let down her guard yet. They were out of food, out of water, and their only lead had already been questioned and investigated by the FBI before Raleigh had been arrested. If her assistant was responsible for framing Raleigh for taking that money, the feds would've uncovered the evidence.

She ran her hands through her snarled hair, the ends frizzing with the added humidity outside. Light gray wallpaper and navy bedcovers urged her to close her eyes. She slipped onto the edge of a pale padded bench at the end of the bed, skimming her palms down her jeans. The same flooring in the main part of the house ran lengthwise through this room, same color of white upholstery giving a serene, peaceful feeling to the entire house.

Peace. When was the last time she'd felt something even remotely close to peace?

She wanted to sink into it. Wanted to believe nothing outside this room existed, that she hadn't been falsely charged with fraud and embezzlement, that there wasn't a killer targeting her. Raleigh studied the streaks of water trailing down the large windows. What would it be like to live here? Raise her daughter here? What would it be like to wake up next to Beckett in this very bed? Raleigh moved to smooth the wrinkles from the deep-colored comforter but hesitated at the sight of the dirt still caking her hands and fingernails. No. This wasn't her bed. This wasn't her house. This wouldn't ever be her life. Not as long as she was a fugitive.

Not as long as Beckett only saw her as a criminal.

"The perimeter's secure." Footsteps echoed down the hallway before mesmerizing blue eyes settled on her, and her heart gave a small jerk in her chest. The traitor. "And we now have running water and power after a small, but very serious, electric shock I wasn't prepared for."

"Beckett, I…" She pushed up off the bed. The life they'd had together, their relationship, had been equally ripped right out from under them, and there was nothing they could do to get it back. Beckett would never let himself see her as anything more than the enemy he'd dedicated his career—his life—to hunting, and she was so tired of watching the people who'd claimed they cared walk away. She'd given everything to hang on to him after her arrest until it'd felt as though her heart had dried up. Too much had changed between them. She'd changed, but neither of them would be able to walk away from this unharmed. For the first time in a long time, she wasn't willing to sacrifice what was left of herself to hold on to that hope she could fix this. Gravity increased its grip on her at the realization, the desertlike cracks left over from heartbreak filling. "I'm sorry. For all of this. You had every right to distance yourself from me after my arrest. You were protecting yourself, and I understand that now. It was wrong of me to put you in that position in the first place, but I need you to believe I wasn't reaching out to you to use your job with the Marshals to my advantage. I just needed… you. You were all I had left."

He lowered his attention to the floor. No response.

"I can't keep running. I'm going to be a mom in a few months, and the only way I can do that job justice is to make this baby girl a priority and to give her a life she deserves. Give her some stability." She smoothed her palms over her still-damp shirt, but reassurance didn't surface this time. "Even if that means her growing up without me."

Beckett shot his head up, locked his gaze on her. "What is that supposed to mean?"

"Whoever framed me for taking that money is powerful, Beckett. They'd covered all their bases and made sure the evidence pointed to me. This doesn't feel like some desperate move to steal millions of dollars of donation money. It's personal. It's outright destruction. They've planned every move from the beginning, and they're obviously willing to kill me in order to make sure everything goes according to that plan. I'm not going to risk this baby's or your life for the smallest chance of proving I'm innocent." The muscles in her jaw ached with the pressure from her back teeth. "I want you to bring me in. You'll have full custody after she's born. Just…promise me to make sure she's loved, and that she knows I did everything I could for her."

"You told me you could prove you're innocent, and now you want me to bring you in." Strong fingers encircled her arm, tugging her into a wall of muscle. She pressed her palms against his chest, his heart thudding hard beneath her hands. "What's changed?"

"Beckett, this is the only way to make sure you and the baby are safe." Raleigh sucked in a deep breath, and her throat dried. "I've lost too many people in my life. I can't handle the thought of losing her. And... I won't lose you."

"No one is taking you from me. Not again." He crushed his mouth to hers.

Chapter Five

She was willing to turn herself in to protect their baby. To protect him.

The guilty ran, but they never surrendered.

Beckett had been fully committed to giving in to the anger and distance that'd been swirling inside him for the past four months, but then she'd up and asked him to bring her in to the feds. To raise their baby on his own. He wasn't sure what'd happened next other than knowing, deep down, he wasn't ready to let her go that easily, and he had pulled her right into him and kissed her.

He opened his mouth wider, took everything she had to give and more. Slipping both arms around Raleigh, he pulled her against him as tight as humanly possible. An explosion of need seared through him as he consumed her. Enough to decimate everything he'd been holding on to since her arrest. The anger, the betrayal, the fear of the past, of realizing the person he'd trusted the most had become nothing more than a common criminal. Reckless, untamed desire for the woman in his arms took control to the point he barely had enough sense to pull away to take a breath.

Damn it. She was everything he remembered, everything he'd wanted, and he wasn't sure it was possible to ever get enough of her. These past few months—the isolation, the loneliness—disappeared in an instant as she penetrated the seam of his mouth with her tongue, and the entire world threatened to drop right out from under him.

She gasped as he trailed his mouth along the tendon at her throat, fingers fisting in his shirt for balance. "Beckett."

His name on her lips only intensified the craze singing through his veins. Lean muscle flexed under his fingers as he maneuvered them back toward the single bed. A feral growl escaped his throat as she threaded her fingers through his hair and redirected his mouth to hers. Capturing his bottom lip between her teeth, she bit down, and electricity lightninged down his spine. No matter how many times he'd tried to move on, to forget her, she was just so damn perfect. Compelling, passionate and wild. Every cell in his body wanted every cell in hers, and he didn't have the strength to pull away.

Her knees hit the edge of the mattress, and the muscles down her spine tensed under his touch. "Beckett, we need to stop. This isn't...this isn't what I want."

He gripped her hips, drawing back. His lungs battled to keep up with his racing heart rate, his entire body lit up from a single brush of her mouth against his. Raw. Unbalanced. Warmth swirled in those green eyes, and his gut clenched with unsatisfied desire. Dimly, he understood this was a bad idea. He was a marshal tasked with bringing her in to answer for not appearing before the judge, and while they were having a baby together, that didn't make his job any less of a reality. She was right. She couldn't keep running, couldn't hide forever. That wasn't the kind of life either of them wanted for this baby. "You're right."

He sucked in a breath between his teeth as she swept her tongue along the edges of her mouth. Why couldn't they go back to before she'd been arrested? To the moment when neither of them had been anything more than two people intent on living out the rest of their lives together. No secrets. No lies. No careers driving them apart. What they'd had together then hadn't been flawless, but it couldn't compare to any other personal encounter he'd experienced. She'd been a bright light in a sea of past darkness. For a while, she'd been his.

"I shouldn't have kissed you. I'm sorry. I…" Missed this connection. Missed her. Running one hand through his hair, Beckett put space between them, their exhalations mingling for a few breaths. No matter how this investigation ended, it'd never be the same as it once was. There was too much history between them, too much doubt.

He'd meant what he had said before. He'd fight like hell to ensure nobody—not even the US Marshals Service—could take her and this baby from him, but his offer of protection couldn't equate to anything more than that. Partnerships thrived on trust, and until they were able to prove she had nothing to do with those stolen donation funds, he couldn't trust her. "It won't happen again."

"I think that's for the best." Nodding, Raleigh swiped the back of her hand against her kiss-stung lips, the slight hint of brown sugar from the granola settling on his tongue. She hiked her thumb toward one of the closed doors attached to the bedroom. "I'm going to shower before we figure out our next move. It's been a rough couple of days, and it's going to take a while to get all this dirt off."

Their next move. Right. Because there was still a gunman out there ready to rip her and their baby out of his life, and they only had one lead when it came to clearing her name of the embezzlement charges.

"Good idea. In the meantime, I'll see if I can find us something to eat." And maybe run off the heat still simmering under his skin to cool down in the rain. What the hell had he been thinking, kissing her like that? He'd set the lines between them, and it'd taken less than twenty-four hours for him to break his own rules. Guess that'd always been the problem when it came to Raleigh. He hadn't been thinking. Not when he'd run to help her during the mugging all those months ago. Not when they'd fallen into bed together that same night, and not when he'd almost handed in his resignation from the Marshals after her arrest. Beckett headed toward the hallway and started to close the bedroom door behind him. Distance. He needed to clear his head, and he sure as hell wasn't going to get the chance sticking around here.

"Beckett, wait." Her voice slipped through the crack in the door, and the hairs on the back of his neck stood on end.

He slowed. Long, dirt-stained fingers wrapped around the edge of the door to pry it wider. Perfectly shaped brows smudged with dirt, a shallow laceration across one sharp cheekbone, light pink lips with a bit of beard burn on one corner. None of it took away from the flawless beauty and strength underneath as she leveled those mesmerizing green eyes on him. She toyed with the bandages he'd secured along her forearms.

"You saved my life, even though I'm sure it was the last thing on your mind," she said. "If you hadn't been there when that gunman tried to shoot me, I'm not sure I'd be standing here, and I wanted to thank you. For protecting us."

Hell, no matter how many times he'd convinced himself he had her pegged, she'd deliver a devastating uppercut and sucker punch him with the unexpected. Raleigh wasn't innocent, not in the least, but she sure wasn't acting like a criminal either, and he had no idea what to do with that information. "Part of the job."

"Is that all this is to you? What this baby and me are? A job?" A wave of vulnerability cracked through her carefully controlled expression as though he'd somehow gotten beneath her skin, but Beckett had been played before. Every change in body language, every look, every sweep of her hands over her stomach was meant to manipulate and confuse him. This intelligent, ambitious, beautiful woman only wanted one thing: to survive. He knew better than to believe any of what she'd told him had been used for anything other than getting her way. She only let him see what she wanted him to see, same game as his old man played until the day Hank got up and left Beckett and his mother behind, and he wasn't going to let himself fall prey again.

"I'll be back to check on you in twenty," he said. "There're alarm sensors on all the windows, so I'd stay away from them if I were you. Can't be too careful."

The fine lines between her brows smoothed. "Thanks for the advice, Marshal."

She pushed the door closed, the lock engaging loud in his ears. The sound of water hitting tile registered through the thin wood a few seconds later. He gripped his hand around the doorknob to keep himself from barging back in that room and telling her the truth. He had to focus. They had one chance to get to Emily Cline, Raleigh's assistant, without alerting the feds or the Marshals Service he'd found his fugitive, and he wasn't going to waste it.

A loud trill cut through the tension-charged haze in his head, and Beckett reached for the phone in his back pocket. Saved by the bell. He swiped the green button to answer the call as his boss's name registered and brought the phone to his ear. "Remington, what can I do for you?"

"Deputy Foster." Disappointment slid into the chief deputy's voice and pooled dread at the base of his spine. So much for holding off his team. "I'm surprised you answered the phone. Seems like you've hit a snag in your recovery assignment of Raleigh Wilde."

Beckett leaned one shoulder into the wall beside him, folding one arm across his chest. The butt of his weapon scraped along his forearm. "Why on earth would you think that?"

"I'm going to let you figure that one out on your own." Finnick Reed and Jonah Watson, damn fine marshals he'd worked countless cases with, and they'd just been sent in to take over his. Damn it. "I've got an unregistered vehicle that once belonged to Ms. Wilde's deceased aunt parked next to your SUV at a cabin out at East Lake, bullet casings near the tree line, two sets of footprints heading into the woods, and another leading to a set of tire tracks we haven't been able to identify."

His back teeth ached from the pressure in his jaw, and Beckett straightened. Of all the successful fugitive recoveries he'd worked over the past decade, she'd brought in two other marshals? "You sent them to check up on me."

"Wouldn't you in my position?" Remi asked. "I gave you this assignment because you told me you could handle it, but from the crime-scene photos I'm looking at, that doesn't seem to be the case at all. Tell me I'm wrong, Beckett. Tell me you're not on the run with a known fugitive in some last-ditch effort to fix what went wrong between the two of you, and I'll reassign Watson and Reed another case."

Beckett turned toward Raleigh's door, her earlier question still echoing through his head. Was this just a case to him? Or more? Remington Barton hadn't gotten to her position as chief deputy of the USMS Oregon district office by avoiding the tough conversations or backing down from the challenges she'd faced as a female in their chosen profession. She was confident, persuasive and one of the best marshals he'd ever had the pleasure of working beside. She wasn't going to let this go. He tightened his grip around the phone. The second he revealed Raleigh was pregnant with his kid, Remi would order him out of the field and pull in another marshal for the recovery.

No. This wasn't just another case to him. Never had been. Not when it came to the woman on the other side of that door. He'd given Raleigh his word to see this through, to protect her and the baby, and that was exactly what he was going to do. But, more than that, that familiar scent of hers woven into his clothes, the feel of her soothing circles on his chest after he'd woken up from another fresh nightmare… She helped settle the agitation and restlessness permanently etched into his bones, and for the first time in longer than he wanted to admit, he felt like he could finally breathe. Who else had been able to do that for him but her?

"Beckett?" Remi asked. "Tell me I'm wrong."

Beckett slid his shoulder up the wall and straightened. "You're wrong."

He ended the call.

Searing heat trailed along her skin and cleared the dirt and leaves from her scalp, but no amount of hot water could make her forget that kiss. She…hadn't expected that. And she hadn't stopped it either. She and Beckett had been together for six months before her arrest, but that kiss had taken her by surprise. Electrically charged, heated, almost starved. She could still feel the bruising indentations of his fingers in her lower back as he'd fought to bring her closer. Almost like he'd been missing a puzzle piece and wanted her to fill the empty space. The difference between the man she'd been with before her arrest and the one who'd kissed her as though he hadn't been able to breathe unless connected to her mouth still rocked through her. Raleigh brushed the pads of her fingers across her lips, flinching at the immediate sting at one side. *No one is taking you from me.*

Taking her from him? Or taking the baby?

She stepped from the shower, air from the vent above fighting to cool the frantic rush of desire still heating her from head to toe—in vain. Drying off with one of the towels hanging nearby, she wrapped herself in a robe dangling on the back of the bathroom door. The same tile that'd lined the fireplace in the main living room added to the modern farmhouse feel of the bathroom. Her reflection skewed in gold light fixtures and plumbing as she ran her fingers through her freshly washed hair.

Didn't matter what he'd meant before, or why he'd kissed her. No matter how much she wanted his presence and intentions to be for her, he'd made it clear that wasn't the case. He was here to do a job, and she couldn't let their past—however short it'd been—cloud her judgment now. She'd worked too hard to distance herself from falling back into old patterns, especially when it came to relying on others. She'd fight to clear her name of the fraud and embezzlement charges, with or without his help, move on with her life, and give this baby the life and love she deserved. She'd gotten by this far on her own. She'd learned to be strong, resilient, driven. Having Beckett here didn't change that.

Raleigh stepped into the large walk-in closet attached to the bathroom, running her fingers through the clothes that'd been left behind by who she assumed were the previous owners of the house before the marshals had seized the property. Dark suit jackets, white shirts and an array of colorful ties hung on one side, the other filled with silk scarves, brand labels, heels and lingerie. Checking back over her shoulder, she skimmed her fingers across the soft fabrics and lace. Her arrest had forced her to leave her possessions behind, including all of her clothing, just as this couple had been forced.

She'd worn the dirt-caked jeans, flannel shirt and cotton underwear from her aunt's cabin in desperation. She'd discarded them on the unique tile a few feet away, but she couldn't stand the thought of putting them back on. Not after reliving the gut-wrenching memory of her brother's last moments.

She wasn't desperate anymore. She didn't have to rely on the pain, anger and resources from the past to carry her through the present. Because she wasn't alone this time. Her heart jerked in her chest as footsteps echoed down the hallway toward the bedroom door.

Three quick knocks accompanied that deep, all-too-familiar voice. "Raleigh, you okay?"

She pulled back her shoulders to counteract the instant warmth pooling at the base of her spine. She wasn't physically alone anymore, but emotionally? She couldn't depend on anyone but herself. "I'll be out in a minute."

"Okay," Beckett said. "I found us something to eat when you're ready."

His boots echoed off the dark hardwood flooring installed throughout the house at his retreat, but the flood of heat refused to drain from her system. He'd always had that effect on her. One word, one touch, and an internal explosion destroyed her all over again without warning. But she'd meant what she'd said. She appreciated his help, but she couldn't afford the distraction getting involved with him offered. Not with their baby's life at stake.

Checking the label of the chunky dark green cable sweater in front of her, she tugged it from its position on top of a row of shelving. The sweater cost more than three months' salary at the foundation, but it fit, and she wasn't about to turn down clean clothes. A fresh start. She pulled a pair of black leggings, a white T-shirt and a set of nude lace lingerie from the drawers stacked against one wall and dressed quickly. The bra-and-panty set wasn't practical for surviving a gunman in the middle of the Oregon wilderness, but it'd been the least sexy item compared to the rest of the options in those drawers. Besides, it wasn't like anyone was going to see it but her. Least of all Beckett Foster.

Facing the mirror, she ran her fingers through her hair once again, but there seemed to be a lightness—a glow—to her skin now. Whether it was from the rush of heat from Beckett's kiss, or something…deeper, she didn't know. Didn't care. Scooping her dirty clothes from the floor, she deposited them into the garbage can under the vanity and shut the cabinet door. Mentally and physically. She had to move on, had to give this baby a real shot of happiness.

She had to leave the past behind.

Raleigh followed the maze of hallways back into the custom chef's kitchen. White cabinets adorned with gold fixtures surrounded a large steel fridge. The island became the focus of the entire space with navy blue shiplap and cascading white marble down each side as Beckett set two plates on the surface. For an instant, she was back in the bedroom, wondering what it'd be like to wake up to this sight every morning, live here, raise a family here.

Beckett half turned toward her. "You want cheese and crackers with deli turkey or a grilled cheese sandwich? I wasn't sure what you or the baby would be in the mood for, so I made both."

"Is it embarrassing to admit I want to eat all of it?" A laugh bubbled past her lips, something foreign since… She couldn't remember how long.

"Oh. Guess you're technically eating for two, right?" He focused his attention on the fridge, his hands flat on the marbled island. "Okay. I can eat the pickles Reed left in the fridge. He's the only one who likes the damn things."

"I'm joking." She threw one hand out, palm first, as another laugh escaped her chest. "Partly. I could eat it all, but I'll take the sandwich. Deli meat is frowned upon when pregnant."

A smile tugged at the corners of her mouth. When was the last time someone had made her something to eat? While she wasn't sure what Beckett had put together would last long between the two of them, he'd obviously put thought into it, having cut the sandwich down the middle to make it easier to eat. Her stomach clenched at the sight of gooey yellow cheese running over the edges of toasted, buttery bread, but she couldn't drown the thought that none of this was for her. Not really.

He'd cleaned her wounds, given up the last of his water, offered his protection. All of it because of the baby. Not out of any kind of loyalty or feelings for her. So then why had he kissed her? "You happened to have cheese, bread and cold cuts here?"

"Two marshals from my office were here a couple days ago installing new dead bolts and sensors." He handed her the plate with the grilled cheese sandwich and turned back toward the fridge. "When we seize a property, we like to make sure the previous owners can't get back in."

"I don't suppose they'll mind I borrowed some of their clothes, then." She took a seat on one of the distressed-metal bar stools as silence settled between them.

Beckett turned his head partially toward her.

"I'm sorry about your brother. I didn't realize how many details were missing from the police reports, and I made assumptions about you I shouldn't have." Setting two water bottles onto the countertop, he skidded one toward her. He leveraged both hands wide against the cold surface of the island, gaze down, and her skin prickled. "My father stole millions of dollars from hardworking Americans when I was a kid by getting them to invest in his Ponzi scheme." He twisted the cap off the bottled water and swallowed several mouthfuls. Strong muscles along his throat flexed and released. He set the bottle down carefully, then dented the plastic in a strong grip, knuckles fighting for release through the back of his hand. "They didn't have any clue he'd been stealing from them for years until the feds caught wind. They trusted him with their hard-earned money, depended on him to ensure they had a future, then lost everything in the blink of an eye. That's why I became a marshal. I've been hunting him ever since, but I lost his trail soon after he dropped off the radar."

The muscles down her spine hardened vertebra by vertebra. Her mouth dried as the nail he'd driven into her heart when he'd disappeared after her arrest settled deeper. She sat a bit straighter, not sure how to respond, what to say. "You've never talked to me about your family. Before…"

"I don't have a family." His voice graveled. "Hank Foster made sure of that when one of the people he swindled came looking for him and shot and killed my mother instead."

What? A forgotten sensation spread through her with a deep inhalation. Something she hadn't felt since that first time she'd realized he was never going to return her messages or her calls after she'd been arrested. That he was never going to live up to his promise to stay by her side, no matter what happened. Breathlessness overwhelmed her control. His mother had been murdered? Why hadn't he told her? She could've done something—anything—to help him through that pain, to support him, to comfort him, but he'd kept it all to himself. Why? With her next breath, the answer slipped to the tip of her tongue. He hadn't revealed that part of his past for the same reason she hadn't told him about her brother up front: to bury the darkness deep, to hide from it. But there was no hiding for either of them. Not anymore. "Beckett, I'm so sorry. How old—"

"Sixteen." He let go of the bottle, the plastic making a cracking sound with the sudden release of pressure. "After I found out about your arrest, I was right back there. I was that sixteen-year-old kid witnessing the damage a single act could inflict on so many lives firsthand, and done by someone I trusted, no less. Someone I thought cared about me."

Air stalled in her throat. He'd really believed she'd stolen that money. Not because of the prosecution's case pristinely wrapped in shiny paper but because he'd already learned the people who were supposed to care about him could turn on him at the drop of a hat. The same lesson she'd learned when her aunt had taken the single most important person in her life away. Twenty-four hours ago, they'd stood on the opposite sides of the law, but it seemed they weren't that different after all. Her fingers tingled as Raleigh reached across the cold marble and wrapped her hand in his. Blue eyes blazed at the contact, but she wouldn't pull away. Not this time. "I cared about you—"

A bullet exploded through the window above the kitchen sink.

And found its mark.

Chapter Six

"Beckett!"

Raleigh's voice pierced through the sudden rush of pain, and he held on to that invisible anchor as tight as he could while reaching for his service weapon. A flash of movement registered through the darkness closing in around the edges of his vision. Raleigh. He had to get her out of here, had to get her somewhere safe.

Long fingers pried him from off the cold marble island, the surface no longer white. She pulled him into her and forced him to sit against the oven's stainless-steel surface. Hell. The shooter who'd ambushed them at the cabin had caught up with them. Beckett locked his back teeth as another wave of agony rolled through his shoulder. The bullet hadn't gone straight through. If it had, he wouldn't have been the only one bleeding out. "You have to go. Get out of here. I'll hold them off as long as I can."

"That better be the blood loss talking. I'm not leaving you here to fight a gunman alone." She pressed her hands on either side of his shoulder, trying to apply pressure to the wound, but it wouldn't do him any good right now. They had to keep moving. He had to keep her and the baby safe. Raleigh glanced up over the countertop, toward the window the bullet had shattered on the way into his shoulder. "You've been shot. Tell me what to do."

"Find something in this kitchen I can use to stop the bleeding." He set his head back against the cool steel behind him, and a bit of the pain ebbed. He nodded toward four drawers stacked one over the other on one side of the island. "That should help long enough for us to get out of here. Try those drawers."

Keeping low to the ground, she crawled on her hands and knees and opened one drawer after the other. Her hands left bloody prints on the pale hardwood, and his insides jerked. She was wasting time she didn't have. The shooter had taken the shot that would leave Raleigh the most unprotected, and it was only a matter of time before their attacker tried to force their way inside to get to her.

"I don't want to think about why they have this in the kitchen, but it's the best we've got." She faced him, sliding back toward him on both knees, and held out a length of clear plastic tubing. With quick, sure movements, she wrapped the tubing around the space between his shoulder and neck and below his armpit, then lifted her gaze to his. Waiting. At his nod, she tightened the makeshift tourniquet as hard as she could, and white streaks shot across his vision.

A scream escaped up his throat. Latching on to her hand, he leveraged his heels into the floor and pressed his back against the oven as hard as he could to compensate for the pain. He couldn't afford to pass out. Not as long as there was an active shooter out there targeting the woman at his side. She adjusted her grip in his hand, the pain draining the longer she held on to him, but he didn't have time to wonder how that was possible. Neither of them did. He knocked his head back into the oven. "Damn it all to hell. The next time that bastard shoots at me, he better put me down."

"You said the other marshals on your team installed new locks and alarm sensors on all the doors and windows." Placing her hands alongside his rib cage, she helped pull him to his feet, and his heart rate hiked into overdrive. Hints of the shampoo she'd used in the shower dived into his lungs, something sweet. Like lavender and honey. "Tell me that will be enough to keep the shooter out."

Beckett clamped a hand to his shoulder, the gun heavy in his grip. "As long as the power is on—"

An audible electrical surge reached his ears.

Turning toward the now blank LED light over the burners on the stovetop, he pulled his phone from his jeans with his injured hand and tapped the screen. No service. Maneuvering Raleigh behind him, Beckett stepped around the wall blocking his view from the front door. The alarm panel installed beside the door had gone dark, which meant no contacting his team, local police, the feds. Nobody. They were on their own. "They cut the power from the backup generator. Whole system's down."

"I counted three exits when we got here. Front door, back door and that side door across the living room. Not to mention the windows." Her fingers slipped over his arm as though the mere contact with him could steady the frantic tone in her voice. She studied the wide expanse of open field between the house and the tree line to the west. "They can't cover them all. We could get to those trees without them knowing we left the house. Make a run for it."

"I'm not taking the chance they didn't come alone." His gaze dipped to the slight bulge along her lower abdominals. The stakes were too high. Dropping the magazine out of his weapon, he counted three rounds left after the shoot-out at the cabin and slammed it back into place. He'd left his extra ammunition in his SUV back at her aunt's cabin, and the rounds Raleigh had buried in backpacks all over that forest didn't fit his weapon. Damn it. There were too many windows in this place, too many sight lines and not enough bullets to keep Raleigh safe. For all they knew, whoever'd stolen that money from Mothers Come First could've contracted the job to tie up loose ends out to a professional. "Get behind me and stay there. Anything happens, use me as a shield."

She did as he asked, the spot where her fingers had held on to him still warm. Her exhalation brushed against the back of his neck as she lowered her voice. "Please tell me you have a plan to get us out of here."

"The previous owner had a car in the garage when we seized the property." Beckett scanned the property through the wall of windows on the other side of the house, heart in his throat. He slid his phone from his pocket and handed it to her. "I'm going to get you to it. Then I want you to get as far from here as you can. Lie low until I can come for you. Understand? If I don't make it out, don't come back here."

"I told you," she said. "I'm not leaving you here to fight alone."

"You're pregnant with my baby, Raleigh. I think I'm entitled to put your safety first—" Movement caught his attention from one of the windows. Beckett twisted around and lunged, colliding with her. "Get down!"

They hit the floor hard as another bullet ripped past overhead. Adrenaline dumped into his veins, and the pain in his shoulder dimmed. Hauling her into his chest with his uninjured arm, he got them both to their feet and pulled her into the hallway for cover. He raised the gun and took aim around the smooth corner of the wall, firing once. Twice. Glass shattered onto the hardwood floor, but Beckett wasn't going to stick around to see if he'd hit the target. Raleigh was the priority. Getting her to that vehicle was the priority. "Go!"

Light gray walls and unfamiliar artwork blurred in his vision as they raced past the small home office and bedrooms branching off the hallway. Blood trickled along the inside of his arm, coating his palm. Wouldn't take long for the shooter to figure out where they'd gone. All they had to do was follow the trail Beckett was leaving behind, but he'd be waiting for them. One bullet. That was all it would take to keep Raleigh safe.

She wrenched the garage door open and disappeared inside mere steps ahead of him.

Darkness enveloped them as Beckett charged through the door. He couldn't see a damn thing with the automatic lights out of commission. Raleigh's heavy breathing cut through his senses, and he reached out for her. Soft, damp hair slipped through his hand, triggering his heart rate to slow slightly. They made their way to the front of the garage. The faster he got her away from here, the sooner she'd be safe. That was all that mattered. "We'll have to open the door manually."

"We'll be giving up our position if we do that," she said. "We can still make it to the trees."

His heart beat hard behind his ears, but through that dull sound gravel crunched beneath heavy footsteps outside the garage door. Her outline took shape beside him as his eyes slowly adjusted to the darkness. Beckett pulled her flat against him and lowered his mouth to her ear. "They already know we're here."

And seeing as how the shooter had tracked them here so quickly, it looked like they weren't going to stop until they got what they'd come for. Raleigh.

He shifted his weight between both feet, tension tightening the tendons between his neck and shoulders. Pain slithered across his back and down his left arm as he held on to her. "Get in the car. Last time I checked, the keys were in the middle console. The second I get that door open, I want you to floor it as hard as you can." He felt more than saw the hesitation in the hardness of the muscles along her arm. "You went into hiding to protect our baby. I'm going to need you to do that again. Promise me you'll get as far from here as possible."

She nodded. "I promise."

The sound of footsteps died. One second. Two. Raleigh slipped into the luxury car and started the ignition as Beckett reached for the small red manual release attached to the garage door. The moment he opened this door, they'd be exposed. Vulnerable. Fumes built inside the enclosed space and burned down his throat, but he wasn't going to make the first move. He adjusted his grip on the gun. He had one shot left. What was their attacker waiting for?

Gunfire tore through the metal door, white streaks of light piercing through the small holes. A click registered. The shooter was reloading. Beckett pulled the release, and the garage flooded with sunlight as the door shot up the track. "Now!"

The car shot backward, barely missing the single masked shooter dressed in head-to-toe black, and spun around toward the dirt road leaving the property. The shooter had reloaded and took aim at the car, but Beckett was already running. He collided with a wall of lean muscle, the bullet in his shoulder screaming in protest. The shooter's weapon slid into the dirt, out of reach, as Beckett fought for control. Sunlight glinted off metal as he shoved to his feet. He dodged the first swing of the assailant's blade, then the second. He struck out, bone meeting flesh, and the suspect stumbled back. The shooter raised his weapon to take the final shot. Raleigh had almost made it to the fence, but the car was crawling to a stop. No. *No, no, no, no.* She had to keep going. She had to get out of here.

His opponent recovered fast. Charging with the knife in one hand, his attacker went for the soft tissue in Beckett's gut. He managed to dodge the fatal strike to his organs, but Beckett wasn't fast enough to block the next move with his injured shoulder.

The blade sank deep into his right thigh. A scream lodged in his throat as the shooter hit him in the left kidney, then the right, and his gun discharged. Lightning struck behind his eyes a split second before he hit the ground. The bastard followed through with a kick to his ribs. The sickening crunch of bone crushed the air from his lungs. He couldn't breathe, couldn't think. He strained to get a visual on the car. On Raleigh.

Fire engulfed the sky.

The explosion rocked through him, a wall of dust fleeing in the wake of red-and-orange flames shooting into the air, and his entire world shattered. "Raleigh!"

Grip on the knife in Beckett's leg, the shooter stood above him and pulled the weapon free. Then wiped it clean with one sleeve. "None of this would've had to happen, Marshal Foster, if Raleigh would've just taken the fall like she was supposed to."

Not a man's voice. Who the hell had come after...? Beckett struggled to hang on to consciousness, but he'd lost too much blood. He couldn't keep his eyes open, and he fell into blackness.

Twigs and thorns tore at her skin as Raleigh rolled into the bushes. Heat—so much heat—seared over her exposed skin. She raised her hand in front of her face to block the burn, but there was nothing left to see. Flames consumed the dry brush around her from the pile of twisted metal. The car had been wired to explode. If she hadn't gotten out once she'd realized the electrical system was failing, she wouldn't have escaped in time.

She pushed her hair out of her face, the crisp edges of dried leaves tickling her palms in the strands. She turned back toward the house. The shooter. They must've gotten to the vehicle before she and Beckett had. How? The house's alarm system had been engaged before the power had gone off-line. Had they slipped inside before then or had they been waiting to make

their move since Beckett had brought her here? She
didn't know. Didn't care. She had to find Beckett, had
to make sure he was okay.

Raleigh pushed to her feet and headed back toward
the house. She'd made him a promise, but that'd been
before her only means of escape had exploded. Now she
had to go back. Breathtaking pain speared through her
side as the adrenaline from the explosion drained. She
tugged at the sweater she'd borrowed from the previous
owner…and froze. Blood. A wave of dizziness flooded
through her at the sight. A thin piece of jagged shrapnel, a quarter inch wide in some areas and a few inches
long, protruded from her right side beneath the thick
cables of yarn. She couldn't risk infection spreading to
the baby. She had to remove the shrapnel and clean the
wound. Raleigh struggled to breathe evenly through
the pain, to stay on her feet.

Whoever had stolen that money didn't only want
her dead. They were trying to destroy her completely.
Who would do this to her? Who would risk shooting
a US marshal for the chance of making sure she never
uncovered the truth?

She scanned the dirt road leading back toward the
house and stumbled forward. Shifting her sweater over
the wound, she spit to counteract the dirt stuck to the inside of her mouth. There was a first-aid kit in the house.
She remembered seeing it in the garage. "Beckett."

Her throat burned as black smoke billowed into the
sky and shadowed the ground in front of her. She forced
one foot in front of the other until she reached the garage. No sign of Beckett or the… Her chest constricted.
Drag marks carved into the dirt threatened to trip her

as the weight of her upper body pulled her around the side of the house. Beckett. Crusted blood flaked in her palms from trying to slow his bleeding in the kitchen.

He had to be here. He had to be alive. She'd come back to her aunt's cabin in desperation, but having him here these past eighteen hours had forced her to confront the demons she'd been hiding from her whole life. One kiss. That was all it'd taken to replace the pain, the loneliness and isolation with something she hadn't felt in so long, hadn't believed was meant for her—even for those brief seconds. He'd given her a glimpse of hope.

And she wasn't leaving without him.

Dry dirt gave way to green grass as Raleigh followed the drag marks to the large barn across the property. Her legs threatened to collapse right from under her as she caught sight of one of the main doors partially slid back on its track. Hadn't it been closed when they'd arrived? Pressing her back against the opposite door, she twisted her head to see inside, instincts on high alert. Ice slid through her as she caught sight of the body in the middle of the floor. "Beckett!"

Dried grass crunched under her boots as she rushed inside and dropped beside him. His chest rose and fell in shallow rhythms. He was alive, but unconscious. Her hands hovered above the bloody stain spreading across his shirt from where he'd been shot in the shoulder, the tubing she'd tied still in place, but now there was a second wound in his thigh. She had to stop the bleeding. Applying pressure on his thigh, she pressed her weight into him. "It's going to be okay. I'm here. I'm here. Stay with me."

Pulling the phone he'd given her from her back

pocket with her free hand, she noted a mere glance of her reflection in the cracked glass. The phone must've been destroyed when she'd rolled from the car. She couldn't call anybody. Tears burned in her eyes. She wasn't trained for this. She wasn't a doctor. Raleigh forced herself to take a deep breath. But neither of those things was going to stop her from trying to save his life. "Hold on a little bit longer. I'm going to get you out of here."

"You're not going anywhere." Another reflection in the shattered glass hiked her pulse into dangerous territory, and Raleigh lunged to the side. The phone slipped from her hand as she turned to confront her attacker, but a hand fisted the hair at the side of her head and thrust her into the floor. The world tilted on its axis as black shoes slipped into her vision. Crouching beside her, the masked shooter—maybe the same one from the cabin, she didn't know—gripped her chin in one hand. "I was hoping it didn't have to come to this, Raleigh, but you wouldn't follow the script we gave you. Like I told your marshal over there. None of this would've happened if you'd taken the fall for stealing the donations like you were supposed to."

Recognition flared as brown eyes settled on her, and something inside Raleigh broke. She'd been right all along, but knowing who'd betrayed her didn't make the truth any easier. The pain in her side intensified the deeper she breathed. "You can take the mask off, Emily. You, of all people, should have the guts to face me after what you've done."

"You always were too smart for your own good. I told my employer we should've gotten rid of you as soon as you started looking into those transfers, but they've always had a soft spot for you. Don't ask me why." A gun materialized in Emily Cline's hand as her former assistant pulled the thick ski mask over her head and tossed it a few feet away. Long black hair had been sleeked back in a low ponytail, accentuating the fullness of the woman's nose and lips. The same smile her assistant had greeted her with every morning Raleigh had walked into her office tugged at the corners of her mouth. Emily ran her free hand over the frizzed hair trying to escape, the gun still aimed directly at Raleigh. Thick arched eyebrows drew together to form three small lines as her former assistant used the barrel of her weapon to move a piece of hair out of Raleigh's face. "As far as I'm concerned, you were the perfect patsy, someone we could use and discard like so many others have done before. That's why we targeted you, Raleigh. All those foster families, your aunt. Even the marshal over there. You weren't good enough for any of them. Nothing you did could make them love you, and now you've outlived your use for us."

The words carved through her, just as Emily had meant them to. Heat rushed into Raleigh's face and neck, her heart rate spiking at the base of her throat. She diverted her gaze to the floor, not willing to let her attacker know exactly how deep she'd cut, but she couldn't keep her attention from straying to Beckett lying there, bleeding on the ground.

The fact she'd been rejected—betrayed—by so many had made her an easy target to Emily and whoever else had framed her for stealing those donation funds, and her heart tightened in her chest. Because Emily was right. Nothing she'd done had made any of those families want to keep her, made her aunt love her, and despite the fact she and Beckett had been together for six months, in the end, he'd walked away from her, too.

If it'd been as easy as her getting arrested to tear them apart, then what they'd had… It hadn't been real. At least, not for him, but that didn't change the fact Beckett was her baby's father, and she'd do whatever it took to make sure their daughter was loved by both of her parents as long as she could help it.

"From what it sounds like, you're just a fixer, Emily. You're not the brains behind the plan to embezzle from the foundation. You're a pawn, like me. So who's the one making the moves?" She dug the tips of her fingers into the barn floor, hay bending under her grip as Emily stared her down. Air pressurized in her lungs the longer her former assistant had the gun trained on her, but if there was a chance she could find out who Emily worked for—and stay alive in the process—she'd take it. She wasn't going to die here. "Do you really believe you won't outlive your use to whoever you're working for when all of this is over? That they'll protect you when the truth comes out?"

A low laugh escaped Emily's throat as she shook her head and straightened. Lowering her voice, the shooter leaned in as though she were about to tell Raleigh a secret. "Everything that's happened these past few months—the forged signatures on the transfers, the offshore accounts in your name and the shell companies—that was all me. My plan, my execution. Only now I wish I would've killed you sooner. Would've saved me a whole hell of a lot of trouble."

Emily aimed the gun at Raleigh's chest, and every cell in Raleigh's body screamed in warning. She couldn't stop a bullet, but she wasn't going to go down without a fight either. Beckett was losing blood. Fast. Pressing her heels into the floor, she ignored the pain tearing through her side where the shrapnel shifted beneath her sweater and prepared to rush her former assistant as fast as she could.

Movement registered from behind the shooter, and she realized Beckett was conscious. She kept her gaze on Emily as he fought to get to his feet. Was he going to attack from behind? He'd already taken a bullet to the shoulder and what looked like a knife wound to his thigh. How much more blood could he lose before his body started shutting down? Her mouth dried. Desperation clawed up her throat. They had to get out of here, but without Emily in cuffs, the shooter would keep coming after them, and they wouldn't have any proof to clear Raleigh's name. Raleigh had to give Beckett a chance. Before Emily realized he'd gotten to his feet. "If you kill me, the secondary account you and your partner have been hiding from the FBI will be exposed."

Emily kept her expression hard as stone aside from the slight downturn of one corner of her mouth. A piece of straw snapped under Beckett's boot, and the shooter twisted around, finger on the trigger.

And fired.

Chapter Seven

"No!" Long dark hair and a flash of red against white blurred in front of him as Raleigh tackled the shooter to the ground. She was alive. The explosion… She must've gotten free of the blast, but now the shooter who'd tried to kill her was scrambling for the gun.

The bullet burned across the surface of his arm but missed puncturing another hole in his body. Beckett stumbled forward, dizzy. Every nerve ending in his leg screamed for relief. The attacker's knife hadn't gone too deep, but there was a possibility he was losing blood a lot faster than he'd originally calculated. He closed in on the two women struggling for the weapon.

That flash of red along Raleigh's white T-shirt. A sickening twist knotted his gut. She could've been injured in the explosion. He had to get her out of here. Had to get her help. What if it affected the baby? Neither of them would forgive themself if something happened to their daughter. His injured leg dragged behind him, and a single kick from the attacker knocked him off-balance. He hit the ground, his shoulder reminding him there was still a piece of steel lodged deep in the muscles of his shoulder.

Wrapping her gloved hands around Raleigh's throat, the woman she'd called Emily fought to smother his future right in front of him. Raleigh's legs kicked out in an attempt to loosen the other woman's grip, but the shooter had the advantage, and she knew it.

"Get your damn hands off of her." A growl built in his chest as he reached out for the nearest item he could use as a weapon—a shovel—and swung. Hard. The metal reverberated off bone into his hands, and the shooter collapsed onto her side. Strained coughing kicked his heart rate into overdrive as Raleigh struggled to sit upright, and he tossed the shovel. Crouching beside Raleigh, he skimmed the angry red skin along her neck. "Tell me you're okay. Is the baby okay?"

"I think so." Her hand shook above her wound as she pulled the oversize green sweater away. She nodded, out of breath. Wild green eyes focused on the woman unconscious beside her. "It was her. Emily. She pretended to be my assistant so she could ensure all the evidence of the missing funds pointed to me like we thought. She set up the offshore accounts in my name, forged my signature on the transfers. All of it, but she wasn't working alone."

"She had a partner." Clarity slid through him for the first time since he'd caught up to her in that old cabin less than twenty-four hours ago. Hell. Had it really only been a day? Beckett pulled a set of cuffs—the same set he'd secured Raleigh with—and dragged Emily's wrists behind her back. Slight movements from the hay in front of her mouth said she was still alive, but she'd have to deal with a hell of a headache when she woke. "Makes sense. My guess is she's a professional. She's been trained in weapons and hand-to-hand combat better than most of the deputies on my team. Someone like that is usually only good for one thing— following orders. She was hired. Emily probably isn't even her real name. Most likely a cover planted inside the foundation."

He hauled Emily from the floor and dragged her upright against one of the empty horse stalls, his leg threatening to give out with each step. Sweeping the shooter's gun from the floor, he tucked it into his empty shoulder holster. Where his service weapon had ended up, he had no idea. Right now, it didn't matter. He'd just make damn sure Emily never laid another hand on Raleigh again. Ever.

"Whoever sent her to kill us is going to know she didn't finish the job. If they were willing to hire someone like this in the first place, there's nothing stopping them from doing it again." Raleigh wedged her boots into the hay-covered floor until her back pressed against the opposite stall from Emily. Clutching her side with one hand, she slid her palm across her lower abdominals with the other, as though seeking assurance the small life inside was still there after nearly being blown to pieces. Fresh blood spread beyond the border of where her sweater skimmed the waistband of her jeans. Color drained from her face as she shook her head slowly. "We're still in danger. We'll always be in danger as long as I'm a loose end. It's never going to stop."

"I'm going to find who did this. I give you my word. I'm not going to let anyone hurt you again. Understand?" Crouching as best he could in front of her, he swept her sweater out of the way, one hand cradled at her lower back as he studied the piece of shrapnel in her side. Shallow exhalations brushed against the overheated skin of his neck despite the frigid temperatures outside. Ripping his coat from his shoulders, he bit down on the groan working up his throat from the bullet wound. "You're losing blood. Stay as still as you can while I find something to get that metal out."

"This wasn't how I imagined seeing you again." Her lashes brushed against the tops of her cheeks. Letting her hand fall to the top of her thigh, she revealed the bloodstained handprint across the white T-shirt she wore. Directly over where their baby would be.

"How exactly did you think it would play out?" He had to keep her talking, had to get her to hang on. Because despite the mess they'd made of their relationship, he still gave a damn about what happened to her. Her and their baby. Beckett shoved to his feet. He pushed the pain and weakness in his leg to the back of his mind. Red-and-white decals drove him toward the large first-aid kit hung against one wall of the barn. Clean her up. Get her to safety. Nothing else mattered.

His heart stalled in his chest as he turned at her lack of response and noted the slackness in her expression. He hauled the kit from the wall and limped back to her side. The kit skidded across the cement, bits of dust and hay digging into his knees. Framing one hand along her jawline, he brushed her hair out of the way with the other. She was breathing but unconscious. Sweat built in a thin layer along her temples. Couldn't be an infection. Not this fast. "Raleigh, open your eyes."

No answer.

No. He maneuvered her flat onto her back, raised

his voice and checked her pulse at the base of her throat. "Raleigh."

"Looks like I've done my job after all." The thud of Emily Cline setting her head back against the warm-colored wood of the stall reached his ears. "Although I have to admit, Raleigh Wilde wasn't nearly as easy to surprise as her partner, but this was a lot more fun. A challenge."

"Calvin Dailey." Of course Emily had killed him. Because the only person who could clear Raleigh's name couldn't be left to the chance he'd never talk to the feds in the future. Beckett didn't bother looking at the woman sent to ruin Raleigh's life as he spun the first-aid kit latch toward him. He riffled through the contents, pulling alcohol, cotton pads and an emergency sewing kit from inside. "Say another word, and I'll make sure you don't wake up a second time."

"Promises, promises, Marshal Foster." Emily Cline's laugh pooled dread at the base of his spine. "But don't forget, I was able to insert myself into a global foundation and operate without raising any red flags from the executives for over a year, and the only way I could've done that was by doing my research. I know you." The weight of her attention constricted the air in his chest. "Your moral code you pride yourself on so highly doesn't let you see in anything but black and white since you realized your father was the reason you lost your mother. At least, until yesterday, when you decided that woman was worth risking your career and everything you believed in. You're finally seeing the world isn't black-and-white. No matter how many criminals you've put away to prove otherwise, I know you won't kill me in cold blood. You don't have it in you."

Beckett's hands hovered above Raleigh's wound, blood trickling from the shrapnel with every shallow breath she took. His ears rang at the sight. He couldn't breathe. Couldn't see anything in front of him but the dark outline of his mother bleeding to death on the floor of their farmhouse all those years ago. His vision swam, his heart pounding hard behind his ears to the point he thought he might pass out. The only person who'd ever supported him, who'd always been there for him, had slipped away as easily as water draining from a tub.

No. Not the only person. Beckett forced himself back into the moment. If it hadn't been for Emily Cline and whoever else was involved in embezzling that money from the foundation, Raleigh wouldn't have been arrested, wouldn't have left him. He hadn't been able to help his mom then. It'd been too late for her, but it wasn't too late for Raleigh. Beckett raised his gaze to the woman merely hired to take everything that he cared about from him. "You don't know a damn thing about me or what I'm capable of."

"The problem isn't me knowing what you're capable of, Marshal. It's how little you know about me." The cuffs rattled as Emily leaned forward, stretching her arms straight behind her. She wound her legs beneath her and brought her cuffed wrists to the front. In less time than it'd taken to put her in the cuffs, she was suddenly standing. She moved fast, diving forward for the gun he'd set down a few feet away while trying to take care of Raleigh's injury.

Beckett lunged, but he wasn't fast enough. Hand

gripped around steel, he bit back the scream of pain as Emily's boot crushed down hard on the wound in his shoulder. In less than a few seconds, he found himself at the wrong end of the gun.

"I'm sure you can understand the kind of pressure I'm under to finish this job, Marshal Foster. So forgive me if I'm not willing to let you save her life first." The shooter increased the pressure on his shoulder. "You're unarmed. You don't have a vehicle or any way to contact your team out here. You can chase me if you want. I might even enjoy it, but that means arresting your suspect or leaving Raleigh here to bleed out. What's it going to be? Uphold the oath you made as a deputy or break that legendary moral code of yours to save a fugitive?"

Blood pooled beneath one side of Raleigh's body. She was running out of time, but bringing Emily Cline in would clear her name of the embezzlement charges and give their baby the future he and Raleigh both wanted. Beckett tried pulling his arm out from under the weight of the shooter's foot, but the pain limited the use of the muscles across his back and down his arm. Twisting his head up, he locked his attention on his attacker. If he went after Emily, he wouldn't have a future. Period. But if he let Emily slip away, Raleigh would spend the rest of her life looking over her shoulder. And so would their daughter.

Not happening.

Beckett rolled out from under her boot and swung a hard right toward her jaw. Emily dodged the hit, and his momentum pulled him forward. Agony tore down his spine as the shooter cracked the butt of her weapon at the base of his skull. He went down beside Raleigh, dirt filling his mouth and lungs. His hand pressed against hers as Emily stood above him. His body wouldn't obey his commands. Raleigh. He had to get up. "Stay away from her."

The shooter's weak smile broke through the darkness as she crouched next to him, dark hair sliding into her face, but her brown eyes didn't reflect the coldness visible a few minutes ago any longer. "We all have our roles to play, Marshal. This is mine."

UNCONSCIOUSNESS RIPPED OUT from under her as throbbing tore through her side. Sunlight speared her retinas, blinding her until the outline of someone in front of her took shape. She pressed her feet into the floor to stand, but something kept her pinned in the chair she'd been set into. Rope? Raleigh tugged at her wrists, the bark scratches along her forearms still stinging. Not rope. The edges of the material were too sharp. Zip ties. She blinked against the wide spread of blood across her T-shirt. The piece of shrapnel had been removed, but she was still bleeding. Her throat burned as she cleared a coat of dirt layering her mouth and raised her head from her chest. "Beckett?"

"I'm afraid he won't be able to save you this time." The dark shape in front of her shifted. Her eyes adjusted slowly, but she didn't need to see who'd tied her to the chair against one of the horse stalls to recognize that voice. "Unfortunately for him, he won't be saving anyone when this is over."

"Emily. What are you...?" Dizziness flooded through her, blurring the fine lines around the woman's wide brown eyes. Nausea churned in her stomach. The baby. She hadn't eaten in a few hours and her blood sugar had dipped. Raleigh shook her head to clear the tension working down her spine. "What did you do to him?"

"Nothing a surgeon can't fix, and as long as you're straight with me, I can get him to a hospital in time." Emily gripped a pair of rounded pliers typically used in shoeing horses and clenched between the teeth a jagged piece of shrapnel. The same piece of shrapnel that'd been embedded in Raleigh's side. Her former assistant had removed the sliver, and the blood trickling down Raleigh's side flowed more freely. She discarded the pliers and the jagged metal onto the floor. "But you don't have long at all."

She was bleeding out.

"What do you want?" She pulled her inner wrists apart, but there wasn't any room to maneuver. Emily had made sure of that.

"Who else aside from Marshal Foster and Calvin Dailey did you tell about what you found during your little off-the-books investigation?" Sunlight reflected off a long piece of steel as Emily pulled a blade from her back.

What she'd found? She hadn't found anything in the four months she'd been looking for whoever'd set her up to take the fall for the embezzlement charges. All she had was a theory with no proof to back it up. What she had found, she was sure the feds had already combed through. The offshore accounts and wire transfers, it all pointed to her. That was the entire point of Emily's and her partner's operation, wasn't it? "I'm not telling you anything until I know Beckett is safe."

A low-pitched laugh blustered from between the shooter's lips. Raleigh eyed the heavy metal pliers her former assistant had forgotten about.

"Every second you waste here is another second your marshal doesn't have, and I'm starting to lose my patience with you, Raleigh." Emily stood, the blade gripped tight in one hand. She shifted her weight between both feet as though forcing herself not to end this interrogation prematurely. Which, if she were being honest with herself, Raleigh appreciated. "Who else knows about the secondary account, the one the feds haven't linked to the missing donations? I recovered the hidden file on your laptop you stashed in the safe at the cabin. I know you found it, and Marshal Foster is running out of time."

Raleigh had threatened to expose the account in an attempt to make Emily reconsider spilling more blood, but it'd been mostly bravado at the time. She'd taken a shot in the dark after calculating how much money had been taken from the accounts she'd overseen for the foundation and the amount the FBI had reported missing during their investigation. The numbers didn't match up, which meant Emily and whoever else she was working for hadn't funneled everything into one account. There had to be another or maybe several, and the feds had no idea they existed.

"Either I see Beckett or you risk going back to your boss empty-handed with a whole lot of blood leading back to you." She was taking a risk making demands. The back of her neck prickled, and she stretched her hands to work out a cramp along one tendon. A sharp, slightly rounded edge caught on her heated skin. The

head of a nail? She slipped her thumb around the metal.
If she could get her wrists closer to the stall door, she
might be able to break the zip tie without Emily noticing. She just had to keep her former assistant distracted
long enough to come up with a plan to get Beckett out
of here. "I don't think you want that. You've accounted
for everything in your operation. You've been planning
this for a long time, and there's a lot of money at stake.
How is it going to look to your employer when you fail?
Do you think they'll let you walk away?"

"If I were you, I'd worry about yourself. Because
when this is over, I'm going to enjoy watching the life
drain from your eyes." Emily closed the distance between them and pressed cold steel against her throat.

The tip of the knife cut into the oversensitized skin
below Raleigh's jaw, but she refused to flinch. Refused
to give up an ounce of confidence.

"Funny, here I was thinking the exact same thing."
Raleigh tried to relax the muscles down her back, but
the pain in her side stole the air from her lungs. Un-
sticking her hair from her face with one shoulder, she
followed Emily's path into one of the other stalls.

Her former assistant slid the stall door back on its
rails, exposing the man unconscious in the hay. Emily
locked dark brown eyes on her from less than ten feet
away, and Raleigh's gut clenched. Beckett. "You know,
I started watching you—studying you—long before I
walked into your office that first day, Raleigh. I know
you. I know what drives you, what scares you, even
how far you're willing to go to protect the people you
care about."

"I didn't realize this was a therapy session." Raleigh

straightened her arms a bit more, then set the edge of the zip tie around her wrists on top of the partially exposed nail head behind her. Interlocking her fingers together, she applied as much pressure as she dared without giving away her attempt to escape. "Is this where you tell me all the reasons I keep people at arm's length or what my dreams really mean?"

"Not at all. It means I can pretty much do anything to you physically, mentally, emotionally, and nothing will get beneath that guarded exterior of yours. I could threaten and torture you all day, and I might get lucky, but neither of us has the time for that, do we? Quite admirable, in fact. Some of the best operators I've known can't withstand pain as long as you can, but Marshal Foster, on the other hand?" Emily sidestepped out from in front of the stall door where Beckett lay and unholstered the gun from beneath the black jacket she wore. She took aim at Beckett, and ice flooded through Raleigh's veins, straight to her heart. "Do you think he'll last long? I mean, I've already shot him and stabbed him, but how long do you think he'll hold on if I put another bullet in him? Should we see?"

The zip tie slipped from the nail behind her back as Raleigh turned her attention to the man who'd risked his life to protect her and their baby. "He has nothing to do with this. You know that."

"You brought him into this when you reached out to him after your arrest. You made him part of this." Emily raised her voice and slipped her finger over the trigger of the gun. "Now you have five seconds to tell me who else knows about that account before I put an-

other bullet in him and make you watch him die before
I kill you for good measure. Five…"

Raleigh increased the pressure against the zip tie
around her wrists. "The second account is yours, isn't
it? The one whoever hired you promised you'd walk
away with after this was all over?"

"Four…" Emily readjusted her grip on the weapon.
"You don't have to do this," she said. "Please."

Her former assistant turned to Beckett. "Three, Raleigh. You're running out of time."

Raleigh lifted her wrists above the nail before slamming her hands down onto the nail. The zip tie snapped,
and she rushed forward. Catching Emily around the
middle, she tackled the shooter to the floor. A gunshot
exploded loud in her ears, but she couldn't focus on
that right now. Pure adrenaline and desperation burned
through her. Fisting Emily's jacket by the collar, she
slammed the gunwoman back into the cement as hard
as she could.

Her attacker stopped fighting, Emily's brown eyes
wide. The lines around her mouth and eyes softened
with unconsciousness. The air rushed from Raleigh's
lungs as she loosened her grip on the woman beneath
her. Her fingers ached with the amount of force she'd
used, just as they had all those years ago. She could still
feel the edges of the rock digging into her hand as she'd
brought it down against her aunt's head that day. Staring at the blood crusted in her palms, she pushed away
from Emily. Raleigh fell back, barely able to keep herself upright. Whether from the blood loss or the rush
of memories clouding her focus now, she didn't know,
but she couldn't wait for Emily to come around. Her

former assistant had been right. There wasn't anything she wasn't willing to do to protect the people she cared about.

They had to get out of here. She had to get Beckett help.

"Beckett." Her hands shook as she got to her feet and reached for him. "Come on. You have to get up. We need to get out of here."

A groan rumbled through his chest, and Raleigh couldn't stop the burst of relief escaping as she battled the burn of tears. Because if she didn't have this small release, she feared she might shatter right here on the floor. He was going to make it. She had to believe that, but first, she had to get him on his feet. "I'm going to help you stand, okay? We can do this."

She collected Emily's gun from where her former assistant had dropped it. Maneuvering his uninjured arm across her back, she ducked her shoulder beneath his side and forced his upper body up. Panicked seconds ticked by as she used the last of her remaining strength to get him to his feet and wedged him against her side. Her pain receptors caught fire as they headed for the main door. Emily hadn't moved. Hadn't given any sign she'd be regaining consciousness, but Raleigh wasn't willing to wait around for that to happen. The shooter wouldn't have walked here in case she had to make a quick getaway. Emily had to have a vehicle nearby, possibly hidden. She and Beckett just had to find it.

Before either of them collapsed from blood loss.

Chapter Eight

"Raleigh." Her name slipped past his lips as they stumbled from the stall into the main part of the barn together. His head hurt. Hell, his whole body hurt, but it was nothing compared to the sight of so much blood spreading across her shirt. "Stop. You need—"

"We need to keep moving." Her fingers fisted tight in his shirt as she struggled to take most of his weight. How she was able to keep walking and drag his injured butt at the same time, he had no idea. Seemed no matter the circumstance, she was determined to prove how strong she could be, but Raleigh didn't need to prove anything to him. She never had. Well, other than her innocence. "She's not going to be out for long."

Emily Cline. Damn it. She was right. They had to get out of here. The woman had been sent to tie up loose ends, to make sure Raleigh never got the chance to clear her name, and she wouldn't stop until the job was done. As much as Raleigh's former assistant had researched him, he knew her kind, too, and he wasn't going to wait around to see how far the shooter would go to complete her mission. They'd lost this battle, but he sure as hell would find out who was behind this war.

He'd do whatever it took, for however long it took, to take them down.

"I've got you. Keep your weight on me." Raleigh led them through the main barn door and out into the open. The toe of his boot dragged behind him as the stab wound weakened his right leg, but she didn't show any signs of slowing despite her uneven exhalations. Keeping her gaze dead ahead, she directed them toward the nearest spread of pines to the west. "We're going to make it. I promise. We just need to retrace Emily's footprints back to her vehicle, okay?"

He'd been an idiot. Even if Emily hadn't caught up with their trail, how the hell had he ever convinced himself Raleigh had taken that money? Every sacrifice she'd made was for the people she cared about. She hadn't reached for his backup weapon at her aunt's cabin to make another run for freedom but to give them a chance of survival during the shoot-out. She could've disappeared in the middle of the night when they'd made camp, but instead she'd soothed him when the nightmares came for him. Then she'd offered to turn herself in to keep him and their baby safe. Criminals didn't do that.

The evidence had been all right there, perfectly staged and easily accessible to anyone who'd come to investigate the missing donation funds, made it look like she'd turned into the kind of criminal he hated the most, the kind that hurt others to gain for themselves. The kind of criminal like his father, a man who didn't give a damn about the consequences of his selfishness. But that wasn't Raleigh. Never had been. Everything she'd done had been for the benefit of others, especially their unborn baby. "I trust you."

He meant it, too. They were going to make it. Because Raleigh Wilde never looked a challenge in the face and backed down, and he couldn't help but admire her for that. When it'd come right down to it, he'd been a coward when he'd cut her out of his life after her arrest. He hadn't wanted to feel the pain of losing another person he'd given a damn about to the wrong side of the law, so he'd convinced himself he hadn't known her at all, hadn't loved her. Hadn't been compromised in any way, but it'd all been a lie.

Her grip strengthened around his arm draped along her shoulders. "Is it too soon to remind you I suggested we make a run for the trees when the first bullet went through the window?"

"You can say I-told-you-so as much as you want after we get the hell out of here." He set his back teeth against the throbbing ripping through his shoulder with each swing of his arm. There was only twenty feet left between them and the tree line. As soon as they reached cover, he'd take a look at her wound. From the amount of blood plastering her sweater to the shirt beneath, he figured she had maybe ten—fifteen—minutes at the most before she collapsed. She was one of the most ambitious, driven and impressive women he'd ever known, and that included the chief deputy of his division. Then again, she could only push herself while pregnant for so long before all that fire ran out. This woman was nothing like he'd come across before, but that didn't make her immune to the things the rest of the mere mortals on earth physically succumbed to. Infection, blood loss, exhaustion. "We need to get you to the hospital."

Ten feet until they'd reach the trees. Green grass bled to dying wildflowers and slightly cooler temperatures in the shade of the pines.

"I...can't. I'm still a fugitive, Beckett. If I go there... they'll take me into custody." Her hand slipped from his waist. Color drained from the patches of red along her face and neck, those mesmerizing green eyes suddenly distant. Her breathing changed, growing more shallow, uneven. She stumbled forward.

Beckett caught her a split second before she collapsed, but her weight and the lack of strength in his right leg pulled him down along with her. Gravel cut into his palms as he braced himself from landing on top of her. She was still conscious. Barely. He scanned the rest of the property for any sign Emily had followed their trail. They couldn't wait for her to catch up. A scream built in his chest as he worked his uninjured arm under her lower back and hauled her up over his shoulder in a fireman's hold. His leg throbbed. She was right. She was on the FBI's most wanted list. They couldn't walk right into a public hospital without alerting local PD and the feds. She'd be taken back into custody, and he'd have to answer for not bringing her in. "I've got someone who can help. A former combat medic. He's a marshal. I trust him."

But could they take the risk?

"Then that'll have...to be good enough for me," she said. "I can walk. You're still...bleeding."

Pressure should've released from behind his sternum as they crossed the tree line. They weren't out of the woods yet, metaphorically speaking, but they at least had a chance to disappear, to find cover. He should've been there for her after the arrest. He should've known better than to believe she'd taken that money, especially after showing him that first sonogram of the life they'd created together. He'd promised to always be there for her, no matter the circumstances, because that was what she'd needed. Someone she could trust, rely on, someone who cared about her after she'd been discarded by so many others, but he'd run at the first sign of trouble. "You might be out to prove to the world how strong and resilient you are, but that doesn't mean you don't need someone to take care of you every now and then."

Beckett adjusted his grip at the back of her knees. He wouldn't run again.

"Not to the world." Her voice softened, somehow distant yet reverberating down his spine at the same time. "Just…you."

"You don't have to prove anything to me." He was the one who'd betrayed her, but he'd spend the rest of his life making it up to her if that was what it took. Beckett pushed deeper into the woods, that knot of uncertainty growing bigger in his gut. It wouldn't take much for the shooter to catch up with them, considering the amount of blood he was leaving behind on his own and the fact Emily wasn't carrying another person on her back, but he wasn't going to stop following the shooter's prints in the mud. Not until Raleigh was safe.

Up ahead, sunlight glinted off tinted glass, and Beckett slowed. A dark SUV had been parked in the thickest part of the woods to cover Emily's approach to the ranch, and he'd never been more thankful at the sight of a standard black vehicle in all his life. "Almost there. Just hang on. I'll get you out of here."

Silence descended around them. Moss-covered pines towered overhead, blocking sunlight from reaching the forest floor in some spots, and the hairs on the back of his neck rose on end. Damp wood and earth tickled his senses. Something was wrong. Well, other than they were fifty miles from the nearest hospital. Hell, from the nearest town.

Cold metal pressed to the back of his neck, and Beckett froze, air stuck in his lungs.

"I'm not leaving without her, Marshal." Emily's voice shook, but the barrel of a gun pressed to the base of his skull remained steady. She must've had a backup neither him nor Raleigh had noticed. One wrong move, and she'd pull the trigger.

Raleigh didn't have that kind of time. Neither of them did.

"You're already looking at the entire US Marshals Service coming down as hard as they can for attempted murder of a federal agent, Emily." His head throbbed, his pulse loud behind his ears. He didn't have a weapon and happened to be holding the one thing she wanted that he wasn't willing to give up—Raleigh. "You can end this now. All you have to do is let me get her to a hospital, and I can put in a good word with the district attorney after you turn yourself in and admit your part in all of this."

"You're right." Emily cocked the gun. "I can end this now."

Beckett tightened his hold on the woman in his arms and launched himself off to the right. The gun went off next to his ear. High-pitched ringing threw him off-balance, but he caught himself before letting Raleigh hit the ground. Rolling, he released his grip on her and shot to his feet before Emily could target him again. He wrapped one hand around her wrist and shoved to get the shooter as far from Raleigh as he could. One strike to her midsection. Two. He positioned her arm over his shoulder, hauled her over his back and slammed her onto the ground.

The rush of her lungs emptying didn't slow her for long. Swinging the gun toward him, Emily shot to her feet with a rolling growl escaping her chest. "You're only making this harder on yourself, Marshal. On both of you."

"Go to hell." Beckett reached out, wrapped one hand around the gun barrel and crushed his knee against her wrist. The gun disappeared into the underlying brush. He dodged the left hook aimed at his face and blocked the second attempt as he backed low out of her reach, but his leg slowed him down. Her knee landed hard against his jaw, and he stumbled back.

"Been there. Only this time you and your fugitive are coming with me." Emily spread her stance, ready to charge.

Three distinct gunshots exploded from a few feet away.

Emily pulled up short, brown gaze wide. Dropping her chin to her chest, she let her mouth fall open as blood spread across her front before collapsing face-first into the dirt. Dead.

Beckett located the second shooter, and his gut twisted. "Raleigh."

She held a hand to her bleeding side, dark hair wild around her face. Exhaustion etched deep lines around compelling green eyes staring down at the woman she'd shot. She lowered the gun, expression smooth and distant. "She can't hurt us anymore."

HE FELL TO his hands and knees, one hand over the stab wound in his thigh.

"Beckett!" Raleigh rushed forward. She'd neutralized the threat by shooting Emily, but he was still in danger of going into shock. Soon he'd lose enough blood to cause his organs to start shutting down one by one. She had to get him out of here. Emily's SUV. It was the only chance they had. Sliding her free hand across his muscled back, she forced him to sit up, fire igniting along her side. "We need to get to the car. Come on."

Her head pounded, fatigue overwhelming, but she wasn't going to give up on him. Because he hadn't given up on her. He'd had the chance. He could've brought her in after he'd discovered her hiding at the cabin, but he hadn't. He'd chosen to help clear her name, even if it'd been for the sake of their baby. He'd made the choice to break that legendary code of his and given his word to a fugitive. Now it was her turn to help him.

Raleigh dragged him in to her side, letting out the scream of pain that'd been building since she'd escaped the fireball set to kill her, and found a small rush of release. Something real and raw she hadn't felt in years. One step toward the shooter's vehicle. Two.

"Raleigh, stop," he said.

"No." She stumbled, unable to keep hiding the pain, unable to ignore the hurt she'd shouldered all these

years. It crashed down around her as she battled to get
Beckett to the SUV. Tears burned as mountains of uncertainty, doubt and effort slipped from the dark crev-
ices she'd held on to protect herself. She'd convinced
herself everything she'd been through—all the trauma,
the betrayal, the shame—had carved her into a strong,
emotionally impenetrable woman who never faltered,
never failed, never relented. Who'd learned to rely on
no one but herself, but she was so tired of holding it all
together, tired of being numb. Day by day, she'd sys-
tematically become a black hole of nothingness to everyone around her after the incident on that beach, most
recently Beckett. Invisible, unknown, void of anything
to the naked eye, but over the past eighteen hours the
man at her side had forced her to face the light, to feel,
and she couldn't hide anymore. "I'm not letting you die
out here. She doesn't get to win. She doesn't get to have
this control over us."

"Find…" he said. "Reed."

"Reed?" Emily's gun still in hand, she hefted Beckett against the hood of the passenger side and fumbled
for the door. The truth of the matter was she wouldn't
have survived the past few hours without Beckett. She
owed him her life—hers and the baby's—and she'd
never be able to pay that back, but she was going to
try. She wrenched the door open and maneuvered him
to sit against the front seat before hoisting his legs inside. "Stay awake, damn it."

Rounding the front of the SUV, she clutched on to
the hood as a rush of pain gutted her from the inside.
The bleeding in her side hadn't slowed, but she couldn't
stop now. Not after everything they'd survived. She

closed her eyes, nails digging into the vehicle's paint. "You can do this. You have to do this."

Because she couldn't lose him. Not again.

The pressure in her gut released after a few seconds, and she pushed one foot in front of the other until she reached the driver's-side door. After hauling herself into the seat, she set the gun between her and Beckett and pressed the ignition button.

The engine growled to life for a few moments, then cut out.

Raleigh hit the ignition a second time, one hand tight around the steering wheel. Her heart thudded hard in her chest. Seconds slipped away. She punched the start button again. "Come on."

Nothing.

She slammed the palm of her hand against the steering wheel. Emily had to have a safety feature in place that prevented anyone else from taking off with her vehicle. Every minute she wasted here was another minute Beckett didn't have. Her hands trembled as she pulled the release for the door and slid from the car. Using the SUV for balance, she slipped her hand along the cool metal until she reached the front of the vehicle a second time and hesitated as her fingers traced the edge of the hood. The metal didn't line up, as though the hood had been popped. Hope flooded through her as she inserted her hand between the hood and the SUV's main frame and lifted slightly. The hood released, and she dropped it back into place. She slid back behind the steering wheel and pushed the ignition button. "We're going to make it. Stay with me."

The engine growled to life, and everything inside her

released. She pulled the vehicle out of Park and maneuvered beyond the patch of pines as best she could before aiming the SUV toward the main road. Dirt kicked up alongside the vehicle on either side of them as she sped away from the ranch, away from Emily. Beckett's head swung toward the passenger-side window, but she didn't need to see his face to know he was running out of time. His shirt and jeans were already soaked through, and there were only so many pints of blood he could lose before he hit the point of no return. Raleigh floored the accelerator, Oregon countryside blurring through the side windows. The nearest hospital was at least fifty miles from here, but Beckett had said he knew of a combat medic. Someone he trusted.

She slid one hand across her abdomen, patches of dried blood starching her borrowed sweater. Bringing Beckett to a former combat medic, a marshal—someone she didn't know—would expose her, put her at risk. Was that the Reed he'd been telling her to find? Raleigh slid her attention to the bloodied man in the passenger seat. She'd have to take the chance. She'd have to trust him. "This baby deserves to know her daddy, Beckett, so I'm not letting you off that easy. If you're not going to hang on for me, do it for her."

The shooter's phone slid from one side of the middle console to the other as Raleigh took the turn onto the national forest road 21. The cell Beckett had given her had been crushed when she'd jumped from the car before it'd exploded, but there was a chance she could recover the SIM card. Gravity pulled at every cell in her body. Her eyes were heavier than a few minutes before as adrenaline drained from her veins, but she couldn't stop. One hand on the wheel, she tugged his phone from her back pocket. The screen was broken, sharp edges digging into her skin, but from what she could tell, the side of the phone hadn't been damaged all that much. She might be able to save the data card. Eyes on the road, she carefully and slowly pried the small green chip free and replaced Emily's with Beckett's. The screen lit up, and something inside of her threatened to break.

It'd worked.

But… A pitiful moan of defeat escaped her mouth. Her thumb hovered above the ten-button configuration of numbers. The phone was asking for a password. Beckett's password. Neither the facial recognition nor the touch identification would work until he'd entered the six-digit code since she'd transferred the SIM card. Damn it. She had to think.

Most people used the same passwords across devices and accounts. There had to be a code he frequently used, something easy to remember. She just had to remember any instances she'd seen him use it. Only, if she entered the wrong code three times, his entire contact list, along with any other data on the phone, would be erased, and she'd have no idea how to reach the person he'd called Reed. If that was even his contact's real name. Locking her jaw against the pain, Raleigh tugged on the wheel as the road curved around. They'd almost reached the Paulina Lake Campground. From there, she could either head south on the national forest road 500 or keep heading west, but she had no idea where this Reed person was, where he lived, if he could help them at all, and she wouldn't know any of that until she was able to get into Beckett's contact list.

Her blood pressure spiked. He'd already lost too much blood. How much longer before his body decided to shut down for good? "Okay. Six digits. Birthday?"

Using her thumb, she punched in the numbers for his birthday into the phone, but the passcode reset. Wrong sequence. Too easy. She had two tries left before the phone locked her out permanently and erased all the data on the SIM card. The split off ahead was coming up too fast, and Raleigh pressed her foot onto the brake pedal. "Beckett, I need you to wake up. I can't get into the phone without your password."

No response.

"Come on!" She forced herself to breathe as the main sign for the campground slid into view. She'd have to stop. She'd have to risk a few more minutes Beckett didn't have. The gunshot wound in his shoulder, the injury to his thigh… This was all her fault. She'd brought him into this mess, and she had no idea if she was going to be able to get him out of it. "Okay. You can do this, Wilde. You can do this."

She tried his mother's birthday next, but the small bubbles at the top of the screen reset again.

Nausea swirled in her stomach. They weren't going to make it. At least, not to the former combat medic. She'd have to take him to a public hospital. She'd have to risk being arrested a second time, never seeing her daughter once the birth was over, but if it'd save his life, she'd do it. For him.

Her gaze slipped to his empty shoulder holster and a flash of memory lit across her mind. That was it. It had to be. His gun safe. He'd kept it under his side of the bed when they'd been together. It'd had an electronic lock with a six-digit passcode, which… She inhaled on a shaky breath. Which had been the day they'd met. Raleigh pulled the vehicle off to the side of the road, her heart in her throat. He wouldn't have kept the same digits. Not after everything that'd happened between them, but she didn't have a whole lot of other options either. Most people didn't change their passcodes over time. Too hard to remember when habit had already rewired the neural pathways in their brains, but that didn't mean his hatred for her—for what she'd been accused of—wouldn't break that habit. Her hand shook as she entered the date, her lungs fighting for a full breath.

The screen went black.

Chapter Nine

"Gotta hand it to you, Foster. When you're trying to piss someone off, you go for the knockout," a familiar voice said. "It's amazing you're still alive. Thanks to me."

Beckett slid back into consciousness breath by slow, agonizing breath. Waves of soft light cascaded over the pale wood paneling overhead, one side of his body cold from the floor-to-ceiling windows stretching along one wall. He shot upright on the modern sofa—the kind with angles rather than cushions—automatically searching the space as his nervous system vaulted into his fight-or-flight response. He'd recognized the voice, but the man perched in one of those ridiculous wicker satellite chairs looked as though he'd aged years in the span of only a few days. Or maybe Beckett was superimposing what he felt like over the marshal who'd obviously saved his life. But where did that leave Raleigh? If she'd brought him here, she'd put herself at risk for arrest. "Reed."

"Yes?" Finnick Reed, former combat medical specialist turned US marshal, clutched a bag of cookies in one hand, rooting through the contents until he found one good enough for his particular tastes. Blue eyes lightened with the help of the firelight dancing on the television screen built into the side of a kitchen island across the room. Despite everything he'd seen, everything he'd been through, the ex-soldier fit perfectly with the stainless-steel, modern feel of the cabin.

Beckett's head pounded as he settled back against the awkward, uncomfortable sofa. Stars peppered the night sky through the windows. How long had he been out? Bits and pieces filtered through the haze clouding his memories. The barn, Raleigh leading them into the woods. Emily Cline's eyes widening seconds before she hit the ground. All of it fought for his focus as he listened for movement throughout the rest of the house. No movement. No sign of her. He clutched the edges of the sofa, his clothing stiff with patches of blood. "Where's Raleigh?"

"You mean the fugitive you told to contact me to save your life so you could put not only your entire career with the Marshals on the line but mine, as well?" Reed dived his hand into the bag for another cookie, crumbs catching in the clean-cut beard around his jaw and mouth. "That Raleigh?"

Blistering rage exploded through him while the deputy sat there as if nothing in the world mattered but those damn cookies. "If you handed her over to the feds, I swear to spend the rest of my life—"

"Relax, Foster. You trusted me for a reason." Reed tossed the bag onto the coffee table between them, mouthing something that looked a whole lot like "wow" as he leaned forward. "She's on the bed upstairs asleep. The woman could barely stand on her own, let alone carry your sorry hide up those stairs by herself, but she stood by you until I gave her doctor's orders to rest after a transfusion of her own. You've only been unconscious for four hours." Reed motioned to the other end of the sofa, where the barest of impressions dipped in the cushion. "I hit my elbow on the doorjamb bringing your unconscious body inside my house, if you care to know."

"I don't." She'd stayed with him despite the shrapnel injury in her side. Always putting others first, even at the cost of her own life. Hell, if he hadn't sent her running, she wouldn't have even been near that car when it'd exploded. The shooter had done enough research to look into Beckett's background. He should've known Emily Cline had just as easy a way into the seized property records. Or her partner did. Beckett rubbed at his eyes as the throbbing in his head echoed behind his ears. "How is she?"

He couldn't ask about the baby. As much as he trusted the deputy, that information was Raleigh's to share, and he doubted she'd let her pregnancy slip. Especially to someone she didn't know.

"Not in cuffs," Reed said.

"You know what I meant." Aside from the jokes and the constant sarcasm, Finnick Reed had watched Beckett's back enough times to earn his trust. A groan worked through his chest as he shifted his position on the couch. His shirt and jeans had been ripped to expose the stained gauze over both wounds.

"She didn't lose as much blood as you did, but she wouldn't let me patch her until I was able to get your bleeding under control and your vitals stable. Studied every move I made until I sewed in the last stitch like she was waiting for me to make a mistake. Something tells me I don't want to know what would've happened if I had." Reed stretched. His vintage-wash T-shirt emblazoned with a superhero logo rode higher. As if Reed was some modern-day, real-life hero—to himself and any woman who happened to be passing through his life. Who wore a threadbare T-shirt with formal trousers? Finnick Reed. That was who. The deputy stood, making his way around the black glossy kitchen island toward the refrigerator. He pulled two water bottles from the shelves and retraced his steps to hand Beckett one. "Both of you are damn lucky I answered the phone, and that I happen to keep stores of blood in my freezer instead of tater tots. Drink up. The headache is only going to get worse."

Beckett didn't give a damn about his headache right then, but he took the water anyway. The cold penetrated through the plastic straight down to bone, kept him grounded. There were only two things that mattered right now. Raleigh and their baby, and the danger closing in on them both, but he couldn't risk moving them until Raleigh had a chance to recover from the fight with Emily Cline. Unscrewing the cap to the bottle, Beckett took a long swig. "You could've turned us both in, saved yourself a whole lot of trouble."

"Now, where's the fun in that?" A smile tugged at one corner of Reed's mouth, deepening the laugh lines on either side of a nose that'd been broken one too many times. "Gotta tell you, having a woman like that show up on my doorstep in the middle of the night, not my worst day. Could've done without the blood on my couch, though. Next time remember it's supposed to stay on the inside of your body."

"I'll try to keep that in mind." Beckett wiped a thin layer of crusted blood onto his jeans from his hand. Hell, they were ruined anyway. "Give us until sunrise. Nobody has to know we were ever here."

Reed set his water bottle on the coffee table, untouched. Overgrown light brown hair lost its shape as the former combat medic interlocked his fingers between his knees. "Is it worth your career, Foster? What you're doing here. Is it worth risking everything you believe in, and the people who've watched your back all these years? Because I read her file. I saw the prosecution's case. Everything—all the evidence—led back to her." The deputy pointed his index finger at him as he stood, his shadow casting across Beckett's knees. "So whatever you have in mind, you better do it fast. The longer you wait to bring her in, the worse it'll get. Not just for you. For all of us."

Beckett twisted his grip around the water bottle, the plastic cracking. He put most of his weight into his uninjured leg, shoved to his feet and stretched out one hand. "Thanks for the help, Reed."

"Glad there was still time I could." Reed shook his hand, then headed for the front door. He pulled a deep tan trench coat from off the rack near the alarm panel and slid his arms into each sleeve. "You owe me a new couch, and one keep-my-name-out-of-a-crime-scene-report card."

Damn it. Emily Cline's body. Sooner or later, he'd have to answer for that, considering the shooter had taken his service weapon off him and Raleigh's prints would be discovered on the weapon that killed her former assistant. Their prints and DNA were all over that ranch. It wouldn't be hard for forensics to place them at the scene, but it looked like Reed had bought them some time. "You got it."

A burst of cold air slithered into the new holes in his clothes as Reed closed the door behind him. Within seconds, the growl of an outdated, muscled engine filled the cabin and headlights flashed. Beckett didn't wait around to watch the deputy make his way down the mountain through the windows. Not when every instinct he owned was begging him to search her out. He headed for the thick black handrail off one side of the kitchen leading up to the next level. The same color of sleek wood paneling followed him up the stairs and rounded the wide expanse of the master bedroom. A large queen-size bed took up most of the space in the center of the room, a minimalistic rack with hangers off to one side. Matching nightstands with lamps, light carpet, modern art hanging above the bed tied in the modern but rustic theme, and in the center of it all, the woman who made it all disappear.

Raleigh lay on one side, faced away from him. Long damp hair spread across the dark gray pillowcase. The clothes she'd been wearing were discarded on the floor, spots of bright red blood so stark against the white fabric of her undershirt, and his gut clenched. She'd stayed with him, watched over him, as Reed had worked to keep him from bleeding out, even at the risk of injuring herself further. That drive of hers, the one that pushed her to be the best, to get the job done, that had built her into the woman he'd fallen in love with all those months ago, kept her from seeing the consequences of putting everyone but herself first. She could've died out there.

They could've lost the baby, but she was the reason he was standing here. She was the reason he hadn't given up hope.

"Stop standing there and get in the bed." Her sleep-coated voice sent heat through his veins. She rolled onto her opposite shoulder, hypnotizing green eyes settling on him, and the past two days slid to the back of his mind.

"There's plenty of room on the floor." Exhaustion dug into his muscles as he slipped off his boots and tossed his destroyed pants onto the floor, her gaze following his every move. Pressure built behind his chest, but not the same kind as when they'd been facing off against a professional killer. No, this was something deeper, more exposing. They'd been through hell together, and he guessed that made them more alike than he'd originally believed.

"Your chivalry is going to tear your stitches." She maneuvered back onto her side, the outline of the same gauze and tape Reed patched him with visible through the oversize superhero T-shirt she'd donned. "Besides, we're adults. I think we can keep our hands to ourselves."

It wasn't her hands he was worried about. After everything they'd been through at the ranch, he wanted nothing more than to hold her against him, to make sure she was real and this wasn't some nightmare he couldn't wake up from. Medical tape pulled at the hairs across his thigh, stinging. He went for the folded clothes on the bottom shelf of the clothing rack. He and Reed weren't the same size, but close enough to make the two-people-one-bed situation a little less awkward. Pain arced through him as he shoved both feet into a pair of sweats meant for someone less bulky than he was and threaded his arms into another one of Reed's superhero tees. He approached the bed, locking on the exhausted, intelligent woman under the sheets. "Enjoying the show?"

"It's been so long since I've seen the show, I've got to enjoy it while I can get it." Her laugh lit up the parts of him that hurt the most as he slipped between the warm sheets. Within seconds, he'd forgotten all about the pain as Raleigh pressed her back against his chest, a perfect fit against him. "Don't move a muscle, Marshal Foster."

Beckett rested his cheek against the crown of her head and closed his eyes. "I'm not going anywhere."

SHE TRACED THE outline of the gauze taped to his shoulder through the soft T-shirt he'd borrowed. His chest rose and fell in easy rhythms as morning sunlight pierced through the edges of the curtains. Nothing like before when she'd found him unconscious in that barn fighting for breath. He was warm and rough, and she didn't dare stir for fear of ruining this perfect moment. They'd survived. Somehow. He'd protected her when every second leading up to right now she'd doubted his promise, doubted he would keep his word, but he'd been there. Made sure they'd made it off that ranch alive.

Grazing his split bottom lip with her thumb, she gave in to the explosive memories of that gut-wrenching kiss they'd shared before the bullets had started flying. She could still taste him. His underlying flavor of peppermint and wildness, but that kiss had been more than pure physical desire. It'd been a hit to the invisible barriers she'd been building all her life, the distance she'd put between her and everyone around her. The cracks had started spreading when they'd been together for those short few months, but after her arrest they had filled with a clear ice she hadn't let anyone break through. Only now… Now for the first time, she felt herself trying to break down that barrier, break through the distrust and hurt. He might've originally defended her as some part of that moral code of his or out of obligation to their baby, but he'd still saved her life. He'd still kept his word to be there for her, even when he'd had the chance to leave her behind, and the numbness from that destructive black hole inside that'd always felt unwanted—unloved—eased a bit. Her insides warmed as she settled her chin against his uninjured shoulder and studied the movement behind his closed eyelids. "How long have you been pretending to be asleep?"

Piercing blue eyes matched the smile tugging at one corner of his mouth. He slid his hand over hers, positioned directly over his heart. The rhythmic beat pulsed through her, ensured this wasn't just some dream. He was here. He was real. "Who says I'm pretending?"

"You never were a good liar." A laugh bubbled up her throat as she leveraged her elbow into the mattress to see his face better, something that seemed to come easier the longer he was around. The stitches in her side stretched but stayed in place. "So do you make it a requirement of your friends to store extra bags of blood, or is that part of Reed thinking he's a superhero?"

"The shirts." His chest shook with a laugh, followed by a groan as he clutched the wound in his shoulder. "Yeah, don't ask me why, but there's not a single shirt in his possession that doesn't have some kind of super-hero logo on it. The guy's obsessed."

"That was clear while he was stitching you up. Kept telling me all about one of the movies he saw last week. I had no idea what he was talking about." She hadn't really had time to keep up on anything outside her own personal investigation into whoever'd stolen from the foundation's donations accounts other than a few baby books. "Guess I've been out of the loop for a while. I don't even know if you're living in the same apartment, or if you started seeing someone else after we…"

Air caught in her lungs. He'd kissed her back at the ranch. He wasn't the kind of man to kiss a woman while another waited for him to finish up his assignment, but that didn't mean he hadn't quickly moved on after her arrest. Didn't mean he hadn't replaced her.

"You're asking if I've been with anyone else since we split up?" he asked.

She shouldn't care. They weren't together anymore, and they didn't have plans to change that in the future. No matter what happened with the investigation, they'd agreed to be active in their daughter's life, but tension still flittered down her spine as she put a few more inches of space between them. Part of her did care—too much—and she wasn't sure what to do with that. She didn't like this feeling—this hope—he'd changed his mind about cutting her from his life after discovering the truth she'd been framed. Because anytime she'd given in to that sensation, she'd always been the one to get hurt, the one left behind. She moved to get out of the bed. "I'm sorry. It's not any of my business."

Calloused fingers wrapped around her arm, preventing her from escaping the warmth of the sheets, and she turned back into him. Beckett leveled his gaze on her, and everything inside her balanced on the edge of some invisible cliff waiting for his answer. One word. That was all it would take, and she'd fall. He released his hold on her arm and threaded his fingers through the hair at the base of her neck. "There hasn't been anyone but you, and when we were out there together, fighting to stay alive, I realized I didn't want there to be."

His admission cut through her, and her mouth dropped open. "What?"

"I made a mistake. After your arrest." Sliding his hand down her neck, along the most sensitive part of her throat, Beckett followed the trail of her collarbone. Fire erupted in the wake of his touch. In the past few months she'd known her body could feel pain, trauma, betrayal and numbness, usually more than one at a time, but she'd never felt this. This...connectedness to another human being. This craving. The muscles along his arm rippled as he ventured over her sternum and scorched a path toward her navel, resting where their baby thrived. "After we fled into the woods, you said I was so determined to make you the enemy, I refused to see if there was the tiniest shred of evidence proving your innocence. And you were right."

Her heart jerked in her chest. Deep down, she'd known that to be true, but there'd still been a piece that'd wanted her to be wrong. Hearing him admit it now... She didn't know what to say to that. Didn't know what he wanted her to say.

"I was so angry about what my father did to our family, I've been blinded from seeing anything other than the black and white in front of me. Good vs. bad. Guilty vs. innocent. People who hurt others vs. those who don't." He fisted his hand and dug it into the mattress between them. He cast his gaze down, refusing to meet her eyes. "Whenever I asked about your family, you dodged the question or would change the subject. I felt like you were keeping me at a distance the entire time we were together, hiding something, and after I got my hands on those sealed records, I was so positive I was seeing the real you for the first time. The criminal you didn't want me to know about. There were so many similarities between your case and my father's, I automatically equated all of that hatred and rage I had for what he'd done with you, but I was wrong. About everything, and I'm sorry. I know you had nothing to do with stealing those donations, and I'll spend the rest of my life trying to make up for my mistakes if that's what you need from me."

Tears burned in her eyes as the last of the barrier she'd built between them shattered.

"I'm sorry, too. Keeping my past from you had nothing to do with you and everything to do with me, Beckett. I never meant to keep you at arm's length. I just… wasn't ready to face it yet. All that pain, the consuming shame every time I thought about what'd happened with my brother." Raleigh framed his face with one hand, forcing him to look up at her. The dark, swirling blue depths of his eyes broadcast the internal war struggling to break through the surface. His beard tickled her palm as she stroked her thumb along his jaw. "But being with you these past couple of days, having to relive that part of me, confronting it openly and honestly, has finally forced me to get rid of this weight that's been suffocating me for years. You did that for me, and that counts for a lot more than you give yourself credit for."

"You give me too much. I told you I'd always be there for you. Then I disappeared when you needed me the most." He turned his mouth into her palm, anchoring her hand against his face with his, and kissed the sensitive skin below her fingers. "I was a coward, and you deserved a whole hell of a lot better than me."

"Good thing I'm the one who gets to decide what I deserve." Raleigh leaned into him, pressing her mouth to his softly. After everything they'd been through, how much he'd risked to keep her safe, coupled with his apology, the hurt she'd been holding on to for the past few months released a bit of its grip from her chest. Heat raced down her neck and across her shoulders as he rotated onto his back, dragging her with him, and a smile broke through her control. "I think you misunderstood. Right now, what I deserve looks like a US marshal making me breakfast."

"You got it." His laugh resonated through her, and she fought to memorize every second. There'd been times after her escape from federal custody she'd tried to remember that laugh, what it'd been like to wake up beside him, how it'd felt to have him warm her when a draft came through their apartment. In the end, they'd just been fragments of memory, but this… She'd never forget this. Beckett slid his legs over the side of the bed, then turned to press his hands into the mattress as he claimed her mouth in a dizzying kiss. The sweats he'd borrowed from Reed outlined thick lines of muscles in his legs and calves, and she couldn't help but enjoy the view. "Eggs, waffles and sausage coming right up. Don't go anywhere."

She'd been running for the past four months, constantly looking over her shoulder, worried she wouldn't have the chance to clear her name before being taken back into custody. But here, she felt safe, protected, wanted. She wasn't going anywhere. "Wouldn't dream of it."

Chapter Ten

A baby.

He hadn't gotten the chance to fully consider what that meant. They'd spent the past two days running for their lives and trying not to get shot, but the news was starting to sink in now. Beckett shot his arm out to flip the eggs in the pan. Fried. Just the way she liked them. The timer of the waffle iron chirped, the entire kitchen a mess of waffle mix, eggshells, milk and cooking oil. Hell, their daughter wasn't even here yet, and the sinking sensation of doubt had already started creeping in. How were they supposed to do this? Clearing Raleigh's name of the embezzlement charges would take work, but the fact she'd escaped federal custody and gone on the run could make it so she'd have to serve some jail time. For how long, he didn't know. Guess it depended on the judge, but she'd broken the law, and while people changed—while he'd changed—the law didn't.

Right now, he couldn't fully tell the woman he'd left in that bed was pregnant, her body almost as lean as he remembered. He didn't know a whole lot about babies, but that baby wouldn't wait around for her mother to pick a good time to make her debut. Beckett slid two eggs onto a plate and set the pan back on the stovetop. He hadn't asked to be a father, but he was going to be one anyway. He wasn't going to avoid his responsibility to that baby's creation. He had a steady job with the Marshals, an apartment. He could support their daughter while Raleigh got back on her feet. They'd have to work out a custody-and-visitation agreement after she was born, or...

His gaze settled on the stairs leading up to the single bedroom. Or maybe this thing between him and Raleigh could be more. Maybe he could have everything he'd ever wanted. Everything they'd both wanted for themselves but never got the chance. A family without secrets, without lies and resentment or loss. Just the three of them.

The smoke detector pealed from overhead, shocking Beckett back into reality. Within seconds, the rest of the detectors joined in from all over the cabin. His ears rang as he dashed to get the waffle burning in the iron free with a fork and his hands. Smoke dived deep into his lungs. Blistering heat burned his fingertips until he finally got the blackened mess free of the metal and into the kitchen sink. After unplugging the device, he flipped on the water and doused the charred remains of Raleigh's breakfast until the smoke cleared. He gripped the edge of the glossy black countertop. His throat burned. Yeah, he was definitely ready to be a dad. At least their daughter would be living off milk for those first few months. No need for her to have to suffer with his cooking skills. He tossed a kitchen towel across the room. "Damn it."

"That's not exactly what I had in mind when I asked

for breakfast, but I appreciate the effort." The sound of bare feet padding down the stairs and across the hardwood flooring raised the hairs on the back of his neck, and suddenly he couldn't think. Couldn't breathe. Dark hair tousled from sleep, Raleigh was a vision unlike any he'd seen before. Long, lean, flawless in nothing but one of Reed's oversize superhero T-shirts, and his chest constricted. She smoothed her hands over the island countertop, the hints of green in the stone almost a perfect match for her eyes. "Need help? I've heard I make a mean glass of orange juice."

He couldn't hold back the laugh escaping his chest. Yeah, she did. "I was the one who said that after you started a fire in my apartment trying to soften the chocolate hazelnut spread in the microwave for your toast."

"Okay, so I accidentally put the jar in the fridge after sneaking some spoonfuls in the middle of the night." She lifted one shoulder in a shrug, angling her chin to the point she actually looked innocent as he wiped down the waffle iron. "I didn't think it would turn into a brick, and I was positive I'd gotten all the foil off the edges before I put it in the microwave."

"That wouldn't have held up in court if my landlord had moved forward with his lawsuit." Pouring the rest of the batter into the now decharred iron, he set the timer. "But now that you mention it, orange juice would be great."

"I'm on it." She moved around the counter, all grace and beauty as though the past couple of days hadn't affected her in the least or that they hadn't nearly died out there, and hell, he admired her for that. He'd spent the entire night envisioning how far he would've gone if Emily Cline had finished what she'd started, if he'd lost Raleigh and their baby. She ducked her head into the fridge, her shirt hugging her in all the right places, but Beckett could only zero in on the stain blossoming through the shirt from her side. "Any word from Reed or your office about the mess we left at the ranch? Can't imagine they're too happy—"

"You're bleeding again." He dropped the fork he'd been holding while waiting to pry the waffle free and closed the distance between them. The tang of metal on granite resonated in his ears as she closed the fridge, and she stared up at him. He threaded his hand between her arm and her rib cage to get a better look.

Arching the bottle of orange juice overhead, she studied the spread of red across her side. "Damn. I have a feeling Reed isn't going to let me raid his closet anymore after he finds out about this."

"Sit down." He unplugged the waffle iron, took the bottle of orange juice from her and set it on the counter, then maneuvered her back until her knees hit the edge of one of the kitchen chairs. A combination of her natural scent and Reed's sank in his chest like a rock as she sat, and a dose of fire burned through him. He trusted the deputy, respected the hell out of him, but Beckett would break the bastard's nose if he came anywhere near what was his. Dropping to one knee, he suppressed the groan as the stitches in his thigh protested. His. What the hell was wrong with him? Two days ago he'd been fantasizing about handing her over to the feds, and now he was thinking of all the ways they could make a life for their daughter if given the chance. "I need you to…let me see the wound."

Which meant seeing anything going on under that shirt.

"Right. Not weird at all. Just exposing myself to a man who I used to sleep with so he can see what's wrong with my stitches. Not a big deal." The words carried a hint of sarcasm, that specific tone she'd use to neutralize any situation she didn't want to confront. She rolled her shirt higher, exposing long lines of pale, smooth skin and the pattern of moles he'd memorized that first night they'd been together. Tasteful beige underwear edged with lace skimmed the tops of her thighs, and suddenly he didn't dare touch her. Not something so perfect, so beautiful. So deserving of better than anything he could offer.

But he'd try. Because he couldn't let the anger he'd held on to for all these years—the hatred for what his father had done—touch her or their baby. Neither of them deserved to feel that kind of pain or to feel the effects of his past trauma, and for the first time as he stared up at Raleigh, he realized he didn't either. Every decision Beckett had made over the past twenty years had led him to this moment, led him to becoming a US marshal. His father had led him here. He protected the innocent because he hadn't been able to protect his mother when he was sixteen. He hunted fugitives because he hadn't been able to find any kind of evidence of Hank Foster or the money he'd stolen after the son of a bitch had disappeared. He went out of the way for the men and women he worked with because he couldn't stand the thought of losing anyone else to the people he brought to justice. Everything he did, everything he said, was because of someone else's actions, and hell, that moment of losing the only family he'd had left had controlled him his entire life.

But it wasn't just him anymore. He was going to be a father to a baby girl, a coparent with Raleigh, and he couldn't let the past dictate his future. Not anymore. He wasn't sure he'd ever be able to forgive his father for what he'd done, but that single event didn't have to control him from here on out. Didn't have to hold him back from being happy. He had the power to choose, to let go, move on.

And he was choosing this.

Right here. Right now. Choosing Raleigh. Choosing their baby.

They were going to be a family.

"Beckett?" His name on her lips raised the temperature of the room by at least ten degrees. Or was it his heart rate that couldn't keep up with the rest of his body? Bloodied gauze lined with tape crinkled at the edges as she breathed. Raleigh tried to get a better look at the wound. "You look like you've seen a ghost. Is it worse than you thought?"

"No. I... You've done everything in your power to protect this baby, even against me, and I can't wait to see what kind of mom you'll be when she's born." He set his hand against her side, her body heat warming him straight down to his bones. His calluses caught on smooth skin as he peeled back the layer of gauze and tape. Thankfully, the stitches Reed had sewn in hadn't torn, but he'd need to clean out the area around the wound again and change her dressing. "I know I was another person in the long line of people who've hurt you, but if you'll let me, I'd like to be there for you both. Appointments, parenting classes, the birth. I can help with setting up the nursery or finding you an apartment when this is over, or if you want a custody agreement, I'll respect that, too. Whatever you're willing to let me have, I'll take it. I just don't want to screw this up. If you give me the chance, I want to be there for you and the baby, to prove I can keep my promises."

Her mouth parted. Her eyes went wide. "You want to do this together?"

"More than anything," he said.

"I don't…" Tension shot across his shoulders as mere seconds slipped past one after the other. Raleigh licked her lips, his attention homing in on the softness of her mouth before she nearly knocked him out cold with that gut-wrenching smile of hers. "I'd like that, but only on one condition. You have to change all of her dirty diapers."

Beckett laughed as he straightened on his knees and threaded his hand through the hair at the base of her neck. "You got a deal."

HE WANTED THEM to have another chance. To be a family.

Raleigh slipped from the bed, the hardwood floor cold under her bare feet as she reached for her discarded clothing a few feet away. They'd spent nearly the entire day talking, debating baby names, imagining what a combination of the two of them would look like, and she stretched all the stiff muscles she'd forgotten existed. Her stitches tugged at the fresh gauze he'd taped over her side, and she stopped short of straining the wound farther. It'd been a long time since she'd felt much of anything, but she felt this. Whatever this was between her and Beckett. The tightness in her chest had lightened. It was easier to breathe. They'd been together for six months before the FBI had arrested her, but the connection they'd shared over the past few days somehow seemed different. Stronger. Changed.

What that meant for the future—if they had one as anything more than coparents—she didn't know, but after everything that'd happened, she was willing to find out. As much pain and hurt she and Beckett had caused one another, they'd agreed on one thing from the beginning: giving their daughter the life she deserved. Most of all she deserved two parents who would always be there for her, always love her, no matter what. Hypothetically, if those parents lived together in the same home, even loved each other, their baby could have a better shot at happiness.

Studying him from over her shoulder, she couldn't help but smile at the idea of waking up to this sight every morning, just as she'd imagined back at the ranch. The only thing missing was the crib that would be positioned nearby in a short few months. Everything else she needed was right in front of her. The smile weakened.

She'd envisioned it so many times after her arrest, but that deep-seated part of her still clung to the fear Beckett would be there for all the appointments and everything that came with preparing to give birth, not for her but for their daughter. Which, honestly, she should be grateful for. There were so many children orphaned by mothers who hadn't made it through the birthing process because the fathers weren't around to take responsibility. So many babies growing up in foster care as she and her brother had. She'd believed him when he'd promised to always be there for them. Because this was his baby, too. He was the kind of man to do whatever it took to ensure their daughter was loved, but he'd promised her the same thing before she'd been arrested. Now she was on the run.

Raleigh clung to her side as she stood, midafternoon sunlight gliding across her skin. Soon, they'd clear her name of the embezzlement charges. She'd have to appear in court for fleeing federal custody, even though she'd been wrongly accused in the first place, but afterward they'd get the chance to move on with their lives. A deeper part of her, one she hadn't dared investigate over these past three days, hoped that he'd meant together. Not as coparents, but as something more.

Her mouth watered as the craving for fresh fruit that'd woken her from her nap consumed her focus.

Padding down the stairs leading to the main floor, Raleigh ignored the colder temperatures on this level and headed for the fridge. Over the past few weeks her body temperature had been slowly climbing higher to the point she'd had to put the air conditioner in her aunt's cabin at risk of freezing up. Cool air cascaded across her exposed skin as she focused on the container of fresh grapes on one shelf. "Your dad makes a mean waffle, but we've got the good stuff now, baby girl."

An electronic ping registered from the small living room, which really only consisted of a modern-looking gray couch, a coffee table and barely any leg room. Popping the plastic grape container, Raleigh carried her snack toward the phone she'd taken from the shooter's vehicle on the coffee table. She wrapped her fingers around the thin frame. The screen lit up again as she raised the phone. It vibrated in her hand. An incoming call, but not from Beckett's contact list off his SIM card. The number wasn't stored in his contacts, but Raleigh knew that number. She'd dialed it over a hundred times over the years. "Calvin?"

She dropped the container of grapes. Both the local police department and the US Marshals had reports from the EMTs at the scene that he'd lost too much blood in his house for him to survive. Or was this whoever'd attacked him? Whoever'd framed her for stealing all that money? The phone stopped vibrating. A notification for one missed call slid across the screen. A different-pitched ping reached her ears as a new message arrived. She couldn't read it without entering Beckett's password. Raleigh glanced up the stairs, listened for any kind of movement before swiping her thumb across the screen. She had to know.

The screen bled from black to a white background with five words highlighted in a blue bubble.

"Pick up the phone, Raleigh." The thin metal frame vibrated again, startling her. Another incoming call from the same number. Her mouth dried. Hand shaking, she hit the green answer button on the screen and brought the phone to her ear. "Hello?"

"Raleigh, thank goodness you're okay." A graveled exhalation filtered through the phone as her former business partner's familiar voice nearly forced her to collapse in relief. "They haven't gotten to you yet."

"Calvin? I thought… They told me you were…" She

turned toward the windows, looking out over the expanse of the trees and mountains. The cabin sat higher
up the mountain, and she was afraid their connection
wouldn't last long. He'd been declared missing less than
two days after his wife, Julia, had called the authorities
when she'd found the blood in their home, and the local
police hadn't recovered a body. Calvin had to know the
Marshals and the FBI were keeping up-to-date on his
personal phone through phone records. They'd notice
the call to this phone. They'd run the number and pin-
point where she was, who she was with. They couldn't
waste time. "Tell me you're okay. All that blood at the
scene—"

"I'm alive, but I barely made it out of my house. Your
assistant, Emily, she was torturing me for information
about another account, one the feds haven't linked to
the investigation, but I didn't know anything. I only
had what you'd shown me before the FBI showed up at
the office." His unsteady breathing pierced through the
slight ringing in her ears. He was out of breath. Possibly
injured. "After I escaped, I ran. I got rid of my credit
cards and tried to stay off the radar. I've been staying at
a motel outside of Portland, but I think I might've been
followed. What the hell is going on? Are you safe?"

"I'm safe." She'd done this. She'd brought him into
this. Pressing one hand against the cool window, she
forced herself to breathe through the heat climbing her
neck. Cold worked down her arm and into the center
of her chest. She'd ruined an innocent man's life trying to uncover the truth to save her own. "Calvin, this
is all my fault. They came after you because I showed
you the evidence I'd uncovered concerning the missing

donations. They couldn't get to me while I was in federal custody, so they targeted you, and I'm so sorry. I'm going to fix it. I promise. I'm going to find the people who are doing this."

"Raleigh, listen to me. This isn't your fault. Just be sure to watch your back. Don't trust anyone. Understand? Especially the feds. Who knows how far this reaches?" Static preceded a loud thump on his side of the line. Calvin lowered his voice to a whisper. "I think they found me. Take care of yourself and remember what I said. Don't trust anyone."

The line died.

"Calvin?" Raleigh checked the screen. The timer had frozen. He'd hung up on her, and fear slithered through her. She called the number back, but it went straight to voice mail. Her heart rate hiked into dangerous territory as she tried again.

Heavy footsteps echoed down the stairs, and she instantly deleted the record of her former business partner's call and message. Calvin had been targeted because of her, which meant someone had intel that she'd reached out to him in the first place. "Raleigh? I thought I heard you talking to someone. Everything okay?"

Don't trust anyone. Especially the feds. Calvin's warning played over and over in the back of her mind as she faced Beckett. She'd known and worked with Calvin Dailey for years. Not just within the foundation but personally. She had no reason not to trust him. They were still in danger, and if he was sure he was being followed back to wherever he'd been hiding, she had to keep her guard up, too. Because Calvin was right. They

didn't know how far the corruption within the foundation extended, and she wasn't going to put his life—or
his family's lives—any more at risk than she already
had. Her gut clenched. Which meant, as much as she
hated the idea, she couldn't tell the US marshal standing in front of her Calvin was still alive. At least, not
until they found whoever was behind the threat to Calvin's and her lives. She tried to school her expression,
the phone still in her hand, but even she could tell her
smile was forced. "I'm fine."

"The grapes scattered across the entire floor say otherwise." Suspicion played across his expression, and her
heart sank toward her stomach. He was one of the best
marshals in the state. Reliable, cautious, supportive.
The second she committed to keeping him in the dark,
she'd destroy any kind of relationship they'd rebuilt, but
Calvin's life had been put in danger because of her. It
would be again if she exposed the fact her former business partner was still alive. She wouldn't be able to live
with herself if something happened to him. Or Beckett.

"Funny story. The baby craves fresh fruit almost
constantly, so I came downstairs to get a snack, and I
couldn't find the remote for the TV, so I picked up your
phone." Half-truths were the best kind of lies. More be-
lievable. She slid her hand over her stomach for reassurance she was doing the right thing. Instead, a hint
of the numbness Beckett had helped dissolve closed
in. "Turns out I'm not so great at the words game as I
thought. I may have lost my temper and the game to
someone named Watson."

She was taking a shot in the dark. That was the other
deputy marshal on his team, wasn't it?

"I've been close to deleting that game a dozen times because of him. I swear the bastard has the entire English dictionary memorized." A smile pulled the lips she'd been kissing less than a few hours ago thin. He closed the space between them, sliding warm hands down her arms, and relief coursed through her. Beckett took the phone from her hand and set it back on the table before heading toward the fridge. "Come on. I'll make you a proper snack. Anything you and the baby want."

She eyed the phone as she followed him into the kitchen. "Sounds perfect."

Chapter Eleven

There had to be something in the FBI's reports they could use.

Beckett used the trackpad on Reed's laptop to scroll through the FBI's and Portland Police Bureau's investigation files. Interviews of anyone who had access to the donation funds, including Emily Cline, witness statements from the foundation's financial services division, bank account and routing numbers, evidence logs from the scene at Calvin Dailey's home and lists of documents taken off the foundation's servers—it was all here.

It all pointed to Raleigh as the primary suspect.

Whoever'd set this entire game in motion had covered their bases. The feds' case had practically been gift wrapped for them with a damn bow and a silver platter, but Beckett wouldn't let them win. Raleigh was innocent. The proof was in the bullet wound in his shoulder, the stab wound in his thigh and the piece of shrapnel in her side. Emily Cline had been hired by whoever'd taken that money to tie up loose ends. That'd included the mother of his child. It was a miracle they'd gotten out of there alive, but the nightmare wasn't over. Not until they uncovered who'd framed her for embezzling those funds. Until then he'd make damn sure they never got another shot at her.

The sun dipped behind the surrounding mountains and cast rays of pink and orange across the main level of the cabin. Beckett slid his attention to the sleeping woman on the couch, the circles under her eyes lighter than a few days ago. They'd spent most of the afternoon talking about the baby, what symptoms Raleigh had been feeling up to this point, checking her wound. She'd even let him put his hand over her stomach in hopes he'd feel a kick. Didn't work, but despite the resentment he'd wedged between them, he'd missed having someone this close, someone he could trust. Damn, if he were being honest with himself, he'd simply missed her. Her fight, her drive, her dedication to make any given moment more awkward between them. A short laugh burst from his chest, but quickly died as reality set in. Only problem with disappearing into the bubble they'd created together was it didn't stop the real world from going on, and it wouldn't solve this case.

But he would. For her, for their family and their future. Because no matter how many times he'd tried to convince himself otherwise, she'd gotten under his skin.

Beckett turned back to the laptop and started where this had all begun. The foundation's accounts. According to Raleigh, nearly twenty people had access to that money, and he'd dig into every single one of them until he got a hit. He paged through the statements collected at the beginning of the investigation, then checked the real-time balances of the accounts and leaned away from the computer.

"That can't be right." All of the affected accounts had been frozen the moment the FBI caught wind funds were missing. The entire foundation had been shut down from operating as long as the case was ongoing. So why was there a difference between the account statement logged four months ago and the current funds in the account? None of that money should've been accessible. He clicked through to the transfer history, noting the user ID below each amount moved from the account. Dozens of transfers leading up to Raleigh's arrest, all totaling one penny short of ten thousand dollars, the threshold unflagged by the federal government, but the last transfer—the largest of them all—had been made one day after Raleigh's arrest. Before the bank had frozen the accounts on the feds' order. Only she couldn't have made that transfer while she'd been in FBI custody. He grabbed his phone and used the calculator app, subtracting the difference between the original statements and the current balances. His low whistle pierced through the silence. One million dollars had gone missing the day after the accounts had been frozen, in addition to the original fifty-point-five million.

He could take this to the district attorney. He could show the transfers—all of them—hadn't been conducted by Raleigh but by someone else using her credentials, but it wasn't hard evidence. The DA would argue she had someone working on the inside, or that Beckett's judgment had been compromised. That she could've gotten access to a device without the feds knowing, or any number of valid variables. The sight of her on his phone as he'd come downstairs a few hours ago flashed across his memory, but he pushed that theory into the small black box at the back of his mind. She didn't have anyone on the inside. She wasn't transferring funds out of her own charity's accounts, and his judgment hadn't been compromised. He knew exactly who she was and what she was capable of. Beckett paged through the more recent statements. The money had to have gone somewhere, to another account the feds hadn't flagged. All he had to do was find the leak, and this would be over.

"You figured out there's more money missing." Movement pulled him from focus as Raleigh pushed upright in his peripheral vision, one hand on her side, but she refused to let her expression show how much pain she was in, and his gut tightened. Always out to impress, to prove she was the strongest.

"Have you suddenly developed the ability to read my mind?" He pressed back into the bar-stool cushion and ran a hand through his hair as frustration took hold. Nobody could move that much money without tipping off the executives or the FBI, considering Raleigh's arrest had put the entire foundation under the microscope. There had to be a reason it hadn't been flagged. "Or is it some kind of sixth sense that comes with being pregnant?"

"Maybe it's Reed's shirt giving me extra abilities." Her laugh resonated through him as she slid one hand across his shoulders. The scrape of her nails across his skin raised the hairs on the back of his neck, eliciting remnants of the electricity they'd shared during that kiss back at the ranch. Raleigh studied the laptop's screen. "I saw the difference in the statements a few weeks after my arrest. IT was supposed to cut off my access, and for a while I think they had, but then I saw a single transfer notification sitting in my email when I logged in a few weeks ago. Someone had turned my access back on and had used it to make one more transfer after my arrest. And to make it look like I was the one who'd done it."

Clear green eyes connected with his as she leaned into him. Her voice hollowed, and it took everything in him not to give in to his explosive need for her bubbling to the surface. "When Emily had me tied to that chair in the barn, she confirmed my suspicion there'd been additional funds funneled out of the accounts into one the feds hadn't flagged yet, but at the time, the only thing I could focus on was you. I didn't know if you were alive, if you were dead, what the hell I'd gotten you into. I've already lost everyone I care about, Beckett. I didn't want to lose you, too. Not again."

"Hey, hey, listen to me." Beckett stood, pulling her in to his chest. Right where she belonged. A perfect fit against him. As though she'd been specifically made to fill the hole he'd been living with nearly his entire life. She hooked both arms under his, caging him between her elbows. Her vanilla scent tickled the back of his throat, and he breathed her in with every last ounce of spare room he had in his lungs, making her part of him. Forever. As he wrapped her in his arms, the world—his sense of justice, integrity, service, everything he thought he'd been standing for all these years—crashed down around them. Even at the threat of torture and pain from a malicious killer, his fugitive had put herself at risk. For him. Damn it all to hell, he loved her for it. Was in love with her. "You didn't get me into this, remember? I came after you. I made the choice to see this through until the end, and we're not done yet. We've survived this long. You, me and our baby. As long as we're together, that's all that matters."

Nodding, she splayed her hand over his heart, her hair catching on his beard under his chin. "Together."

"We're going to figure this out. We're going to find whoever framed you. No matter what happens, I'm not giving up. I'm not going anywhere. I'm here for you and the baby." Beckett combed his hands through her long dark hair. "It'd take a tedious amount of patience and power to hide behind the hundreds of transfers it's taken to pull a heist like this off. Every step they've made is recommitting to building a case against you that would require months if not years of planning. Which executives have been at the foundation the longest aside from you?"

"Calvin and I started the foundation three years ago." Raleigh slid out of his arms, swiping at her face. "I guess the next executive would be one of our lower-level chief officers. She took over some of my duties about a year ago. Everyone else has been with the foundation for less time than that."

His instincts prickled. "How did you and Calvin meet?"

"At another charity event. I was trying to find investors on my own, and we happened to be seated at the same table. We got to talking. I told him my idea to provide expectant mothers with resources and education to help lower birthing mortality rates, and he wanted to help." She folded her hands into one another as she talked. "We worked together to raise the initial capital we needed to bring education and services to mothers here in Oregon, then spent the next few months writing pitches to local businesses and corporations for donations before we went national."

"You didn't run a background check on Calvin?" he asked. "Didn't ask why he was so interested in helping accelerate your work? Why he approached you?"

"Approached me? I just told you we were seated at the same table at another charity event. What do you mean?" Mesmerizing green eyes narrowed on his. She took a step back, taking the heat she'd generated deep below his skin with her. Color drained from her face, and he reached out for her in case she lost her balance. She shook her head. "You can't…you can't possibly think Calvin had anything to do with this. He was attacked because I brought him into this. I went to him with the evidence I'd collected, and now he's missing."

She held on to her side, and a different theory hit him in the gut. The blood. Reed had an entire freezer full of stored bags of blood in case of emergency. For a former combat medic and a US marshal, that wasn't entirely unusual, but what if whoever'd framed Raleigh had had the same idea?

"You're right. He's missing, but I don't think you had any part in that. The Portland Police Bureau hasn't found a body. Just a lot of DNA evidence that could've been easily planted with a few bags of stored blood." Beckett gripped her arms, compelling her to look up at him. To at least face the idea it was a possibility. "You didn't bring your business partner into this at all. It was the other way around. Raleigh, I think Calvin Dailey stole that money, framed you for embezzlement and faked his death to get away with it. You've been a mark from the beginning."

IT WASN'T POSSIBLE. Calvin wouldn't...

A high-pitched ringing filled her ears as she pulled out of Beckett's reach. Three years of conversations, of dinner parties, of late-night pitch writing came into question in a matter of seconds. Her hands shook as she pushed one through her hair. Calvin had escaped a hired killer. Not faked his death. He couldn't have stolen all that money. Wouldn't have framed her. They were friends, partners in building something they could be proud of. Right? He wouldn't...he wouldn't do this to her.

Raleigh closed her eyes as a wave of dizziness washed over her. The timing of his disappearance, the fact he'd known how to reach her on Beckett's phone. The easy answer would be to put his face in that dark silhouette that'd been at the front of her mind since her arrest. The pieces fit better than she wanted to admit. Calvin could have planned this from the beginning. He could've been the one to frame her to take the fall. Because she was an easy mark. Just like Emily Cline had accused her of being.

"Talk to me." Beckett's grip on her arms held her up as the entire world she'd built threatened to shatter right in front of her. "Tell me what's going through your head."

"I... I need some air." She didn't know what else to say, what to think. She couldn't breathe without her chest tightening, and it felt as though the walls were closing in on her. She had to get out of here. Tugging out of Beckett's hold, she pushed past him toward the sliding back door of the cabin. She moved on autopilot, and within seconds, freezing air worked deep into her lungs. The outdoor scent of pine and earth—more pronounced than Beckett's natural aroma—filled the dark, empty spaces clawing for escape inside. Raleigh clutched on to the wood railing with everything she had. She'd barely processed the fact she was pregnant with Beckett's baby and had unshouldered the emotionally traumatic weight she'd carried her entire life, and now she was supposed to accept her closest confidant had turned her into a criminal? The muscles in her jaw ached as she clenched her back teeth. No. Anger blotted out the beauty and expanse of wilderness stretching miles in every direction as she dug her fingernails into the railing. If Calvin was responsible for her arrest—for everything—he hadn't just done this to her. He'd put her baby at risk, and she wasn't going to let him get away with it.

The sliding glass door protested on its track from behind. She didn't have to turn around to know he'd followed her. Her back warmed as Beckett drew near, and right then she wanted nothing more than to pretend he wasn't a US marshal and she wasn't his fugitive, but hiding from the truth didn't change anything. Hiding problems didn't heal them. She had to face it.

"He's alive. Calvin. He called me on your phone." Raleigh notched her chin over her shoulder, keeping him in her peripheral vision as he settled both elbows against the railing beside her. "That's who I was talking to right before you came downstairs. He convinced me Emily Cline had tortured him for information on the secondary account, like she'd threatened us, and I believed him. I agreed to keep his secret because I thought I was the one who'd put him in danger by coming to him with the evidence in the first place. I lied to you." Heat climbed her neck and into her face. She'd lied to a US marshal, but it was more than that. She'd lied to him, the one person who'd willingly positioned himself between a hired gunwoman and her and promised to protect their unborn baby, and she hated herself for it. She'd have to accept the consequences, whatever they may be, and her heart hurt thinking of all the possibilities of what that meant. Of losing him again.

Because over the past few days, she'd let herself care about him again. Cleaning her wounds from the bark, giving up the last of his food and water for her, taking on a professional killer so she could escape. He'd carefully chiseled his way through the hardened exterior she'd built from being unwanted for most of her life, and now there was nothing left. Nothing but him. Whether he'd kept his word to see this investigation through to the end because of the pregnancy, his job with the Marshals or for her, it didn't matter. He'd made her feel wanted, desired even, and she'd hang on to this feeling as long as she could.

"You were right. I was just another mark, easily manipulated because building that foundation from the ground up made me feel valuable, like I was doing something good with my life for once. Calvin must've seen me for exactly what I was when we'd met. Desperate. Weak." Splintered wood bit into her palms. Emotion bubbled past her careful control. "I thought I was doing the right thing protecting Calvin, but that doesn't excuse the fact I lied to you. So I understand if you want to rethink our agreement concerning our daughter. We can work something out to where you won't have to see me after this is over—"

"Men like Calvin Dailey are master manipulators, Raleigh—that's their job. They enjoy hurting people and reaping the rewards of their hard work. No matter how many lives they destroy in the process." He was speaking from personal experience, and her stomach revolted. He'd lost his mother because of a con man. She could only imagine the thoughts running through his head right then. Hands intertwined, he stared out over the tops of the trees, gaze distant. Stars materialized overhead and added a bit of brightness to the blue of his eyes. He straightened, facing her before closing the small space between them. The length of his body pressed into hers, and she was forced to look up at him. He swiped her hair back from her face, and in an instant, warmth lightninged through her. "As long as I've known you, you've put everyone else's needs before your own. That's not weakness, Raleigh. That's courage, and it's one of the reasons I fell in love with you a long time ago. We're going to get through this, but only if we work together. We have to trust each other. No more secrets. No more lies."

Love? Her mouth parted, directing his attention straight to her lips, and an electrical zing lit up her insides. "You love me?"

"Out of all of that, that's what you choose to focus on during this conversation?" His smile pulled at something deep inside her as she lifted her arms behind his neck, careful of the wound in his shoulder. His hands dipped to her waist as though he needed her to anchor him right there on the back deck, and Raleigh was more than happy to let him take advantage. His smile disappeared as he settled those bright blue eyes on her. "You've been taking care of everyone else your whole life. It's time to put yourself first, Raleigh. Don't think about what you want for other people. What do you want? Right now, right here. Tell me what you want."

"I've only wanted one thing my whole life." Her mouth dried. She'd never admitted this to anyone, never admitted it to herself. Nobody had asked her what she'd wanted before, but her answer had always been there, waiting on the tip of her tongue from the very first foster home she could remember. It'd burned each time she'd reached out to someone, only to be used and discarded all over again, as Calvin was doing now. If there was one lesson she'd learned over the years of constant disregard, it'd been the people she'd cared about the most had always had the ability to do the most damage. Including Beckett. Raleigh trailed a path down his arms with her fingertips, memorizing every valley, every ridge in his build beneath the ridiculous shirt he'd borrowed from Reed's closet. "All I've ever wanted was to feel loved by someone as much as I loved them. To have that connection to another person, to be appreciated without any demands, expectations or manipulations. Not because I served a purpose at that moment in their life or because they have an obligation to me." A heaviness lifted from her chest, making it easier to breathe as she looked up at him. "Someone to love me... for being me."

Seconds ticked by, a full minute. Her heartbeat

echoed at the base of her skull. She needed him to say something. Anything.

"There's only one thing I've ever wanted from you." Beckett raised his hand, rough calluses catching on the skin of her jaw as he scorched a path from her earlobe to her chin. Heated sensations battled the cool air slicing through the trees, but a shiver still racked her spine. Not from the temperatures. From him. Always from him. "That's for you to be happy. No conditions, expectations or demands. After everything you've been through in your life, you deserve a happily-ever-after. I don't care if you're pregnant with my baby or someone else's. You're not an obligation to me, and I want to be the one to give you everything. Every second of every day, I'll spend the rest of my life proving it to you, if that's what you need. Starting now."

He reached into his back pocket, pulled a piece of folded white paper free and handed it to her.

"What is this?" Confusion flooded through her. Dry corners slipped against her fingertips as she unfolded the single piece of paper and read the first few lines. Her heart threatened to beat straight out of her chest as understanding hit. "This is a letter of resignation from the US Marshals Service. Dated the day after my escape from federal custody."

Before he'd known she was pregnant.

"I was going to come after you one way or another, Raleigh Wilde," he said. "Because I'm not finished with you."

Tears burned in her eyes. Sincerity laced his words and anchored into the familiar sea of blackness she'd held on to inside for so long. From that single point something new chased back the loneliness, the isolation.

Raleigh lifted up onto her toes and brought his mouth level with hers. The slightest graze of his lips sent a rush of frantic sensation through her. His beard tickled the sensitive skin around her chin and cheeks, heightening her five senses to a whole new level. Carefully curated control—the kind she'd always needed to protect herself from becoming too attached to anyone around her—slipped through her fingers as he dug his hands into her lower back and maneuvered her back through the open sliding glass door. He loved her, and for the first time she could remember, freedom, unlike anything she'd experienced before, coursed along every nerve ending she owned, every muscle, every bone, until she felt like she might explode. "I believe you."

A moan escaped up his throat as Beckett directed her toward the counter, then hauled her onto the island, the cold of the granite more shocking to her central nervous system than she'd expected. The pain from both the bullet wound in his shoulder and the stab wound in his thigh must've spiked when he'd lifted her, but her marshal never let it show. Didn't so much as break their kiss. He was only focused on her, and a different kind of warmth penetrated through the layers she'd built over the years. "Back at the ranch, you told me this wasn't what you wanted. So I'm going to need you to be clear right now. What do you want from me?"

She loved him, too.

"You, Beckett." Her fingers ached as she fisted his

shirt and positioned him between her knees. Pressure released from beneath her rib cage as she breathed into his mouth. "All of you."

Chapter Twelve

Something had changed between them. Something significant he couldn't explain, but the resulting awareness he'd experienced after Raleigh had admitted her deepest desire to be valued above all else didn't press him to dig deeper. She'd trusted him, where so many others had let her down before, and he'd do whatever it took to deserve that trust.

Of all the stories his daughter would hear about her mother when she was old enough, they wouldn't be about fear or loss or manipulation. No. She'd know how strongly, bravely and fearlessly Raleigh fought for her when the world threatened to bring her down. This baby would grow up knowing how to rely on herself through every battle, every struggle that pushed back at her, because of the example of the woman asleep beside him, and Beckett couldn't wait to see it for himself.

Raleigh hadn't felt important to anyone her entire life, but she was everything to him.

And he wasn't about to lose her again.

He slowly drew his legs over the edge of the bed, soreness rocketing through him. There had to be something he was missing in those files, something not even the FBI had caught.

"If you think you're getting out of this bed, Marshal, think again." A smile pulled at her kiss-burned lips as she lay facedown beside him. She shifted beneath the sheets, hypnotic green eyes settling on him as she rolled onto her side. Raleigh wedged one arm under her head, all that gorgeous hair stark against the white pillowcase, and wiggled her eyebrows higher in a feigned attempt at seducing him. "I'll share some of the chocolate I found under the mattress if you reconsider."

A laugh reverberated through him. Damn, he loved her. The mattress dipped under his knee as Beckett planted a kiss on her forehead, afraid anything more would, in fact, stop him from getting out of the bed. He straightened. Collecting another set of clothes from Reed's clothing rack, he shoved his feet into a pair of jeans slightly tighter in the waist than he was used to. "As much as I'd love to break into Reed's weird, secret collection of mattress food, Calvin Dailey is still a suspect we need to look into. Until we're certain he's the one behind those missing funds, you're in danger, and if you want me to be able to pay child support for our daughter, I've got a job to do."

Raleigh sat up on the bed, the sheet clasped against her chest, and he couldn't look away. Temptation to do exactly as she asked flared as he forced himself to reach for a clean T-shirt from the rack. "That's the first time you've said *our* daughter."

"You're right." He slumped onto the bed beside her, his hand automatically reaching for the slightly firm section of her stomach where their baby grew. Beckett kissed her bare shoulder. "Guess it finally feels like we're on the same team."

"Always." She lifted his chin with one finger and slipped her mouth over his, and he was lost in her all over again.

"That's cheating." His laugh filled the room a second time, and it took every last ounce of strength and determination he had left to pull away. "I'm going to check out the transcripts from Calvin's interview conducted by the feds. Feel free to join me after you're dressed."

"Fine, but I'm keeping all of the mattress chocolate for myself," she said.

He made his way down the stairs. On the main level, he righted the laptop he'd pushed across the kitchen island to get to Raleigh and brought it out of sleep mode. Hell, his shoulder and thigh still hurt after that one, but at the time, the pain hadn't bothered him at all. He'd just wanted her. His blood heated at the memories of his name on her lips, the feel of her surrounding him, the echo of exhalations as they'd climbed into ecstasy together. But as long as the threat was still out there, neither Raleigh nor their baby would be safe, and he'd never live with himself if something happened to her on his watch. Not when they could give each other everything they'd ever wanted. Needed.

Beckett clicked through the FBI's case file straight to the interviews and statements. Calvin Dailey had been interviewed by an agent shortly after Raleigh's arrest, but nothing in the transcript gave them a leg to stand on that he was their man. What'd he expect? A full confession? The son of a bitch had claimed he hadn't known anything about Raleigh dipping into the foundation's funds, despite her official statement she'd handed over the evidence she'd collected straight to him two weeks before an anonymous tip pinned her as the FBI's primary suspect. But according to Calvin's statement, it'd sure broken his heart when he'd found out. Yeah, right. Beckett shook his head. Guys like Calvin Dailey were all the same, but Beckett had experience with his kind, and he sure as hell wasn't going to let another con man destroy his future. "Let's see if that's even your real name."

Logging in to the Warrant Information Network—WIN—used by marshals all over the country to conduct investigations, run warrant searches, handle threat management and keep an eye on witnesses in WIT-SEC, he typed the suspect's name into the search bar and hit Enter.

And froze as the man's photo stared straight back at him.

His knees threatened to drop right out from under him as nausea worked up his throat. He gripped the edge of the counter. The suspect was older, slightly worn around the edges, but Beckett would recognize that face anywhere. His instinct to check into the foundation's CEO had been right. Calvin Dailey wasn't the man's real name. Hell, Beckett wasn't even sure he'd ever known his real name, but he knew at least one other alias for the feds to trace.

"Reed seriously needs to consider the kind of chocolate that's worth stashing." Light footsteps padded down the stairs at his back as the muscles down his spine hardened. "Good chocolate is not supposed to have a diet aftertaste. I don't care how much he paid for it. None of that was worth saving."

His hands shook as the rage he'd tried to contain these past few days exploded through him. Adrenaline surged into his veins, the pain in both wounds pushed to the back of his mind. Everything about this case had felt too close, too familiar. He'd ignored those initial suspicions, attributed his feelings to the situation between him and Raleigh, but he'd been wrong from the start. "You knew, didn't you?"

"About the chocolate?" She crossed into his peripheral vision as she wrenched the refrigerator door open and reached inside for a bottled water. "I wish. Now I can't get that taste out of my mouth. Brushing my teeth didn't help."

"You were helping him this entire time, and I was too blinded to see it." The main level of the cabin blurred as Beckett turned on her, and those bright green eyes widened. The past year came into excruciating focus. The mugging, their whirlwind romance, her arrest, the pregnancy. Hell, even him finding out Calvin Dailey was still alive had probably gone off without a hitch. Every step had been meticulously timed and executed. Because if there was one thing he knew about that man in the photo, Calvin Dailey—whoever the SOB would become next time around—never did anything halfway. When he set out to destroy lives, he succeeded. Only Calvin Dailey wouldn't have been able to do it alone. "I've been racking my brain, wondering how on earth someone in the foundation was able to steal that much money without anyone else noticing but you. Now I know. You're working with him."

Venom dripped from his words as Beckett closed the distance between them. The tendons in his fingers ached as he curled them into fists. Had any of it been real, or had he just taken the bait?

"What are you talking about?" Color drained from her face, but she couldn't fool him. Couldn't pretend. Not anymore. What'd looked like vulnerability was a carefully constructed emotional response catered to him, to his reactions. Like the good con woman she was supposed to be, and everything he'd felt for her, every promise out of his mouth, ground into dust inside him. Raleigh tried to counter his approach until her back hit the refrigerator. There was nowhere for her to go this time. Nowhere for her to run. Not from him. "Beckett."

"You've been working with him this entire time, haven't you? Using me," he said.

The muscles along her throat flexed as she swallowed, the water bottle still clenched between her hands. "You're accusing me of partnering with Calvin Dailey to steal from my own foundation. Based on what evidence?"

"Come on. We both know that's not his real name." He struggled to control the fire burning through him as he reached for the cuffs he'd left on the counter beside the keys to the SUV. Cool metal pressed against his palm. "You might as well call him Hank Foster when you're talking to me."

"Calvin Dailey is...your father?" Disbelief coated her words. She stared up at him, her mouth parted slightly as though she were surprised by the information. Hank had certainly taught her well. Her exhalation reached his ears. She shook her head. "Beckett, I swear to you I had no idea—"

"Stop lying!" He slammed his free hand against the fridge above her head, his control razor thin. He'd survived the past twenty years living off his anger—his hatred—for that man, but with her he'd nearly forgotten that feeling. Now the familiarity of that rage wrapped around him. Supported him. Protected him from being that sixteen-year-old kid holding his mother on the floor as she died in his arms. He backed off and collected his shoulder holster loaded with one of Reed's backup weapons from the counter, threading his arms through the supports. "I'm guessing you didn't expect to be arrested four months ago. Your partner threw you under the bus because that's the kind of bastard he is, and as a backup plan you thought you could use me as a get-out-of-jail-free card. You'd appeal to my sense of justice, seduce me, and later down the road, you'd disappear." Beckett turned to her, lasering her with his glare. "Just tell me one thing. Was the pregnancy his idea or yours?"

Her expression smoothed, any hint of the vulnerable, soft woman she'd been slipping away by the second. In her place, the self-assured, driven fugitive he'd always known existed surfaced. "You didn't answer my question. You're accusing me of partnering with a con man to steal from my foundation. What evidence have you found to support that theory?"

"I don't need evidence. You're already a fugitive." Beckett let his hands slip from the refrigerator and pushed away. Grabbing her right arm, he spun her around and secured one cuff around her wrist. Then the other. "Raleigh Wilde, you are under arrest."

THE CUFFS CLICKED loud in her ears, and the invisible black hole he'd helped repair over the past few days engulfed her from the inside. Raleigh bit back the scream working up her throat as her heart shattered into a million unrecognizable pieces, worse than before, but she wouldn't cry. She wouldn't show weakness. Not in front of him. She'd trusted him, believed he'd keep his promises this time, and from the hardness in his expression, there was nothing she could say to make him see the truth. But that didn't stop her from trying. "You're making a mistake, Beckett. I didn't know Calvin was your father. I swear—"

"I'm not interested in anything you have to say. Now walk." His voice lacked the slightest hint of the emotions he'd shown her while they'd been here, and the empty space inside only spread faster. He'd said he'd fallen in love with her, that he'd be there for her and the baby. Had it all been a lie? Beckett gripped the cuffs between her wrists and maneuvered her toward the cabin's front door. "I risked my career for you, put my life on the line for you, and this is what I get for trusting a fugitive. The second I hand you off to the FBI, I'm going after Hank, and I'll never have to deal with you again. My lawyer will be in touch to make arrangements for custody after the baby is born."

He was going to take her baby from her.

"No." Raleigh wrenched out of his hold, twisting around to face him, and he automatically reached for the weapon he'd borrowed from Reed's arsenal upstairs. Her gaze lowered to his hand, then rose back to those defensive blue eyes. Would he shoot her? Would he risk his daughter's life out of his misdirected hatred for the man who'd threatened to destroy them? "I didn't have anything to do with Calvin—" she closed her eyes as disbelief reared its ugly head and forced herself to breathe evenly "—Hank stealing that money. If after everything we've been through together, you still don't believe me, I can handle that. But you don't get to pretend what we had didn't mean anything to you and drive off into the sunset without facing me."

The veins along his forearms seemed to strain to break through the thin skin there, his hand still positioned over the gun in his holster. "What you can or can't handle no longer concerns me."

"Tell me you don't believe me." She battled to keep her face expressionless. She wouldn't back down until he said the words, until he confirmed her deepest, darkest fear. She wouldn't let him see how much his betrayal hurt, how he'd broken her down to nothing all over again. She wasn't going to let him see the destruction he'd caused. Not just for her but for their daughter. Raleigh stepped into him. "Lie to my face. Tell me you don't love me so we can both move on with our lives after you realize what you've done."

One second. Two.

"How could I love someone like you?" His words came through gritted teeth. "I don't even know you, and neither will our daughter."

The effect hit her as though she'd been impaled with a piece of shrapnel all over again. Her throat burned with the sob building at the edges. She'd forgotten how to breathe, how to move, and all she could do was nod as numbness spread through her. No thoughts. No sensations. Just a sea of comforting black she'd been retreating into her whole life. "Then let's get this over with."

Beckett reached over her shoulder and disabled the alarm panel before spinning her toward the door. Cold air worked under the superhero T-shirt and pale gray sweats she'd borrowed from Reed's clothing rack as he led her outside. Her bare feet caught on the splinters sticking out from the aged front porch of the cabin, but she kept moving at his insistence. Dark stains spotted the stairs as they descended, a bloody trail of breadcrumbs leading them to the SUV she'd used to get them to safety. When she'd believed he could finally move past the hatred that'd been tearing him apart since he was sixteen years old.

She'd been wrong.

Raleigh focused on the SUV as they approached. She could run. She could head straight for the trees and never look back, but she'd spend the rest of her life looking over her shoulder if she ran. Because Beckett Foster would never stop searching for her or for his daughter. The best chance she had of giving their baby the life she deserved—a family—would be to prove her innocence and fight for custody. No matter how long it took. No matter how much it hurt.

"What did Hank promise you if you helped him steal all that money? A cut of his share? That he'd leave the entire foundation in your hands and let you live out the rest of your life in peace?" His humorless laugh broke through the slight ringing in her ears. He wrenched the back passenger-side door open but held her arm to keep her from getting in. The keys jingled in his hand as he unlocked one cuff and hauled her hands above her head before securing her to the handle above the seat. Beckett stepped aside as she got in, his hand resting on the outer edge of the door. "I think him hiring Emily Cline to take you out tells you exactly what kind of man you've gotten involved with. Because of you our baby— my baby—is in danger, and if anything happens to her, it's on you. I hope you can live with that."

Nothing she said, no amount of evidence she presented to the contrary, would alter his belief about her or satisfy his anger. She doubted hearing it from the source of all that hatred would do any good either. Beckett had spent his entire life fighting to counterbalance the evil his father had carried out. She only hoped he understood it'd be a lifelong battle. Not with Hank Foster but with himself. She stared at the back of the front headrest as best she could with both hands secured over her head. "If it's all the same to you, I'd rather not talk the rest of the trip back to Portland."

"You got it." He slammed the door, the force quaking through her as she followed his movements through the windshield. Not yet. She couldn't break apart yet, but every step he took around the front of the SUV sealed her fate. He'd take her back to Portland. He'd hand her over to the FBI, and she'd never see him or her daughter again. Of all the promises he'd made over the past few days, this would be one he'd never break.

Tears burned in her eyes, and she ducked her chin to her chest as he pulled himself into the driver's seat. He didn't love her, but she'd been through this before and survived. With every foster family who hadn't been able to handle her violent attempts to protect her brother, with being forced to live with an aunt who'd only used them for an extra paycheck, with the loss of friends after her arrest. Then why, after so many others had discarded her out of selfishness, did Beckett's admission hurt this much? He'd distanced himself from anything that had to do with her after her arrest four months ago, just as he was doing now. Why was this time any different?

Staring out the window, she couldn't focus on anything other than her opaque reflection in the glass. The answer was there, drowning in the storm of feelings reminding her she'd always be unwanted, worthless, unloved by everyone around her. That storm had built her into the woman who'd do whatever it took to succeed emotionally, professionally and physically, but this time...this time she'd let him in. She'd let her guard crumble for the off chance of building a life for their daughter, one where their baby would never doubt she was loved. But now Raleigh would have to be the one to suffer the consequences.

The SUV's engine vibrated to life, and Beckett directed them down the single dirt access road leading down the mountain. The cuffs hit against the handle above her head as the vehicle climbed over wayward rocks and dips in the road. His gaze lifted to the rear-view mirror, connecting with hers for the briefest of moments, and her gut clenched. The trip back to Portland would take at least two hours. She could do this. For hers and Beckett's daughter. *You never know how strong you are until being strong is the only choice you have.* Her brother's words echoed as a memory of him reaching down to help her to her feet after a particularly nasty fight with another foster brother landed her with two broken fingers and a bloody nose. She didn't have a choice now, but she'd sure as hell make sure her daughter did.

She caught movement through the windshield a split second before a bullet penetrated through the glass. Beckett's pain-filled groan filled the silence, and Raleigh ducked low as best she could in her seat as he veered the vehicle off the road. Her heart throbbed at the base of her skull. "Beckett!"

"Damn it. I'm fine." Cold air rushed through the hole in the glass as Beckett reached for his gun. He clutched his side. Blood spilled between his fingers, and before he could unholster his weapon, he slumped in his seat. Unconscious.

"Beckett?" Raleigh leaned forward as much as she could to reach him, but the cuffs kept her secured. She couldn't get to him. The road forced the SUV to course correct, and they were once again headed down the mountain, increasing speed as they approached a sharp turn ahead. She pulled at her restraints, a desperate growl slipping past her control. The pines up ahead were growing larger through the windshield. They were going too fast. They were going to crash.

Sitting back in her seat, she braced for impact as best she could. The vehicle's tires caught on the edge of the opposite side of the dirt road, and the vehicle flipped. The ground rushed up to meet her window. A scream tore past her lips as rocks shattered through the glass and scraped along her shoulder, but before she could take another breath, the SUV rolled again. The tree line and the ground blurred as her stomach shot into her throat. Then everything was still. Absolutely still.

A low thump reached past the haze closing in. Her body felt as though she'd been burned as cold air met the fresh layer of raw skin under the cuffs and the gravel embedded in her shoulder. She clutched the handle Beckett had cuffed her to and tried to sit up, broken glass and debris shifting under her heels, but the SUV had landed upside down in the middle of the road. There was no up. A deep groan reached past the echo of her uneven breathing, and her heart jerked. "Beckett."

The series of thumps grew louder. Closer. Footsteps? Hinges protested loud in her ears as her passenger-side door ripped open, and she closed her eyes to block the piercing sunlight as a dark outline closed in.

"Hello, Raleigh," a familiar voice said. Cold metal slipped between her skin and the cuffs before the steel links snapped. Her arms relaxed onto her chest as a second, more muscular outline reached in and pulled her from the vehicle. "You and I have some unfinished business to discuss."

Chapter Thirteen

"So this is what dying feels like." Beckett gripped the ambulance bay door as the EMT threaded another stitch into his side. His pain receptors screamed in protest, but lucky for him, the bullet had been a through-and-through. A few more stitches and a clean dressing and he'd be back out there hunting his fugitive.

"Stop getting shot, and you wouldn't have to go through this again." Chief Deputy Remington Barton adjusted the AR-15 strapped over her shoulder, barrel pointed down. A black long-sleeved T-shirt peeked out from under her dark tactical vest with US Marshals spread across the back. The radio specifically designed to reach the rest of the deputies on their team had been strapped to one side of the Kevlar, grazing her short black hair, but it was those intense blue eyes that said she was ready for the coming fight. Prepared to protect her team and get the job done. "Want to tell me I'm wrong about how close you are to this investigation again?"

He wasn't going to dignify that question with a response. Helicopter blades thumped loud from overhead. Last he'd checked, the dogs had tracked Raleigh's trail north, but they'd lost her scent as soon as she and whoever'd gotten her out of the SUV had crossed the river about two hundred feet into the woods. They had the entire Oregon US Marshals Service working this manhunt, but Raleigh was smart. She'd managed to escape federal custody once. He should've expected her to try again. "Any sign of her?"

"The footprints we tracked disappear at the river. Looks like whoever'd shot you and pulled her from the SUV carried her out, but we managed to pick up tire tracks on the other side until they meet up with the main road." Remi studied the scene as the sun arced over the western half of the sky. "Whoever was behind the wheel most likely headed west, but enough time passed between the accident and when we arrived on scene, they could be anywhere right now. We're running matches to narrow down the make and model of the vehicle from the tires and putting checkpoints in place. We'll catch her."

"She won't go back to her aunt's cabin. Too risky." Damn it. There was a piece of this case he wasn't seeing, something his gut had been trying to tell him from the start. He just couldn't think straight enough to figure it out. "What about Calvin Dailey? Any luck tracing the call he made to my cell?"

No. Not Calvin Dailey. Hank Foster. His bastard of a father was still hurting anyone he came into contact with, consequences be damned, only this time Beckett would be ready for him. He'd do whatever he had to, to make sure the SOB didn't hurt Raleigh. For his daughter's sake. Pressure built behind his chest as he studied the wreckage. He'd cuffed her to the handle above the back seat. She wouldn't have had any way to fight off the shooter if she was, in fact, innocent, as she'd claimed. The new set of stitches in his side stung, keeping him in the moment. There was no point imagining what'd happened after the crash. Raleigh wasn't innocent.

"The call was rerouted using an internet service. No location, but we've got units at the foundation and his home, and his photo and a list of possible aliases sent to every law-enforcement agent and officer in the state." Remi's ocean-blue gaze locked on him as Beckett shoved to his feet, her mouth lifting at one corner. "I'm sorry. Are you wearing one of Reed's superhero T-shirts?"

He stared her down. "They were the only clean clothes he had on hand."

"If you say so." The chief deputy surveyed the other marshals around them, her expression weary as she stepped into him and lowered her voice. The side of her weapon caught on his shirt. After reaching into her pants pocket, she handed him a thin piece of paper. "There was something else we found while we were following Wilde's trail to the river. Something I have a feeling you wouldn't want anyone else to know about."

Beckett smoothed the thin paper, and a crushing weight took hold of his insides.

The ultrasound.

"You two were together twenty weeks ago," Remi said. "The baby's yours. That's why you wanted to help her clear her name."

Panic cemented his feet in place. His blood pressure spiked as he ran one hand through his hair. Raleigh had done everything she could to hang on to the evidence of her pregnancy these past three days. Hell, she'd slept with the ultrasound right next to the damn bed and kept it in her sweats pocket when she was up walking around the cabin. He ran his fingers over the fresh fold marks. No exceptions. She never would've left this behind.

Not unless she'd been unconscious.

Or taken against her will.

Which could mean… Raleigh was in danger. "Where did you find this?"

"Northwest. About fifty feet past the tree line." Authoritative blue eyes steadied on him, but Beckett was already maneuvering around his superior. "Beckett, she's a fugitive. You knew that when you took on this assignment, and I can't protect you if—"

"I don't need your protection. I'm going to save my family. With or without your help." The scene vanished to the back of his mind as he headed for the nearest SUV. Raleigh was out there. She was in the hands of a killer who'd used her to play out his sick game, and Beckett had accused her of being one of the masterminds. Damn it, how could he have been so stupid? He'd let his hatred for Hank Foster destroy the last remaining chance he had of moving on with his life, of having everything he'd ever wanted, because he couldn't let go of the past. If his father so much as broke a hair on her head, he'd kill the man himself.

His boots sank in the damp earth as Beckett wrenched open the door to Remi's SUV and climbed inside. Within seconds, he'd flipped the vehicle around and accelerated down the mountain. Pines thinned at the bottom of the road, his hands aching from his grip on the steering wheel. "I'm coming. I'm going to find you."

He had to think. Hank had spent the past three to four years as Calvin Dailey, but the man would still have his own habits, locations he would've visited over and over aside from the foundation or his home. Things the con man had been doing for so long, no alias could change. Beckett slowed at the bottom of the hill and shoved the vehicle into Park. He shouldered out of the SUV and rounded the hood. Dips in the old dirt road tried to trip him up, but that didn't stop him from crouching beside the fresh set of tire tracks. Remi had mentioned the driver of the vehicle had most likely turned west to head back to Portland, but this set of muddied tracks leading off the dirt road said otherwise.

East. Toward Mount Vernon.

Beckett straightened, gaze following the length of single-lane asphalt road about a mile off. The bastard was taking her back to where this had all begun twenty years ago. "He's headed to the ranch."

New stitches stretched across his wound tight as he hauled himself back into the driver's seat. Adrenaline brought everything into focus as he dropped the magazine out of the sidearm he'd borrowed from Reed's home arsenal and counted the rounds. There were no guarantees Hank had been working alone when he'd taken Raleigh. He'd hired Emily Cline to do his dirty work, but Beckett wouldn't be caught off guard this time. Not when his entire future was at risk.

He put the SUV in Drive and turned east on 26.

An undeniable rift tore through him at the thought of losing that future, at the thought of what he'd accused Raleigh of doing, at the thought of having to go back to the place where he'd lost everything that'd mattered to him as a kid. He'd spent most of his life trying to recover from the single event of losing his mother to violence, of having a father who'd chosen to hurt people. He'd put himself through high school, gotten his criminal justice degree, worked the ranch with his own two hands and gotten away from it all, but somewhere in the process he'd convinced himself he didn't need anyone. There'd been one person in this world he could rely on when times got tough: himself. But deep down, somewhere he hadn't dared look in a long time, he knew he couldn't spend the rest of this life angry. On edge. Alone. Not when there was a woman out there who'd helped him forget all of that over these past few days, who'd…freed him from the control Hank Foster had held over him since he'd been sixteen years old.

Hell, he needed that weight gone. Needed her.

Raleigh had given him a reason to let the past die. She'd given him something to look forward to after all these years. One look from her—one touch—and the chaos he'd warred with for twenty years calmed, and he couldn't give up on that. Because she hadn't given up on him. Now it was his chance to return the favor.

Beckett reached for his phone, the screen brightening as he raised it, and sent the ranch's coordinates to the rest of the team. He pressed his boot flat against the accelerator to push the vehicle faster. The ultrasound he'd tossed into the passenger seat sat stark in his peripheral vision against the muted background. He reached for it, switching his attention between the dark photo of his and Raleigh's growing baby and the road ahead.

He'd known the day he'd have to face Hank was coming, and if there'd ever been a reason better than to settle the past, it was to save the two people who held his future. "I'm coming, Raleigh. For both of you."

EVENING LIGHT SLANTED at her feet through the old slats nailed over the only window in the room.

Raleigh rolled her head to one side. The out-of-date wainscoting at her back dug into her spine, her hands restrained overhead to some kind of exposed metal plumbing. Dust danced in the rays of sun, making it hard to decipher between the white spots still clinging to her vision and spores. Chunks of drywall littered the peeling linoleum flooring near the legs of an old kitchen set with a single chair. A vanity dresser took up most of the opposite wall, an odd choice considering this room had obviously once been a kitchen, but the framed photos lining the bottom of the mirror told of a family-centered space.

She closed her eyes as pain splintered through one side of her head. She and Beckett had been in an accident, which accounted for gravel embedded in the first few layers of skin of her shoulder. Beckett. He'd been shot, and… She couldn't remember anything after that. Light green flowered wallpaper curled along her side as Raleigh pulled at the rope to sit up.

"I always loved this wallpaper," someone said from beside her.

She jerked as far away from that voice as she could, but the ropes didn't have much give. Her heart shot into her throat as she realized how close he'd gotten. "Calvin. What…what are you—"

"Took us three months to agree on this paper." His navy blue suit jacket and slacks accentuated dirt and dust streaking along his tall frame. Dark brown shoes knocked against hers as she leveraged her heels into the aging floor. Calvin's arms framed either side of his head, blocking her view of his face, but she'd know that voice anywhere. She'd trusted that voice for three years, never knowing what kind of man he really was, how far he'd go to hurt the people who cared about him the most. Not just her but Beckett, the families he'd conned twenty years ago, the women who wouldn't get the help they needed from the foundation they'd started together. Gray stubble peppered what she could see of his jaw, the wrinkles at the edges of his mouth somehow more pronounced.

He twisted his entire upper body to face her, steel-blue eyes putting her directly in his crosshairs, and her gaze lifted to the rope wrapped strategically around his wrists. Just like she'd been restrained. "My first wife and me. She would've liked you, you know. I knew the moment I met you at that charity function all those years ago, she would've liked you. In some ways you remind me of her. Headstrong. Stubborn. Guess she had to be, considering she'd been married to a man like me."

"You mean the kind of man who steals money from innocent, hardworking families and people in need?" Raleigh couldn't keep the bitterness out of her tone, even with them both tied to the same damn line of plumbing. He obviously hadn't been the one to cause the crash when the shooter had put a bullet in his son, but that didn't make Calvin——Hank——innocent either.

"I know who you are, Hank Foster. I know what you've done and the people you've hurt."

His chin dipped toward his chest, that all-too-familiar voice tainted with something she couldn't quite put her finger on. "Beckett."

"He told me everything. You target innocent victims, prey on marks you can manipulate into doing what you want, consequences be damned." Years of trust, of friendship, slipped away as she faced him, and Calvin suddenly looked far older than she remembered. He might not be the current threat, but that didn't make him any less dangerous. He'd stolen victims' life savings, retirements, everything they'd had, and disappeared as though it'd never happened. "Was that what I was for you? Another mark in the long line of easy targets? Is that why you approached me at that charity event? You saw something you could take advantage of and turn a profit, no matter how many people got hurt in the process."

"You were never a mark, Raleigh, and I never profited from our foundation. Not a single penny. All my salary checks for the past three years? I donated them right back into the foundation we built together. I didn't want any of it." Hank Foster set the crown of his head back against the wall, staring up at the dilapidated ceiling threatening to crash down on them at any moment. He closed his eyes. "I stole that money twenty years ago. I did, and it destroyed my family. It got my wife— Beckett's mother—killed, left my son orphaned, and I've never been able to forgive myself since. The day I heard about what'd happened to her, that Beckett had been there to witness the entire thing, I gave it all back to the people I'd stolen from. Every dime." He locked trusting blue eyes on her. "When I met you, when you reminded me so much of my late wife, I realized starting this foundation with you would be a step in the right direction to fixing what I'd done. It might never be able to make up for all those people I hurt—especially my son—but I'll spend the rest of my life trying."

Truth resonated in his voice, and an acrid taste filled her mouth. Her stomach knotted. Everything that'd happened since the moment she'd been arrested had been carefully planned, calculated, but the tired-looking man restrained next to her didn't fit that description. Emotions she'd shut down after Beckett had arrested her and accused her of partnering with the thief surged to the surface. Relief, fear, guilt and curiosity tumbled over one another, and she didn't know which to process first. Her throat seized. "You…didn't steal the money, did you?"

"No." Footsteps echoed off the walls of an adjacent room, and Calvin turned toward the sound. "But I know who did."

A familiar outline centered in the doorway across the room, and a rush of memories materialized. The comfortable—almost caring—voice Raleigh hadn't been able to place after the crash, the oversize bolt cutters that'd snapped the links of her cuffs, the surprising strength it'd taken to pull her from the wreckage. Her attacker's long, lean frame shifted beneath a denim jumpsuit, shiny brass buttons and jewelry reflecting the dim light. Caramel highlights stood out from the waves of long blond hair fluttering around the woman's shoulders, and there, that beautiful, straight smile that'd welcomed Raleigh into her home so many times over the years flashed wide.

"Julia," she said.

Julia Dailey, Calvin's current wife, revealed the pistol in her hand. "I'm glad to see the little hit on the head I gave you didn't cause too much damage, Raleigh. There's still a lot we need to talk about since you shot the woman I sent to get me the information I needed from you."

Air evacuated from Raleigh's lungs as her fingers recalled the feel of pulling that trigger. She'd done it to save Beckett's life, just as she'd wielded that rock to save her brother's, but the blood was still on her hands. Always would be. "You hired Emily Cline to kill me."

"Yet here you are. Stubborn and determined as ever. I've always liked you. There was a point over the past few years I'd considered you a daughter, seeing as how Calvin and I never had children of our own, but you refused to play your part in my plan. Bringing Calvin's, or should I say Hank's, son into the investigation... Well, I couldn't have that. I've worked too hard and for too long to let you take this from me." Dark brown eyes settled on Calvin. Drywall debris skidded across the aged linoleum as Julia's muddied boots carved a path through the kitchen. Pink-tipped fingers smoothed over the gun in her left hand as Julia crouched beside her husband. "I lost count of how many times he'd tell me a story about Beckett, or his wife, or this place and how happy they'd been before she'd died. No matter how much I tried to be there for him, to be the wife he could be proud to have on his arm, I never came close to her, did I, Hank? Not once. Fifteen years of feeling unwanted, used, alone."

Dejection surfaced as she rested the barrel of her gun over Calvin's heart. "Do you have any idea what that kind of pain does to a person?"

"You feel worthless. Underappreciated." Raleigh's throat dried as echoes of Beckett's accusations of conspiring against him and her own foundation pierced straight through her. Her heart pounded loud behind her ears. She knew what that kind of pain did to a person, what it'd done to her over the years. But what hurt more? Having it done by the one person in the world who'd convinced her she'd been valuable, who'd promised to always be there for her. For their daughter. Her voice hollowed as she retreated into the familiar sense of numbness she'd cultivated over the years. Only that space had shrunk over the past few days to the point she could barely get a grip. "You convince yourself there must be something wrong with you, that you're not worth being loved, and that there's no point in getting close to anyone because they're just going to discard you anyway. So you go numb to deal with the rejection, whether it's real or not, to feel like you have the slightest bit of control."

But it was a lie. Because there was always the chance someone would come along and rip that control away. As Beckett had done for her. He'd broken through her internal armor. He'd forced her to confront and question her deepest beliefs about herself, to feel things she'd closed herself off from for so long, and Raleigh feared she'd never be able to rebuild that wall. She didn't have the strength.

The weight of Julia Dailey's attention constrained the air in her lungs. A distance infused her voice, her expression smooth, and suddenly Raleigh had a vision of what her future looked like if she continued down this path. "Spoken like someone with firsthand experience. I think I'll be doing you a favor by putting you out of your misery sooner rather than later."

"Where is my son, Julia?" Calvin asked.

"You know, for a con man, you didn't do a very good job covering your tracks." Julia pushed to her feet. She studied the cracks in the walls, the single chair at the kitchen table, kicked at a stray root that'd worked through the flooring. "You've always talked about coming back here, renovating the property, working the land like you used to. You never told me the exact location, but it wasn't hard to find once I did a bit of digging through public records and put all the pieces together. Fitting this is going to be the place they find your body."

Calvin tried to lunge for his wife but came up short as the ropes held him back, and Raleigh pressed her lower back into the wall to counter the fear clawing through her. "Where is my son!"

"Don't worry, Hank. You'll be joining him very soon." Julia's low-pitched laugh filled the room. Her gaze flickered to Raleigh, her weapon still aimed at her husband. "Both of you will. Just as soon as Raleigh hands over my money."

Chapter Fourteen

Beckett parked the SUV about a quarter mile down the road from the ranch he'd grown up on and hit the headlights. Shadows closed in around him, and he shouldered out of the vehicle. Cool air mixed with dirt and the slight spice of trees as he rounded to the cargo area and popped the latch. Righting the storage container every deputy marshal under Remington Barton's purview was required to carry, he unhinged the lid and took what he needed. He strapped the extra Kevlar vest to his chest, the wound in his shoulder and side lighting up with a renewed edge of pain, and maneuvered the AK-15 strap over his neck. Extra mags and ammunition, a flashlight with fresh batteries and an additional handgun. Armed, he shut the case and secured the hatch.

His father had surprised him by hiring Emily Cline to do his dirty work, but the con man wouldn't see him coming this time. Neither would anyone who got in his way.

Keeping low, Beckett moved through the trees surrounding the property he hadn't ever expected to step foot on again. His boots suctioned in the mud with each step, the gear he carried getting heavier by the second, but he only pushed himself harder. Whoever'd opened fire on him and Raleigh had left the scene of the accident more than an hour ago. Hank had obviously needed Raleigh for something—maybe to access the secondary account she'd uncovered during her own investigation—but that didn't leave much time.

Twigs snapped under his weight as he circled closer to the fenced property line and crouched behind one of the largest pines to the west to get his bearings. He'd memorized every foot of this place and the surrounding woods when he'd been a kid, but a lot had changed since then. The stable roof had started caving in the middle, the wooden fence posts sagged toward one another and nature had overgrown the family cemetery less than fifty feet off to his left. The top of one tombstone—his mother's—stood out against the backdrop of night. Nobody had been here to take care of the land after he'd joined the Marshals, and for that he was sorry. He'd held the deed and paid the taxes all these years, but the thought of coming back here, of reliving that fearful night… It'd been too much.

Until now.

Beckett surveyed the shadows, focused on the slightest hint of movement near the main house.

There. At the southeast corner. His finger slipped alongside the trigger of the rifle he carried close to his chest as a single armed operative tossed a cigarette at his feet and ground out the ashes. Movement pulled Beckett's attention to the other side of the house. Another gunman, not quite as large as the first, but Beckett would assume just as deadly. Both his shoulder and thigh wounds burned in remembrance of the kind of violence Emily Cline had been capable of—of the type of people Hank had hired to keep his hands clean—and Beckett double-checked that the sonogram of his and Raleigh's baby was still in his pocket. He'd been trained in criminal apprehension for the past fifteen years, and nothing would stop him from getting to his fugitive. Raleigh was all he had left.

He hauled himself between the backer rails of the fence and took cover behind the west side of the stable. The second operative disappeared behind the house. Twenty feet separated him and his target. He had to move. Now. Back to the stable wall, he gripped the rifle between both hands and approached the far side. The odor of cigarette smoke and sweat burned the back of his throat, and Beckett pulled up short of rounding into the gunman's sights and raised his weapon. Hesitation pulsed through him. He couldn't take the shot. Not without tipping off the second operative and whoever Hank had inside with Raleigh. He couldn't force her abductors to panic and do something brash. Damn it. Beckett repositioned the rifle at his back. His hands curled into fists.

He rushed forward. Beckett closed the distance between them fast, rocketing his fist into the side of the gunman's face. Bone crunched under his knuckles, but one shot didn't take the hired gun down. Clamping on to the operative's shoulder, he hiked his knee into the man's gut. The gunman blocked the hit with a groan, fisted Beckett's vest and threw him to the ground. The air crushed from his lungs a split second before a fist landed a hard right hook to his jaw.

Beckett's eyes watered as agony ripped through his

head, but he managed to dodge the second hit aimed at his face and pushed to his feet. Dirt worked into his lungs as he wrapped the guard in his arms from behind and threw the man to the ground. Keeping hold of one wrist, he threaded the bastard's arm between his thighs and increased the pressure on the gunman's shoulder until a pop broke through their heavy breathing. A scream gurgled up the man's throat, and Beckett hauled the heel of his boot into the guy's head, knocking him unconscious.

"There goes the element of surprise." The gunman's scream had most likely given away his position. He unwound his legs from around the guard and got to his feet, but not fast enough.

The barrel of a pistol scratched the oversensitized skin along his scalp. "Drop the rifle, kick it away. Slowly. Along with any others you're carrying, Marshal Foster."

"You know me?" The muscles down his back hardened with battle-ready tension. The second operative. Damn it. Beckett turned his head enough to keep the gunman in his peripheral vision as he raised his palms shoulder height. He had no intention of giving up the rifle or any other weapons.

"I know enough." The second man tugged Beckett's backup weapon from his shoulder holster, along with the extra magazines he'd stocked on one side of his vest. A strong hand grasped Beckett's wounded shoulder and shoved him down before maneuvering the rifle strap over his head. "On your knees."

"If you say so." The pain flaring from the gunshot wound stole the oxygen from his chest but kicked his central nervous system into high gear. He'd come here to save Raleigh and his baby, and he wasn't leaving without them. Loose rocks ground into Beckett's knee as he turned around and shot both hands into the gunman's wrist and pushed upward. A gunshot arced wide before he pried the steel from his attacker's hand and tossed the weapon, but he couldn't let that slow him down. Straightening the shooter's arm, Beckett hauled his attacker into the side of his childhood farmhouse face-first.

The shooter wrenched his wrist out of Beckett's hold and swung a hard left hook. White lights raced across his vision as the hit threw him off-balance. He stumbled back, throwing his hands up to block the next hit, but his assailant was too fast. Another punch knocked his head straight back on his shoulders. Beckett struck out with a solid hit, but the gunman caught his fist and twisted until the muscles in his arm screamed. He shot his injured arm forward, connecting with the side of his attacker's head, but at the cost of tearing the stitches Reed had sewn in only recently. Undeniable agony tore through him, but he couldn't stop. Not until he'd found Raleigh.

The last rays of sun reflected off the gun he'd pried from the operative's grip, and Beckett lunged at the same time as his attacker. He wrapped his hands around the familiar weight of the weapon and shot to his feet before the mercenary had a chance to strike. Blood trickled down his arm beneath his shirt as he widened his stance and brought up the gun. "How many more of you did Hank hire? I need to know so I can be sure I have enough bullets when the time comes to shoot you."

"You've got it all wrong, Marshal." His attacker swiped at the blood from his mouth, spitting the excess at the ground. A low laugh penetrated through the ringing in his ear from the gun going off so close to his head. "You're not the one calling the shots here."

Multiple sets of footsteps echoed off the overhanging porch of the farmhouse. Another two operatives materialized on either side of him, two more at his back. He was outmanned and outgunned, and they knew it. Well, hell. He'd walked right into Hank's trap, just as the bastard had probably intended from the beginning, and he'd been stupid enough—desperate enough—to follow along. Beckett shook his head, a laugh escaping past his mouth as he tossed the pistol in his hand into the dirt. "All right, then. Take me to the shot caller."

Two operatives flanked him from behind, one shoving him forward. His boots echoed off the old wood porch he'd spent so many summers running up and down as a kid. Hell, he could still see where his mother had recorded his height every year before school started on the front doorframe. The second gunman swung the porch screen wide and motioned him inside. As though Beckett had needed an invitation to walk inside his own damn house.

Peeling paint, splintered wood, rusted hinges. He ran his hand down along the corner of the doorframe. When this was over, when Hank was behind bars where he belonged and Beckett had cleared Raleigh's name of embezzling the money from the foundation, he'd come back here. He'd make this place the home his daughter deserved, somewhere Raleigh would feel safe. If she gave him the chance.

He crossed the threshold, the heaviness of mold and dust thick in his lungs. The outline of the brick fireplace demanded attention as they herded him through the main room toward the kitchen. Four operatives at his back, two outside. Not counting however many Hank had with him at all times. A man like that, who destroyed people's lives, was bound to have a few enemies. However, Beckett only had focus for the woman who'd had the guts to put a gun to Raleigh's head as he rounded into the small kitchen he used to know so well. The mother of his baby had been tied to an exposed length of plumbing. He shot forward, those captivating green eyes wide as the men behind him pulled him back. "Raleigh."

Pain exploded across the back of his head as one of the mercenaries at his back hit him from behind, and Beckett collapsed onto his knees. Raleigh's scream barely registered through the gag in her mouth, and the rage he'd become so familiar with over the years surged. Darkness closed in around the edges of his vision, but he had enough sense to make out the person holding the gun wasn't his father after all. That mistake went to Julia Dailey, Calvin Dailey's wife.

"I've never looked forward to family reunions, Marshal Foster," Julia said. "But I can't tell you how long I've been waiting to meet you."

HE WAS BLEEDING.

Raleigh pulled at her restraints as one of the gunmen used the butt of his weapon to keep Beckett in line. He dropped to his knees, and her heart dropped with him. Her protest faded behind the piece of fabric Julia had shoved into her mouth when it became clear her men were under attack, and now the cause of that disruption was outnumbered and outgunned. One gunman pulled Beckett upright by the wound in his shoulder. Pain contorted his expression, and every cell in her body caught fire. She couldn't get to him, but one way or another, she'd make sure he got out of this alive.

"Perfect timing, Marshal. Ms. Wilde was about to transfer the money I've worked so hard to keep for myself back into my account." Julia increased the space between her and Raleigh, then swept the gun up. And took aim directly at Beckett. "That makes you the perfect motivation she needs to follow through."

"Glad I'm good for something other than a punching bag." Beckett swiped at his bloodied mouth, every bit the defensive, reliable marshal she'd fallen in love with over the past few days, and her insides clenched. "But you took something that belongs to me, so forgive me if I'm not in the family-reunion mood, ma'am."

Belonged to him? Did that mean…? Her heart shot into her throat.

He'd come here for her, to save her.

Her pulse throbbed at the base of her neck. Scouring the debris around her and Hank, Raleigh forced herself to focus on finding something—anything—that could cut through the ropes around her wrists. Desperation flooded into the tips of her fingers as she clawed at the thousands of threads making up her restraints. The second Julia forced her to log in to that account, Beckett would be out of time. They all would. She shifted her legs a few inches wider, and a soft scraping registered over the low drone of voices. A single piece of broken tile. Her mouth parted slightly. It must've broken off from the old countertop a few feet away. If she could somehow get it into her hands, she could cut through the ropes.

One look at Hank and she realized he'd made the same connection. He nodded. Blue eyes, not nearly as bright as his son's, shifted to Julia.

"Damn it, Julia, this is between you and me, and you've made your point." Hank struggled against the ropes, but it was no use. At least not without something to cut through them. "You were right. I never committed to you, even after we were married, and I'm sorry. I'm sorry I never gave you a fair chance. I'm sorry I never got over my wife. I'll blame myself for what happened to her every day for the rest of my life, and that guilt didn't leave much for anything else, especially you." Rough exhalations controlled the rise and fall of Hank's shoulders. "But you know as well as I do Raleigh and my son have nothing to do with this. They don't deserve to pay for the mistake I made. Please, let them go. I can get you the money. You and I can work this out. Together. We can start over."

Julia closed her eyes and lowered the weapon to her side, and Raleigh used the backs of her thighs to shift the piece of broken tile between her and Hank. The woman's expression smoothed as the fight seemingly left her shoulders. "You have no idea how long I've been waiting to hear those words, Hank." She opened her eyes, and the muscles in Raleigh's legs seized. "But your apology is fifteen years too late."

Julia raised the gun and fired.

The bullet ripped into Hank's chest, and Raleigh

couldn't hold back her muffled scream as blood splattered against one side of her face. Beckett cringed in his handlers' hold. The stain rapidly spread across Hank's white shirt, every second she couldn't stop the bleeding slipping through her fingers. Hank stared down at the wound as air hissed through his teeth, and he set his head back against the wall. "I just had this shirt cleaned."

"I underestimated you, Raleigh." Julia unpocketed a phone from her jumpsuit, the screen a bright beacon in the overcrowded kitchen, and handed it off to one of the men at her side. "You uncovered an account the FBI had no idea existed—my account—and drained everything I'd stolen from the foundation without me noticing, but you've always been impressive." She didn't so much as look at her husband as he bled out beside Raleigh, and a coldness worked through Raleigh's veins. Who was this woman? How hadn't Raleigh seen her for what she was until now? "Do you know how long it's taken me to plan this? I accounted for every step, every setback, for years before I put anything in motion, but I never expected you to run with my money."

The sun had gone down, intensifying the shadows along Beckett's jaw, the bruising and crusted blood darker than before. Confusion swirled through the crystal-blue eyes she hadn't been able to get out of her head for the past four months. "What the hell is she talking about? What did you do?"

"Go on, Raleigh. Tell him you're innocent, that he had you all wrong, and you fully intended to give the money you've taken from me back to the foundation where it belongs," Julia said. "Do you think he'll believe you this time, or does he already know the truth? That you're the one thing he hates most in this world. That you're exactly like his father."

Raleigh slid her attention to Beckett. He'd accused her of lying to him before, and he'd been partly right. Not about conspiring to steal all that money from the foundation with his father—or Julia—but because she'd stolen it back. Every dime. Emily Cline had set up the secondary account to funnel small increments without the FBI's notice at Julia's instruction, but she'd done it in Raleigh's name, with her personal information, to make the case against Raleigh stronger in case the feds caught on. Only that'd also given Raleigh access to the funds. Over one million dollars the FBI had no idea had been taken, a small percentage compared to the original fifty million that'd been stolen right out from under her nose. Her mouth dried as Beckett's expression hardened.

Julia reached out, soft skin sliding against Raleigh's cheek as she pulled the gag low. Hank struggled to breathe beside her but didn't warrant a single consideration from the woman who'd been married to him for fifteen years.

"I don't care where you moved it. I only want it back. Once I confirm the funds have been returned, you'll walk out of here alive. We can all move on with our lives and be happy in the knowledge that, after tonight, Hank and Beckett Foster won't ever be able to hurt us again." Julia stood. Centering the gun used to shoot her husband back on Beckett, she leveled her gaze on Raleigh. "Don't do as I ask, and I'll make it look like you killed the next man in the Foster lineup before his father bleeds out, which, from the looks of it, shouldn't be much longer. Is that what you want me to tell your daughter when she grows up, Raleigh? That her mother killed her father, a US marshal, and will spend the rest of her life behind bars?"

Nausea curdled in her stomach as Raleigh looked up at Julia. "What?"

"You didn't think I knew about the baby? I told you, Raleigh. I've planned for every setback of this plan. I'll be the only family she has left when this is all over, so getting custody won't be difficult when you're back in the FBI's possession." Julia had framed her for embezzling from the foundation she and Hank had built from the ground up. She'd hired mercenaries to keep her hands clean, shot her husband, who couldn't forgive himself for his past mistakes, and now the woman was threatening to kill the man Raleigh had stupidly fallen in love with and take her daughter from her. There was no way Julia would let them walk out of here alive. "Or you can put the money back where you found it and start your life over. Just you and your baby. Isn't that what you've always wanted? What you deserve?"

A predatorial growl registered a split second before Beckett shoved to his feet. He disarmed the gunman to his right and pulled the trigger. Once. Twice. Both men collapsed to the floor, and her marshal twisted around, putting Julia in his sights.

The nearest gunman cut the rope around Raleigh's wrists and wrenched her into his chest by her hair. In a matter of seconds, he pressed a long, cold blade against her throat. Hints of body odor rolled off his leather jacket, and Raleigh swallowed to counter the fear clawing through her. Two more guns for hire took position beside the door Beckett had come through, weapons trained on him. One wrong move, and she'd lose everything. "Beckett, no."

His gaze flickered to hers—cold, detached—and she lost feeling beneath her rib cage. She'd been wrong before. He'd tracked her back to his childhood ranch not because he'd realized he'd made a mistake accusing her of conspiracy or to prove he hadn't meant what he'd said. But because he was a US marshal assigned to recover his fugitive. Just as he'd always claimed.

"I've worked too hard for this. I deserve that money after what your father put me through," Julia said. "Shoot me, and you won't only lose him, Beckett. You'll lose your entire family."

"No, he won't." Fire simmered beneath the surface of Raleigh's skin. She closed her grip around the broken piece of tile she'd grabbed as the hit man with the knife had hauled her off the floor. Sharp stone cut into her palm, but the pain kept her grounded, focused, and Raleigh shot her elbow back into the gunman's gut. Following through with a knee to his face when he doubled over, she didn't bother watching him hit the floor as she turned on Julia. "Because we're not going any—"

Pain burned through her as Julia's gun discharged, and Raleigh froze. One second. Two. She followed the spread of blood across her shirt, so much closer to her navel than the piece of shrapnel from the car explosion. She stumbled back and touched the entry wound. Tears burned in her eyes before she tripped over one of Hank's feet and fell backward. She hit the floor, out of breath.

"No!" Beckett's yell reverberated through her, followed by three more gunshots.

She couldn't see him, couldn't move. She'd been shot. Then silence. Strained breathing echoed around her after a few seconds, but she didn't have the strength to get up. "Beckett."

Chapter Fifteen

The rhythmic pulse of the machines recording her body's stats grated against the headache at the base of his skull. Three days. Raleigh should've come around from the anesthesia by now, but there wasn't any sign she intended to open her eyes and her doctors couldn't tell him anything more than he'd have to be patient. Things like this happened after experiencing the kind of trauma she'd been through.

Beckett leaned forward in the chair he'd set up beside her hospital bed. The surgeons had pulled the slug from her without any complications. He just needed her to wake up, and when she did, he'd be here. He wasn't going anywhere. Ever again.

He'd been such an idiot—for so many reasons, but more recently about the money she'd stolen from Julia Dailey, about conspiring with his father to steal from her own foundation. Raleigh hadn't taken those funds for her personal gain, as he'd feared. She could have. She could have run and never looked back, taken his daughter with her, and hell, he wouldn't have blamed her after what he'd done. But she hadn't. Instead, she'd proved once again to be a better person than he'd ever be, and she'd put them right back where they belonged.

In the foundation's accounts.

With Julia Dailey in federal custody, the FBI had had no other choice than to drop the accusations against Raleigh and close their investigation into the foundation. Beckett pressed his elbows against his knees and swiped his hand down his face. She was free, but at this rate, there was a chance he'd lose his fugitive all over again. The worst part was he'd brought it on himself.

Time had slowed when Julia had pulled that trigger. He'd watched the bullet leave the gun and race toward Raleigh. Only he hadn't been fast enough to stop it. With his entire future at risk, Beckett had turned his weapon on the two operatives behind him and left Julia Dailey to stand on her own. He'd secured his father's wife to the same pipe she'd tied Raleigh to as he'd waited for backup and the medical chopper, but every minute had felt like an hour.

A knock registered softly from behind, and Beckett swiped his hand down his face before standing to face the visitor. She hadn't had many over the past few days. Apart from him, the list mostly consisted of nurses, doctors and his team to update him on the investigation, but the last person he'd expected to set foot near the mother of his child darkened Raleigh's doorway.

Hank Foster.

"What the hell are you doing here?" Beckett stepped into the bastard responsible for this entire mess. If it hadn't been for his SOB father, for all the people he'd hurt, Raleigh wouldn't have been shot in the first place. She wouldn't have been targeted by Emily Cline or framed for stealing from the foundation. She wouldn't have been arrested and forced to go on the run to avoid their daughter growing up without her parents.

"I was discharged a couple hours ago, and one of the other marshals you work with told me you haven't left this room since Raleigh got out of surgery after he was done questioning me." Hank offered him a white foam box, eyes downcast. The man Beckett had spent twenty years of this life hating with every fiber of his being had the guts to look ashamed, apologetic. "I thought we could both use some real food, and I remembered you liked waffles, so I ordered some from that old diner we used to visit when you were a kid."

"Don't you dare say her name, Hank." The frustration, the anger, the desperation he'd been holding back since Beckett had stepped off the Life Flight chopper three days ago broke through the invisible dam he'd built in preparation for this moment. "You're the reason she's here. You're the reason your wife framed Raleigh and hired a hit woman to kill the best thing that's ever happened to me. No matter how far I've distanced myself from you, from what you've done, I'm the one who's still paying the price for your mistakes. First with Mom, now Raleigh. You put her in danger. You put my baby in danger, and I'm not going to let you anywhere near either of them. Ever. Do you understand? I'm done with the past controlling my life, dictating every decision I make, and I'm done with you."

Hank retracted the box into his chest, the outline of bandages clear between the unbuttoned section of his shirt. "I'm sorry, Beckett. For everything. Your mother was killed because of me. Because of my selfishness.

I was never arrested for what I did, but I've spent the past twenty years working to make that right, to be the father you deserve instead of the one you got. I don't know if it's possible given what's happened over the past few days, but I'll spend another twenty years trying, if that's what it takes. I'll keep the foundation going. I'll help as many people as I can, and if you decide to change your mind about where we go from here, I'll be waiting." Hank nodded, and in that moment, he suddenly looked older than a few minutes ago. Setting the box of waffles on a nearby table, he adjusted the suit jacket draped over his arm. "I'm proud of you, son. You're going to be a great father to that little girl, the kind she deserves."

"No thanks to you." Whether he'd said that more for himself or to Hank, he didn't know. He didn't care. Hank had apologized for what'd happened to his mother, accepted responsibility for Julia's actions, but that wouldn't erase two decades' worth of hatred and anger. Their relationship—if they'd ever have one— would take more than a single conversation to heal, but at least he'd made his opinion on the matter clear.

"You've got one hell of a fighter on your hands, son, but if you want to be around much longer, eat the damn waffles. You look like you're going to fall over," Hank said.

The fight drained from Beckett as he turned back toward the bed and slid his hand in Raleigh's, but he could still feel Hank at the door. Fine. Beckett would let him see the damage he'd caused, how he'd almost destroyed the only family Beckett had left. He smoothed his thumb over her scabbed knuckles, and Raleigh's hand jerked in his. The hollowness under his rib cage intensified as his gaze shot to her face. "Raleigh?"

She squeezed her eyes shut, then opened them slowly. Hypnotic green eyes lifted to his, and relief flooded through him. Her chest collapsed on a strong exhalation as she shook her head. She licked dry lips, and he reached for the plastic mug provided by the hospital at the side of her bed. He set the straw against her mouth for her to take a drink, but her voice still graveled from the grogginess of being out cold for three days. "Beckett."

"I'm here. It's okay." Beckett kept her hand in his as he took his seat in the chair beside the bed. "You were shot. Three days ago at the ranch. You were Life-Flighted here to the hospital in Portland where the surgeons were able to remove the bullet, but it took you a while to shake off the anesthesia."

"The baby." Panic infused her expression as she slid her free hand over her stomach above the sheets. Tears welled in her lower lash line, and she strengthened her grip on his hand. Raleigh fought to sit up straight, but the pain in her expression said her wound wouldn't let her get far. "Please tell me she's okay. Tell me the bullet didn't hurt—"

"She's fine." He brought her hand against his mouth, planting a kiss on the thin skin below her knuckles as he helped her settle back against the pillow. "Everything is fine. Julia Dailey was arrested, the charges against you were dropped, all of the missing donation funds have been returned to the foundation, and our daughter is exactly where she's supposed to be."

"Okay." She nodded, the distant haze in her eyes revealing she was still trying to get her bearings. After everything she'd been through, he wouldn't be surprised if it'd take her more than a few minutes to adjust. Hell, might even take months, and he intended to help her through it every step of the way. "I remember the gunshot, the blood on my shirt and that I couldn't see you after I fell. I thought I'd lost you both."

"You didn't lose anything. I'm here, she's here, and we're not going anywhere. It's over." Beckett worked small circles into the space between her index finger and thumb. His chest tightened at the fear still swirling in her gaze, and he repositioned her hand over his heart. He focused on the light blue veins running along the length of her arm. "Everything that happened was because of me. Julia wouldn't have gotten her hands on you in the first place if I hadn't let my own anger get in the way of seeing the truth, but when I saw who Calvin Dailey really was, that my father was part of this, I lost it, Raleigh."

Heat seared along his nerve endings at the memory, at the pain he'd put her through after he'd given his word to always be there for her. This woman had reached straight into his chest and claimed his heart, and he'd had no idea what he was supposed to do with that. Until now. "I couldn't see straight. I was fitting evidence into the puzzle that had nothing to do with the case, and I was scared. I've been disconnected for so damn long—living in the past—that I'd convinced myself I'd spend the rest of my days walking this earth alone, but then you came along. You kept me grounded even when I thought we wouldn't make it. You gave me purpose, and I was scared of losing that, of losing you and our baby. So I found a reason to make you the enemy to avoid having to feel that pain ever again. I was stupid for considering you'd been involved with Hank's next con, and I'm sorry. I'm sorry for breaking my word to always be there for you when you deserved so much better. I can't promise I won't be an idiot in the future, but I sure as hell won't ever doubt you again. If you'll just give me the chance to prove it."

She tugged her hand from his and set it over her slight baby bump. The muscles in her throat worked to swallow. She kept her expression neutral as she raised her gaze to his. The answer was so clear in those beautiful green eyes, the pain he'd caused evident, and his gut soured. "I don't know if that's possible anymore. I haven't felt important to anyone my whole life, Beckett. Everyone I've let get close has walked away once I didn't serve a purpose for them anymore, but when we were in that cabin, you made me feel like I could've been important. That you saw me just for me and not something to be used." She tilted her head to one side, tears sliding down her cheeks. "I was falling in love with you, dreaming about waking up next to you every morning on that ranch the marshals seized, taking family trips into town, teaching our daughter how to ride her first horse. It felt so real. I wanted it to be real." Her voice hollowed. "But I realized it'd been a fantasy. All of it. Because until you recognize you have people who want to be there for you—that you're the one who's been pushing them away—there isn't going to be room in your life for me or for our daughter."

His throat threatened to swell shut. "What are...what are you saying?"

"I'm saying we're always going to be connected because of this baby. There's no denying that," she said, "but I'm going to let the lawyers handle everything from here."

SHE SHOULDN'T BE HERE.

Raleigh stepped out of the old four-door sedan she'd purchased a few days after being released from the hospital. Her car, her apartment, her belongings, it'd all been taken by the state once she'd been arrested, but that was behind her now. It was time to start over, fresh, but she hadn't planned on ever coming back here.

Her past had been burned clean, and she was going to take advantage. If it hadn't been at Beckett's insistence they meet here to review the paternity and custody papers before their lawyers submitted them to the courts, she never would've driven out here. She'd made it clear in the hospital she'd hand off any legal matters concerning their daughter to her lawyer, negating any reason for them to have to see each other until the baby was born, but he'd sounded desperate over the phone. Broken.

She couldn't deny she was hurting just as badly at what'd happened between them.

She breathed in the slight hint of pines and hay for a few moments. Yellowing grass swayed in the breeze as she followed the dirt road leading to the main farmhouse. The seized property looked the same as it had a few weeks ago—when Emily Cline had caught up with them—but where fear had controlled her then, beauty met her now. She burrowed into her coat as the large barn at the edge of the property demanded her attention before she stepped onto the house's pale front porch. She lifted her hand to knock before the door swung inward.

And there he was.

A tingling sensation bubbled inside her as his gaze studied her from head to toe. His beard seemed thicker, the lines around his eyes and mouth a little deeper as though he hadn't slept in a while, and her heart hiccuped in her chest. It'd been only two weeks since she'd woken to find him next to her hospital bed, but so much had changed since then. Those brilliant blue eyes brightened, and she fought the rush of need she'd been working to bury as it seeped through the cracks in her shattered armor. He was handsome as ever with the white long-sleeved shirt, jeans, boots and no visible signs of his blood or anyone else's staining his clothes, and it took her a few breaths to remember why she was here. "I didn't think you'd come out here."

"You wanted me to double-check the paperwork before we go to court." Raleigh folded her arms across her chest. The siding beside the door smelled of fresh paint the longer she stood there, but there was no reason the US Marshals would be fixing the place up unless they were getting it ready for public auction. A strange heaviness settled in her gut at the thought. For the past few weeks she'd been staying in a hotel room while the FBI concluded their investigation, but soon she'd have to find a more permanent place. She and Beckett had almost been killed right near here, but that didn't detract from the sense of peace—of home—she'd experienced before the gunwoman had fired that first bullet. "If we're going to make this coparenting thing work, we're each going to have to make an effort. This is mine."

"I appreciate it." He shifted back on his heels, motioning her through the door. "Come in."

She stepped over the threshold, that immediate feeling of calm washing over her. Warmth flooded over the exposed skin of her neck and hands from the fireplace as she took in the wall of windows and pale gray-and-white decor. Everything looked the same, felt the same. Only they weren't. Not with Beckett.

He'd taken responsibility for his mistake in accusing her of conspiracy, in arresting her mere hours after promising to always be there. His admission of letting the anger he'd held on to all these years get in the way of his judgment still echoed in her head when she lay alone at night. He'd asked for another chance, and she'd been so tempted to give it, to forget he'd turned his back on her all over again. But she couldn't.

Because what would stop him from turning his back on her the next time? What would stop him from leaving her as an only parent when all that anger clouded his judgment again?

In that moment, Raleigh had imagined having to explain to their baby girl why her father had disappeared. She'd seen the disappointment in her daughter's eyes so clearly, experienced that feeling of being unwanted by the man she'd look up to, heard their child convincing herself she wasn't worth loving. That single image had broken what was left of Raleigh's heart in a matter of seconds, but she had the power to make sure it never became reality. By coparenting with Beckett as agreed, but nothing more. No commitment. No emotions. Nothing that he could use to hurt her or their daughter down the line.

Closing the door behind her, Beckett moved ahead of her deeper into the house. His boots echoed off the dark hardwood flooring, each step a physical and invisible wedge between them. "I've got the documents in the kitchen and some snacks if you need. I know it's a long drive, and I'm guessing you probably didn't think to pack anything to eat before you left."

"I didn't." She followed him into the kitchen and ran her fingers across the cold white granite of the kitchen island as he rounded behind it. A stack of documents and pens had been positioned on one side, along with a couple of bottled waters and an assortment of fresh fruit. The weight of his attention constricted the air in her lungs. She reached for the papers. "You could've emailed me the documents. We didn't have to meet all the way out here."

"The papers aren't the only thing I wanted to have you look over." Beckett came around the island, every muscle across his chest and along his shoulders flexing and releasing with each step, and her skin prickled with his proximity. A combination of pine and hard work dived into her lungs as he slid something across the granite. The scrape of metal jarred her back from the edge of leaning into him.

Keys? Raleigh pinched the metal ring between her index finger and thumb, studying them as though she'd be able to recognize them at a glance. "What are these for?"

"This place." Beckett pressed his palms onto the stone as he leveled that blue gaze on her. "It's yours."

What? Her throat got tight. "I'm sorry. I think my

brain left my body there for a second. Can you repeat that?"

"In the hospital you told me you'd imagined waking up here every day, of teaching our daughter to ride, that it'd all felt real when you were here. So I bought the property back from the Marshals Service before it could go to public auction, and I'm giving it to you. These papers aren't for custody of our daughter. They're to sign the deed to this place over to you." He stepped into her, unbearably close, which forced her to look up at him, and she suddenly didn't have the mind to confirm what the papers said.

She only had attention for him. For all that dark hair she'd run her fingers through a dozen times, for the strong tendons between his neck and shoulders she'd held on to when they'd been on the run for their lives, for the softness of his mouth when he'd kissed her. She planted her hand against his chest, her head urging her to push him away, to regain her composure, but the familiar beat of his heart under her palm reverberated through her.

He'd bought her the ranch?

"I know why you wanted the lawyers involved, and you had every reason to get as far from me as you could these past couple of weeks. Seeing how this anger I've carried around has hurt you and any chance I have at being a father to that baby girl brought me to the lowest point of my life." He lowered his gaze to her hands as he took them both in his. "I've been hanging on to it as a crutch for so long, I wasn't sure I could get by if I had to let it go, but you leaving made me realize I wanted you more than I wanted to hate Hank. I'm not sure I'll ever be able to forgive him for what he's done, but I'm willing to try. For you. For our baby."

He smoothed calming circles into the backs of her hands, and she was overtaken by need. By the feeling of complete and utter destruction she'd been trying to ignore since she'd been discharged from the hospital. "I can't take another second being apart from you. I can't live the rest of my life handing off our daughter at neutral locations or only seeing you for a few minutes at a time every couple of weeks. I can't pretend I'm okay with the thought of you finding someone else or being with anyone other than me. I can't. I'm in love with you, Raleigh, and I want to work to make you and our daughter happy for the rest of our lives. And that means I'm not going anywhere. Ever."

He released her and dropped to one knee.

"What are you doing?" She slid her hand over her stomach, waiting for reassurance as she'd done a hundred times over the past few months, but she couldn't think straight. Couldn't breathe. He'd bought her a ranch to show he loved her. She'd gotten so used to people walking away over the years, to pretending their actions hadn't hurt, but the truth was Beckett had cut deeper than them all. He'd cut through her sense of worthlessness, her feeling of being unwanted by everyone around her, cut through the numbness she was comfortable living with the rest of her life. Where others had left her empty and exhausted, he'd made her whole and given her a gift no one else had ever before: hope for the future.

"Raleigh Wilde, I love you." Beckett pulled a small black box from his front pocket and flipped it open. In the center of lush cream silk was a simple solitaire embedded in a thick band, and the connection she'd relied on during those terrifying few days of their secret investigation flooded through her. "Will you marry me?"

"Yes." She fell into him and wrapped her arms around his neck as she straddled him right there in the middle of the kitchen floor. Her kitchen floor. He held on to her, and everything she'd ever wanted came within reach. A stable home, a partner who had her back, a family. It was all hers. Raleigh slid her mouth over his, her heart threatening to beat straight out of her chest. "I love you, too, but the next time you feel the need to arrest me, you better be ready for the fight of your life."

Beckett wrapped her in the circle of his arms. "The next time I feel the need to arrest you, I promise to give you a head start."

* * * * *

COMING SOON!

We really hope you enjoyed reading this book.
If you're looking for more romance, be sure to
head to the shops when new books are
available on

Thursday 7th
January

To see which titles are coming soon, please visit
millsandboon.co.uk/nextmonth

LET'S TALK

Romance

For exclusive extracts, competitions
and special offers, find us online:

[f] facebook.com/millsandboon

[🐦] @MillsandBoon

[📷] @MillsandBoonUK

Get in touch on 01413 063232

For all the latest titles coming soon, visit

millsandboon.co.uk/nextmonth

MILLS & BOON

THE HEART OF ROMANCE

A ROMANCE FOR EVERY KIND OF READER

MODERN

Prepare to be swept off your feet by sophisticated, sexy and seductive heroes, in some of the world's most glamourous and romantic locations, where power and passion collide.
8 stories per month.

HISTORICAL

Escape with historical heroes from time gone by. Whether your passion is for wicked Regency Rakes, muscled Vikings or rugged Highlanders, awaken the romance of the past.
6 stories per month.

MEDICAL

Set your pulse racing with dedicated, delectable doctors in the high-pressure world of medicine, where emotions run high, passion, comfort and love are the best medicine.
6 stories per month.

True Love

Celebrate true love with tender stories of heartfelt romance, the rush of falling in love to the joy a new baby can bring, and focus on the emotional heart of a relationship.
8 stories per month.

Desire

Indulge in secrets and scandal, intense drama and plenty of hot action with powerful and passionate heroes who have it all: wealth, status, good looks…everything but the right woman.
6 stories per month.

HEROES

Experience all the excitement of a gripping thriller, with an romance at its heart. Resourceful, true-to-life women and strong fearless men face danger and desire - a killer combination!
8 stories per month.

DARE

Sensual love stories featuring smart, sassy heroines you'd want as best friend, and compelling intense heroes who are worthy of
4 stories per month.

To see which titles are coming soon, please visit
millsandboon.co.uk/nextmonth

JOIN US ON SOCIAL MEDIA!

Stay up to date with our latest releases, author news and gossip, special offers and discounts, and all the behind-the-scenes action from Mills & Boon...

 millsandboon

 millsandboonuk

millsandboon

MILLS & BOON

HISTORICAL

Awaken the romance of the past

Escape with historical heroes from time gone by. Whether your passion is for wicked Regency Rakes, muscled Viking warriors or rugged Highlanders, indulge your fantasies and awaken the romance of the past.

MILLS & BOON

MODERN

Power and Passion

Prepare to be swept off your feet by sophisticated, sexy and seductive heroes, in some of the world's most glamourous and romantic locations, where power and passion collide.

MILLS & BOON
DARE

Sexy. Passionate. Bold.

Sensual love stories featuring smart, sassy heroines you'd want as a best friend, and compelling intense heroes who are worthy of them.

MILLS & BOON
True Love
Romance from the Heart

Celebrate true love with tender stories of
heartfelt romance, from the rush of falling
in love to the joy a new baby can bring,
and a focus on the emotional
heart of a relationship.

MILLS & BOON
MEDICAL
Pulse-Racing Passion

Set your pulse racing with dedicated, delectable doctors in the high-pressure world of medicine, where emotions run high and passion, comfort and love are the best medicine.